W9-CYB-454

DICTIONARY
OF THE
KHAZARS

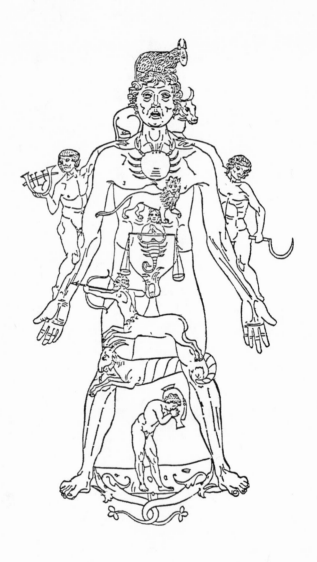

DICTIONARY

OF THE

KHAZARS

A LEXICON NOVEL IN 100,000 WORDS

MILORAD PAVIĆ

TRANSLATED FROM THE SERBO-CROATIAN
BY CHRISTINA PRIBIĆEVIĆ-ZORIĆ

This is the FEMALE EDITION of the Dictionary.

The MALE edition is almost identical. But NOT quite. Be
warned that ONE PARAGRAPH is crucially different.

The choice is yours.

ALFRED A. KNOPF NEW YORK 1988

Here lies the reader
who will never open this book.
He is here forever dead.

LEXICON

COSRI

(A DICTIONARY
OF THE DICTIONARIES
ON THE KHAZAR QUESTION)

RECONSTRUCTION OF THE ORIGINAL
1691 DAUBMANNUS EDITION
(DESTROYED IN 1692), INCLUDING
ITS MOST RECENT REVISIONS

CONTENTS

The author assures the reader that he will not have to die if he reads this book, as did the user of the 1691 edition, when *The Khazar Dictionary* still had its first scribe. Some explanation regarding that edition is in order here, but for the sake of brevity the lexicographer proposes to strike a deal with his readers. He will sit down to write these notes before supper, and the reader will take them to read after supper. Thereby, hunger will force the author to be brief, and gratification will allow the reader to peruse the introduction at leisure.

1. A History of *The Khazar Dictionary*

The event discussed in this lexicon occurred sometime in the 8th or 9th century A.D. (or there were several similar events), and this subject is commonly referred to by scholars as "the Khazar polemic."[▽] The Khazars[▽] were an autonomous and powerful tribe, a warlike and nomadic people who appeared from the East at an unknown date, driven by a scorching silence, and who, from the 7th to the 10th century, settled in the land between two seas, the Caspian and the Black.[*] It is

---

[*] A review of the literature on the Khazars was published in New York (*The Khazars, A Bibliography*, 1939); a Russian, M. I. Artamonov, wrote a monograph on the history of the Khazars in two editions (Leningrad,

known that the winds that brought them were masculine winds, which never bring rain—winds with a yoke of grass, which they trail through the sky like a beard. One Late Slavic mythological source mentions the Kozije Sea, which could be taken to mean that there was a sea called the "Khazar Sea," since the Slavs called the Khazars "Kozars." It is also known that the Khazars established a powerful empire between the two seas, preaching a to-us-unknown faith. When their husbands were killed in battle, Khazar women would be given a pillow to hold the tears they would weep for the warrriors. The Kazars entered the annals of history when they went to war against the Arabs and concluded an alliance with the Byzantine Emperor Heraclius in 627 A.D., but their origins remain unknown and all traces of them have vanished, leaving nothing to show by what name or people one should look for them today. They left in their wake a graveyard by the Danube, although it is not sure it is really Khazar, and a pile of keys surmounted by silver or gold triangular coins, which Daubmannus ✿ believed had been minted by the Khazars. The Khazars, and the Khazar state, vanished from the stage of history as a result of the event that is the main concern of this book—their conversion from their original faith, unknown to us today, to one (again, it is not known which) of three known religions of the past and present—Judaism, Islam, or Christianity. The collapse of the Khazar Empire followed soon after their conversion. A Russian military commander of the 10th century, Prince Svyatoslav, gobbled up the Khazar Empire like an apple, without even dismounting from his horse. In 943 A.D. the Russians went without sleep for eight nights to smash

---

1936 and 1962), and, in 1954, in Princeton, D. M. Dunlop published a history of the Jewish Khazars.

the Khazar capital at the mouth of the Volga into the Caspian Sea, and between 965 and 970 A.D. they destroyed the Khazar state. Eyewitnesses noted that the shadows of the houses in the capital held their outlines for years, although the buildings themselves had already been destroyed long before. They held fast in the wind and in the waters of the Volga. According to a 12th-century Russian chronicle, Oleg was already called archon of the Khazar state by the year 1083, but by that time (the 12th century), another people—the Kuman—were already to be found on the territory of what had once been the Khazar state. There are very few material remnants of Khazar culture. No public or private inscriptions have been discovered, no trace of the Khazar books mentioned by Halevi,✿ or of their language, though Cyril✝ notes that they prayed in the Khazar language. The sole public building excavated in Suwar, on erstwhile Khazar territory, is probably not Khazar, but Bulgar. Nor was anything noteworthy found in the excavations at Sarkel, not even traces of the fortress we know the Byzantines built there for the Khazars' use. After the fall of their state, the Khazars are barely mentioned. In the 10th century a Hungarian chieftain invited them to settle on his territory. In the year 1117 a group of Khazars went to Kiev to see Prince Vladimir Monomakh. In Pressburg, in 1309, Catholics were forbidden to enter into matrimony with Khazars, and in 1346 the decision was confirmed by the Pope. That is about all there is.

The Khazars' act of conversion, which was to seal their fate, occurred in the following way. According to ancient chronicles, the Khazar ruler, the kaghan,▽ had a dream and sought three philosophers to interpret it for him. This was a matter of importance to the Khazar state, because the kaghan had decided to convert, to-

3

gether with his people, to the faith of the sage who would give the most satisfactory dream interpretation. Some sources assert that, when the kaghan made his decision that day, the hair on his head died, and although he felt it happen, something nevertheless drove him on. And so it was that a Moslem, a Jewish, and a Christian divine— a dervish, a rabbi, and a monk—were to be found at the kaghan's summer residence. Each received a knife made of salt as a gift from the kaghan, and they began their debate. The sages' viewpoints, their contest based on the tenets of their three different faiths, the characters involved in, and the outcome of the "Khazar polemic" aroused keen interest and strongly conflicting opinions about the event and its consequences, the victors and the vanquished, and through the centuries they became the subject of repeated debate in Hebrew, Christian, and Moslem circles; all this continues to the present, although the Khazars have long since ceased to exist. Sometime in the 17th century there was a surprising renewal of interest in Khazar affairs, and the immense body of studies concerning the Khazars was systematized and published in Borussia (Prussia) in 1691. Among the items examined were samples of triangular coins, names inscribed on old rings, images painted on a pitcher of salt, diplomatic correspondence, portraits of writers in which all the book titles etched in the background were transcribed, reports from spies, testaments, voices of Black Sea parrots thought to speak the extinct Khazar language, painted scenes of music-making (from which musical annotations drawn on score books were deciphered), and even a tattooed human skin, not to mention the Byzantine, Hebrew, and Arab archival material. In short, everything that the imagination of 17th-century man could tame and turn to his own advantage was drawn on. And all this was collected between the covers of one dictionary.

An explanation for the awakened interest in the 17th century, one thousand years after the event, was left by a chronicler in the following obscure sentences, which read: "Each of us promenades his thought, like a monkey on a leash. When you read, you always have two such monkeys: your own and one belonging to someone else. Or, even worse, a monkey and a hyena. Now, consider what you will feed them. For a hyena does not eat the same thing as a monkey. . . ."

In any case, in the said year of 1691 the printer of a Polish dictionary, Joannes Daubmannus ⚙ (or a successor under his name), published a listing of sources on the Khazar question in the one format that made it possible to include the sundry material that had been amassed and lost through the centuries by those who, with quills in their earrings, use their mouths as ink bottles. The work was published in the form of a dictionary about the Khazars and entitled *Lexicon Cosri*. According to one (Christian) version, the book was dictated to the publisher by a monk named Theoctist Nikolsky,[A] who had found various material about the Khazars on an Austrian-Turkish battlefield and had memorized it. Daubmannus' edition was divided into three dictionaries: a separate glossary of Moslem sources on the Khazar question, an alephbetized list of materials drawn from Hebrew writings and tales, and a third dictionary compiled on the basis of Christian accounts of the Khazar question. This Daubmannus edition—a dictionary of dictionaries on the Khazar Empire—had an unusual fate.

Among the five hundred copies of the first dictionary, Daubmannus printed one with a poisoned dye. This poisoned copy, with its gilded lock, had a companion copy with a silver lock. In 1692 the Inquisition destroyed all copies of the Daubmannus edition, and the only ones to remain in circulation were the poisoned copy of the book, which had escaped the censors' notice, and the auxiliary copy, with its silver lock, which accompanied it. Insubordinates and infidels who ventured to read the proscribed dictionary risked the threat of death. Whoever opened the book soon grew numb, stuck on his own heart as on a pin. Indeed, the reader would die on the ninth page at the words *Verbum caro factum est* ("The Word became flesh"). If read simultaneously with the poisoned copy, the auxiliary copy enabled one to know exactly when death would strike. Found in the auxiliary copy was the note: "When you awake and suffer no pain, know that you are no longer among the living."

From the legal case concerning the 18th-century Dorfmer family and its inheritance, we see that the "gold" (poisoned) copy of the dictionary was passed down from one generation to the next in this Prussian family: the eldest son received one half of the book, and the other children each received one quarter, or less if there were more of them. The rest of the Dorfmer inheritance—orchards, meadows, fields, houses, water, livestock—was divided up with each section of the book, and for a long time the book was not associated with the deaths that occurred. Once, when pestilence struck down the livestock and there was a drought, someone told the members of the household that every book, like every girl, could turn into the witch Mora, that her spirit could go out into the world and infect and torment those around her. Therefore, into the book's lock should be placed a small wooden cross, like those put in a girl's mouth when she turned into this witch, so as not to release its spirit to plague the world and the household. This they did with *The Khazar Dictionary*—a cross was placed on its lock as over a mouth—but matters only got worse, and members of the household began to choke in their sleep and die. The family went to the priest and told him what was happening, and the priest came and removed the cross from the book; that very same day the plague ended. He told them: "Be careful, in future, not to place the cross on the lock like that, when the spirit is residing outside the book. It fears the cross and, not daring to go back into the book, it wreaks havoc all around." And so the little gilded lock was bolted and *The Khazar Dictionary* remained on the shelf for decades, unused. From that shelf at night could be heard a strange rustling sound that emanated from the Daubmannus dictionary, and some diary notes kept at the time in Lvov say that built into Daubmannus' lexicon was a sandglass, made by Nehama, a man familiar with the Zohar and able to speak and write at one and the same time. This Nehama claimed that in his own hand he recognized the consonant "he" of his Hebrew language, and in the letter "vav" his own male soul. The hourglass he had built into the binding of the book was invisible, but, as you read you could hear the trickle of the sand in the utter silence. When it stopped, you had to turn the book over and continue reading it the other way around, back to front, and therein the secret meaning of the book was revealed. Other records relate, however, that the rabbis did not approve of the attention their compatriot Nehama paid to *The Khazar Dictionary,* and the book was subject to periodic attack by learned men from the Jewish community. The rabbis had no quarrel with the orthodoxy of the Hebrew sources for the dictionary, but they could not agree with the claims of the other sources. Finally, it must be said that the *Lexicon Cosri* did not fare well in Spain either, where, in the Moslem [Moorish] community, an eight-hundred-year ban was placed on reading the "silver copy"; since that period has yet to expire, the ban still applies. This act can be explained by the fact that families that originally came from the Khazar Empire were still to be found in Spain at the time. It is written that these "last Khazars" had an unusual custom. When they came into conflict with someone, they would try at all costs to imprecate and curse him while he slept, yet were careful not to awaken him with their invectives and curses. Evidently they believed that such imprecations had a stronger effect, and that curses worked faster when the enemy was asleep.

2. Composition of the Dictionary

It is impossible to tell what the 1691 Daubmannus edition of *The Khazar Dictionary* looked like, since the only remaining exemplars, the poisoned and the silver (companion) copies, were both destroyed, each in its own part of the world. According to one source, the gilded copy was destroyed in an utterly ignominious way. Its last owner was an old man from the Dorfmer family, famous for his ability to judge a good sword, like a bell, by its sound. He never read books and used to say, "Light lays its eggs in my eyes like a fly lays larvae in a wound. We know what that can spawn. . . ." Greasy foods were bad for the old man, and every day, when no one in the house was looking, he would lower a page of *The Khazar Dictionary* into his bowl of soup to skim off the fat and then throw away the telltale leaf. And so it happened that, before anyone in the house even noticed, he had used up the *Lexicon Cosri*. The same source says that the book was embellished with drawings, which the old man did not want to use because they spoiled the taste of the soup. These illustrated pages of the dictionary were the only ones to be preserved, and they could still perhaps be located today, provided one could ever identify, amid the trails of a path, that first trail, from which all others followed. A professor of Oriental studies and medieval archeology, Dr. Isailo Suk,[†] is believed to have owned a copy or transcript of *The Khazar Dictionary,* but after his death nothing was found among his possessions. Hence, only fragments of the Daubmannus edition have reached us, just as sleep leaves a dusting of sand in the eye.

On the basis of these fragments, cited in writings that disagree with the author or authors of *The Khazar Dictionary,* it has been firmly established (as mentioned above) that the Daubmannus edition was a sort of Khazar encyclopedia, a collection of biographies or hagiographies of individuals who had in any way crossed the firmament of the Khazar Empire, like sparrows flying through a room. Lives of the saints and of other individuals who participated in the Khazar polemic, in recording and studying it through the centuries, provided the foundation of the book, and everything was divided into three sections.

The composition of the Daubmannus dictionary, consisting of Hebrew, Moslem, and Christian sources on the Khazars' conversion, also serves as the basis for this second edition, a decision that was made, in spite of the lack of source material for the dictionary and the insurmountable difficulties this posed, after the lexicographer had read the following lines from the Khazar lexicon: "A dream is a garden of devils, and all dreams in this world were dreamed long ago. Now they are simply interchanged with equally used and worn reality, just as coins are exchanged for promissory notes and vice versa, from hand to hand. . . ." In such a world, in such a phase of that world, this was a responsibility one could indeed accept.

Here it is important to bear in mind the following.

The publisher of this second edition of *The Khazar Dictionary* is perfectly aware that Daubmannus' 17th-century material is not reliable, that it is largely based on legends, that it is something like a feast eaten in a dream, and that it is caught in a web of various ancient misconceptions. Nevertheless, this material is offered here for the reader to inspect, since this dictionary does not concern itself with the Khazars as we see them today, but is, rather, an attempt to reconstruct the lost Daubmannus edition. Contemporary findings about the Khazars are used only as unavoidable supplements to the fragments of the unpreserved original.

It is also necessary to mention that, for understandable reasons, it was impossible to preserve the order and alphabetical arrangement of the Daubmannus dictionary, in which three alphabets and three languages were used —Greek, Hebrew, and Arabic—and in which dates were given according to the three calendars of the three above-mentioned groups. Here all dates are calculated according to a single calendar, and a translation of Daubmannus' sources and his entries in three languages is given in a single language. In the 17th-century original all the words were arranged differently and, in changing from one language to another, the same name would appear in different places in each of the three dictionaries (Hebrew, Arabic, and Greek), because letters do not follow the same sequence in every alphabet, just as book pages are not always turned in the same direction, and, in the theater, leading actors do not always make their entrances from the same side of the stage. Indeed, the same principle would apply to each new translation into any other language, because the material for this dictionary on the Khazars would inevitably have to be grouped differently in each new language and new alphabet, so that the entries would always appear somewhere else and the names would acquire an ever-changing hierarchy. Hence, important entries in the Daubmannus edition, such as St. Cyril,[†] Judah Halevi,[✿] Yusuf Masudi,[𝕮] and others, do not appear in the same place here as in the first edition of *The Khazar Dictionary*. This is certainly the main shortcoming of the current version in relation to the Daubmannus edition, since only someone who can read through the sections of one book in their proper order can create the world anew. This approach was adopted, however, because it is impossible to reproduce Daubmannus' alphabetical order.

All these shortcomings need not be considered as a major drawback: the reader capable of deciphering the hidden meaning of a book from the order of its entries has long since vanished from the face of the earth, for today's reading audience believes that the matter of imagination lies exclusively within the realm of the writer and does not concern them in the least, especially with regard to a dictionary. This type of reader does not even need a sandglass in the book to remind him when to change his manner of reading: he never changes his manner of reading in any case.

3. How to Use the Dictionary

For all its problems, this book has preserved some of the virtues of the original Daubmannus edition. Like that one, it can be read in an infinite number of ways. It is an open book, and when it is shut it can be added to: just as it has its own former and present lexicographer, so it can acquire new writers, compilers, and continuers. It has a register, concordances, and entries, like a holy book or a crossword puzzle, and all the names or subjects marked with the small sign of the cross, the crescent, the Star of David, or some other symbol can be looked up in

11

the corresponding book of this dictionary for more detailed explanation. Words under the sign

†   are to be found in "The Red Book" of this diction-
       ary (Christian sources on the Khazar question)

☽   are to be found in "The Green Book" of this diction-
       ary (Islamic sources on the Khazar question)

✡   are to be found in "The Yellow Book" of this
       dictionary (Hebrew sources on the Khazar ques-
       tion)

Entries marked with the sign ▽ will be found in all three
dictionaries, and those with the sign ∧ are in Appendix I
at the back of the book.

   Thus, the reader can use the book as he sees fit. As
with any other lexicon, some will look up a word or a
name that interests them at the given moment, whereas
others may look at the book as a text meant to be read
in its entirety, from beginning to end, in one sitting, so
as to gain a complete picture of the Khazar question and
the people, issues, and events connected with it. The
book's pages can be turned from left to right or from
right to left, as were those of the Prussian edition (Hebrew and Arab sources). The three books of this dictionary—Yellow, Red, and Green—can be read in any
order the reader desires; he may start with the book that
falls open as he picks up the dictionary. That is probably
why in the 17th-century edition the books were printed
in three separate volumes. The same has not been done
here, for technical reasons. *The Khazar Dictionary* can
also be read diagonally, to get a cross-section of all three
registers—the Islamic, the Christian, and the Hebrew.
The best way to use this method is to work in threes,
either by choosing entries with the sign ▽ (which are to
be found in all three dictionaries), such as the words
"Ateh," "kaghan," "Khazar polemic," or "Khazars," or
by choosing three different persons connected by the

same role in the history of the Khazar question. This gives the reader an integral picture of the entries in the three different books of this dictionary, which tell of the participants in the Khazar polemic (Sangari, Cyril, Ibn Kora), of its chroniclers (Al-Bakri, Methodius, Halevi), or of students of the Khazar question in the 12th century (Cohen, Masudi, Brankovich) and in the 20th century (Suk, Muawia, Schultz). Of course, among these triads one should not forget the three who come from the three hells, the Moslem, the Hebrew, and the Christian (Ephrosinia Lukarevich, Sevast, Akshany). They have covered the longest journey to reach this book.

But the reader should not be discouraged by such detailed instructions. He can, with a clear conscience, skip all these introductory remarks and read the way he eats: he can use his right eye as a fork, his left as a knife, and toss the bones over his shoulder. That will do. He may, of course, wander off and get lost among the words of this book, as did Masudi, one of the writers of this dictionary, who wandered into other people's dreams, never to find his way back. In that event, the reader has no other choice than to begin in the middle of any given page and forge his own path. Then he may move through the book as through a forest, from one marker to the next, orienting himself by observing the stars, the moon, and the cross. Another time he will read it like the buzzard that flies only on Thursdays, and here again he can rearrange it in an infinite number of ways, like a Rubik cube. No chronology will be observed here, nor is one necessary. Hence, each reader will put together the book for himself, as in a game of dominoes or cards, and, as with a mirror, he will get out of this dictionary as much as he puts into it, for, as is written on one of the pages of this lexicon, you cannot get more out of the truth than what you put into it. After all, this book need never be read in its entirety; one can take half or only a part and stop there, as one often does with dictionaries. The more one seeks the more one gets, and the lucky discoverer will ultimately have in his possession all the links connecting the names in this dictionary. The rest will be for others.

4. Preserved Fragments from the Introduction to the Destroyed 1691 Edition of the Dictionary (translated from the Latin)

1. The author advises the reader not to tackle this book unless he absolutely has to. And if he does touch it, let it be on days when he feels that his mind and sense of caution probe deeper than usual, and let him read it the way he catches "leap-fever," an illness that skips over every other day and strikes only on feminine days of the week.

2. Imagine two men holding a captured puma on a rope. If they want to approach each other, the puma will attack, because the rope will slacken; only if they both pull simultaneously on the rope is the puma equidistant from the two of them. That is why it is so hard for him who reads and him who writes to reach each other: between them lies a mutual thought captured on ropes that they pull in opposite directions. If we were now to ask that puma—in other words, that thought—how it perceived these two men, it might answer that at the ends of the rope those to be eaten are holding someone they cannot eat. . . .

8. Take care, my friend, not to be too obsequious and not to curry favor overly with those who hold their authority in a ring and their power in the sweep of a sword. They are always surrounded by people who pay

court not willingly or out of conviction, but because they have to. And they have to because they have a bee showing on their cap or lard hidden in their armpit, they were caught doing wrong and are now atoning for it; their freedom is on a leash, and they are ready to do anything. Those high up, who rule over everybody, know and use this well. Take care, therefore, that they do not perceive you as one of that lot, innocent though you may be. This is exactly what will happen if you ever praise them in excess or overly pander to them in that crowd of sycophants: they will associate you in their minds with lawbreakers and criminals and will think you are another one with a mote in your eye and that you do nothing of your own free will or out of conviction, but because you must in order to atone for your sins. Such people are rightly despised and kicked around like dogs or forced to commit the same sorts of acts they committed before. . . .

9. As for you, the writer, never forget the following: the reader is like a circus horse which has to be taught that it will be rewarded with a lump of sugar every time it acquits itself well. If that sugar is withheld, it will not perform. As for essayists and critics, they are like cuckolded husbands: always the last to find out. . . .

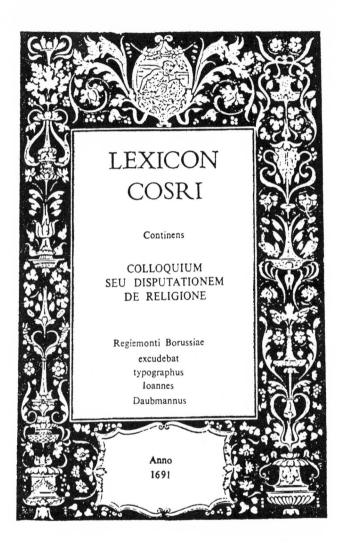

LEXICON
COSRI

Continens

COLLOQUIUM
SEU DISPUTATIONEM
DE RELIGIONE

Regiemonti Borussiae
excudebat
typographus
Ioannes
Daubmannus

Anno
1691

Title page from the original (destroyed)
1691 Daubmannus edition of
The Khazar Dictionary
(Reconstruction)

THE
RED
BOOK

CHRISTIAN SOURCES
ON THE
KHAZAR QUESTION

ATEH▽ (9th century)—the Khazar princess whose role in the polemic concerning the Khazars'▽ conversion was decisive. Her name is taken to be the term for the Khazars' four states of consciousness. At night she wore a single letter on each eyelid, inscribed as are those put on the eyelids of horses before a race. The letters came from the proscribed Khazar alphabet, in which each letter kills as soon as it is read. They were written by blind men, and the ladies-in-waiting shut their eyes when they attended to the princess in the morning, before her bath. Thus, she was protected from her enemies while she slept. This, for the Khazars, was the time when a person is the most vulnerable. Ateh was a beautiful and pious woman, and the letters suited her perfectly. Seven kinds of salt stood on her table at all times, and she would always dip her fingers in a different salt before taking each piece of fish. This is the way she prayed. They say she had seven faces, like her seven salts. According to one legend, every morning she would pick up a mirror and sit down to draw; a male or a female slave, always someone different, would come to pose. And every morning she would create a new, hitherto unseen image of her own face. According to other stories, Ateh was no beauty at all, but she would train her face in the mirror and compose her features into a lovely expression and a pretty shape. These beauty exercises required tremendous physical effort, and as soon as the princess was alone and could relax, her beauty would dissolve like her salt. In any event, in the 9th century a Byzantine emperor used the term "Khazar face" to describe the famous philosopher and Patriarch Photius, which could have meant either that the Patriarch was related to the Khazars or that he was a hypocrite.

According to Daubmannus,✲ neither was the case. The term "Khazar face" referred to the characteristic of all Khazars, including Princess Ateh, of starting each day as someone else, with a completely new and unfamiliar face, so that even the closest of kin were at pains to recognize one another. Travelers recorded just the opposite: that all Khazar faces were identical, that they never changed, and that this created problems and caused confusion. Whatever the case may be, the result is the same, and a Khazar face epitomizes a face that is hard to recall. This may also explain the legend that Princess Ateh showed a different face to each of the participants in the Khazar polemic at the kaghan's▽ court, or even that there were three Princess Atehs—one for the Moslem, another for the Christian, and a third for the Hebrew scholar and dream interpreter. The fact is, however, that her presence at the Khazar palace was not recorded in the Christian source of the time, written in Greek and translated into Old Slavonic (*The Life of Constantine of Thessalonica, St. Cyril*), but, according to *The Khazar Dictionary,* something like a cult of Princess Ateh once existed among Greek and Slavic monastic circles. This cult originated in the belief that Ateh had defeated the Hebrew theologian in the Khazar polemic and had adopted Christianity along with the kaghan, about whom it is uncertain whether he was her father, her husband, or her brother. Two of Princess Ateh's prayers were preserved in their Greek translation, and although they were never canonized, Daubmannus cites them as her "Our Father" and "Hail Mary!" The first of these two prayers reads:

On our ship, my Father, the crew swarms like ants: I cleaned it this morning with my hair, and they crawl up the clean mast and strip the green sails like sweet vine leaves into their anthills: the helmsman tries to tear loose the helm and haul it off on his back like spoils to feed and live on for an

*entire week; the weakest among them pull at the salty rope
and disappear with it into the bowels of our floating home.
Only thou, my Father, hast no right to their kind of hunger.
While they devour speed, to thee, my heart, thee, my only
Father, belongs the quickest part. Thy food be the shattered
wind.*

Princess Ateh's second prayer seems to explain the
story of her Khazar face:

*I have memorized my mother's life and, like in a play, I
act it out in front of the mirror every morning for an hour.
This has gone on day after day for years now. I don my
mother's robes, holding her fan, my hair done like hers,
plaited into the shape of a woolen cap. I enact her in front
of others as well, even in the bed of my beloved. In moments
of passion I cease to exist, I am not me, but her. For I enact
her so well that my own passion vanishes and only hers
remains. In other words, she has already stolen my every
touch of love. Yet I do not begrudge her, because I know
that she too was once robbed in the same way by her own
mother. If someone were now to ask me why I act so much,
I would say: I am trying to give birth to myself anew, but in
a better way. . . .*

It is known that Princess Ateh never managed to die.
Nevertheless, a record of her death exists and is inscribed
on a knife embellished with tiny holes. This isolated and
not particularly plausible story is cited by Daubmannus,
not, however, as a story about how Princess Ateh actually
died, but about how it could have happened had she
been able to die at all. Just as wine does not turn the hair
gray, so this story cannot cause anyone harm. It reads:

THE FAST MIRROR AND THE SLOW

One spring Princess Ateh said: "I have grown accustomed to my thoughts, as to my dresses. They always
have the same waistline, and I see them everywhere, even

at crossroads. Worst of all, they make it impossible to see the crossroads any more."

One day, hoping to amuse her, the princess's servants brought her two mirrors. They were much like other Khazar mirrors. Both were made of shiny salt, but one was fast and the other slow. Whatever the fast mirror picked up, reflecting the world like an advance on the future, the slow mirror returned, settling the debt of the former, because it was as slow in relation to the present as the other was fast. When they brought the mirrors to Princess Ateh, she was still in bed and the letters had not yet been washed off her eyelids. She saw herself in the mirrors with closed lids and died instantly. She vanished between two blinks of the eye, or better said, for the first time she read the lethal letters on her eyelids, because she had blinked the moment before and the moment after, and the mirrors had reflected it. She died, killed simultaneously by letters from both the past and the future.

B RANKOVICH, AVRAM (1651–1689)— one of the authors of this book. A hired diplomat in Edirne and to the Porte in Constantinople, a military commander in the Austro-Turkish wars, a polyhistor and a learned man. Brankovich's donor portrait was painted on the wall of the Church of St. Paraskeva in Kupinik, the Brankovich family estate. There he was shown with his kin, offering on his sword the completed Church of St. Petka to his great-great-grandmother, the despot and saint, the holy mother Angelina.

Sources: Information about Avram Brankovich is scattered in Austrian intelligence reports, especially those compiled for Prince Badensky and General Veterany by one of Brankovich's two scribes, Nikon Sevast.[†] Some attention was devoted to Avram Brankovich by his relative Count George Brankovich (1645–1711) in his Walachian chronicle and his extensive Serbian chronicles, the relevant sections of which, unfortunately, have been lost. Brankovich's final days were described by his servant and master of the sword, Averkie Skila.[†] A chronology of Brankovich's life and work can best be assembled on the basis of the written confession sent to the Peć Patriarch from Poland by Avram Brankovich's second scribe, Theoctist Nikolsky,[Λ] and on the basis of the icon depicting the miracles of St. Elias the prophet, because Brankovich adapted every scene from the life of his saint to events in his own life, recording it all on the back of the painting.

"Avram Brankovich hails from a family that moved from the South to the Danubian basin after the Serbian Empire fell to Turkish rule," wrote Nikon Sevast in his confidential report to the Viennese court. "Family members swept up in the move to abandon territory that had fallen into Turkish hands migrated to the Lipova and Yenopolje provinces in the 16th century. It has been said ever since that the Brankoviches of Erdély count in Tzintzar, lie in Walachian, are silent in Greek, sing hymns in Russian, are cleverest in Turkish, and speak their mother tongue—Serbian—only when they intend to kill. They come from western Herzegovina, from the environs of Trebinje, from the town of Korenići, near Lastva in Gornje Police, whence they derive their second family name, Korenići. Since the time of their migration, the Brankoviches have held a respected position in Erdély, and for two hundred years now they have had the best wine in Walachia; whence the maxim 'They can get you drunk on their tears.' While distinguishing themselves in military battle on the border of two centuries and two states—the Hungarian and the Turkish—the Brankovich family also provided a number of distinguished clerical figures in their new territory along the Mureşul River, in Yenopolje, Lipova, and Pankota. Moses Brankovich, as Bishop Matthew, was a metropolitan of Yenopolje, and the walnuts he tossed into the Danube were always the first to reach the Black Sea. Solomon (named Sava I when he was bishop of Yenopolje), his son, and uncle to Count George Brankovich, governed the Yenova and Lipova eparchy without ever dismounting from his horse and drank exclusively in the saddle until Lipova was taken from the Turks in 1607. The Brankoviches claim that they are descendants of the Serbian despots Brankovich, but it is difficult to determine the origin of their property. There is a saying that everything gained between Kavalla and Zemun in Tzintzar dreams actually goes into the Brankovich bag of booty. Their jewels are as cold as vipers, birds cannot fly over their lands, and folk poems already confuse them with the ruling families. The Brankoviches are the patrons of monasteries in Walachia and on Mt. Athos in Greece; they build fortresses and churches, like those in Alba Reale in Kupinik or in a place called Teus. Prince Sigmund Rakoczy has bestowed colonies, heaths, and noble titles upon the female members of the Brankovich clan, and through the female line of the family the Brankoviches are related to the Sekels of Erdély, and thus one part of their property was obtained from the Sekels as a dowry. It is worth mentioning that in the Brankovich family inheritances are meted out according to the color of one's beard. All heirs with red beards (which they inherited from the female side, since the Brankoviches take red-haired women for wives) relinquish priority to the black-bearded men, whose beards testify that they descend from the male line. The Brankoviches' possessions are currently valued at nearly twenty-seven thousand forints, and produce an annual revenue estimated at over fifteen hundred forints. Their family heraldry may not be the most reliable, but their wealth is both undisputed and as firm as the ground on which they ride, and for over two hundred years the smallest coin never once escaped their chests of gold.

"Avram Brankovich arrived in Constantinople lame,

with a raised heel, and there is a story circulating here about how he was crippled. When Avram was a mere boy of seven—so the story goes—the Turks raided his father's property and on the road encountered a small contingent from the court, accompanying the child on a walk. When they saw the Turks the escorts fled, leaving Avram and an old man who deftly staved off all the horsemen's attacks with a long stick, until their leader hurled a spear that he had kept between his teeth, hidden in a piece of reed. Struck, the old man fell, but Avram, who had a stick of his own in his hand, swung it with all his might and caught the Turk by the boots. Yet, for all the despair and hate behind the boy's blow, it was not enough. The Turk only laughed and rode off, ordering the village to be burned down. Years passed like turtles, Avram Brankovich grew up, and the event was forgotten, for there were other battles to be fought, and Brankovich now led soldiers of his own, bearing a flag on his sleeve and a reed with a poisoned spear in his mouth. Once they came across an enemy spy traveling with his son, a mere boy, on the road, carrying only a stick and looking innocent enough. One of the soldiers recognized the old man, spurred his horse toward him, and tried to tie him up. But the old man defended himself so tenaciously with his stick that everyone thought there was a secret message rolled up in it. Then Brankovich withdrew the poisoned spear and killed the old man. At that same moment, the boy struck him with his own stick. He was barely seven years old and, truth be told, not with all the force of his hatred and love could he have harmed Brankovich. All the same, Brankovich laughed and fell as if he had been cut down dead.

"That blow left him lame in one leg, so he gave up the military and was brought by his relative Count George Brankovich into the diplomatic corps in Edirne,

Warsaw, and Vienna. Here in Constantinople, Branko-vich works for the English envoy and has an apartment in a spacious castle on the Bosporus, between the castles Yoroz Kaleshi and Karatash. On the first floor of the castle, Brankovich built exactly one-half of the church dedicated to his great-great-grandmother Angelina, who was declared a saint by the Eastern church, while the other half of the church is located in Erdély, where Brankovich's father comes from.

"Avram Brankovich cuts a striking figure. He has a broad chest the size of a cage for large birds or a small beast, and is often the target of murderers, for there is a popular poem saying that his bones are made of gold.

"He arrived in Constantinople and travels on a tall camel that is fed on fish. The animal strides so smoothly beneath him that wine does not spill from the glass set in its harness. Since earliest childhood Brankovich has slept not at night, like the rest of the saucer-eyed world, but only during the day; no one knows exactly when he tucked in his hair and gave up day for night. But even at night, when he is awake, he cannot settle down in one place for long, as if he had fed on another's tears. Hence, two plates, two chairs, and two glasses are always set for him at the dining table, and in the middle of a meal he will suddenly jump up and change his seat. Similarly, he cannot stay with one language for long: he changes them like mistresses and speaks Walachian one minute and Hungarian or Turkish the next, and he has begun to learn Khazar from a parrot. They say he also speaks Spanish in his sleep, but this knowledge melts by the time he is awake. Recently someone in one of his dreams told him a poem in an unintelligible language. He re-membered the poem, and in order to interpret it, we had to find someone skilled in the languages Brankovich does not know. This led us to a rabbi, and Brankovich recited the memorized verses for him. There were not many, and they went:

לִבִּי בְמִזְרָח וְאָנֹכִי בְּסוֹף מַעֲרָב
אֵיךְ אֶטְעֲמָה אֵת אֲשֶׁר־אֹכַל וְאֵיךְ יֶעֱרָב
אֵיכָה אֲשַׁלֵּם נְדָרַי וָאֱסָרַי בְּעוֹד
צִיּוֹן בְּחֶבֶל אֱדוֹם וַאֲנִי בְּכֶבֶל עֲרָב
יֵקַל בְּעֵינַי עֲזֹב כָּל־טוּב סְפָרַד כְּמוֹ
יֵקַר בְּעֵינַי רְאוֹת עַפְרוֹת דְּבִיר נֶחֱרָב׃

Having heard the beginning, the rabbi interrupted Brankovich and continued to recite the remainder of the poem from memory. Then he wrote down the name of the author. The poem had been written back in the 12th century, and had been compiled by a man named Judah Halevi.✢ Since then Brankovich has also been learning Hebrew. His daily occupation, however, is entirely practical. For he is a man of many talents, and his smile is alchemy among the other knowledges and skills of his face.

"Every evening, as soon as he rises, he prepares himself for war. In fact, he practices his speed with the saber with a locally renowned expert, a Copt by the name of Averkie Skila, whom Kyr Avram hired as a servant. This Averkie has one ravenous and one Lenten eye, and all the wrinkles of his face are tied up in a swathed knot between his brows. He possesses the most complete description and list of every saber move ever performed, and, before adding new ones to his handwritten manual of saber techniques, he personally tests them on human flesh. There is a spacious hall with a carpet the size of a small meadow where Lord Brankovich and the aforementioned Copt lock themselves in and practice with their sabers in total darkness. Averkie Skila usually takes one end of the camel's reins in his left hand; Kyr Avram takes the other, and in his right hand holds the saber, which weighs the same as the one held there in the dark by Averkie Skila. Slowly they coil the rein around their elbows, and when they sense each other's nearness they ruthlessly strike out at each other in the deafening darkness. Songs of Brankovich's speed are sung to the strains of the gusle. Last autumn I saw him stand beneath a tree, his saber drawn, waiting for the wind to blow; as the first fruit dropped, he slashed it with his saber in mid-air, splitting it in half. He has a harelip, and grows whiskers to hide it, but his teeth show through when his mouth is closed. He looks as if he has no lips and his whiskers grow on his teeth.

"Serbs say that he loves his native land and is both candle and salt to his people, but he has habits that are strange and unbefitting to his calling. He does not know how to put an end to a conversation and never seizes the moment when it is time to get up and leave. He always drags it out and tarries too long, leaving people more confused at the end than when they first met him. He smokes hashish prepared specially for him by a eunuch from Kavalla, and by no other. But, strangely enough, he has no constant need for opium, and in order to maintain himself thus, he periodically sends a messenger with a sealed chest of hashish as far as Pest, whence he receives it unopened, under the same seal, two months later, just when he knows that he will again need opium. When he is not traveling, his enormous camel saddle, with its little bells, stands upright in the spacious library and serves as a standing desk on which one can write and read. In the rooms around him are piles of household articles that look intimidated, but nowhere in his immediate vicinity are there, nor will there be, two identical objects. Every object, animal, and person around him must be from a different village. Among his servants he has Serbs, Romanians, Greeks, and Copts, and recently he hired a Turk from Anatolia as a valet. Kyr Avram has a large and a small bed, and when he is reposing (he sleeps only during the day) he moves from one bed to the other. While he sleeps, his valet, an Anatolian by the name of Yusuf Masudi, ^Ɛ watches him with a look that fells birds. When awakened, Kyr Avram sits in bed and, as if out of fear, sings troparia and contakia in honor of his ancestors, whom the Serbian church has declared saints.

"It is impossible to determine the extent of his interest in women. A life-size wooden monkey with an enormous penis crouches on Brankovich's table. Kyr Avram is sometimes wont to say, 'A woman without a behind is like a village without a church!,' but that is all. Once a month my lord Brankovich goes off to Galata, always to the same fortuneteller, and she reads the cards the old way, very slowly. The fortuneteller has a special table for Brankovich, and she throws a new card on this table whenever the wind changes outside. Which wind blows determines what card will fall on Brankovich's table, and so it has been for years. Last Easter a southerly wind blew as soon as we entered, and she was able to offer him a new prophecy:

" 'You are dreaming of a man with a mustache, one half of which is gray. Young, with red eyes and glass fingernails, he is heading for Constantinople, and soon the two of you will meet. . . .'

"This news so pleased our master that he immediately ordered a golden ring to be placed in my nose, and I barely managed to dissuade him from such kindness. . . .

"Aware of the Viennese court's great interest in the plans of my lord Brankovich, I can say that he is a person who tends to his future like a garden—with special attention and zeal. He is not one of those who will journey through life on the run. He settles his future very slowly and conscientiously. He uncovers it piece by piece, like an unknown shore; first he clears it, then he builds on the best site, and finally he rearranges the objects inside at great length. He tries not to let his future slow down its pace and growth, but he also takes care not to rush ahead of it. It is a kind of race: the quickest is the loser. At present, Kyr Avram's future is like a garden where a seed has already been planted, but only he knows what will sprout. Still, the direction in which Brankovich is heading can perhaps be determined from a tale whispered about him. It is:

THE TALE OF PETKUTIN AND KALINA

"Kyr Avram Brankovich's elder son, Grgur Brankovich,[†] thrust his slipper into the stirrup early and drew his saber steeled with camel dung. His frilled and blood-stained vestments had been sent from Gyüla, where Grgur lived with his mother, to Constantinople to be washed and ironed under his father's supervision, to dry in the perfumed breeze from the Bosporus, to bleach in the Greek sun, and to return to Gyüla with the first caravan.

"Avram Brankovich's second, younger son was at the time stretched out somewhere in Bachka behind a motley stove built like a church, and he was suffering. It was rumored that the devil had pissed on him and that the child would get up at night, flee from the house, and clean the streets. For at night Mora sucked him, she nibbled at his heels, and man's milk flowed from his breasts. In vain did they drive a fork into the door and with their spit-covered thumb between their fingers make the sign of the cross over his chest. Finally, a woman advised him to pass the night with a knife soaked in vinegar and, when Mora fell upon him, to promise to lend her salt in the morning and then to stab her with the knife. The boy did so: when Mora began to nurse at his breast, he offered her a loan of salt, stabbed her, and heard a cry in which he recognized a voice he had known long ago. The third morning, his mother arrived from Gyüla, in Bachka, asked for salt at the door, and dropped dead. On her was discovered a knife wound; when he licked it, it was sour.... From that moment, the boy was left weak with horror, his hair began to fall out, and (according to what the healers told Brankovich) he lost one year of his life with every hair that fell out. They sent Brankovich locks of the child's hair, wrapped in jute. He attached them to a soft mirror painted with the child's image, and so knew how many years his son had left to live.

"However, almost no one knows that Kyr Avram, besides those two sons, also had a foster son, if that is the right word for him. This third, foster, son had no mother. Brankovich created him out of mud and read him the Fortieth Psalm to awaken and breathe life into him. When he came to the lines 'I waited patiently for the Lord; and he inclined unto me, and heard my cry. He brought me up also out of an horrible pit, out of the miry clay, and set my feet upon a rock, and established my goings,' the church bell in Dalj rang out three times, and the young man moved and said:

" 'At the first ring I was in India, at the second in Leipzig, and with the third ring I entered my own body....' Then Brankovich tied a Solomon's knot in the boy's hair, hooked a hawthorn-wood spoon into his pig-tail, bestowed the name Petkutin upon him, and released him into the world. Around his own neck he placed a rope with a rock, and stood through the liturgy for the fourth week of the holy Lenten fast with this collar around his neck.

"Of course, the father also had to build death into Petkutin's breast (so as to have everything just like the living). At first, this embryo of his end, this small and still-unfledged death inside Petkutin, was timid and rather stupid; it had little need for food and had stunted limbs. But it was already infinitely pleased that Petkutin was growing, and he grew enough that soon his ornate sleeves were so large that a bird could fly in them. Yet the death within Petkutin soon became quicker and smarter than he was, and was the first to sense the dangers. Then it seemed to acquire a rival, who will be discussed later. It became impatient and jealous and drew attention to itself by making Petkutin's knee itch. He would scratch the knee and his nail would inscribe letters on his skin, which could then be read. This is how they corresponded. Death was especially intolerant of Petkutin's illnesses. But Petkutin's father had to provide him with illness so that he would look more like a living being, because illness serves as a pair of eyes for living beings. Brankovich tried, however, to make Petkutin's illnesses as innocent as possible, and favored him with a flower-fever, which appears in the spring when the wild grass grows and the flowers dust the wind and water with pollen.

"Brankovich installed Petkutin on his estate in Dalj, in a house where the rooms were always full of grey-hounds that were keener on killing than on eating. Once a month the servants combed the carpets with cards and pulled out balls of long different-colored hairs resembling dogs' tails. As time passed, the rooms in which Petkutin lived took on the same special colors, by which Petkutin's quarters could be recognized immediately from a thousand others. The imprints and grease spots that he and his sweat left behind on glass doorknobs, pillows, seats, and supports, on pipes, knives, and glass stems, created a rainbow of hues peculiar to him alone. It was a kind of portrait, icon, or signature. Brankovich sometimes found Petkutin inside the mirrors of the spacious house, built into the green silence. He taught him to reconcile inwardly autumn, winter, spring, and summer with the water, earth, fire, and wind which man also carries in his bowels. The enormous work to be done lasted ages; Petkutin acquired calluses on his thoughts, his mnemonic muscles were stretched taut, and Brankovich taught him to read one page of a book with his left eye and one with his right, to write Serbian with his right hand and Turkish with his left. Then he instructed him in literature, and Petkutin began to succeed in finding traces of the Bible in Pythagoras' writings and signed his name as quickly as catching a fly.

"Overall, he became a handsome and educated young man, and only occasionally did he exhibit barely noticeable signs that he was unlike others. For example, on Monday evenings he could take a different day from his future and use it the following morning, in place of Tuesday. When he came to the day he had taken, he would use the skipped Tuesday in its place, thereby adjusting the total. Under these conditions, of course, the connecting seams of the days could not fit together properly, and cracks appeared in time, but this matter only gladdened Petkutin.

"This was not so with his father. Brankovich was forever doubtful about the perfection of his creation, and when Petkutin reached the age of twenty-one, the father decided to test him and see how he competed in every regard against real human beings. He thought: 'The living have tested him; now he must be tested by the dead. For only if the dead are deceived and, upon seeing Petkutin, think that a real man of flesh and blood is standing before them, one who first salts and then chews, can the experiment be considered a success.' And, having come to this conclusion, he found Petkutin a bride.

"Since landowners in Walachia always take with them a bodyguard and a soulguard, Brankovich occasionally did the same. Among his soulguards he had a Tzintzar who used to say that everything on earth had become truth and who had a very pretty daughter. The daughter had taken all her best features from her mother, who after birth remained forever ugly. When the girl turned ten, her mother, with what had once been pretty hands, taught her how to bake bread, and her father summoned her, told her that the future is not water, and died. The girl wept such torrents for her father that ants were able to climb up to her face on her tears. She was left an orphan now, and Brankovich arranged for her to meet Petkutin. Her name was Kalina. Her shadow carried the scent of cinnamon, and Petkutin discovered that she would fall in love with any man who ate cornelian cherries in March. He waited for March, ate his fill of cornelian cherries, and invited Kalina for a walk along the Danube. When they parted, she removed the ring from her finger and threw it into the river.

"If something good happens to somebody—she explained to Petkutin—it should always be spiced with some small unpleasantness, so that the moment is better remembered. One always remembers the unpleasant longer than the pleasant things in life. . . .

"In short, she liked Petkutin, Petkutin liked her, and the wedding took place that same autumn to great rejoicing. The groomsmen at the wedding said their good-byes and kissed farewell, since they would not be seeing one another for months; then they threw their arms around one another and left to make the rounds of the brandy stills. When spring came, they finally sobered up, took stock of their surroundings, and, following the long winter stupor, laid eyes on and recognized one another again. Then they returned to Dalj and saw off the new-lyweds on the traditional spring excursion, shooting their guns in the air. One should know that on their spring outings or excursions, newlyweds from Dalj usually go as far as the ancient ruin, with its lovely seats of stone and its Greek darkness that is thicker than any other darkness, just as a Greek fire burns brighter than any other fire. This is where Petkutin and Kalina now headed. From afar, Petkutin looked as if he were driving a team of black horses, but when he sneezed from the scent of a flower or cracked his whip, a cloud of black flies would rise from the horses and one could see that they were white. This, however, bothered neither Pet-kutin nor Kalina.

"That winter they had fallen in love. They ate by turns from the same fork, and she drank wine from his mouth. He caressed her until her soul groaned within her body, and she worshipped him and begged him to urinate inside her. She would laughingly tell the other girls that nothing scratches better than the three-day beard of a man who has been making love. But she thought to herself: 'The moments of my life are dying like flies gulped down by fish. How can I make them nourishment for his hunger?' She begged him to bite off her ear and eat it, and she never closed drawers or cup-board doors behind her, so as not to break her luck. She was a quiet girl, because she had grown up in the silence of her father's endless reading of one and the same prayer, which always drew the same kind of silence around it. And now it was the same as they set off on their excursion, and this pleased her. Petkutin held the reins of the coach around his neck and read a book, while Kalina chattered. They played a game along the way. If she spoke a word that he happened to be reading just then in his book, they would switch roles, and she would do the reading and he the guessing. Thus, when she pointed to a sheep in the field and he said that he had just reached the place in his book where a sheep was mentioned, she scarcely believed him, and took the text to see for herself. And indeed, in the book it was written:

> *And when I had with prayers and supplications*
> *Entreated them, the nations of the dead,*
> *I took the sheep and cut their throats above*
> *The pit, and the black blood ran out. And then*
> *There gathered out of Erebus the ghosts*
> *Of the departed dead; unwedded youths*
> *And brides, and old men that had suffered much. . . .*

"Having guessed correctly, Kalina now began to read what followed:

> *And many wounded by the bronze-tipped spears,*
> *Men slain in fight with bloody harness on them.*
> *From every side they swarmed around the pit*
> *With eerie cries, and pale fear seized on me. . . .*
> *For me, I drew my sharp sword from my side*
> *And sat there, suffering not the strengthless shadows*
> *O' the dead to venture near the blood, until*
> *I had made question of Teiresias.*

"Just as she came to the word 'shadow,' Petkutin noticed a shadow cast by the ruin of a Roman theater by the road. They had arrived.

"They entered by the actors' entrance, placed the bottle of wine, mushrooms, and blood sausages they had brought with them on a large rock in the center of the stage, and quickly retired into the shade. Petkutin gathered dry buffalo droppings and some mud-caked twigs, carried all this to the stage, and lit a fire. The sound of its crackling carried clearly all the way to the farthest seat in the last row at the top of the theater. But outside the arena, where wild grasses mixed with the scent of cranberries and laurel, nothing of what was taking place inside could be heard. Petkutin salted the fire to rid it of the smell of dung and mud, then washed the mushrooms in wine and tossed them and the blood sausages onto the smoldering cinders. Kalina sat and watched the setting sun change seats in the theater, moving toward the exit. Petkutin walked about the stage and, noticing the names of bygone occupants of the seats carved in front of each row, began to read out the ancient unfamiliar words:

" 'Caius Veronius Aet . . . Sextus Clodius Cai filius, Publilia tribu . . . Sorto Servilio . . . Veturia Aeia . . .'

" 'Don't summon the dead!' Kalina warned him. 'Don't summon them—they'll come!'

"As soon as the sun had departed from the theater she removed the mushrooms and blood sausages from the fire and they began to eat. The acoustics were perfection itself, and each bite they took carried singly and with equal clarity to every seat, from the first to the eighth row, but everywhere in a different way, echoing the sound back to them at center stage. It was as if the spectators whose names had been carved into the fronts of the stone seats were eating together with the couple, or at least were greedily smacking their lips with every bite. One hundred and twenty pairs of dead ears were eavesdropping at pricked attention, and the entire theater was chewing along with the married couple, hungrily sniffing the aroma of the blood sausages. When they stopped eating, the dead stopped too, as if a morsel had got stuck in their throat, and they waited tensely to see what the young man and woman would do next. At such moments, Petkutin was especially careful not to cut his finger while slicing the food, because he had the feeling that the smell of human blood might throw the spectators off balance and that, as quick as a shooting pain, they might attack him and Kalina from the gallery and tear them apart, driven by their two-thousand-year-old thirst. He felt himself shudder, drew Kalina toward him, and kissed her. She kissed him, and they could hear the sound of 120 mouths kissing, as though those in the gallery were kissing too.

"After the meal, Petkutin threw the remainder of the blood sausages into the fire to burn and then doused the flames with wine; the sizzling of the dying fire in the theater was accompanied by a muffled 'Pssssss!' He was just about to return the knife to its case when the wind blew unexpectedly, depositing pollen on the stage. Petkutin sneezed and cut his hand. Blood spilled onto the warm stone and began to smell. . . .

"At that moment 120 shrieking and howling dead souls descended upon them. Petkutin drew his sword, but they pulled Kalina apart, tearing her live flesh piece by piece until her cries became one with those emitted by the dead, and until she herself joined in devouring the still-uneaten parts of her own body.

"Petkutin did not know how many days had passed before he realized where the theater's exit was. He wandered about the stage around the dead fire and the remains of dinner until something invisible picked up his mantle from the ground and threw it over its shoulders. The empty cape came up to him and addressed him in Kalina's voice.

"Frightened, he embraced her, but beneath the fur and in the depths of her voice he could see nothing but the purple lining of the mantle.

" 'Tell me,' Petkutin said to Kalina, clasping her in his arms, 'I feel as if some terrible thing happened to me here a thousand years ago. Someone was torn apart and devoured, and his blood still lies on the ground. I don't know if or when it really happened. Whom did they eat? You or me?'

" 'Nothing happened to you; they didn't tear you apart,' replied Kalina. 'And it happened just a while ago, not a thousand years ago.'

" 'But I do not see you. Which of the two of us is dead?'

" 'You do not see me, young man, because the living cannot see the dead. You can only hear my voice. As for me, I do not know who you are and cannot know until I have tasted a drop of your blood. But calm down—I do see you, I see you very well. And I know that you are alive.'

" 'But, Kalina!' he cried. 'It's me, your Petkutin. Don't you recognize me? Just a moment ago, if it was a moment ago, you kissed me.'

" 'What is the difference between a moment ago and a thousand years ago when things are the way they are now?'

"At those words Petkutin withdrew the knife, raised his finger to the spot where he imagined the invisible lips of his wife to be, and cut himself.

"The drop of blood released its smell but did not spill onto the stone, for Kalina eagerly awaited it on her lips. Once she recognized Petkutin, she screamed and tore him apart like carrion, greedily drank his blood, and tossed his bones into the theater, whence came the others in a swarm.

"On the same day this happened to Petkutin, Kyr Avram Brankovich wrote the following words: 'The experiment with Petkutin has ended successfully. He performed his role so well that he fooled both the living and the dead. Now I can proceed to the more difficult part of my task. From the small to the large undertaking. From man to Adam.'

"And so we come to the plans of Kyr Avram Brankovich. The plans on which he is staking his future are tied to two key persons. One is Brankovich's distinguished relative Count George Brankovich, about whom the Viennese court certainly has more information than we do here. The other is an individual whom Kyr Avram calls Kuros (which means 'boy' in Greek) and whose arrival he awaits here in Constantinople as the Jews await the coming of the Messiah. As far as can be discovered, Brankovich does not know this individual personally, does not even know his name (thus the Greek nickname), and sees him only in his dreams. But this individual appears to him regularly in his sleep, and when Brankovich dreams, he dreams of him. According to Master Avram's own description, Kuros is a young man, one half of his mustache is gray, he has glass fingernails and red eyes. Brankovich expects to meet him one day and, with his help, to discover or achieve something he very much desires. In his dreams Brankovich has learned from his Kuros to read from right to left, in the Jewish manner, and to dream dreams from their end to their beginning. These unusual dreams in which Kyr Avram turns into Kuros, or, if you like, into a Jew, began many years ago. Brankovich himself says that his dream first appeared in the form of a restlessness that, like a stone thrown into his soul, fell through it for days, stopping only at night, when his soul fell along with the stone. Then, however, his dream took complete control of his life; he became twice as young in his dream as in reality. First birds, then his brothers, and finally his father and mother disappeared from his dreams forever, saying goodbye as they parted. Subsequently, all the people and cities that belonged to his surroundings and memories disappeared from his dreams without a trace, until finally he too disappeared from this totally alien world of dreams, as though at night, while dreaming, he turned into a completely different person, whose face, seen in the mirror of the dream, frightened him, as if his mother or sister had grown a beard. This other person had red eyes, a mustache, half of which was gray, and glass fingernails.

"In these dreams, as he took leave of everyone, Brankovich dreamed of his late sister the most, but each time she would lose some part of her familiar appearance, and would acquire parts of a new, unfamiliar, different body belonging to somebody else. First she exchanged her voice with the unknown person into whom she was being transformed, then the color of her hair and her teeth, until only her arms still embraced Brankovich, with increasing passion—the rest was no longer her. And then, one night, a night so thin that two men, one standing in Tuesday and the other in Wednesday, could shake hands, she came to him completely transformed, so beautiful that the very sight of her frightened people away. She threw herself around his neck with double-thumbed hands. At first he almost fled from her out of his dream, but then he yielded and picked one of her breasts like a peach. And, as if he picked his days from her as from a tree, she offered him a different fruit each time, each one always sweeter than the last, and he slept with her during the day in different dreams the way other men sleep with their mistresses at night in borrowed homes. When one of her double-thumbed hands periodically emerged from these embraces, he was unable to determine which hand she was using to caress him, since they did not differ. But this dreamed love so truly and completely exhausted him that he was almost entirely drained from his dreams into his bed. Then she came to him one last time and said:

" 'He who curses from a bitter soul will have his wish granted. Perhaps we shall meet somewhere in another life.'

"And Brankovich never found out if she had said that to him, Kyr Avram Brankovich, or to Kuros, the double with the gray half-mustache from his dream, into whom Brankovich was transformed while he slept. For he had long since stopped feeling like Avram Brankovich in his dreams. He felt completely like the man with the glass fingernails. For years he hadn't limped in his dreams, as he did in real life. In the evenings he felt as if he were being awakened by someone else's fatigue; in the mornings he felt as though he might fall asleep, because somewhere someone felt rested, alert, and awake. He had eyelids that would shut whenever someone else's would open. He and his anonymous double had connecting vessels of energy and blood, and this strength flowed from one to the other, the way wine is poured from one container into another to keep from souring. As the one became more and more rested and energetic at night, while he dreamed, the energy would increasingly desert the other, edging him toward fatigue and sleep. Most horrifying of all was when one of them would suddenly fall into a sleep in the middle of the street or wherever he might be, as though it were not sleep but the echo of someone's momentary awakening. Recently, while observing the eclipse of the moon, Kyr Avram fell into a sleep so suddenly that he immediately began to dream he was being whipped, and he was entirely unaware that in falling he had struck his head, cutting himself in the same place on his forehead where he had been struck with the whip in his dream.

"It is my impression that this whole affair—involving both Kuros and that fellow Judah Halevi—is directly tied in with a project my lord Brankovich and we, his servants, have been working on for years. This is a glossary, or an alphabetized list, that could be called *The Khazar Dictionary*. He has been working on it tirelessly with a fixed goal. Brankovich had eight camel-loads of books brought to Constantinople from the Zarand district and from Vienna, and more are still arriving. He has sealed himself off from the world with walls of dictionaries and old manuscripts. I, who have experience with colors, inks, and letters, recognize each letter by its smell in the damp night, and, lying in my corner, I read by their smells entire pages of the sealed and rolled scrolls that lie somewhere in the attic of the castle. Kyr Avram prefers to read in the cold, clothed only in a shirt, subjecting his body to shivers, and the only part of his reading he considers worth remembering and noting in the book is what penetrates the shivering to reach his attention. Brankovich's card file, created along with the library, encompassed a thousand pages, covering a variety of subjects: from catalogues of sighs and exclamations in Old Church Slavonic prayers to a register of salts and teas, and enormous collections of hair, beards, and mustaches of the most diverse colors and styles from living and dead persons of all races, which our master glues onto glass bottles and keeps as a sort of museum of old hairstyles. His own hair is not represented in this collection, but he has ordered that strands of it be used to weave his coat of arms with a one-eyed eagle and the motto 'Every master embraces his own death.'

"Brankovich labors over his books, collections, and

card files every night, but he has devoted himself with utmost secrecy and special attention to compiling an alphabetized list, a dictionary on the conversion of the Khazars▽—a long-lost tribe from the Black Sea coast that buried its dead in boats. It is a sort of family tree, a catalogue or collection of biographies of all the people who, a few hundred years ago, participated in the Khazars' conversion to Christianity, or of those who later left some written account of the event. Only Theoctist Nikolsky and I, Avram Brankovich's two scribes, have access to his *Khazar Dictionary*. This precaution is probably due to Brankovich's consideration of various heresies in this work, not only Christian, but also Jewish and Mohammedan: our Peć Patriarch would be sure to save for Kyr Avram one of his anathemas which he counts every August on the Day of St. Anne's Ascension, if he knew what he was up to. Brankovich possesses all the available information on Cyril† and Methodius,† the Christian enlighteners and missionaries who participated on the Greek side in the Khazars' conversion. One of the main difficulties, however, is that he is unable to alphabetize the Jewish and the Arab representatives in the Khazars' conversion, although they too took part in the event and in the related polemic conducted at the court of the Khazar kaghan.▽ Not only has he been unable to learn anything about the Jew or the Arab other than that they existed, but neither he nor any Greek source he could find on the Khazars knows their names. His men made the rounds of Walachian monasteries and Constantinople's cellars in search of Hebrew and Arabic documents on the Khazars' conversion, and he himself even came here to Constantinople, whence the missionaries Cyril and Methodius had once been sent to the Khazar capital to convert the Khazars, in order to find manuscripts and people interested in the event. However, you cannot rinse

a well with mud, and he has found nothing. He does not
believe that he is the only person interested in the Khazars, or that in the past no one outside the circle of the
Christian missionaries who left behind information on
the Khazars, no one from St. Cyril to the present day,
studied them. Certainly some dervish or Jewish rabbi—
he contends—knows some particulars about the life and
work of the Jewish or Arab participant in the polemic,
but such are not to be found in Constantinople, or they
simply don't want to say that they know. He presumes
that, aside from the Christian sources on the Khazars,
there also exist extensive Arab and Jewish sources on the
same question and people, but something is preventing
the individuals working on this from meeting and collat-
ing their knowledge, which, if only it could be pooled,
would provide a clear and complete picture of everything
concerning this question.

" 'I don't understand,' he often says. 'I probably always
stop thinking about everything too early, and then these
things remain half-formed inside me and reveal themselves only as far as the waist. . . .' In my opinion, the
reason for Kyr Avram's excessive interest in such an
insignificant matter is not difficult to explain. My lord
Brankovich concerns himself with the Khazars for the
most selfish of reasons. He is trying to cure himself of
the dream that holds him captive. The Kuros of his
dreams is also interested in the Khazar question, and
Kyr Avram knows this better than we do. The one and
only way for Kyr Avram to free himself from his dream
is to find this stranger, and only through the Khazar
documents will he find him, because they are the only
trail leading to him. I think this stranger has the same
thing in mind. Their encounter, therefore, is as inevitable
as the encounter between jailer and prisoner. Thus, it is
no wonder that lately Kyr Avram has been practicing so

intently with his master of sabers. He detests his Kuros so much that he will swallow his eyes like bird's eggs. As soon as he grabs hold of him . . . This is but a supposition. If, however, it is inaccurate, then we must recall Avram Brankovich's words about Adam and his successful experiment with Petkutin. In that event he is dangerous, his intentions will have unforeseeable consequences, and his *Khazar Dictionary* is but a bookish preparation for forceful action. . . ."

With these words, Nikon Sevast's report on Avram Brankovich comes to an end. Sevast was unable, however, to report to anyone on his master's final days, since both master and servant were killed on a Wednesday shrouded in fog, somewhere in Walachia. A record of this event was left by another of Brankovich's servants, the above-mentioned master of sabers, Averkie Skila. This note looks as though Skila had written it on the ground with the tip of his weapon, dipped in ink, while holding down the paper with his boot.

"On the last evening in Constantinople prior to his departure"—wrote Averkie Skila—"Papas Avram assembled us in his hall, which overlooked three seas. Green winds blew from the Black Sea, blue, translucent winds from the Aegean, and dry, bitter winds from the open Ionian Sea. Our master was standing by the camel saddle, reading, when we entered. Anatolian flies were feasting before the rain, and he defended himself and beat them off with a whip, unerringly hitting the bites on his back with its tip. We had already finished our regular practice session with the sabers that evening, and had I not taken his shorter leg into account, he would have slashed me wide open in that darkness. He was always faster at night than during the day. Now he had a bird's nest instead of a gaiter on his shorter leg, because it was a better warmer.

"We sat down, the four of us who had been called in —myself, two of his scribes, and the valet Masudi, who already had everything for the trip prepared in a green feedbag. We each took a spoonful of cherry preserves sprinkled with hot pepper and drank a glass of water from the well that stands here in the room but echoes somewhere in the castle's cellar, burying our voices. Then Papas Avram paid us and said that whoever wanted to could stay. The rest would go with him to war, to the Danube.

"We thought that that was all he had to say to us and that he would not detain us any longer. But Brankovich had a peculiar trait: he was always at his wisest just when he was parting with his interlocutors. He would pretend ineptness on these occasions and always left his company a little later than what is considered polite and natural. He always overstepped the moment when everything had already been said, when everyone had long since removed their masks and showed themselves as they were when alone. So he dallied on this occasion too. He squeezed the Anatolian's hand, surreptitiously observing the others. Then suddenly between Masudi and Nikon Sevast there flashed a violent hatred, a hatred that had gone unnoticed until then and had been diligently hidden by both parties. This occurred when Masudi said to Kyr Avram:

" 'Sire, allow me to return a favor before we part. I shall tell you something that will bring you great joy, for you have long yearned to hear it. The one you dream of is named Samuel Cohen. ✿'

" 'He lies!' Sevast cried out unexpectedly, grabbing Masudi's green feedbag and hurling it into the burning

hearth. Surprisingly quietly, Masudi turned to Papas
Avram and, pointing to Nikon Sevast, said:

" 'Look at him, Sire. He has only one nostril in his
nose. And he pisses with his tail, like all satans.'

"Papas Avram took the parrot that was clutching the
lantern in its claws and lowered both to the floor. In the
light one could see in Nikon Sevast's nose a solitary
black, undivided nostril, the kind that devils have. Then
Papas Avram said to him:

" 'So you are one of those who dare not change their
shoes?'

" 'Yes, I am, Sire, but I am not one of those whose
shit stinks of fear. I do not deny that I am Satan,' he
admitted without hesitation. 'I only say that I belong to
the underworld of the Christian universe and sky, to the
evil spirits of the Greek lands, and to the Hades of the
Eastern Orthodox faith. Just as the sky above us is divided between Jehovah, Allah, and God the Father, so
too is the underworld divided between Asmodeus, Iblis,
and Satan. I happen to have been caught on the soil of
the present Turkish Empire, but this does not give Masudi or other representatives of the Moslem world the
right to judge me. That can be done only by representatives of the Christian faith, whose jurisdiction alone can
be recognized in my case. Otherwise, Christian or Jewish
judges may start judging those of the Moslem underworld if they fall into their hands. Let Masudi think
about this warning. . . .'

"To this Papas Avram replied:

" 'My father, Yoanikie Brankovich, had some experience with your kind. Each of our houses in Walachia
always had its own small witches, tiny satans, and vampires, with whom we supped. We sent after them vampire killers and Sabbat's children, gave them a sieve to
count the holes, and found their dismembered tails lying

around the house, picked blackberries with them, tied them to the door or to an ox and whipped them as punishment, and closed them up in wells. One night in Gyüla, Father came across an enormous snowman seated on the hole of the latrine. He struck him with the lantern, killed him, and went to dinner. Dinner was cabbage soup with boar meat. He tasted the soup and, all of a sudden—plop!—his head fell into the bowl. He kissed his own image sticking out of the bowl and drowned in the cabbage soup. Right there before our very eyes, before we realized what was happening. To this day I recall that while he was drowning in the soup he acted as though he were embracing a woman, put his arms around the wooden bowl as if he were holding not a boar but the head of another being. In short, we buried him as if we were wrenching him from someone's powerful embrace. . . . And we threw his boot into the Mureşul so that he would not become a vampire. If you are Satan, as indeed you are, then tell me the significance of my father, Yoanikie Brankovich's, death.'

" 'You will discover that for yourself, without my assistance,' Sevast replied, 'but I will tell you something else. I know the words that sounded in your father's ears when he died. They are: "A bit of wine to wash my hands!" This rang in his ears while he was dying. And now one more thing, so that you do not say that I sucked all this out of my hollow bone.

" 'You have been working on the Khazar alphabet for decades, so allow me to add something to your *Khazar Dictionary*.

" 'Listen, then, to what you do not know. The three rivers of the ancient world of the dead—the Acheron, the Phlegethon, and the Cocytus—today belong to the underworlds of Islam, Judaism, and Christianity; their flow divides the three hells—Gehenna, Hades, and the icy hell of the Mohammedans—beneath the one-time Khazar lands. And there, at the junction of these three borders, are confronted the three worlds of the dead: Satan's fiery state, with the nine circles of the Christian Hades, with Lucifer's throne, and with the flags of the Prince of Darkness; the Moslem underworld, with Iblis' kingdom of icy torment; and Gebhurah's territory, to the left of the Temple, where the Hebrew gods of evil, greed, and hunger sit, in Gehenna, under Asmodeus' rule. These three underworlds do not interfere with one another; their common borders are drawn by an iron plow, and no one is allowed to cross them. It is a result of your inexperience that you have misconceptions about these three underworlds. In the Jewish hell, in the state of Belial, the angel of darkness and sin, it is not Jews who burn, as you think. Those like yourself, all Arabs or Christians, burn there. Similarly, there are no Christians in the Christian hell—those who reach the fires are Mohammedans or of David's faith, whereas in Iblis' Moslem torture chamber they are all Christians and Jews, not a single Turk or Arab. Imagine Masudi, who fears his own horrible yet so-familiar hell, but finds himself in the Hebrew Sheol or the Christian Hades instead, where I will be waiting for him! Instead of Iblis, he will come upon Lucifer. Just imagine the Christian sky above the hell in which a Jew does penance.

" 'Take this as a powerful and ultimate warning, my lord, as the greatest words of wisdom! Have nothing to do with things that involve the three worlds of Islam, Christianity, and Judaism here on earth, so that we may have nothing to do with their underworlds. For those who hate one another are not the problem in this world. They always resemble one another. Enemies are always the same, or become so with time, for they could not be enemies otherwise. It is those who actually differ among themselves who pose the greatest danger. They long to meet one another, because their differences do not bother them. And they are the worst. We and our enemies will combine forces to fight those who allow us to differ from them and do not let this difference disturb their sleep; we will destroy them in one fell swoop from three sides. . . .'

"To this Kyr Avram Brankovich said that there was still something unclear to him. He inquired:

" 'Why haven't you done this yet—if not you, because your tail has yet to fall off, then those who are older and more experienced? What are you waiting for, while we are building a house for our Father?'

" 'We are waiting for time, my lord. Besides, we devils cannot take a step until you humans have taken yours. Each of our steps must fit in your footstep. We are always one step behind you, we eat our dinner only after you have eaten yours, and, like you, we cannot see the future. So you are always first, and we follow. But let me tell you this too: you have not yet taken a single step that would impel us to pursue you. Yet, if you or any of your descendants ever do so, we will catch up with you on a day in the week whose name shall go unmentioned. For the present, however, everything is all right, because there is no way for you and that red-haired Kuros of yours to meet, even if he should show up here in Constantinople. If he dreams of you as you dream of him, if he constructs your reality in his sleep as his reality is constructed in yours, then the two of you can never look into each other's eyes, for you can never be awake at the same time. Still, do not try our patience. Believe me, my lord, it is much more dangerous to compile a dictionary on the Khazars out of strewn words, here in this peaceful castle, than to go to war on the Danube, where the

Austrians and the Turks are already fighting; it is much more dangerous to wait here in Constantinople for an apparition from your dreams than to unsheathe your saber and charge at the enemy—something, Sire, you do well. Think it over. Go to wherever you were going without worry, and don't listen to this Anatolian who dips his oranges in salt. . . .'

" 'As for the rest, Sire,' Sevast concluded, 'you may, of course, turn me over to the Christian spiritual authorities and let the court for devils and witches deal with the matter. But, before you do so, allow me to ask you just one question. Do you believe that your church will exist and be able to pass judgment in three hundred years, as it does today?'

" 'Of course I do,' replied Papas Avram.

" 'Then prove it: exactly two hundred and ninety-three years from now, we will meet again, at this same time of year, for breakfast here in Constantinople, and then you will judge me just as you would today. . . .'

"Papas Avram laughed, gave his consent, and killed another fly with the tip of his whip.

"We cooked the wheat porridge at dawn, wrapped it and the pot in a pillow, and put it in a traveling net to warm Papas Avram while he rested. We started out on our journey by boat across the Black Sea and then upstream along the Danube. The last of the swallows were flying on their backs, and the Danube reflected their black backs instead of their white stomachs. We entered fogs, but they moved, carrying through the woods and across Djerdap a hard, deafening silence into which all other silences flowed. On the fifth day, near Kladovo, we were welcomed by a cavalry unit from Erdély that was covered with bitter Romanian dust from the other side of the water. As soon as we found ourselves in Prince Badensky's camp, we learned that Count George had himself set out for the battlefield, that Generals Haydersheim, Veterany, and Heisel were already prepared to attack the Turkish positions, and that for two days now the barbers had been running around them, shaving and combing them in mid-stride. That same night we witnessed the incredible expertise of our master.

"The seasons of the year were in flux, the mornings cold, but the nights still warm—summer until midnight, autumn at dawn. Papas Avram selected a saber, they saddled his horse, and a small division of cavalry with live doves in their sleeves rode out to him from the Serbian camp. They smoked long-stemmed pipes as they rode and blew rings of smoke around their horses' ears. Brankovich mounted up, and he too was given a lighted pipe; as they went off in a shroud of smoke to receive their orders from General Veterany, a cry suddenly rang out in the Austrian camp:

"'Naked Serbs are coming!' And indeed, behind the cavalrymen appeared a division of infantrymen who had thrown everything off themselves save their caps. Naked, they passed through the light of the campfires as if through gates, and behind them, in the darkness, moving swiftly, came their naked shadows, twice as old as they were themselves.

"'Are you really going to attack in the dark?' Veterany inquired, stroking a dog so tall it could slap a man in the mouth with its tail.

"'Yes,' replied Kyr Avram, 'the birds will show us the way.'

"Above the Austrian and Serbian positions was a hill called Rs where rain never fell; there stood a Turkish fortress with cannons. For three days now they had been

55

unable to approach it from any side. The general told Brankovich to attack the fortress.

" 'If you capture the position, light a green fire of maplewood stick,' added the general, 'so that we know how to orient ourselves.'

"The cavalrymen received their order and rode off, smoking their pipes. Shortly afterward we saw ignited pigeons soar up above the Turkish position—one, then a second, and a third—and we heard a little gunfire, and Papas Brankovich and the cavalrymen returned together to the camp, still smoking on their long-stemmed pipes as before. Surprised, the general asked why they were not attacking the cannons. Papas Avram pointed silently to the hill with his pipe. A green fire was blazing, and the Turkish cannons could no longer be heard. The fortress had been taken.

"The following morning, Papas Avram, worn from the night's battle, was resting in front of his tent, and Masudi and Nikon Sevast sat down to play dice. For the third day running, Nikon was losing an enormous sum, but Masudi would not stop the game. They must have had some terribly strong reason to have stayed there, Brankovich in his sleep and the two of them in their game, when the bullets started raining down on them. In any case, their reasons were stronger than mine: I took refuge in a secured shelter. Just then Turkish soldiers attacked our trench, slashing everything that stirred, and directly behind them came Sabljak Pasha© of Trebinje, who looked only at the dead, not at the living. Rushing onto the battlefield behind him came a pale young man with a half-gray mustache, as though only half the man had aged. Embroidered on Papas Avram's silk vest was the Brankovich coat of arms, with the one-eyed eagle. A Turkish soldier raised his spear, and lunged at the embroidered bird with such force that the iron blade went through the sleeping man's chest and could be heard hitting the rock beneath him. Awakening in death, Brankovich raised himself up on one arm, and the last thing he saw in his life was the young red-eyed man with glass fingernails and a half-gray mustache. Then Brankovich broke out in beads of perspiration, and two streams of sweat joined together in a knot at his neck. The arm he was leaning on began to shake so badly that, despite his wound, he looked at it curiously and pressed down with all his weight to steady it. But it continued to twitch for some time, slowing like a plucked string; when it had become quite still, he fell on the arm without uttering a sound. That same instant, the pale young man collapsed into his own shadow, as though felled by Brankovich's look, and the feedbag he carried on his shoulder rolled away.

" 'Is that Cohen who was killed?' cried the pasha, and the soldiers, thinking that one of the gamblers had shot at the young man, immediately slashed Nikon Sevast to pieces, the unthrown dice still in his hand. They then turned toward Masudi, but he said something in Arabic to the pasha, warning him that the pale young man was not dead, just asleep. Masudi thereby prolonged his own life by one day: the pasha ordered him to be slain by the sword not that day, but the one following, which is what happened."

Averkie Skila concluded his report on Avram Brankovich as follows: "I am a master of sabers and I know: when you kill, it is different every time, just as it is different with every new woman you take to your bed. Later, some you forget and some you do not; then again, some of those you killed, like some of the women you bedded, never forget you. The death of Kyr Avram Brankovich is remembered. It happened like this. The pasha's boys ran out from somewhere with a trough of

warm water, bathed the limp body of Kyr Avram, and
turned him over to an old man who wore around his
neck a third shoe that was filled with scents, balsams,
and hemp. I thought he would heal Papas Avram's
wounds, but instead he rubbed him with bleach and
rouge, shaved and brushed him, and took him thus
groomed to Sabljak Pasha inside the tent.

" 'Yet another naked Serb,' I thought. He died in that
tent the following morning. That was 1698, according to
the Eastern church's calendar, on the day of the holy
martyr Eutychius. As Avram Brankovich breathed his
last breath, Sabljak Pasha went out in front of the tent
and requested a bit of wine to wash his hands."

B RANKOVICH, GRGUR —see "Stylite."

C HELAREVO (7th–11th century)—archeolog-
ical site with a medieval graveyard near the Danube in
Yugoslavia. The settlement that nourished the graveyard has not been found. It is not known exactly who is
buried in the Chelarevo graveyard, but it bears clear
signs of the Avars, yet the objects found inside the graves
show a Persian influence, and menorahs (Jewish seven-
branched ceremonial candlesticks), other Jewish symbols,
and the odd Hebrew inscription have been found inside
as well. Preserved at the Kerch site in the Crimea are
tiles with the same type of menorah as those found at Chelarevo. All this has led experts to conclude that in the Novi
Sad area (where the Chelarevo site is located) there are
finds that differ from the usual Avar remains, suggesting
that we should perhaps consider the existence of some

MENORAH FROM CHELAREVO

other substratum, which moved to the Pannonian plains prior to the arrival of the Magyars. There are preserved writings to confirm this. An anonymous notary of King Bela, Abdul Hamid of Andalusia, and Cinnamus all believed that this area along the Danube was settled by a people of Turkish origin (Ismailians) who claimed to be descendants of settlers from Khorezm. All this seems to show that the ancient burial site in Chelarevo belonged in part to the Judaized Khazars. Dr. Isailo Suk,[†] an archeologist and Arabist from this region, who worked on the excavations at Chelarevo in their earliest stages, left a note not discovered until after his death. The note concerns not only Chelarevo, but also his opinions on it. It reads: "Regarding the issue of who is buried at Chelarevo, the Magyars would like them to be Hungarians or Avars, the Jews would like them to be Jews, the Moslems Mongols, but no one wants them to be Khazars. Yet they most probably are. . . . The cemetery is full of broken menorah-decorated pottery. To the Jews, a broken pottery dish is the mark of an undone, lost person, and this is a graveyard of an undone and lost people, which is what the Khazars were at this place and perhaps at this time."

CYRIL (Constantine of Thessalonica or Constantine the Philosopher) (826 or 827–869 A.D.)—Enlightener of Eastern Christianity, Greek representative in the Khazar polemic,$^\triangledown$ one of the apostles of Slavic literacy. Seventh child of Leo the Drungar, who conducted military and administrative affairs for the Byzantine court in Thessalonica, Constantine held a number of official and diplomatic posts and was raised amid the stark icon-free churches of the iconoclasts who were then in power in Constantinople. They included a number of Thessalonicans, and Constantine learned from men who were leading iconoclasts. Leo the Mathematician, who taught him Homer, geometry, arithmetic, astronomy, and music, was an iconoclast and a relative of Constantinople's Patriarch (837–843 A.D.), the iconoclast John the Grammarian; he maintained ties with the Saracens and their Caliph Mamun. Another of Constantine's instructors, the famous philosopher and later Patriarch Photius, who taught him grammar, rhetoric, dialectics, and philosophy, was called the Christian Aristotle and, along with Leo the Mathematician, helped to launch the humanistic renaissance in which the Byzantine world once again considered itself a descendant of ancient Hellenic lineage. Photius practiced hermetic and proscribed sciences, as-

trology and magic; the Byzantine emperor called him
"Khazar face," and there was a legend circulating at
court that in his youth Photius had sold his soul to a
Hebrew sorcerer. Constantine loved languages; to him
they were as eternal as the winds, and he changed them
as the Khazar kaghan did women of different faiths. In
addition to Greek, he studied Slavonic, Hebrew, Khazar,
Arabic, Samaritan, or languages written in the Gothic or
"Russian" script. He grew up and later lived with an
insatiable wanderlust. He always carried a rug with him
and used to say, "My home is where my rug is"· he spent
the better part of his life among tribes so wild that, after
shaking hands, he always had to count his fingers. Only
illness provided some sort of island of peace in his life.
As soon as he fell ill, he would forget every other language save his own. There were always at least two
causes for his illnesses. When the Thessalonican party of
iconoclasts was removed from power in 843 A.D. and the
cult of icons was reintroduced following the death of
Emperor Theophilus, Constantine was forced to take
shelter in a monastery on the coast of Asia Minor. He
thought, "And God has retreated to make room for the
world. Our eye is the target of the objects before it. They
all aim at it, not the opposite." He was then compelled
to return to the capital, to speak out publicly against his
own former teachers and countrymen, and to defend
icons. "It is only an illusion that our thoughts are in our
heads," he then concluded. "Our heads and we as a
whole are in our thoughts. We and our thoughts are like
the sea and the stream that runs through it—our body
is the current in the sea, but our thoughts are the sea
itself. Hence the body makes room for itself in the world
by forging through thoughts. And the soul is the sea-
bed of the one and the other. . . ."

He then abandoned yet another of his former teachers

CONSTANTINE OF THESSALONICA,
ST. CYRIL, FROM A 9TH-CENTURY FRESCO

—his elder brother, Methodius,[†] who had never attacked anyone of like mind. Cyril saw himself leaving
behind his one-time spiritual father and brother, and
taking the lead.

In his service to the Constantinople court, first he was
archon of a Slavic province, then he studied at the
imperial school in the capital, as a priest became the
patriarchate's librarian at the Church of St. Sofia in Constantinople, and a professor of philosophy at the University of Constantinople, where, owing to his exceptional
erudition, he was granted the honorable title of "Philosopher," which he carried to his death. But he held fast
to a different view and to the seaman's conviction that

the meat of smart fish is harmful and tougher than that
of stupid fish. Only the stupid eat both the stupid and
the smart, whereas the smart pick and choose the stupid.

Having spent the first half of his life fleeing from
icons, he spent the second half carrying them like a
shield. It transpired, however, that he could grow accustomed to the icon of the Holy Mother, but not to the
Holy Mother herself. Many years later, in the Khazar
polemic,▽ when he compared her to the servants in the
kaghan's entourage, he compared her not to a woman
but to a man.

Then half his century passed and half his life was
spent.

He took three gold coins and placed them in his bag,
thinking, "The first I will give to the horn blower, the
second to the church singers, and the third to the singing
angels on high." And so he set out on his endless journeys. Never was he able to mix the crumbs from lunch
with the crumbs from dinner. He was constantly on the
move. In 851 A.D. he went to the Arab caliph in Samarra,
near Baghdad, and when he returned from his diplomatic mission, he saw in the mirror the first wrinkle on
his forehead and called it "the Saracen wrinkle." The
year 859 A.D. was drawing to a close, and he became
coeval with Alexander the Great, who died at thirty-
three, which was Constantine's own age now.

"There are more people my own age below ground
than above," he thought now, "people from all time
periods, from the era of Ramses III, from the labyrinth
of Crete, from the time of the first siege of Constantinople. One day, when I am below ground, I too will be the
same age as many of the living. But, aging here, above
ground, I betray the dead who are younger than I am."

And then came yet another siege of the city whose
name he bore. While the Slavs besieged Constantinople
in 860 A.D., Constantine was setting a trap for them in

the quiet of his monastic cell in Asia Minor's Olympus —he was creating the first letters of the Slavic alphabet. He started with rounded letters, but the Slavonic language was so wild that the ink could not hold it, and so he made a second alphabet of barred letters and caged the unruly language in them like a bird. Only later, when it had been tamed and taught Greek (for languages learn other languages), could the Slavonic language be caught in the original Glagolitic, rounded letters. . . .

Daubmannus relates the following story about the genesis of the Slavic alphabet.

It was no easy task to tame the barbarians' language. One quick three-week-old autumn, the brothers were sitting in their cell, trying to write out the letters that men would later call Cyrillic. They were not getting anywhere. From the cell you could clearly see half of October, and in it the silence was one hour's walk long and two hours' walk wide. Then Methodius called his brother's attention to four jugs standing on the window of their cell, but outside, on the other side of the bars. "If the doors were locked, how could I get to one of those jugs?" he asked. Constantine broke one of the jugs, then drew the fragments piece by piece through the bars and into the cell, where he reassembled the jug, bonding it with saliva and clay from the floor beneath his feet. This they now did with the Slavonic language: they broke it in pieces, drew it into their mouths through the bars of Cyril's letters, and bonded the fragments with their saliva and the Greek clay beneath the soles of their feet.

That same year, the Byzantine Emperor Michael III received a legation from the Khazar kaghan,$^\triangledown$ who had requested that a person capable of explaining the fundamentals of Christian doctrine be sent to him from Constantinople. The emperor turned for advice to Photius, whom he called "Khazar face." It was an equivocal move, but Photius took the request seriously and recommended his protégé and disciple Constantine the Philosopher, who, with his brother, Methodius, set out on his second diplomatic mission, called "the Khazar mission." On the way, they stayed in Kherson, in the Crimea, where Constantine studied the Khazar and Hebrew languages, preparing for the diplomatic assignment that awaited him. He thought: "Every man is the cross of his own victim, but nails go through the cross too." When he arrived at the court of the Khazar kaghan, he met representatives of the Moslem and Jewish religions, whom the kaghan had also invited, and Constantine entered into the polemic with them, holding the "Khazar Orations" which Methodius later translated into Slavonic. Having refuted the arguments of the rabbi and the dervish representing Judaism and Islam respectively, Constantine the Philosopher persuaded the Khazar kaghan to accept Christianity, taught him that it does no good to pray to a broken cross, and left with a second, Khazar wrinkle on his face.

As the year 863 A.D. drew to a close, Constantine became a contemporary of the philosopher Philo of Alexandria, who died in his thirty-seventh year, which was now Constantine's own age. He completed the Slavic alphabet and left with his brother for Moravia to be among the Slavs he knew from his native land.

He translated church writings from Greek into Slavonic, and a crowd of people gathered around him. They had eyes where horns had once obviously been, wore snakes around their waists, slept with their heads turned south, and tossed fallen-out teeth over the house. He watched them pick at their snot with their fingers and whisper prayers as they ate it. They washed their feet without taking off their shoes, spat into their food before meals, and added their barbarian masculine and feminine names to every word in the "Our Father," so that the "Our Father" rose like bread and simultaneously disappeared, and every three days it had to be cleaned of the chaff and could be neither heard nor seen for all the wild names that swallowed it. They found the smell of carrion irresistible; they were quick-witted; they sang most beautifully, and he cried as he listened to them and watched his third, Slavic wrinkle trickle down his forehead like a drop of rain. . . . After Moravia, in 867 A.D. he went to the Pannonian Prince Kotsel, and from there to Venice, and he entered in debate with the Trilinguists, adherents of the view that only the Greek, Hebrew, and Latin languages were worthy of the liturgy. The Venetians asked him, "Did all of Judas kill Christ, or not quite all?" And Constantine felt a fourth, Venetian wrinkle appear on his cheek, cutting and crossing his face with the older Saracen, Khazar, and Slavic wrinkles, like four nets thrown over the same fish. He gave the first gold coin from his bag to a trumpeter to start blowing his horn and asked the Trilinguists how the army would respond to the call if the trumpet's signal was not understood. The year was now 869 A.D., and Constantine's thoughts turned to Boethius of Ravenna, who had died at the age of forty-three. He was now the same age. The Pope invited him to Rome, where he succeeded in defending his principles and his Slavonic liturgy. With him were Methodius and his students, who were baptized in Rome.

Reflecting on his life and listening to the chanting in

the church, he thought: "Just as a man gifted for a job performs it reluctantly and clumsily when he is ill, so a man not meant for the job will perform it with equal reluctance and clumsiness though he be healthy. . . ." The Slavonic liturgy was sung in Rome on this occasion, and Constantine gave his second gold coin to the singers. In the age-old manner, he placed the third gold coin under his tongue, entered one of the Greek monasteries in Rome, and died under his new monastic name, Cyril, in the year 869 A.D.

Main Sources: An extensive bibliography of writings about Cyril and Methodius is to be found in G. A. Ilyinsky's *Opit sistematicheskoi kirilo-mefod'evskoi bibliografii* with numerous later additions (Popruzhenko, Romanski, Ivanka Petrovich, et al.). An overview of the most recent research is provided by the new edition of F. Dvornik's monograph, *Les Légendes de Constantin et Méthode vue de Byzance* (1969). Some information relating to the Khazars and the Khazar polemic was provided by the Daubmannus edition of *The Khazar Dictionary, Lexicon Cosri*, Regiemonti Borrusiae, excudebat Ioannes Daubmannus 1691, but that edition was destroyed.

D REAM HUNTERS —a sect of Khazar priests whose protectress was Princess Ateh.▽ They could read other people's dreams, live and make themselves at home in them, and through the dreams hunt the game that was their prey—a human, an object, or an animal. A note left by one of the oldest dream hunters has been preserved, and it reads: "In dreams we feel like fish in water. Occasionally we surface from a dream and skim an eye over the world on shore, but we again descend with yearning haste, for it is only in the depths that we feel good. During these brief sorties we notice on dry land a strange creature, more sluggish than ourselves, accustomed to breathing in a manner different from our own, and glued to the land with all its weight, deprived of the passion we inhabit like our own bodies. For here below, passion and the body are indistinguishable, they are one and the same thing. That creature out there, that too is us, but a million years from now, and between it and us, aside from the years, lies a terrible calamity that has befallen it, because that creature out there has separated the body from passion. . . ."

One of the most famous dream readers was reportedly named Mokaddasa Al-Safer. [ℰ✿] He was able to probe into the deepest recesses of secrets, to tame fish in people's dreams, to open doors in people's visions, to dive deeper into dreams than anyone before him, straight down to God, for at the bottom of every dream lies God. But something happened, and never again was he able to read dreams. For a long time he thought he had reached the pinnacle and that, indeed, there was nowhere else to take this mystical skill. He who reaches the end of a road needs it no longer, and the road is not given to him any more. But those around him thought differently. They once confided the matter to Princess Ateh, who then explained to them the case of Mokaddasa Al-Safer:

Once a month, on the salt holiday, followers of the Khazar kaghan fight a life-or-death battle against you, my followers and charges, in the outskirts of our three capitals. When night falls, while we are burying his dead in Jewish, Arab, or Greek graves, and mine in Khazar graves, the kaghan quietly opens the copper door of my chamber, bearing a candle whose flame smells and trembles from his passion. I do not look at him, for he resembles all lovers the world over who have been struck in the face by happiness. The two of us spend the night together, but when he departs at dawn I look at his reflection in the shiny copper of my door and can recognize in his fatigue what he intends to do, where he is going from, and who he is.

And so it is with your dream hunter. There is no doubt that he has reached one of the heights of his art, that he has prayed in the temples of others' dreams, and that he has been killed countless times in the souls of dreamers. He has been so successful in his calling that the finest substance in existence—the substance of dreams—has begun to give in to him. And even if he made not a single error in his ascent toward God, and thus it was given to him to see God at the bottom of the dream he was reading, he certainly made some error on his return, while descending into this world from the heights to which he had risen. And for that error he has paid. Beware of the return! concluded Princess Ateh. A bad descent can obliterate the successful scaling of a mountain.

KAGHAN[∇] —title of the Khazar ruler. His capital was Itil, and his summer residence, located on the Caspian Sea, was called Samandar. It is thought that the decision to admit Greek missionaries to the Khazar court was politically motivated. As early as the year 740 A.D., one of the Khazar kaghans had turned to Constantinople for a missionary versed in Christian law. And in the ninth century, the Greek-Khazar alliance needed to be consolidated in the face of a common danger, for by this time the Russians had already nailed their shield to the gates of Constantinople and had taken Kiev from the Khazars. There was another danger as well. The kaghan did not have an heir to the throne. One day some Greek merchants arrived and he received and entertained them. Each and every one of them was short, swarthy, and so hirsute that the hair on their chests had a part like the hair on their head. The kaghan sat amid them like a giant and feasted. A storm was approaching; birds were blindly crashing into the windows, and flies into the mirrors. After the travelers had been led away, laden with gifts, the kaghan turned around in his chamber and caught sight of the leftover morsels of food from the meal. The Greeks' were enormous, like those of giants, while the kaghan's were tiny, like those of a child. He quickly called on his court to remember what the strangers had said to him, but no one could recall a word. On the whole they had remained silent—everyone agreed. Then a Jew from the palace retinue appeared before the kaghan and said he could resolve the kaghan's difficulties.

"Show me," said the kaghan, taking a lick of the holy salt. The Jew led in a slave and ordered him to bare his arm. It was absolutely identical to the kaghan's right arm. "Yes," said the kaghan, "retain him. Retain him and proceed with your work. You're on the right road."

Heralds were then sent out across the entire kingdom, and three months later the Jew brought before him a young man whose feet looked exactly like the kaghan's. He too was retained at the palace. They subsequently found two knees, an ear, and a shoulder—all exactly like the kaghan's. Little by little, a group of young men gathered at the palace; there were soldiers, slaves, rope-makers, Jews, Greeks, Khazars, and Arabs who—if one took a limb or part of the body from each—could be assembled into a young kaghan identical to the one who ruled in Itil. Only the head was missing. It was simply not to be found. And then one day the kaghan summoned the Jew and demanded either the Jew's own head or the kaghan's. The Jew showed no sign of fear, and the surprised kaghan asked him for the reason.

"The reason is that fear struck me a year ago, not today. A year ago I found the head. And all these months I have been keeping it here in the palace, though I dared not show it."

When the kaghan ordered him to show the head, the
Jew brought before him a girl. She was young and
pretty, and her head bore such a resemblance to the
kaghan's own that it could have doubled for it in a
mirror: anyone seeing her image in a mirror would have
thought he was seeing the kaghan, only younger. Then
the kaghan ordered all those gathered at the palace to be
brought to him and commanded the Jew to create another kaghan from their limbs. As the surviving cripples
departed, their limbs assembled into a second kaghan,
the Jew inscribed some words on the brow of the new
creation, and the young kaghan, the kaghan's heir, sat
up on the kaghan's bed. Next he had to be tested, and
the Jew sent him to the bedchamber of the kaghan's
mistress, Princess Ateh.$^\triangledown$ In the morning the princess
sent the real kaghan the following message:

"The man sent to my bed last night is circumcised,
and you are not. Therefore, either he is someone else and
not the kaghan, or the kaghan turned himself over to
the Jews and was circumcised, becoming someone else.
It is for you to decide what happened."

The kaghan asked the Jew what this difference ought
to signify. The latter inquired:

"Will not the difference vanish as soon as you yourself
are circumcised?"

The kaghan was in a quandary and this time asked
the Princess Ateh for advice. She led him to the cellar of
his palace and showed him the kaghan's double. She had
placed him in chains and behind bars, but he had already
broken all the chains and was shaking the bars with
tremendous force. In one night he had grown so large
that the real uncircumcised kaghan looked like a child
in comparison.

"Do you want me to let him loose?" asked the princess. The kaghan was so taken with fear that he ordered

the circumcised kaghan to be put to death. Princess Ateh spat at the giant's brow, and he fell down dead.

The kaghan then favored the Greeks, concluded a new alliance with them, and adopted their religion as his own.

K HAZARS[▽] —Theophanes wrote the following about the origin of the Khazars: "The great Khazar people appeared from the remotest reaches of Bersilia, the first Sarmatia, and ruled the entire area extending from the Black Sea. . . ." In the 5th century, according to Priscus, the Khazars belonged to the Hun Empire and were known by the name of Akatzir. St. Cyril[†] claimed that the Khazars were a people who worshipped God in their own Khazar language, rather than in Greek, Hebrew, or Latin. Greek sources refer to the Khazars as Χαεαροι, but also as Χοτξιροι. The Khazar state extended considerably to the west of the boundary formed by the Crimea, the Caucasus, and the Volga. In June the shadow of the Khazar mountains falls twelve days into Sarmatia, and in December it falls a month's walk to the north. As early as about 700 A.D., Khazar officials resided on the Bosporus and in Phanagoria. Christian (Russian) sources, such as *Nestor's Chronicle,* assert that in the 9th century tribes south of the central Dnieper paid a tribute to the Khazars in the form of one white squirrel pelt or one sword per head. In the tenth century this tribute was paid in the form of money.

Greek sources on the Khazar question are supported by an important document that the Daubmannus[✧] edition refers to as "The Great Parchment." According to this source, a Khazar legation was sent to the Byzantine Emperor Theophilus, and one of the envoys had the

Khazars' history and topography tattooed on his body—
in the Khazar language, but using Hebrew letters. At
the time the envoy had been tattooed, the Khazars were
already using Greek, Jewish, or Arabic letters inter-
changeably as an alphabet for their own language, but
when a Khazar converted he would use only one of the
three alphabets, that of the faith he had adopted. Khazars
who converted to the Greek faith, to Islam, or who
accepted Judaism began to distort their Khazar language,
in the desire to make it look less and less like the language of the Khazars who had retained their original
faith. Some sources, however, do not recognize the incident of the tattooed envoy mentioned by Daubmannus.
They speak instead of a richly decorated dish of salt, sent
to the Byzantine emperor as a gift from which he could
read the Khazars' history, and they believe that the entire
story of "The Great Parchment" was really only the
result of a misread historical source. This rational quali-
fication presents a problem, however. If one accepts the
dish-of-salt version, it is impossible to understand the
remainder of the story about "The Great Parchment,"
which proceeds as follows.

In "The Great Parchment" years were calculated according to the large Khazar years, which took into account only wartime periods, consequently, they had to be
converted into the smaller Greek years. The beginning
of the parchment was lost, because the part of the envoy's
body on which the first and second great Khazar years
had been written had been chopped off at some point as
an act of punishment. The preserved part of the Khazar
tale begins, therefore, with the third large year, in the
7th century (according to modern calculations of time),
when the Byzantine Emperor Heraclius marched on
Persia with the aid of the Khazars, who participated in
the siege of Tiflis under the leadership of their King

Ziebel and retreated in 627 A.D., leaving the Greek troops to face the enemy alone. They believed that all things followed one code when on the rise and another when on the fall, that departures and returns did not come under the same law, and that the same agreements did not apply before and after a victory. After an earthquake even plants grew in a new and different way. The fourth large Khazar year described the Khazar victories over the Bulgarian alliance, when part of that Onogur Hun tribe fell subject to the Khazars and the rest retreated, under Asparuh, westward to the Danube River, to the tribes that whip the wind, grow grass on their heads instead of hair, and have icy thoughts. The fifth and sixth large years (written on the envoy's chest) contained the history of the Khazar Empire's wars during the reign of the Byzantine Emperor Justinian II. After his dethronement, Justinian, expelled and crippled, was imprisoned in Kherson, whence he escaped and fled stark naked to the Khazars, sleeping under heavy rocks along the way to keep from freezing. He was well received at the court of the Khazar kaghan$^\nabla$ and married the kaghan's sister, who adopted the Greek faith and took the name Theodora (from the name of Justinian I's empress), but, in the Khazar tradition, she continued to believe that God had appeared to the Virgin Mary in her sleep and had impregnated her with the dreamed word. This is how Justinian II saved himself among the Khazars the first time. The second time, he was to meet his end with the Khazars; one can flee to them, but not from them. When the legation from Emperor Tiberius arrived at the Khazar court, demanding that Justinian be handed over to the Greeks, he fled once more and headed for the capital. When he again became emperor, Justinian II forgot the Khazars' hospitality, and in 711 A.D. sent a punitive expedition to Kherson, to which he had once been banished and which was now under Khazar rule. This time the move toward the Khazar Empire was to cost him his head. The Khazars were supporting rebel imperial troops (the Crimea was already theirs by this time), and Justinian II and his small son, Tiberius, child of the Khazar princess and the last descendant of Heraclius' dynasty in Byzantium, were killed in the rebellion. In short, the Khazars sheltered the pursued and destroyed the pursuer, who were one and the same person. In the seventh and final large Khazar year given in "The Great Parchment," inscribed on the stomach of the Khazar envoy, there was another tribe of the same name, and this Khazar twin lived far away from the real Khazar tribe; people often confused them with the real Khazars, and travelers from the two peoples would occasionally meet.

These other Khazars tried to take advantage of the similarity in their names, and on the real envoy's thighs there was a warning that similarly tattooed envoys bearing not the Khazar history but that of the other tribe of the same name had been known to appear at the courts of caliphs and emperors. These other Khazars even knew how to speak Khazar, but the knowledge never lasted longer than three to four years, the lifespan of a strand of hair. Sometimes their knowledge came to a halt in mid-sentence and they would be unable to utter another word. The envoy used his powers of persuasion and his tattooed message to show that he was the representative of the real Khazar kaghan and the real Khazars. He also mentioned that at one point the Greeks had linked up with the Khazars' doubles; that was during the period covered by the seventh large Khazar year. In 733 A.D. (by modern calculations), and in the said large Khazar year, Emperor Leo III the Isaurian, an iconoclast, married his son Constantine to Irene, the daughter of the Khazar kaghan. This marriage later produced the Greek Emperor Leo IV the Khazar (reigned 775–780 A.D.). It was at this time that Emperor Leo III was asked to send to the Khazar court a legation to interpret the Christian faith. The request was to be renewed some one hundred years later, during the reign of the Greek Emperor Theophilus (reigned 829–842 A.D.), when the Russian Normans and Magyars menaced the Crimea, the Greek Empire, and the Khazar state. At the request of the Khazar kaghan, Greek engineers built the Sarkel fortress; inside the envoy's left ear one could clearly see a fortress being erected at the mouth of the Don. One of his thumbs showed the Khazar attack on Kiev in 862 A.D., but because this thumb carried a festering wound received in the very same siege, the picture was smeared and remained an eternal mystery. That siege had not yet taken place when the envoy was dispatched to Constantinople; it was two full decades away.

The note on "The Great Parchment" breaks off at this point, and it can be safely said that the individual who created this "excerpt" from the Khazar original only included material concerning Greek-Khazar relations, omitting everything else that had certainly been tattooed on the skin of the Khazar diplomat, thereby leaving the "walking letter" to continue its mission in some other land. This seems to be supported by information that the Khazar envoy ended his life at the court of some caliph by turning his soul inside out and slipping it on like an inverted glove. His torn skin, tanned and bound like a big atlas, held a place of honor in the caliph's palace in Samarra. According to a second group of sources, the envoy had many a nasty moment. First, while still in Constantinople, he had to let his hand be cut off, because an influential man at the Greek court had paid in solid gold for the second large Khazar year, written on the

envoy's left palm. A third group of sources claims that
on two or three occasions the envoy was forced to return
to the Khazar capital, where he had to undergo correc-
tions of the historical and other facts he bore, or where
he was replaced by another envoy, whose skin had been
imprinted with the corrected and revised version of history. He lived—*The Khazar Dictionary* tells us—like a
living encyclopedia of the Khazars, on money earned by
standing quietly through the long nights. He would keep
vigil, his gaze fixed on the Bosporus' silver treetops,
which resembled puffs of smoke. While he stood, Greek
and other scribes would copy the Khazar history from
his back and thighs into their books. It is said that, in
keeping with Khazar tradition, he carried a glass sword,
and that he claimed that the letters of the Khazar alphabet derived their names from foods, the numbers from
the names of the seven types of salt the Khazars differ-
entiated. One of his sayings has been preserved. It reads:
"If the Khazars did better in Itil [the Khazar capital]
they would do better in Constantinople too." Generally
speaking, he said many things that were contrary to what
was written on his skin.

He or one of his successors explained the Khazar
polemic conducted at the court of the Khazar kaghan in
the following manner. An angel once came to the
kaghan in a dream and told him, "The Lord is not
pleased by your deeds, but is by your intentions." He
immediately summoned one of the most prominent
Khazar priests from the sect of dream hunters and asked
him to explain what the dream meant. The hunter
laughed and told the kaghan: "God knows nothing of
you; he sees not your intentions, or your thoughts, or
your deeds. The fact that an angel appeared and rambled
on in your dream only means that it had nowhere else
to spend the night and that it was probably raining

outside. If it did not stay long, that is probably because your dream had a bad stench. Wash your dreams next time. . . ." Upon hearing these words, the kaghan became enraged and summoned foreigners to interpret his dream. "Yes, human dreams have a dreadful odor" was the Khazar envoy's comment on this story. He passed away, because his skin inscribed with the Khazar history began to itch terribly. The itch was unbearable, and it was with relief that he died, glad to be finally cleansed of history.

Khazar Polemic —the event that Christian sources attribute to the year 861 A.D., according to *The Life of Constantine of Thessalonica, St. Cyril,*[†] written in the ninth century and preserved in what is referred to as the manuscript of the Moscow Spiritual Academy and in the 1469 version of Vladislav the Grammarian. In that year of 861 A.D., Khazar envoys came before the Byzantine emperor and said: "We have always recognized only one God, who rules over us all, and we bow to Him facing east, and uphold our other pagan customs as well. The Jews are trying to persuade us to adopt their faith and rites, and the Saracens are offering peace and many gifts to draw us to their own faith, saying, 'Our faith is better than all other peoples' '; therefore, nurturing an old friendship and love, we now turn to you, for you, the Greeks, are a great people vested with imperial power by God; in seeking your advice, we ask you to send us one of your learned men, for if he emerges victorious from the debate with the Jews and the Saracens, we shall adopt your faith."

When the Greek emperor asked Cyril if he would go to the Khazars,[▽] the latter replied that he would embark

on such a journey on foot and in his bare feet.
Daubmannus ✿ believes that what Cyril meant was that
he needed as much time to prepare for his journey as it
would take him to walk from Constantinople to the
Crimea, for at the time Cyril was still illiterate in his
dreams and did not know how to unlock them from the
inside; in other words, he did not know how to wake up
when he wanted. Nevertheless, he accepted the mission,
and in Kherson, where he stopped off along the way, he
learned Hebrew and translated the Hebrew grammar
into Greek in preparation for the polemic at the court of
the Khazar kaghan. He and his brother, Methodius, †
passed Lake Meot and the Caspian gates of the Caucasus
Mountains, where they were met by the kaghan's envoy.
The envoy asked Constantine the Philosopher why he
always held a book before him when speaking, while the
Khazars extracted all wisdom from their chests, as if they
had swallowed it first. Constantine replied that he felt
naked without a book, and who would believe that a
naked man has many robes? To meet Constantine and
Methodius, the Khazar deputy had traveled from the
capital, Itil, to Sarkel on the Don, and to Kherson. He
then led the Byzantine envoys to Samandar, on the Caspian Sea, the kaghan's summer residence, where the polemic was to be held. At court, where the Jewish and
Saracen representatives had already arrived, the question
arose as to what rank Constantine should have at the
dinner table. He responded: "I had a great and very
famous grandfather who was close to the emperor, but,
because he refused the honors bestowed upon him, he
was exiled, and he arrived in a strange land where he
became poor and I was born. I, seeking my grandfather's
one-time honor, have not succeeded in achieving it; you
see, I am only the grandson of Adam."

"You worship the Trinity," said the kaghan in his

dinner toast, "and we worship but one God, as it is written in the books. Why is that?"

The Philosopher replied:

"Books preach the Word and the Spirit. If someone pays you honor but does not respect your word and spirit, while another respects all three, which of the two pays the greater honor?"

The Jewish representative asked:

"Tell us, then, how can a woman place in her womb God, whom she cannot see, let alone give birth to?"

The Philosopher pointed to the kaghan and his first counselor, saying: "If someone were to say that the first counselor cannot receive the kaghan, but that the lowliest servant can both receive him and render him honor, tell me, then, what should we call him: mad or sensible?"

Now the Saracens joined the polemic, and Constantine the Philosopher was asked about a custom he had first encountered in Samarra, at the Saracen caliph's. The Saracens used to place a picture of the devil on the outside of Christian houses; on each Christian door was a figure of some demon. And the Saracens, who had long been trying to poison Constantine, asked him:

"Do you, Philosopher, comprehend the significance of this?"

And he said:

"I see the demonic figures, and I think that Christians live inside, but since demons cannot coexist with them they run outside. And if there are no demon figures outside, it means that they are inside with the household. . . ."

Another badly damaged Christian source on the Khazar polemic has reached us in the form of a legend concerning the Kievites' conversion to Christianity in the 10th century. From the legend, in which Constantine the Philosopher (Cyril) was among the participants in the

Kiev polemic about the three religions (even though he
lived one hundred years earlier), one can recognize a
document that was originally about the Khazar polemic.
If we abstract the additions and revisions of the 10th and
later centuries, this source's report on the Khazar polemic would look roughly as follows.

A Khazar kaghan whose fortunes had flourished in
the wars against the Pechenegs and the Greeks, from
whom he had captured Kherson (Kerch on the Crimea),
decided to adopt a leisurely life after all his military
successes. He wanted to have as many women as the
soldiers he had lost in war. "He had many women," says
a version of this legend published in Venice in 1772 in
the Serbian language, "and, wanting to have women of
all faiths, he not only worshipped various idols, but, out
of affection for his women and mistresses, also wanted
to profess different faiths." This prompted various foreigners (Greeks, Arabs, Jews) to rush to the kaghan with
their envoys, in the hope of converting him immediately
to their own faith. Constantine the Philosopher, sent by
the Greek emperors, was more successful than the Jews
or Saracens in the polemic at the court of the Khazar
kaghan, says this source. But, unable to reach a final
decision, the kaghan kept hesitating, until finally one of
his kin, recognizable as Princess Ateh,[∇] who is familiar
to us from a third source, stepped in. Her people convinced the kaghan to send them out among the Jews,
Greeks, and Saracens to investigate their doctrines firsthand. When this woman's mission returned, it recommended Christianity as the most suitable faith, and the
envoys revealed to the kaghan that his relative, whom
they served, had adopted Christianity long before.

The third source of Christian references to the Khazar
polemic—Daubmannus—believed that the kaghan was
frightened by this news. Consequently, fortune fell to the

Jewish representative after the kaghan discovered that Christians, like Jews, observe the Old Testament. When Constantine confirmed that this was true, the kaghan turned to the Jew, who had fled to the Khazars from Greece and strongly advocated Judaism.

"Of us three dream hunters," the Romaniot told the kaghan, "the only one you Khazars have no reason to fear is me, a rabbi; for neither a caliph, with the green sails of his fleet, nor a Greek emperor, with a cross over his armies, stands behind the Jews. Behind Constantine of Thessalonica come spears and cavalry, but behind me, a Jewish rabbi, trail prayer shawls. . . ."

So spoke the rabbi, and the kaghan now favored him and his arguments, when Princess Ateh intervened in the polemic and once again completely altered the outcome of the conversation. The decisive words in the Khazar polemic, spoken by Ateh to the Jewish participant, were:

You say: Let him who wants wealth turn to the North, and him who wants wisdom to the South! But why do you speak such sweet and wise words to me here in the North and not to Wisdom, who awaits you in the land of your fathers? Why did you not go there, where light lays its eggs, where centuries rub against centuries, to drink the sour rain of the Dead Sea, to kiss the sand that runs in oblique streams like a stretched rope of gold in place of water from Jerusalem's wells? Instead you tell me that I dream of an inky night and that only in your reality is there moonlight. Why do you say this to me?

Yet another week has grown poor and thin. It has spent its most solemn day, which you say begins in Palestine, the day it had so jealously guarded, but whose time has come. It gives it up reluctantly, piece by piece. Take your piece; take your Sabbath and then go. Go to Wisdom and say everything you wanted to say to me. You will be happier. But beware:

to conquer a fortress one must first conquer one's own soul. . . .

But I tell you all this in vain, for you carry your eyes in your mouth and do not see until you speak. My conclusion is this: either your saying is wrong or it is not you expected in the South, but someone else. How else am I to understand why you are here in the North and with me?

Princess Ateh's words startled the Khazar kaghan and he told the rabbi he had heard that the Jews themselves admitted that their God had abandoned and scattered them all over the world. "Do you wish to draw us to your faith so that you may have comrades in your misery, and so that we Khazars may be punished by God as you are and scattered throughout the world?"

The kaghan then turned away from the Jew and again found the most acceptable arguments to be those of Constantine the Philosopher. He and his chief aides converted to Christianity and sent the Greek emperor a letter, cited in Cyril's hagiography, that reads:

"Your Serene Majesty, you sent us a man who has explained to us the glory of the Christian faith in both word and deed, and we are convinced that it is the true faith and are commanding people to baptize themselves voluntarily. . . ."

According to another source, the kaghan, having accepted Constantine's reasons, quite unexpectedly decided to go to war against the Greeks instead of adopting their faith. He said, "You do not beg for faith, you obtain it by the sword!" He attacked them from Kherson and when he had victoriously completed his campaign, he asked the Greek emperor for a Greek princess to take as his wife. The emperor set only one condition—that the Khazar kaghan convert to Christianity. To the great surprise of Constantinople, the kaghan accepted the term, and that is how the Khazars were converted.

METHODIUS OF THESSALONICA

(c. 815–885 A.D.)—Greek chronicler of the Khazar polemic,[▽] one of the Slavic apostles and the enlightener of Eastern Christianity, elder brother of Constantine of Thessalonica, Cyril.[†] Hailing from the family of the Byzantine commander of Thessalonica, Drungar Leo, Methodius tested his talents as administrator of a Slavic region, in all likelihood in the area of the Strumica (Strymon) River. He knew the language of his Slavic subjects, who had bearded souls and in winter carried birds inside their shirts to keep warm. In the year 840 A.D., after a brief period, he left for Bithynia, near the Sea of Propontis, but for the rest of his life he rolled the memory of his Slavic subjects in front of him like a ball. The books cited by Daubmannus[✿] say that he studied there under a monk, who once told him: "When we read, it is not ours to absorb all that is written. Our thoughts are jealous and they constantly black out the thoughts of others, for there is not room enough in us for two scents at one time. Those under the sign of the Holy Trinity, a masculine sign, take in only the odd sentences of their books when they read, whereas we, under the sign of the number four, a feminine number, take in only the even sentences of our books. You and your brother will not read the same sentences from the same book, since our books exist only as a combination of masculine and feminine signs. . . ." Indeed, there was another person from whom Methodius learned—his younger brother, Constantine. At times he would observe that this younger brother of his was more intelligent than the author of the book he was currently reading. Then Methodius would realize that he was wasting his time, close the book, and converse with his brother. Methodius became a monk on the Asia Minor coast in a colony of ascetics called Olympus, where he was later joined by his brother. They watched the sand, swept by the Easter wind, reveal on each holiday yet another ancient desert temple at a new site, showing only enough for them to make the sign of the cross over it and read out the "Our Father," before it was buried again forever. It was then that he began dreaming two parallel dreams, and this led to the legend that he would also have two graves. In the year 861 A.D. he departed with his brother to see the Khazars. This was nothing new for the two brothers from Thessalonica. They had heard of these powerful people from their teacher and friend Photius, who had contacts with the Khazars, and they knew that the Khazars preached their faith in their own language. On orders from the capital, Methodius now participated in the polemic at the Khazar court, both as a witness and as Constantine's associate. The 1691 *Khazar Dictionary* notes that on this occasion the Khazar kaghan$^\triangledown$ told his guests something about the sect of dream hunters. The kaghan despised the sect, which was loyal to the Khazar Princess Ateh,$^\triangledown$ and he compared the futile work of the dream hunters with the Greek story of the skinny mouse who slipped easily enough through the hole into a basket of wheat, but when he had eaten his fill could not get out on his full stomach: "You cannot get out of the basket when you are full. You can do so only when you are hungry, as when you entered. And it is the same with the swallower of dreams; he easily slips through the narrow chink between reality and dream when he is hungry, but when he has caught his prey and picked his fruit, he can no longer return with his fill of dreams, because to leave you must be the same as when you entered. So he must leave his pick-

METHODIUS OF THESSALONICA,
FROM A 9TH-CENTURY FRESCO

ings or else forever remain in dreams. Either way, he is of no use to us. . . ."

After their Khazar journey, Methodius once again retreated to Olympus in Asia Minor; when he saw the same icons there for the second time, they looked tired. He became head of the Polychron Monastery, of which nothing was known for centuries except that it had perhaps been built at the juncture of three measures of time —Arab, Greek, and Hebrew—whence its name.

In the year 863 A.D. Methodius returned to the midst of the Slavs. He wanted to establish a Slavic school under Greek influence, with its own students, a Slavic alphabet, and books translated from Greek into Slavonic. He and his brother had known since childhood that birds in Thessalonica and birds in Africa do not speak the same language, that swallows from the Strumica and swallows from the Nile do not understand one another, and that only albatrosses speak the same language everywhere in the world. With these thoughts in mind, they set out for Moravia, Slovakia, and Lower Austria, gathering around them young men who looked at their tongues rather than listened to what they said. Methodius decided to present a finely decorated stick as a gift to one of the men he and his brother taught. They all hoped he would present it to the best pupil and waited to see who that would be. But Methodius gave it to his worst pupil, saying: "A teacher spends the least time teaching his best pupils, and remains longest with the worst, because the quick ones quickly move on. . . ."

It was in a room with a rotting floor, the kind that nips at bare feet, that Methodius first heard he and his brother had been attacked. Their clashes began with the Trilinguists, German defenders of the concept that worship could be offered in only three languages (Greek, Latin, and Hebrew). In Pannonia, on Lake Balaton, where one's hair freezes in the winter and one's eyes become in the wind like a tablespoon and a teaspoon, Methodius and his brother spent some time in the capital of the region's Slav Prince Kotsel. In battle the prince's soldiers bit as well as any horse or camel; they forced snakes out of their skin with the blows of a rod; their women gave birth in the air, hanging from a holy tree. They tamed fish in the mud of the Pannonian marshes and showed newcomers an old man who prayed by removing a fish from the mud and letting it fly off the palm of his hand like a falcon. And it would actually rise up in the air and fly, shaking off the mud and using its fins as wings.

In 867 A.D. the brothers set out with their followers

and disciples on one of those journeys where every step is a letter, every path a sentence, and every stop a number in a large book. In 867 A.D., in Venice, they entered into another debate with the Trilinguists, and then they arrived in Rome, where Pope Adrian II acknowledged the legitimacy of the Thessalonican brothers' teachings and ordained the Slavic disciples in the Basilica of St. Peter. For this occasion, the Slavonic liturgy was sung in a language only recently tamed; it had been bound and brought from the Balkan expanses to the capital of the world like a small animal in a cage of Glagolitic letters. There in Rome, one evening in the year 869 A.D., while his Slav followers were spitting into one another's mouths, Methodius' brother, Constantine, died as St. Cyril; Methodius returned to Pannonia. He was in Rome a second time, in 870 A.D., when the Pope conferred upon him the title Archbishop of Pannonia and Sirmium, whereupon the Salzburg Archbishop was forced to leave Lake Balaton. When he returned to Moravia in the summer of 870 A.D., Methodius was imprisoned by the German bishops and locked up for two years, during which he could hear nothing but the sound of the Danube. He was brought to trial before a synod in Regensburg, then tortured and exposed naked to the frost. While they whipped him, his body bent over so low that his beard touched the snow, Methodius thought of how Homer and the holy prophet Elijah had been contemporaries, how Homer's poetic state had been larger than the state of Alexander of Macedonia, because it had stretched from Pontus to beyond Gibraltar. He thought of how Homer could not have known all that moved through and was to be found in the seas and cities of his state, just as Alexander the Great could not have known all that was to be found in his own state. He also thought of how Homer had at some point written into his work the name of Sidon and with it, unknowingly, that of the prophet Elijah, fed by birds according to God's will. He thought of how Homer had had seas and towns in his vast poetic state, not knowing that in one of them, in Sidon, sat the prophet Elijah, who was to become an inhabitant of another poetic state, one as vast, eternal, and powerful as Homer's own—an inhabitant of the Holy Scriptures. And finally he wondered whether the two contemporaries had ever met, Homer and St. Elijah, the settler of Galaad—both immortal, both armed only with words, one blind and gazing at the past, the other clairvoyant and obsessed with the future, one a Greek who sang of water and fire better than any poet, the other a Jew who rewarded with water and punished with fire, using his cloak as a bridge. There is a tight pass on earth—thought Methodius finally—one no wider than ten camel deaths, where two men missed each other. This space between their strides is narrower than any gorge in the world. Never had two greater things been so near to each other. Or are we mistaken, like all those whose sight serves the memory rather than the ground beneath us? . . .

After the Pope interceded, Methodius was released, and in 880 A.D., for the third time, he argued in Rome for the legitimacy of his work and the Slavonic liturgy; once again the Pope issued a missive confirming the correctness of the Slavonic Mass. Along with the story of Methodius' beating, Daubmannus also tells how Methodius bathed three times in Rome's Tiber River, as in birth, marriage, and death, and how he took Communion there with three enchanted breads. In 882 A.D. Methodius was received with the highest honors at the court in Constantinople and then at the patriarchate, at whose head sat his childhood friend the Patriarch and philosopher Photius. Methodius died in Moravia in

885 A.D., leaving behind him the Slavonic translations of the Holy Scriptures, the Nomocanon, and the sermons of the Holy Fathers.

In his capacity as an eyewitness and an associate of Constantine the Philosopher in the Khazar mission, Methodius appears twice as a chronicler of the Khazar polemic. He translated Cyril's "Khazar Orations" into Slavonic and, judging by the words of Cyril's hagiography, he edited the texts (dividing them into eight books). Since Cyril's "Khazar Orations" have not been preserved in either the Greek original or Methodius' Slavonic translation, the most important Christian source concerning the Khazar polemic remains the Slavonic hagiography of Constantine the Philosopher (Cyril), completed under the supervision of Methodius himself. Here the date of the polemic (861 A.D.) has been preserved, along with a detailed description of Constantine's speech and those of his unnamed opponents and interlocutors—the Hebrew and Moslem representatives at the Khazar court. Daubmannus gives the following opinion of Methodius: "The hardest to plow are someone else's field and one's own wife"—he notes—"but since every man is stretched on his wife, as on a cross, it devolves that it is harder to bear one's own cross than another's. So too was it with Methodius, who never bore the cross of his brother. . . . For his younger brother was his spiritual father."

SEVAST, NIKON (17th century)—It is believed that at one time Satan lived under this name in the Ovchar gorge on the Morava River, in the Balkans. He was unusually gentle, addressed all men by his own name: Sevast, and worked as the head calligrapher at the

St. Nicholas Monastery. Wherever he sat, however, he left an imprint of two faces, and in place of a tail he had a nose. He claimed that in his previous life he had been the devil in the Jewish hell and had served Belial and Gebhurah, had buried golems in the attics of synagogues, and one autumn, when the birds had poisonous droppings that seared the leaves and grass they soiled, had hired a man to kill him. This enabled him to cross over from the Jewish to the Christian hell, and now in his new life he served Lucifer.

According to other stories, he never did die, but let a dog lick a bit of his blood, then entered the grave of some Turk, grabbed him by the ears, tore off his skin, and put it on. That is why goat's eyes peered out from behind his handsome Turkish eyes. He ran from flint, ate his supper after everyone else, and stole a rock of salt every year. The story goes that he would ride the monastery and village horses in the night; indeed, sunrise would find the animals coated with foam and dust, their manes braided. They say he did this to cool off his heart, because his heart had been cooked in boiling wine. Therefore, into the horses' manes they inserted the seal of Solomon, from which he fled, and this protected the horses from him and from his boots, which always bore the toothmarks of the dogs. He dressed lavishly and painted very good frescoes—a talent, it is said, that was given to him by the archangel Gabriel. On his frescoes in the churches of the Ovchar gorge are inscriptions that, if read in a certain order from painting to painting and monastery to monastery, form a message. It can be assembled as long as the paintings themselves exist. Nikon left this message for himself, for when, in three hundred years' time, he would return from the dead to be among the living; demons, he would say, recall nothing of their former lives, and this, therefore, was how they must get around it. When he first started painting he was not especially successful as an artist. He worked with his left hand; his paintings were fairly good, but they simply could not be remembered; it was as if they would vanish off the wall as soon as no one was looking at them. One morning a dejected Sevast sat in front of his paints and felt a different kind of stillness float into and shatter his own silence. Someone else was present, and keeping silent, but not in Nikon's language. Then Nikon began praying to the archangel Gabriel to grant him the grace of colors. Throughout the ravine at this time, in the monasteries of St. John, the Annunciation, St. Nicholas, and the Visitation of the Virgin, there were always plenty of young monks—icon and fresco painters—who decorated the walls and, in some silent, collective prayer, competed to see who would best paint the saint. Hence, it never occurred to anyone that Nikon Sevast's prayer might be answered. But that is precisely what happened.

In August 1670, just before the day of the seven saintly martyrs of Ephesus, when one starts eating venison, Nikon Sevast said:

"One of the sure paths to the real future (because there is also a false future) is to proceed in the direction of your fear."

And so he went hunting. He took with him the monk Theoctist Nikolsky,[A] who assisted him in copying the books at the monastery. It is probably thanks to that monk's notes that this hunt made its way into the story. Sevast, the story goes, hoisted a greyhound behind him onto the saddle, and they set out to hunt deer. All of a sudden the greyhound leapt from the horse's croup to attack; though Theoctist saw no deer in front of them, the greyhound barked as if it were actually chasing the prey, and slowly something invisible but heavy moved toward the hunters. Twigs could be heard snapping in the underbrush. Sevast behaved like the dog. He stood poised as if there were a deer in front of him; a deer's bellow could, in fact, be heard from very nearby, and from this Theoctist concluded that the archangel Gabriel had finally appeared before Nikon in the form of a deer, a deer that was the soul of Nikon Sevast. In other words, the archangel brought Nikon a soul as a gift. And so Nikon hunted and caught his own soul that morning, and with it struck up a conversation.

"Depths call unto depths in the expanse of your voice; help me with colors to offer your praise!" Sevast cried out to the archangel, or to the deer, or to his own soul, or whatever it was. "I want to paint the night between Saturday and Sunday, and on it so fine an icon of you that even in other places, without seeing it, people will pray to you!"

Finally the archangel Gabriel spoke, and said:

"Preobidev potasta se ozlobiti. . . ."

The monk realized that the archangel was omitting the nouns from his speech, because nouns are for God and verbs for man. The icon painter then replied:

"How will I work with my right hand when I am left-handed?" But the deer had vanished, and the monk asked Nikon:

"What was that?"

The latter answered perfectly calmly:

"Nothing special, all this is but temporary; I am merely passing through here on my way to Constantinople. . . ."

But then he added:

"Move a man from his resting place, and in that resting place are worms, insects as translucent as precious stones and mildew. . . ."

Joy seized him like an illness; he transferred his brush from his left hand to his right and began to paint. Colors flowed from him like milk, and he barely had time to spread them on. Suddenly he knew everything: how to mix India ink with musk, that yellow is the fastest color and black the slowest, taking the longest to dry and show its real face. His best colors were "St. John's white" and "dragon's blood," and he coated his pictures not with lacquer but with a small brush dipped in vinegar to give them the color of radiant air. He painted by feeding and healing everything around him with colors—doorposts and mirrors, beehives and pumpkins, gold coins and peasant shoes. On his horse's hoofs he painted the four evangelists, Matthew, Mark, Luke, and John, and on his own fingernails God's Ten Commandments; on the well bucket he painted Mary of Egypt; on the shutters he painted both Eves, the first Eve (Lilith) and the second Eve (Adam's). He painted on gnawed bones, on his own teeth and others', on pockets turned inside out, on caps and on ceilings. He painted the twelve apostles on live turtles and let them crawl off into the woods. The nights were as quiet as rooms; he would choose the one he wanted, enter, place a lamp behind the board, and paint a diptych. On it he portrayed the archangels Gabriel and Michael passing the soul of a sinner woman to each other through the night from one day to the next, with Michael standing in Tuesday and Gabriel in Wednesday. They walked on the written names of the days, and the pointed letters made blood gush from the archangels' feet. Nikon Sevast's paintings were nicer in winter, in the reflected brightness of the white snow, than in the summer, under the sun. They had then a kind of bitterness about them, as if they had been painted during an eclipse, and the smiles on the faces were extinguished in April and lost until the first snow. Then he would sit down to paint again, and only occasionally, with his elbow, would he shove his enormous penis between his legs so it would not bother him while he worked.

People remembered his new paintings all of their lives; monks from the ravine and icon painters from its monasteries flocked to the St. Nicholas Monastery, as if called by a whistle, to see Nikon's colors. Monasteries began to vie with one another for him, each of his icons brought in as much money as a vineyard, and he painted faster than the fastest horse could run. A record of how Nikon the icon painter worked has been preserved in a book of eight-voice canticles, and this record from 1674 reads:

"Two years ago, on the Day of St. Andre Stratilat, when we begin to eat partridge, I was sitting in my cell at the St. Nicholas monastery," notes the unknown monk in this record, "reading the book of the new-Jerusalem poems from Kiev, and in the adjacent room three monks and a dog were eating: the two idiorrhythmic monks had already finished their dinner, and the painter Sevast Nikon was eating, as was his custom, later. Through the silence of the poems I was reading, I could tell that Nikon was chewing beef tongue that had been beaten against the plum tree outside to make it tender. When Nikon finished his meal, he sat down to paint, and, watching him prepare his colors, I asked him what he was doing.

" 'It is not I who mix the colors but your own vision,' he answered. 'I only place them next to one another on the wall in their natural state; it is the observer who mixes the colors in his own eye, like porridge. Therein lies the secret. The better the porridge, the better the painting, but you cannot make good porridge from bad buckwheat. Therefore, faith in seeing, listening, and reading is more important than faith in painting, singing, or writing.'

"He took blue and red and placed them next to each other, painting the eyes of an angel. And I saw the angel's eyes turn violet.

"'I work with something like a dictionary of colors,' Nikon added, 'and from it the observer composes sentences and books, in other words, images. You could do the same with writing. Why shouldn't someone create a dictionary of words that make up one book and let the reader himself assemble the words into a whole?'

"Nikon Sevast then turned to the window, pointed with his brush to the field outside, and said:

"'Do you see that furrow? It is not a plow that made it. That furrow was made by the barking of a dog....'

"Then he thought for a moment and said to himself:

"'If I paint this way with my right hand when I am left-handed, just imagine how I would paint with my left hand!' And he transferred the brush from his right hand to his left....

"Word of this immediately spread through all the monasteries, and everyone was horrified, convinced that Nikon Sevast had gone back to Satan and would be punished. Indeed, his ears again became as pointed as knives, and it was said that he could slice a piece of bread with his ear. But his talent remained the same; he painted just as well with his left hand as with his right, and nothing changed; the archangel's anathema had not been carried out. One morning Nikon Sevast awaited the prior from the Monastery of the Annunciation, who was coming to arrange for Nikon to paint some altar doors. But no one arrived from the Monastery of the Annunciation that day or the following day. Then Sevast seemed to remember something, read his fifth 'Our Father,' which is recited to put the souls of suicides at peace, and set out for the monastery himself. There he found the prior in front of the church and, in keeping with his custom of calling others by his own name, inquired:

"'Sevast, Sevast, what is it?' Without a word the old man led him into the cell and showed him an icon painter, as young as hunger can be, who was already painting the doors. Nikon stared at the paintings, shocked. The young man flapped his eyebrows like wings and painted just as well as Nikon. He was no better and no worse than he. And then Nikon understood the kind of punishment being meted out to him. It was also rumored that another young man as good as Nikon was working in the church at Prnjavor, and this proved to be true. Soon other mural and icon painters, some not even so young, began one by one to paint better and better; it was as if they had untied themselves from a pier and were setting out for the wide-open seas, and they began to catch up with Nikon Sevast, whom, until then, they had regarded as an unattainable ideal. And so the walls of all the monasteries in the ravine were illuminated and restored, and Nikon went back to the beginning, from his left hand to his right. Unable to bear it, he said:

" 'What is the point of my being an icon painter like the rest? Now everyone can paint like me. . . .'

"He discarded his brushes forever and never painted another picture. Not even on an egg. He wept all the colors from his eyes into the monastery mortar and departed from St. Nicholas Monastery with his assistant, Theoctist, leaving behind him the print of a fifth hoof. Upon leaving he said:

" 'I know a great lord in Constantinople whose pigtail is as thick as a horse's tail and who will employ us as scribes.'

"And he mentioned his name. The name was: Kyr Avram Brankovich."[†]

SKILA, AVERKIE (17th and early 18th century)—of Coptic descent, a fencing instructor, one of the most renowned saber experts in Constantinople at the end of the 17th century. Skila was hired as a servant by the Constantinople diplomat Avram Brankovich.[†] He practiced his saber skills with his master in total darkness, tied to his opponent by a long leather belt. He knew how to heal wounds and always carried with him a collection of Chinese silver needles and a mirror on which red dots outlined the contours of his head and green dots the spreading lines on his face. When wounded or in pain, Skila would stand before the mirror and pierce his own face with the Chinese needles wherever the green dots appeared. His pains would disappear and his wounds would heal, leaving only the odd Chinese letter on his skin. This mirror could heal no one but himself. He always liked to have amusing people around him, and wherever he smoked and drank he paid them well to make him laugh. But he determined the price of every joke differently. Laughter—he believed—can be ordinary when a man laughs at only one thing. That is the cheapest kind. More costly is what makes a man laugh at two or three things at once. But that kind of laughter is rare, like everything else that is precious.

Averkie Skila spent decades painstakingly collecting the best saber strokes from the battlefields and outposts of Asia Minor; he studied them, tested them on living flesh, and finally described them in a text filled with diagrams and sketches showing the various strokes of this ancient art. He could kill a fish in the water with his saber, or at night hang a lantern on a sword impaled in the ground and then, when his enemy was facing the light, attack him from the darkness with a knife. He marked each of these movements with a different sign of the zodiac, and each star of these constellations represented a single death. It is known that by 1689 Skila had already mastered Aquarius, Sagittarius, and Taurus and was in the constellation of Aries. All he needed was practical confirmation of the final saber stroke and this constellation too would be his. The stroke was a snake-like incision that left behind a terrible sinuous, gaping slash; like a mouth it released voices from the wound sounding like the cry of liberated blood. Somewhere on an Austro-Turkish battlefield in Walachia in 1689, Skila, as he himself notes, tested this, his final stroke, and subsequently retired to Venice, where the experiences of this swordsman and saber master were published in 1702 in a book entitled *The Finest Signatures of the Saber*. Included in the book were folios with diagrams of fencing strokes, portraying Averkie Skila as standing amid the stars or, more precisely, in a cage or a net formed by his saber moves. To the uninitiated he seemed to be enclosed in a beautiful, transparent pavilion that he had drawn and constructed in the air around him with a whistle of the saber and a cut of the blade. But this cage was made of such sumptuous shapes and was so light and airy, so full of sweeping turns, floating domes, bridges, arches, and slender towers at each corner, that Averkie Skila looked as though he were enclosed in the flight of a bumblebee whose endless signature in the air had suddenly become legible. Averkie Skila's face was serene behind those completed moves or prison bars, but it had double lips and always looked as though someone else inside him wanted to speak in his stead. He maintained that every wound was a new heart that beat independently; with his saber he made the sign of the cross over these wounds; he had a hairy nose, by which people recognized and avoided him.

An interesting note about Averkie Skila was left by the musician and dream reader Yusuf Masudi. He and Averkie Skila worked as servants for the said diplomat to the Sublime Porte in Constantinople, and he hunted for the specters that travel through people's dreams. He noted that, in cases when two persons dream each other and the one's dream builds the other's reality, a small part of the dream is always left over. These are "the children of the dream." A dream, of course, is shorter than the reality of the one being dreamed, but the dream is always incomparably deeper than any reality, so there is always some dross left over, a "surplus of material" that cannot completely fit into the reality of the person being dreamed, but, rather, spills into and attaches onto the reality of a third person, who consequently experiences considerable difficulties and changes. As a rule, this third individual is in a more complicated situation than the first two; his free will is twice as restricted by the unconscious as that of the other two, because the surplus of energy and material that passes from one dream to the other alternately flows into the spiritual life of the third person, who thereby becomes a sort of hermaphrodite and leans toward one dreamer one moment and the other dreamer the next.

It was Masudi's conviction that Averkie Skila suffered from this type of inhibition of will and was in a dead heat with the two dreamers, whose names Masudi also mentioned. They were Averkie's lord and master, Avram Brankovich, and a man named Cohen,✿ whom Averkie Skila did not even know. In any case, though Skila was like an instrument with the deepest voice and thickest strings, he could only form the skeleton of the melody, the rudimentary, crude sound of his own life. All the rest evaded him and was tailored by others and for others. His loudest cries and greatest achievements took him no further than the level at which others exist painlessly and perform within the mean of their own possibilities.

According to Masudi's version of the events, Averkie Skila did not start his collection of saber strokes for reasons of a professional or military nature, to advance the learning of the art, but, rather, as part of his desperate search for the one stroke that would rescue him from the vicious circle within which he moved, waiting for his tormentors to come within reach of his saber. In his final years he placed great and unreasonable hope in solving his predicament with the aid of a single saber stroke, which, he claimed, was under the sign of Aries. At times he would awaken, his eyes filled with the dried-up tears of sleep; but when he rubbed them, the tears would break and crumble under his fingers like pieces of shattered glass or grains of sand, and from these fragments the Copt was able to tell that these were somebody else's tears, not his.

Be that as it may, the final diagram in the Venetian edition of Averkie's book, *The Finest Signatures of the Saber,* showed Averkie Skila in his cage of broken-line strokes; but the zigzag saber stroke under the sign of Aries was depicted in this sketch as a passage permitting an exit from the cage or net. In the final diagram of his book, Averkie Skila is pictured exiting from the cage of his combat skills through an opening made by this unusual sinuous stroke, and walking, as if through a gate, to freedom. He came out through this slit as through a wound, being born from his astral prison into the world and a new life. And inside his mute outer lips the other, inner lips laughed joyously.

STYLITE (BRANKOVICH, GRGUR)

(1676–1701)—in Eastern Christianity the word "stylite" signifies an ascetic monk who lives his life in prayer on top of a pillar. In the case of Grgur Brankovich, however, the term Stylite served as a nickname, and it was given to him in a very peculiar way. Grgur Brankovich was actually a company commander from the Brankovich family of Erdély and the eldest son of the 17th-century diplomat and military leader Avram Brankovich.[†] He survived his father by only twelve years. It is written that he was spotted like a leopard and very deft at midnight attacks. He wore a precious saber made of seventy metal leaves that had been forged while the blacksmith read out nine "Our Father"s in a row. He himself never heard the nickname Stylite, since he acquired it after the unusual death he suffered while in Turkish confinement. Hasan Agribirdi the Younger, the cannon forger, left a description of his death that made its way into folk ballads, and it was as if Brankovich, through his nickname, became equated with the holy ascetic monks of the Christian church.

According to this description, Brankovich and some cavalrymen accidentally came upon a strong Turkish division by the Danube. The Turks had only just arrived and were sitting on their horses and pissing into the river from their saddles. As soon as he caught sight of them, Brankovich turned to flee. The Turkish commander saw him, but went right on peeing. Only when he had completely emptied his innards and shaken himself off did he pursue Brankovich and take him captive. They tied him and brought him to their camp, beating a drum with their spears. The Turks placed the captured Brankovich on a Greek pillar, and three archers took aim at him. Before they began, however, they told him that if he survived the fifth arrow they would grant him his life and give him a bow and arrows to shoot at the three men who had been shooting at him. He begged them not to shoot two arrows simultaneously, because "he could not count pains, only shots." And so the three shot at him, while he counted. The first arrow hit his belt buckle, entered his intestines, and awakened all the pains that had already been born once during his lifetime. The second arrow he managed to catch with his hand, but the third penetrated his ear and hung there like an ear-ring, and he counted. The fourth missed him and the fifth hit him in the knee, veered off, and penetrated his other leg, but still he counted; the sixth missed again, the ninth riveted his hand to his thigh, and he counted; the eleventh shattered his elbow, the twelfth ruptured his lower back, but still he counted. He counted to seventeen and then fell from the pillar, dead. On that spot sprouted wild grapes—*Vitis sylvestris*—which are never bought or sold, for to do so is a sin.

SUK, DR. ISAILO (March 15, 1930–October 2, 1982)—archeologist, Arabist, university professor in Novi Sad, woke up one April morning in 1982 with his hair under the pillow and a slight pain in his mouth. Something hard and jagged was pressing against it. He inserted two fingers, like slipping a comb out of his pocket, and extracted from his mouth a key. A small key with a gold top. Human thoughts and dreams have their own horned, impenetrable exteriors, which protect the soft inner core from harm, like a shell; thus mused Dr. Suk as he lay there in bed, holding the key up before his eyes. But these thoughts expire on contact with words as quickly as words expire on contact with thoughts. Our portion is only what survives this mutual bane. In short, Dr. Suk blinked with eyes that were as hairy as testicles, and could make no sense of anything. It wasn't the key in his mouth that surprised him so much. After all, think of all the things in a lifetime that a person stuffs into the only mouth he has (if he had more he might pick and choose)! Once, after a binge, he had pulled the whole head of a sow, complete with muzzle, out of his gullet. No, he was surprised by something else. He estimated the key to be at least one thousand years old, and Professor Suk's estimates in archeology were seldom questioned: his professional reputation was uncontested. He put the key into the pocket of his trousers and bit at his mustache. Whenever he bit at his mustache in the morning he would remember what he had for dinner the night before. He would know right away, for instance, that he had eaten *ajvar* and liver smothered in garlic. Sometimes, however, his mustache would quite unexpectedly smell of oysters and lemon or something else that Dr. Suk would never have put in his mouth. Then he would usually remember whom he had discussed dinner with in bed the night before. And so this morning he remembered Gelsomina Mohorovichich. She always thought she had three Fridays until dinnertime. Her smile was well seasoned and her eyes slightly slanted so that her nose wrinkled every time she blinked. Her small hands were lazy and so warm you could boil an egg in them. Dr. Suk would tie up his New Year's gifts with her silky hair, and women would recognize it even when it was cut off.

With these thoughts in his head, his ears freshly shaved and his gaze well honed, Dr. Suk prepared to go out. He was currently in the capital, where he still went to visit his family home. It was in this house that Professor Suk had started his research thirty years before. Since then his studies had taken him farther and farther away, and he could not help feeling that his journey would end in some distant land where hills stood like a sliced loaf of black bread with the odd fir tree sprouting out. Yet his archeological research and his discoveries in Arabistics, especially his study of the Khazars, an ancient people who had long ago vanished from the stage of world events and had left behind the saying that the soul has its own skeleton made of memories, all were associated with this house. The house had once belonged to his left-legged grandmother, from whom he had inherited his left-handedness. Here in the home of his mother, Mrs. Anastasia Suk, Dr. Suk's writings now held the place of honor on the library shelves, bound in the pelts of old fur coats, the kind that smell of currants, and read with special glasses, used by Mme. Anastasia only on formal occasions. Freckled like a trout, Mme. Anastasia carried her name in her mouth like an irritating coin; not once did she answer to it, not, until the end of her days, did she ever utter it. She had fine blue eyes like those of a goose, and her son often found her sitting with one of his books in her lap and a fragment of somebody's name (probably his father's) stuck to her lips, speckled with blood.

Impenetrable and as thick as porridge, the years that Dr. Suk had forded in the last decade, collecting archive material, photographs of old coins, and fragments of salt pitchers to build the pillar of truth had made it increasingly clear that his mother was returning to him from a great distance, coming back to life. She was returning through his advancing years and through his wrinkles, and the older he got the more she settled into his face and body, dislodging his late father's traits and features. He was manifestly growing out of him and into her; now that he was compelled to live alone and do women's work, less and less of his father's dexterity was left in his hands, and more and more often he recognized his mother's gestures in his slow, clumsy fingers. His visits to the family home, which were rare and usually on the occasion of birthdays (as was the case now), also began to change. Now his mother meets him at the door, kisses him on the nose, leads him to the corner where his baby walker had once stood and where now there is an easy chair tied to the door handle like a pig.

"Sashenka, you always neglected me so," she says to her son. "The finest and happiest hours of my life were connected with such excruciating effort that I remember them still. I remember them, which means I remember you too, not as a joy but as a joyful, almost intolerable effort. Why was it so exhaustingly difficult to be happy? Never mind, that has all long since passed like the wind through the willow. Now that I am no longer happy, I have settled down. And yet—look—there is someone who still loves me, who still remembers me!"

And she brings out a bundle of letters he wrote to her.

"Imagine, Sasha, they're from Professor Suk!"

The mother has tied the letters with the hair of Gelsomina Mohorovichich; she kisses them and reads them to him triumphantly, like songs of war, almost forgetting to see him off at the door when he leaves to go back to his hotel to sleep. Or she kisses him goodbye so hastily that he accidentally feels her breasts, like a compote of pears under her dress.

Now, when Professor Suk was entering the third decade of his research work, when his eyes had become quick and his mouth slower than his ear, when his books had been accepted by archeologists and Arabists, there was yet another reason for him to come to the capital. There, one morning, in the huge pretzel-shaped building, Dr. Isailo Suk's name had been placed for the first time in a hat. Although his name had not been drawn then or the next couple of times, now Dr. Suk was being regularly invited to meetings in the building. He would go to these meetings wearing yesterday's smile stretched on his lips like a cobweb, and he would lose his way in the building's corridors, corridors that were circular and in which you could never find the point where you had started from. He thought of how this building was like a book written in an unknown language he had not yet learned, how these corridors were like the sentences of a strange language, and the rooms foreign words he had never heard before. He was not in the least surprised when one day he was told that he was to take an ordinary exam in one of the first-floor rooms, which smelled like a rancid keyhole. On the second floor, where the names were drawn, his books were held in indisputable esteem, but one floor down in this same building he felt short-legged, as though his trousers were getting longer and longer. The people here were subordinate to those up there on the second floor, but here his books were not taken into account, and every year he was subjected to exams, after his identity was carefully checked. The first time he went to take his exam, Isailo Suk was relieved to see that the head of the examining board was an instructor from his faculty, who had recently taken his doctoral orals before a commission Suk himself had chaired, and whom he often saw through the window sitting in the Third Boot Tavern. Dr. Suk was not told his grades after the exam, but the head of the examining board spoke highly of the examinee's potential. And so it was with a feeling of relief that Dr. Suk finished his exam that day and went to see his mother. As usual, she led him into the dining room, where, eyes closed, she held clasped to her breast Dr. Isailo Suk's latest endeavor, with a handwritten dedication by the author himself, and showed it to him. After he had looked politely at the book and at his own signature in it, his mother placed him on a footstool in the corner of the room, with the words Dr. Suk remembered from his childhood—"Just sit there for a while!"—and she explained to him the gist of the scientific undertaking described in the book.

She spoke with a joy that was less like the sadness of a
clown and more like the cheer of some figure from a
tragedy. With considerable accuracy she explained to her
son how Professor Suk had established that the keys
found in a jar from the Crimea had silver, copper, or
gold barbarian imitation coins for handles. A total of 135
keys had been found (Dr. Suk believed that originally
there may have been ten thousand in the jar), and on
each he had discovered a small sign or letter. At first he
thought it was the mark of the locksmith, but then he
noticed that other samples of the same coin, of a somewhat higher denomination, had a second letter, the silver
coin had a third, and the gold, he presumed, a fourth
letter, but not a single gold-handled key had been found.
And then he had a brilliant idea (at this momentous
point she asked him to stop fidgeting and interrupting
her with his questions): he laid out the coins in order of
denomination and read out the secret inscription or message formed when the letters on the coins were put
together—"Ate"; there was still one letter missing (from
the gold coin that had not been found). Dr. Suk believed
that the missing letter could be one of the holy letters of
the Jewish alephbet, perhaps the letter "he," the fourth
letter of the Lord's name. . . . The key bearing it augurs
death.

"Think of the brilliance of it!" she cried, and then,
seeing that his glass was empty, added, "One glass is
enough, two are not!"

Meanwhile, every second spring Dr. Suk's name was
placed in the hat behind the doors with their smell of
rancid keyholes. He was never notified of the fact, nor
did he ever know the outcome. He was coughing at the
time with the feeling that a cluster of tendons had
sprouted from their roots, cutting so deeply into his
shoulders and neck that he could barely break free. The

exams came more frequently now, and there was always someone new heading the examining board. Dr. Suk had a student, a girl who had gone bald at an early age, but at night a dog licked her scalp and thick, colored fur grew on her head. She was plump and could not remove the rings from her fingers; she had eyebrows like small fishbones and wore a woolen sock as a cap. She slept on her mirrors and combs, whistling in her dreams for her little boy, who was lying in bed beside her, kept awake by the whistling. Now she was examining Dr. Suk, with the sleepless, bald child seated next to her. Wanting to get through the exam as quickly as possible, Dr. Suk answered the boy's constant questions. Finally, when it was all over, he went to his mother's house and sat down to eat, but he was so preoccupied with his own thoughts that his mother said worriedly: "Be careful, Sasha, your future will destroy your past! You don't look well. You should find a child to walk on your back."

It was true that unknown varieties of hunger had been lately growing and blossoming inside him, and a viscid, undefined hope would quickly ripen like a fruit only to die when his hunger was assuaged with the first bite he swallowed.

"Do you know how many mouth holes the Jews have?" his mother asked that day as he ate. "I'm sure you don't. I read about it recently somewhere, probably in Dr. Suk's book; at the time he was studying the spread of biblical beliefs in the steppes of Eurasia. On the basis of his findings, in 1959, at the Chelarevo site by the Danube, he established that the area had been settled by a people unknown to us, a people considerably more primitive and anthropologically older than the Avars. He believes that this is the burial site of the Khazars, a people who came down from the Black Sea to the Danube in the 8th century A.D. It's late now, but remind me, when you come for Gelsomina's birthday tomorrow, to read you the exciting page in which he describes it all; it's extremely interesting. . . ."

It was after this promise that Dr. Isailo Suk woke up and found the key in his mouth.

When he stepped out into the street, the afternoon was ailing; a plague of light was blighting the radiance of the sun; an epidemic of boils and rashes spread and erupted across the sky, infecting the clouds, which wilted and sagged in their faltering progress.

The week had received its monthly wash, and Sunday was already a reek in the air, breaking wind like a cripple on the road to recovery. And there in the distance, along the scabby skyline, Suk's spent days shone blue, small, and healthy, devoid of calendar names in the happily vanishing herd, free of him and his worries, leaving dust in their wake. . . .

One of the children who had been playing in the street, swapping pants with the other boys, stopped in front of the newsstand where Dr. Suk was buying the paper and peed on his trouser leg. Dr. Suk turned around with the expression of a man who notices in the evening that he has been going around all day with his fly unbuttoned. Just then, however, an utterly unknown man slapped him in the face as hard as he could. It was cold outside, and Dr. Suk felt the warmth of the assailant's hand through the slap; for all the pain there was something just slightly pleasant about it. He was about to argue with the malapert when he felt the wet trouser leg stick to his calf. Then he was hit by another man, who had been standing behind the first, waiting for his chance. Dr. Suk now realized it would be better for him to move away, which is what he proceeded to do, not understanding a thing except that the second slap had smelled of onions. But there was no time to lose, because other passers-by were converging upon him. There seemed to be something perfectly natural about the way the blows began raining down upon him; Dr. Suk started to feel that the hands behind some of them were cold, and this he found curiously agreeable in the entire disagreeable affair. He had warmed up now. There was yet another fortunate circumstance in this scene. While he had no time to think, because one can do very little thinking in between one blow and the next, he did notice that the slaps were sometimes sweaty and that they were driving him from the Church of St. Mark toward the square, along the road he had intended to take in the first place, the road that led straight to the store where he wanted to shop. So he submitted to the blows, which were bringing him closer to his destination.

Then he came upon a fence behind which nothing had ever been seen or heard. And since he was now forced to run under the unrelenting rain of blows, the slits in the fence merged before his eyes and he saw for the first time (although he had passed there before) that there was a house behind the fence, and that a young man was standing at the window playing a violin. He also noticed the music stand and instantly recognized Bruch's Concerto in G minor for Violin and Orchestra, but he heard no sound, although the window was open and the young man was playing fervidly. Surprised, the pelting rain of blows still upon him, Dr. Suk finally ran into the store that had been the object of his sortie that morning, and breathed a sigh of relief as he slammed the door shut behind him. Inside it was as still as in a cucumber jar; only the corn smelled. The shop was empty, except for a hen nestled in a cap in the corner.

She cocked one eye at Dr. Suk and saw everything edible in him. Then she switched to the other eye and saw all the indigestible parts. She thought for a moment, and finally Dr. Suk appeared in her mind's eye, composed once again of digestible and indigestible parts, and at last she knew whom she was dealing with. As for what happened next, let him tell the story himself.

THE STORY OF THE EGG
AND THE VIOLIN BOW

I stood there in the pleasant cool and I caught the smell of polish. The violins were responding to one another; you could have composed an entire polonaise from their soft sighs, as if composing a game of chess. All you would have had to do was to rearrange the order and the sounds a bit. Finally, out came the Hungarian who owned the instrument shop. He had eyes the color of whey. Red, as though he were about to lay an egg, he displayed a chin shaped like a small belly with a navel.

He took out a pocket ashtray, flicked ashes into it, carefully closed it tight, and asked whether I had not made some mistake: "The furrier is next door. People are always coming in here by mistake." Nobody had come into his store for the past seven days, except by mistake. In fact, his store had no doors; one might say it had the creak of a door but no real doors, just a small shopwindow with a handle that swung open into the shop, letting the customer into a cramped room. I inquired whether he had a small violin for a small young lady, or a midget cello, if they were not too expensive.

The Hungarian turned to go back from where he had come, from where wafted the smell of paprikash. Just then the hen picked itself up from the cap, clucking at its freshly laid egg. The Hungarian carefully took the egg and placed it in a drawer, having first penciled on it a date—October 2, 1982—which I noted with surprise was still several months away.

"What do you want with a violin or a cello?" he asked, turning around at the entrance of his small back room. "You have records, the radio, television. A violin —you know what a violin is? A small violin, my good sir, has to be plowed, sowed, and reaped every year, from here to Subotica, with this here!" And he pointed to the violin bow hanging from his belt like a sword. He drew it out and pulled taut the strings with fingers that wore rings around the nails, as if to hold them in place and keep them from dropping off. Then he abstained from further conversation, and with a wave of his hand again turned to leave. "Who needs it?" he said on his way out. "Buy her something else; buy her a scooter or a dog."

I just stood there in the shop, not coping very well with this decisiveness voiced in such an indecisive, undulating language, like food that may be filling but is unappetizing. Actually, the Hungarian had mastered my language rather well, but at the end of every sentence he would add for dessert a Hungarian word that I couldn't understand. He did this now as he gave me his parting words of advice: "Find something else, sir, to make your little girl happy. This happiness is too difficult for her. And it's belated happiness. Belated," he added through the wafting aroma of the paprikash. "How old is she?" he inquired, assuming a businesslike tone.

With that he disappeared, and I could hear him getting dressed and preparing to go out. I told him Gelsomina Mohorovichich's age: seven. He flinched at the number as though touched by a magic wand. He translated it into Hungarian, obviously able to count only in Hungarian, and a strange smell enveloped the room, the smell of cherries; I saw that the smell followed his change of mood. A glass pipe now appeared in his mouth, through which he sucked cherry brandy. He crossed the shop, stood on my foot as if by accident, took out a small child's cello, and offered it to me, all the while standing on my foot to show me how cramped his shop was. I stood there and, like him, took no notice, except that he was doing this at my expense and I to my own detriment.

"Take this," he said. "The wood is older than you and me together. The lacquer is good. . . . Hear for yourself!"

He strummed the strings. The cello vibrated with a four-note chord, and he stepped off my foot as if the chord could ease all the troubles of this world.

"You hear?" he asked. "Each string contains all the others. But to hear it you have to listen to four different things at once, and we're too lazy to do that. Do you hear it or not? Four hundred and fifty thousand," he said, translating the price from Hungarian. The amount struck me like a rock. It was as though he had peered into my pocket: he knew exactly how much I had. I had been saving it for Gelsomina. It's not all that much, I know, but it took me three years to collect even that. I told him I would gladly take it.

"Take it?" asked the Hungarian, shaking his head disapprovingly. "Sir, is that how one takes an instrument? Don't you want to try it?"

Disconcerted, I looked around the shop for something to sit on other than that cap, as though I really did want to try the cello.

"You need a chair?" he asked. "A duck sits on water, and you don't know what to do even on dry land? You don't know?" Scornfully he took the little cello from me and placed it on his shoulder like a violin.

"Like this!" he said, giving me back the instrument.

I took it, and for the first time in my life played the cello like a violin. De Falla didn't sound too bad in the deep fifths, and I even seemed to hear the notes more clearly through the wood pressed against my ear. Suddenly the Hungarian changed his smell. This time it was the odor of pungent masculine sweat. He took off his coat and was in his undershirt, two gray braided beards suspended from each armpit. He pulled out a drawer, sat on the corner edge, took the cello from me, and played. I was astounded by his marvelous improvisation.

"You play very well," I said.

"I don't play the cello at all. I'm a harpsichordist, and I like the violin. But I can't play the cello. What you heard wasn't music, although you know nothing about it. That was just an arrangement of all the sounds, from the highest to the lowest, so as to judge the capacity and other elements of the instrument. Shall I wrap it up for you?"

"Yes, please," I said, reaching for my wallet.

"That will be five hundred thousand," said the Hungarian.

An icy chill went down my back.

"Didn't you say four hundred and fifty thousand?"

"I did, but that's for the cello. The rest is for the bow. Or don't you want the bow? You don't need the bow? I thought that a fiddle and a bow went together. . . ."

He unwrapped the bow and put it back in the display window.

I stood there at a loss for words, struck dumb. Finally I recovered from all the slaps of before, and from this Hungarian, as from an illness, a hangover or a torpor. I came to my senses, sobered up, and at last stopped playing in this comedy with the Hungarian who picked at his teeth. Actually, I had forgotten all about the bow. I didn't have the money to buy it, and I told him so.

Suddenly, he slipped on his coat—there was a smell of mothballs—and he said:

"I haven't got time, my good sir, to wait around while

you earn the money for the bow. Especially if you haven't been able to do so by the age of fifty. Better you should wait than me."

And with that he made to depart, leaving me there alone in the shop. He stopped at the door, returned, and said:

"Shall we make a deal? You take the bow on the installment plan."

"You're joking?" I replied, no longer willing to play his game and wanting to leave.

"No, I'm not joking. I propose a deal. You don't have to accept it, but at least listen."

The Hungarian lit his pipe with such pride that it was obvious he had already fumigated Pest with it.

"All right, let's hear it," I said.

"You will buy the egg along with the bow."

"An egg?"

"Yes. You saw the egg the hen laid a while ago. Well, that's the one," he said, taking the egg out of the drawer and shoving it under my nose.

Written in pencil on the egg was the date October 2, 1982.

"You'll give me as much for the egg as for the bow, repayable in two years. . . ."

"What did you say?" I asked, not believing my ears. From the Hungarian again came the smell of cherries.

"Are you telling me your hen lays golden eggs?"

"No, my hen does not lay golden eggs, but it does carry something that you and I, sir, cannot lay. It carries days, weeks, and years. Every morning it lays a Friday or a Tuesday. Today's egg, for instance, has a Thursday instead of a yolk. Tomorrow's will have a Wednesday. Instead of a chick, it will hatch a day of life for its owner! What a life! These are not golden eggs, they're time eggs. And I'm offering them to you at a cheap price. This egg, sir, holds one day of your life. It's closed in there like a chick, and it's up to you whether it will hatch or not."

"Even if I were to believe your story, why should I buy a day I already have?"

"Use your head, sir. Think. Do you think with your ears? Why, all our problems in this world stem from the fact that we have used up our days such as they are— from the fact that we can't skip over the worst ones. That's the point. With my egg in your pocket, you're safe from misfortune. When you notice that the coming day is too bleak, you just break the egg and you'll avoid all unpleasantness. In the end, of course, you'll have one day less to live, but in return you'll be able to fry yourself a fine plate of scrambled eggs out of that one ugly day."

"If your egg is really all that valuable, why don't you keep it for yourself?" I said, looking him in the eyes but finding nothing in them that I could understand. He looked at me in pure Hungarian.

"The gentleman can't be serious? How many eggs do you think I already have from this hen? How many days do you think a person can break in order to be happy? A thousand? Two thousand? Five thousand? I have as many eggs as you want, but not that many days. Anyway, like all eggs, these are good for only so long. After a while they go bad and can't be used any more. That, sir, is why I am selling them before they lose their effect. And you aren't in a position to choose. You'll give me a receipt for the loan," he added at the end, scribbling something on a scrap of paper and shoving it at me to sign.

"And can your egg," I asked, "dispense with or save a day or an object—like a book, for instance?"

"Of course, you just have to break the egg on the blunt end. But then you will have missed the chance to use the egg for yourself."

I signed the paper on my knee, paid, was given the receipt; again I heard the hen clucking in the next room as he carefully wrapped the cello with the bow and the egg and I finally left the shop. He came out with me, asked me to pull the door handle tight while he locked the shopwindow; once again I was drawn into one of his games. He went off without a word, then turned back at the corner to add, "Remember—the date on the egg tells you when it expires. After that the egg is no good any more...."

On his way back from the shop, Dr. Suk worried for a while about being attacked again on the street, but all went well. He was thinking about this when the rain caught him in front of the fence where the boy had been playing the violin that morning. As he ran, the slits in the fence merged again before his eyes and once more he saw behind the fence the boy playing the violin at the window. Again he heard no sound, although the window was open. To some sounds he was deaf, to others not. He ran on, nearing his mother's house. His hands fingered his skin like those of a blind man feeling his way; the fingers recognized the direction and the well-trodden path. In his pocket were the key that augured death and the egg that could save him from a deadly day.... The egg was marked with a date, the key with a small gold handle. His mother was still alone; she liked to take a short nap in the late afternoon, and she was sleepy.

"Pass me my glasses, please," she said to her son, "and let me read you that bit about the Khazar cemetery. Just listen to what Dr. Suk writes about the Khazars in Che-larevo:

" 'They lie in family tombs scattered in disarray along the banks of the Danube, but in each the heads are turned toward Jerusalem. They lie in double graves with their horses, they and the animals squint at opposite sides of the world; they lie underneath their wives, who are curled up on their stomachs, but in such a way that they do not see their faces, only their thighs. Sometimes they are buried vertically, terribly aged and almost disassembled from constantly staring up at the sky; they have with them bricks with the name Jehovah or the word *shahor*—"black"—scratched on them. They light fires in the corners of the tombs, keep food by their feet, and a knife at their waist. From grave to grave different animals lie by their side: in one it will be a sheep, cow, or goat, in another a hen, pig, or deer, and in the children's graves they put eggs. Sometimes their implements, sickles or forging and goldsmith tools, lie next to them. Their eyes, ears, and mouths are lidded with pieces of tile bearing the image of the seven-branched Jewish candlestick; the fragment of tile is of Roman origin, dating from the 3rd or 4th century, and the picture on it is from the 7th, 8th, or 9th century. They etched the pictures of the candlestick (the menorah) and other Jewish symbols on the tiles with pointed tools, clumsily, as though in a great hurry, perhaps secretly, as if they dared not make them too good. Or as though they had only a vague memory of the object they were etching, as though they had never seen a candlestick, a shovel for ashes, a lemon, the horn of a ram, or a palm, but, rather, were drawing them from somebody's description. The carved lids for the eyes, mouth, and ears warded demons and *shedim* away from their graves, but these tiles were strewn all over the cemetery, as if some tremendous force, the tide of earth's gravitation, had scattered them to the winds and no single one is any longer in place to stand guard.

It might even be supposed that some undefined subsequent burning need had brought these lids for the eyes, mouth, and ears here from other graves, opening up the way to some demons and closing it off to others. . . .' "

Just then all the doorbells started ringing and guests streamed into the house. Gelsomina Mohorovichich came in, wearing sharp boots, her lovely staring eyes like stones out of a ring. In front of everyone, Professor Suk's mother presented her with the cello, kissed her between the eyes (leaving there a third eye traced by her lipstick), and said:

"Who do you think this present is from, Gelsomina? Guess! It's from Professor Suk! You must write him a nice letter and thank him for it. He's a handsome young gentleman. And I always save the best chair at the head of the table for him!"

Pensive, her shadow so heavy she could kick you with it like a boot, Mrs. Suk sat her guests down to dinner, leaving the chair at the head of the table empty, as though she were still awaiting her most important guest; her thoughts elsewhere, she hurriedly seated Dr. Suk next to Gelsomina and the other young people; the leaves of the well-watered rubber plant standing behind them perspired and wept so that you could hear them drip on the floor.

At dinner that evening Gelsomina turned to Dr. Suk, touching his hand with her burning fingers, and said:

"A person's acts in life are like meals, and his thoughts and feelings like seasoning. Whoever puts salt on cherries or pours vinegar on sweets will fare poorly. . . ."

Dr. Suk was slicing the bread as Gelsomina spoke, and he thought how she had some years for him, and others for the rest of the world.

When he returned to his hotel room after the party, Professor Suk took the key out of his pocket and examined it through his magnifying glass. On the gold coin that served as a handle he deciphered the Hebrew letter "he." He laughed, put down the key, took out of his briefcase the 1691 Daubmannus edition of *The Khazar Dictionary,* and before going to sleep read the entry on *The Wet Nurse.* He was convinced that his was the poisoned copy, where the reader would die at the ninth page, so he never read more than four pages at a time, just to keep on the safe side. He thought to himself, "One should not needlessly embark on a road that brings rain." The entry he chose for this evening was not long:

"The Khazars," wrote the Daubmannus dictionary, "had wet nurses who could make their own milk poisonous. They were in great demand. They are believed to have hailed from one of two Arab tribes that Mohammed had expelled from Medina because they worshipped Mahat, the fourth Bedouin deity. They probably came from either the Khazarai or the Auz tribe. They would be hired to nurse (just once was enough) some undesirable princeling or a rich heir whose fellow heirs wanted him removed. 'Poison-milk tasters' were established as a result; these were young men who would sleep with the wet nurses and suck their breasts just before they were to nurse the children entrusted to their care. Only if their lovers passed unharmed were the wet nurses allowed into the nursery. . . ."

Dr. Suk fell asleep just before dawn, thinking how he would never learn what Gelsomina had said to him that evening. He was totally deaf to her voice.

THE
GREEN
BOOK

ISLAMIC SOURCES
ON THE
KHAZAR QUESTION

AKSHANY, YABIR IBN (17th century)—

Anatolian minstrels (lute and tambourine players) believed that Satan used this name for a while and that he appeared under it before one of the most celebrated lute players of the 17th century—Yusuf Masudi.❦ Ibn Akshany was himself a very deft player. There exists a written record of his fingering for a song, so we know that he used more than ten fingers to play his instrument. He was a good-looking man; he carried no shadow, and his shallow eyes were like two trampled puddles. Although he declined to make public his opinions about death, he conveyed them indirectly through his tales, advising people to read dreams or to gain knowledge about death from the dream hunters. Two proverbs are ascribed to him: (1) "Death is the surname of sleep, but that surname is unknown to us"; (2) "Sleep is the daily end of life, a small exercise in death, which is its sister, but not every brother and sister are equally close." He once wanted to show people just how death operated, and he did so by using a Christian military commander whose name has been preserved: he was called Avram Brankovich,† and he fought in Walachia, where, Satan claimed, every man is born a poet, lives like a thief, and dies a vampire. Yabir Ibn Akshany spent some time as a guard at the turbeh of Sultan Murat, and it was here that an anonymous visitor wrote down some of the things Akshany said:

"The guard locks the gates of the turbeh, letting the heavy sound of the lock fall into the dark interior, as though leaving the name of the key inside. Dispirited, like me, he sits down on the stone beside me and closes his eyes. Just when I think he has dozed off in his part of the shade, the guard lifts his hand and points to a moth fluttering above the entrance to the tomb, having come out of our clothes or the Persian carpets in the turbeh.

" 'You see,' he says to me casually, 'the moth is way up there by the white wall of the doorway, and it is visible only because it moves. From here it almost looks like a bird high up in the sky, if you think of the wall as the sky. That's probably how the moth sees the wall, and only we know it is wrong. But it doesn't know that we know. It doesn't even know we exist. You try to communicate with it, if you can. Can you tell it anything in a way it understands; can you be sure it has understood you completely?'

" 'I don't know,' I replied. 'Can you?'

" 'Yes,' the old man said quietly, and with a clap of his hands he killed the moth, then proffered its crushed body on the palm of his hand.

" 'Do you think it didn't understand what I told it?'

" 'You can do the same thing with a candle, extinguishing it with your two fingers to prove you exist,' I commented.

" 'Certainly, if a candle is capable of dying . . . Now, imagine,' he went on, 'that there is somebody who knows about us what we know about the moth. Somebody who knows how, with what, and why this space that we call the sky and assume to be boundless, is bounded—somebody who cannot approach us to let us know that he exists except in one way—by killing us. Somebody on whose garments we are nourished, somebody who carries our death in his hand like a tongue, as a means of communicating with us. By killing us, this anonymous being informs us about himself. And we, through our deaths, which may be no more than a warning to some wayfarer sitting alongside the assassin, we, I say, can at the last moment perceive, as through an opened door, new fields and other boundaries. This sixth and highest degree of deathly fear (where there is no memory) is what holds and links us anonymous participants in the game. The hierarchy of death is, in fact, the only thing that makes possible a system of contacts between the various levels of reality in an otherwise vast space where deaths endlessly repeat themselves like echoes within echoes. . . .'

"As the guard talks, I decide: If what he tells me is just a matter of wisdom, experience, or erudition, then it does not merit attention. But what if at this moment he simply has a better vantage point than the rest of us, or than he himself had the day before? . . ."

For a while, Yabir Ibn Akshany lived the life of a vagabond, carrying with him his instrument made of white tortoiseshell. He roamed the villages of Asia Minor, played his music, and shot fortunetelling arrows in the air, stealing and begging two sieves of flour a week. He met his death in the year 1699 after Isa in a curious way. At the time, he was touring Thursdaysites (places that held fairs on Thursdays) and, whether seated or standing, he always caused trouble. He would spit in people's pipes, tie together the wheels of their carts, or knot their turbans, making them undo one another's. When he had outraged passers-by to the point that they fell upon him, he would cut their purses and empty their pockets while they lashed out at him in concert. He seemed to be passing time. One day, when he deemed that it had passed, he found a peasant who owned a yellow cow and paid him to bring it to a certain place at an appointed hour. The place had been innocent of all sound for a year. The peasant brought the cow and it gored Ibn Akshany, killing him on the spot. He died easily and quickly, as though he had fallen asleep, and at that moment a shadow appeared beneath him, perhaps simply to receive his body. He left behind his lute of white tortoiseshell, which that very same day began walking, turned back into an animal, and swam off into the Black Sea. The minstrels believe that when Yabir Ibn Akshany returns to this world, his turtle will once more become a white lute and replace his shadow.

He was buried in Trnovo by the Neretva River, at a spot that is still called Satan's Grave. A year later, a Christian from the Neretva area who had known Akshany well went to Thessalonica on some business. There he entered a store to buy a two-pronged fork for piercing two kinds of meat—pork and beef. When the shopkeeper came out to serve him, the man immediately recognized Akshany and asked him what he was doing in Thessalonica when he had been buried a year ago in Trnovo.

"Well, my friend," Akshany replied, "I died, and Allah condemned me forever and a day, and so here I am, a merchant, and I have just about everything imaginable. Only don't ask me for a scale, because I can no longer weigh anything. That's why I sell sabers, knives, forks, and tools, things that are counted, not weighed. I'm always here, except on the eleventh Friday of the year, when I have to be in my grave. But, listen, I'll give you whatever you want on loan if you give me a written promise that you'll return it all as agreed. . . ."

The Neretva man accepted the offer, although it was a day when pipes fizzle and won't draw; he wrote the chit for a date after the eleventh Friday, in the month of Rabi-al-awwal, honed his black cane as sharp as buckwheat seed, and left for home, taking with him all the merchandise he wanted. On his way back, by the Neretva River, he was attacked by a huge boar and only just managed to fend it off with his cane, but not before the animal had torn off a patch of his blue silk belt. When the month of Rabi-al-awwal came around, just before the eleventh Friday, the Neretva man took a pistol and the fork he had bought in Thessalonica and dug up Satan's Grave, only to discover two men lying there. One lay on his back, smoking a long-stemmed pipe, and the other lay sideways, saying nothing. When the Neretva man aimed his pistol at them, the one with the pipe puffed smoke in his face and said:

"I am Nikon Sevast.[†] You can't harm me, because I am buried by the Danube." And with these words he vanished, leaving only the pipe behind in the grave. Then the other one turned around, and the Neretva man recognized Akshany, who now said to him reproachfully:

"Ah, my friend, I could have destroyed you in Thessalonica, but I didn't, I gave you my help. Now you have come to do me in with your faith. . . ."

And with these words Akshany smiled and the Neretva man saw the patch of blue belt in his mouth. . . . Flinching, he turned the gun upside down and fired at Akshany. Akshany lunged out at him, but it was too late: he only nicked the man, because the shot had been fired and had hit him. Akshany roared like a bull, and blood flooded the grave.

When he returned home, the Neretva man put away his weapon and reached for the fork—but it was nowhere to be found. While he was firing the pistol, Akshany had stolen the fork. . . .

According to another legend, Yabir Ibn Akshany

never died at all. In Constantinople one morning in 1699 he tossed a laurel leaf into a pail of water and dipped in his head to wash his pigtail. It wasn't for more than a few seconds, but when he lifted his head from the water and took a deep breath, Constantinople and the empire in which he had washed were no longer there. He was now in the Kingston, a luxury Istanbul hotel, the year was 1982 after Isa, he had a wife, a child, and a Belgian passport, he spoke French, and all that was left floating at the bottom of the sink made by F. Primavesi & Son, Corella, Cardiff, was the laurel leaf.

A T E H $^\triangledown$ (beginning of 9th century)—According to Islamic legend, the Khazar kaghan had a relative living at his court who was renowned for her beauty. Huge, silver-haired watchdogs stood guard outside her chamber, lashing their eyes with their tails. They were trained to stand still, and every so often they could be seen peeing down their front legs, without moving. They rolled consonants like stones deep down in their chests, and before going to sleep they would curl up their tails like ship rope. Ateh had silver eyes; instead of buttons she wore bells, and anyone in the street would know from their sound whether the princess at court was dressing or undressing for bed. But her bells were never heard. Along with brains, the princess was endowed with inordinate slowness. She breathed less than other people sneezed, and in her slowness she abominated anything and anyone who wanted to make her act quickly, even if it was something she herself had intended to do. The lining of this garment of slowness revealed another side when she talked—she never dwelt on one subject for long, and when conversing with people would hop from one subject to another like a bird from branch to branch. But a few days later she would unexpectedly return to the story at the point where she had left off and, unbidden, would proceed with what she had before refused to consider, trailing after her meandering thoughts. This complete nondifferentiation between important and marginal subjects, and total indifference to all topics of conversation, is believed to be a misfortune that befell the princess during the Khazar polemic.[V] Ateh was a poetess, but the only lines of hers to have been preserved are: "The difference between two yeses can be greater than the difference between yes and no." Everything else is merely ascribed to her.

A number of her poems, or texts written under her supervision, are believed to have been preserved in Arabic translation. Authorities on the Khazars and their conversion are especially interested in the poems devoted to the Khazar polemic. These are originally love poems; only later were they used as arguments in the polemic, when chroniclers sat down to record the events. Be that as it may, Ateh took fervid part in the polemic, successfully out-arguing both the Jewish and the Christian participants, and in the end helping the Islamic representative, Farabi Ibn Kora.[©] Together with the Khazar kaghan, her lord and master, she converted to Islam. Sensing that he was losing, the Greek joined up with the Jewish deputy, and together they condemned Princess Ateh to the underworld powers of the two hells—to the Hebrew Belial and the Christian Satan. To avoid such an end, Ateh decided to volunteer for the third hell— that of the Islamic Iblis. Since he could not completely overturn the decision concerning the other two hells, Iblis divested her of her sex, condemned her to forget all her poems and her language, except for one word, *ku*,[©] but he gave her eternal life. He sent her a demon by the name of Ibn Haderash,ⓔ who appeared in the guise of an ostrich and carried out the sentence. And so Princess Ateh was left to live forever; she could return endlessly and without haste to each of her thoughts and each of her words, because eternity had blunted her feeling for what comes before and what comes after in time. Love she could only have in her dreams. That is why Princess Ateh devoted herself completely to her sect of dream hunters, Khazar priests who strove to create a sort of earthly version of that heavenly register mentioned in the Holy Book. Her skills and theirs enabled her to send messages, her own thoughts or others', even objects, into people's dreams. Princess Ateh could reach the dream of someone a thousand years younger, and she could send any object to someone dreaming of her as safely as a messenger riding a horse nourished on wine, only much, much faster. . . . A description remains of one such case. Princess Ateh once placed the key of her bedchamber in her mouth and waited until she heard music and the frail voice of a young maiden uttering the following words:

"A person's acts in life are like meals, his thoughts and feelings like spices. Whoever puts salt on cherries or pours vinegar on sweets will fare poorly. . . ."

As the words were spoken, the key disappeared from the princess's mouth and she knew, they say, that the substitution had been completed. The key had gone to the person for whom the words were intended, the words had come to Princess Ateh in replacement of the key. . . .

Daubmannus✿ claims that Princess Ateh was still alive in his day and that a 17th-century lute player, a Turk from Anatolia by the name of Masudi,ⓔ met and spoke with her. This man was instructing himself in the art of the dream hunters and had in his possession an Arabic version of a Khazar encyclopedia or dictionary, but at the time that he met the princess he was not yet familiar with all of its entries and so could not recognize the word *ķu* when Princess Ateh uttered it. The word comes from the Khazar dictionary and means a kind of fruit; had he known that, Masudi would have realized who stood before him and might have spared himself his subsequent travails; he could have learned more about dream hunting from the unfortunate princess than from any dictionary. But he did not recognize her and let go of his best catch, believing it to be worthless, which is why, according to one legend, Masudi's own camel spat in his eye.

A L-BAKRI, THE SPANIARD (11th century)—principal Arab chronicler of the Khazar polemic.$^\triangledown$ His text was only recently published (*Kunik and Rosen,* 44), translated from the Arabic by Marquart (*Osteuropäische und ostasiatische Streifzüge,* Leipzig, 1903, 7–8). Along with Al-Bakri's, another two reports on the Khazar polemic (i.e., conversion) have been preserved, but they are incomplete, and it is not always clear whether they refer to the Khazars' conversion to Judaism, to Christianity, or to Islam. In addition to Al-Istakhri's report, this part of which has been lost, there is also the report of Masudi the Elder, the author of *Golden Pastures,* who believed the Khazars$^\triangledown$ had abandoned their faith during the reign of Harun al-Rashid (786–809), a time when many Jews were being expelled from Byzantium and from the caliphate to Khazaria, where they were received without resistance. The other chronicler of the polemic was Ibn Al-Athir, but his testimony has not been preserved in its original form—it comes to us from Dimasci. Finally, as the most reliable and most exhaustive source, there is Al-Bakri, who claims that, after the year 731 and the wars with the caliphs, the Khazars accepted peace and Islam from the Arabs. Indeed, the Arab chroniclers Ibn Rustah and Ibn Fadlan mention many Islamic places of worship in the Khazar Empire. They also speak of the "twofold kingdom," which can be taken to mean that at one point Islam was adopted in the Khazar state on an equal footing with some other confession, and the kaghan professed the religion of Mohammed, while the Khazar king espoused Judaism. According to Al-Bakri, the Khazars subsequently converted to Christianity and finally, after the polemic under Kaghan Sabriel-Obadiah in 763, which the Islamic representative did not attend because he was poisoned on route, they adopted Judaism.

Al-Bakri (in the opinion of Daubmannus ✲) believed the crucial moment was when the Khazars first deserted their faith and converted to Islam. The Holy Book has many levels to it—he wrote—as confirmed by the first imam when he says: "Not a single word of this book sent through the Angel descended from heaven without his dictating it to my pen; not one was written without my repeating it aloud, and each he explained to me eight times: the literal meaning and the spiritual sense, the line that is changed by the preceding and the line that changes the succeeding line, mystery and ambiguity, the particular and the general." Following some of the indications marked by the medical authority Zachary Razi, Al-Bakri believed that the three religions—Islam, Christianity, and Judaism—could be taken as three of the levels of the Holy Book. Every nation adopts these levels from the Holy Book in the order that suits it best, thereby expressing its deepest nature. He did not take the first level of meaning into consideration, because this is the literal level, called *avam,* and it is accessible to everyone regardless of his faith. The second level—the level of allusions, of figurative meanings, called *kavas* and understood by the elite—represents the Christian church, and covers the present moment and the sound (voice) of the Book. The third level, called *avlia,* embracing occult meanings, represents the Jewish level in the Holy Book, the level of mystical depth and numbers, the book's alephbetical level. And the fourth, *anbia,* the level of prophetic rays and tomorrows, represents Islamic teaching in its most essential meaning, the spirit of the Book, or the seventh depth of the deep. In first accepting the highest level *(anbia),* and only later the other levels of the Holy Book, and even then not in sequence, the Khazars showed that Islamic teaching suited them best. After that, they never really abandoned Islam, although they went on to convert to Christianity and then to Judaism.

Proof of this is that, before the collapse of the Khazar Empire, the last Khazar kaghan converted back to the faith that had originally been adopted and espoused Islam, as Ibn al-Athir recorded so well.

The report of the Spaniard Al-Bakri was written in carefully chosen Arabic, the same as spoken by the angels, but in the last years of his life, when he was already old, Al-Bakri's style changed. He had started to feed his sixty-seventh year; he was bald, left-handed, and right-legged; and all that he still sported was a fine pair of big eyes, like two small blue fish. One night he dreamed that a woman was knocking at his door. From his bed he could clearly see, through an opening in the door, her moonlit face, which she had powdered with fish flour the way virgins do. When he got up to let her into the house, he found that she was not standing at the door knocking, but sitting on the ground. Seated, she was as tall as Al-Bakri. But when she began to pull herself to her feet, it took so long and she rose so high that Al-Bakri took fright and woke up, only to find himself not in his bed, where he had been dreaming the dream, but in a cage above water. He was a young man of twenty, left-legged, with long curly locks and a long beard, to which an utterly unexplained memory was tied—he was dipping his beard in wine and washing the breast of a girl with it. He did not know a single word of Arabic, and with his jailer, who baked him bread out of ground fly flour, he spoke fluently in a language that the jailer understood but he himself did not. He really knew no language any more, and this was the only trace of his old, prewaking self. The cage hung suspended over the water; when the tide came in, only his head peeked over the waves, but when it went out, he could catch a crab or a turtle with his hand, because then the sea receded and the river rose, and he washed the salt water off with fresh water. He wrote in his cage by using his teeth to cut letters into the shell of a crab or a turtle, but since he did not know how to read what he had written, he dropped the animals back into the water, never knowing what messages he was sending out into the world. At other times, catching turtles at low tide, he would receive messages on their shells and read them, but he never understood a word of what he read. He died dreaming of salty female breasts in a gravy of saliva and toothache, relearning the language of the Holy Book from the tree on which he hung.

FINGERING—a term used in music to designate the most suitable sequence and order for applying the fingers to an instrument to produce the tones. Yusuf

SHAITAN'S FINGERING
(ADAPTED FOR THE GUITAR BY THE SPANISH)

Masudi's fingerings were highly regarded by 17th-century lute players in Asia Minor. "Shaitan's Fingering" denotes a particularly difficult passage.

There is a Spanish version of Shaitan's Fingering used by the Moors. Only its adapted form for the guitar has been preserved, showing that it used an eleventh finger; according to legend, the shaitan used his ten fingers and his tail to play it. Some say Shaitan's Fingering originally meant something quite different—the step-by-step procedure for making gold or the order in which fruits were to be planted in the garden so as to always have fresh fruit from spring to autumn; they say that only later, when it was applied to music, did it turn into a fingering, whereby one wisdom buried and covered up another, older wisdom. Hence, its secret can be translated from one into another language of man's senses, without losing any of its effectiveness.

FRAGMENT FROM BASRA—the title of an 18th-century transcript of an Arabic text presumed to have been part of Joannes Daubmannus'* lexicographic edition. Published in Prussia in 1691 as *The Khazar Dictionary,* the edition was immediately destroyed, and it is therefore impossible to verify the above assertion; nor is it known exactly where the fragment might have appeared in the dictionary. The fragment reads:

"Just as your soul holds your body in its lowest depths, so Adam Ruhani, the third angel, holds the universe at the bottom of his soul. Now, in 1689 after Isa, Adam Ruhani is on the descending curve of his orbit and is approaching the point where the orbit of the moon crosses that of the sun, the hell of Ahriman; hence, we do not, as we might, pursue you dream hunters† and readers of the imagination, who follow him and try to assemble his body in the form of a book. But when in the end of the 20th century after Isa, he follows the ascending orbit of his wanderings, his state of dreams will approach the Creator, and then we shall have to kill you, you who recognize and collect parts of Adam's body in people's dreams and compile on earth a book of his body. For we cannot permit a book of his body to become a state. Do not think, however, that only a few of us insignificant shaitans and demons concern ourselves with Adam Ruhani. At most you will form his fingertip or the mole on his hip. And we are here to stop his fingertip or the mole on his hip from being shaped. Other devils handle people who try to assemble his other extremities. But do not live in illusion. Not one of you has ever even touched the bulk of his immense body, the state of your dreams. The job of spelling out Adam

Ruhani is only in its infancy. The book that is to incarnate his body on earth is still only in people's dreams. It is partly in the dreams of the dead, and it is as impossible to draw out as water from a dry well."

Ibn (ABU) HADERASH —The devil who divested Princess Ateh$^\triangledown$ of her sex. He resided in hell, at the place where the orbit of the moon crosses that of the sun. A poet, he wrote the following lines about himself:

> *When I near their women, Abyssinians*
> *look aghast,*
> *As do Greeks, Turks, and Slavs,*
> *from first to last. . . .*

The poems of Ibn Haderash were compiled by a man named Al-Mazrubani, who collected the verse of demons and in the 12th century assembled a book of demon poetry (compare the Arabic collection of Abul-Ala Al-Maarri, which records this fact).

Ibn Haderash rode a long-striding horse, and the trot of its hoofs can still be heard, one in each day.

Kaghan —title of the Khazar ruler, comes from the Tatar word *khan,* which means "prince." According to Ibn Fadlan, the Khazars buried kaghans under water, in the streams. The kaghan always shared power with a coruler and was senior to him only to the extent that he was the first to be wished a good day. The kaghan usually came from an old ruling, perhaps Turkish family, whereas the king, or bey, his coruler, was a man of the people, a Khazar. A 9th-century document (Yakubi) says that as early as the 6th century the kaghan also had a caliph as his representative. The best record of corule among the Khazars was left by Al-Istakhri. Written in 320 according to the Arabic calendar (932 A.D.), it goes as follows:

"As for Khazar politics and administration, the ruler is called the kaghan of the Khazars. He is higher in rank than the Khazar king (bak or bey), except it is the king who appoints him (gives him the title of 'kaghan'). When they wish to appoint a kaghan, the designee is brought in and strangled with a piece of silk until his breath is almost cut off, and then they ask him: 'How long do you wish to rule?,' and he replies, 'Such-and-such number of years.' If he dies before that term expires, then nothing happens. If not, they kill him as soon as the said number of years is completed. The kaghan has power only in the homes of prominent families. He does not have the right to command, but he is honored and everyone falls prostrate in his presence. The kaghan is chosen from a group of prominent people who have neither power nor money. When it is someone's turn to assume the post, they choose him without examining his property status. I heard from a reliable source that she saw a young man in the street selling bread. It was said that when the kaghan died this young fellow was the only person who deserved to take his place, but he was a Moslem and the title of kaghan is given only to Jews."

The kaghan's corulers were usually excellent warriors. Once, after a battle victory, the loot they captured from their enemies included a cuckoo bird whose cries opened the springs of drinking water. Their enemies then came to live with them. Time began to pass too slowly. They aged in one year as they used to in seven, and they had to change their calendar, which was divided into three months—the month of the sun, the month of the moon, and the month of no moonlight. They were born in

twenty days; they had nine harvests within a single summer, and then nine consecutive winters to eat what they
had reaped. In one day they went to bed five times,
cooked and sat down to eat fifteen times; milk stayed
fresh only on moonless nights that lasted so long that the
people would forget where their paths lay, and when the
day finally dawned they could not recognize one another,
because some had grown up and others had grown old.
And they knew that, when night fell again, it would be
the last they would see of this generation. The letters
inscribed by the dream hunters became bigger and bigger; the tips of the letters were hard to reach; books were
no longer tall enough, and so the dream hunters began
writing on hill slopes; rivers flowed on and on to the
great sea; and one night, while the horses were grazing
in the moonlight, an angel appeared in the kaghan's
dream and said to him:

"The Creator is pleased with your intentions but not
with your deeds." The kaghan then asked the dream
hunters what his dream meant and whence came the
Khazars' misfortune. One of the dream hunters said that
a great man was coming and that time was pacing itself
accordingly. To this the kaghan replied:

"That is not true; we have grown smaller, and that is
where our troubles come from."

He then dismissed the Khazar priests and dream
hunters and ordered that a Jew, an Arab, and a Greek
be brought to him to explain the dream. He had decided
that he and his people would convert to the faith of the
one who provided the best explanation. When the polemic about the three faiths began at the kaghan's court,
he was swayed by the arguments of the Arab participant,
Farabi Ibn Kora,[€] who, among other things, gave the
most satisfactory answer to the following question:

"What illuminates our dreams, which take place in

total darkness, behind our closed eyes? The memory of light, which no longer exists, or the light of the future, which we take like an advance on tomorrow's day, even though it is not yet daybreak?"

"In both instances it is a nonexistent light," replied Farabi Ibn Kora. "Therefore, it does not matter which answer is right, for the question itself should be taken as nonexistent."

The name of the kaghan who adopted Islam has not been preserved. It is known he was buried under the sign of "elif" (the crescent-shaped Arabic letter). Other sources say his name was Katib before he took off his shoes and washed his feet to enter the mosque. When he had finished with his prayers and stepped out into the sun, his old name and shoes were gone.

K HAZARS —in Arabic "Khazar," in Chinese "K'osa"; the name of a people of Turkish origin. The name is derived from the Turkish *qazmak* (to wander, move) or from *quz* (the northern, shaded side of the mountain). Also found is the name Aq-Khazar, meaning "white Khazar," obviously to distinguish them from the black Khazars (Qara-Khazar) mentioned by Al-Istakhri. After the year 552 the Khazars were probably part of the western Turkish Empire and perhaps fought in the campaign launched by the first kaghan of the western Turks against the Persian fortress at Sul or Darband. In the 6th century the area north of the Caucasus was held by the Sabirs (one of the two great Hun tribes). However, in the 10th century the historian Masudi the Scribe says that the Turks called the Khazars "Sabirs." In any event, when Moslem sources mention the Khazars, it is unclear whether they are always referring to the same nation.

The entire nation, including its ruler, appears to have had a double. Hence, the names "white" and "black Khazars" can be seen in another light: since *khazar* in Arabic means both "white" bird and "black" bird, the white Khazars can be assumed to represent the days and the black Khazars the nights. At the beginning of their remembered history, the Khazars defeated a powerful northern tribe called W-n-nd-r, which is mentioned in *Hudu al lam (The Regions of the World)*. This tribe's name corresponds with what the Greeks called the Bulgars—"On-Ogundur." Thus, the first Khazar clashes in the Trans-Caucasus territory would have been with the Bulgars and the Arabs. According to Islamic sources, the first Arab-Khazar war broke out in the Caucasus in the year 642. In 653, in the battle at Balanjar, the commander of the Arab forces was killed and the war came to an end. According to Masudi the Scribe, the capital was moved from Balanjar to Samandar, and finally to Atil or Itil. The second Arab-Khazar war began in or shortly before the year 772, ending in 773 with the defeat of the Khazars. That was during the time of Muhamad Marwan, when the kaghan preached Islam. A map by the Arab geographer Al-Idrisi shows that the Khazar state occupied the lower course of the Volga and Don rivers, including Sarkel and Atil. Al-Istakhri talks about the caravan route from Khazaria to Khorezm; also mentioned is the "imperial route" from Khorezm to the Volga.

Islamic sources say the Khazars were excellent tillers of the soil and fishermen. There is a valley in their land where a great deal of water accumulates in the winter, creating a lake. The fish they breed here become so fat that they can be fried in their own oil. When spring comes, the water dries up, and then they sow fish-fertilized wheat in the valley; it does so well that in the same year and place they have both a fish harvest and a wheat harvest. They are so resourceful that they have oysters breeding on trees. They take a tree by the sea, bend its branches into the water, and hold them down with a rock; within two years the branches become so heavy with oysters that by the third year they break loose from the rock and rise out of the water, bearing a splendid yield of tasty shellfish. The river that flows through the Khazar Empire has two names, because in the same riverbed half of its course runs from east to west, and the other half from west to east. The names of this river are the names of two Khazar calendar years, because the Khazars believe that passing through the four seasons are two years, not one, and that they move in opposite directions (like the Khazars' river). Both years shuffle the days and seasons like cards, mixing winter days with spring, and summer days with autumn. Moreover, one of the two Khazar years flows from the future to the past, the other from the past to the future.

The Khazars carve all the outstanding events in their lives on a stick, and these signs are in the form of animals that represent situations and moods, not events. The owner's grave is built in the shape of the animal that appears most frequently on his stick. Hence, Khazar graves are divided into groups, depending on whether they are shaped like tigers, birds, camels, lynx, fish, eggs, or goats.

The Khazars believe that deep in the inky blackness of the Caspian Sea there is an eyeless fish that, like a clock, marks the only correct time of the universe. In the beginning, according to Khazar legend, all creation, the past and the future, all events and things, melted as they swam in the fiery river of time, former and subsequent beings mixing like soap and water. At the time, to the horror of others, every living thing could create any other living thing; it was not until the Khazar god of salt ruled that beings could give birth only to their own image that an end was put to their willfulness. He separated the past from the future, set up his throne in the present; he walks over the future and flies over the past to keep an eye on it. He creates the entire world out of himself, but he swallows and chews up whatever is old, spitting out a rejuvenated world. The fate of all human races, the book of nations, is inscribed in the universe, where every star represents the nest and the already formed life of a language or people. And so the universe is visible and compressed eternity, in which the fates of human races twinkle like stars.

The Khazars can read colors like musical notes, letters, or numbers. When they enter a mosque or a Christian place of worship and see the wall paintings, they immediately spell, read, or sing whatever is depicted in the painting, icon, or other picture, showing that the old painters knew of this secret and unacknowledged skill. Whenever the Jewish influence in the Khazar Empire grows, the Khazars move away from the paintings and forget the skill they have, but it suffered most during the iconoclastic period in Constantinople and was never fully recovered again.

The Khazars imagine the future in terms of space, never time. Their places of worship are built in a strict, predefined arrangement, which, when connected, forms a picture of Adam Ruhani, the third angel, the symbol of the Khazar princess and her sect of priests. With the Khazars, a character moves from one dream to another, and the Khazars can follow it from village to village. There are priests from the sect of Princess Ateh[v] who follow these figures from one dream to another, writing their biographies like the lives of the saints or prophets, with their deeds and detailed descriptions of their deaths. The Khazar kaghan does not like these dream hunters,[†] but he can do nothing to them. Dream hunters always carry the leaf of a secretly grown plant they call *ku*.[€] When the leaf is placed on a rip in a sail or on a wound, it mends and heals instantaneously, as though by itself.

The Khazar state is organized along very complex lines. Its subjects are divided into those born under the wind (the Khazars) and those born above the wind, meaning that they have come from all over, like the Greeks, Jews, Saracens, or Russians. The Khazars are the most numerous in the empire, the others all consti- tuting very small groups. But the empire's administrative organization is designed not to show this. The state is divided into districts. Those populated by Jews, Greeks, or Arabs are named accordingly, whereas the larger part of the Khazar state, inhabited only by Khazars, is divided into several districts, all with different names. This was done so they would have only one of these purely Khazar districts carrying the Khazar name, while the rest ac- quired their name and standing in the state in other ways. In the north, for instance, an entirely new nation was invented, which gave up the Khazar name, even the Khazar language, and it has a different name for its district. In view of the circumstances and the Khazars' unfavorable position in the empire, many Khazars dis- claim their origins and language, their faith and customs, and pretend to be Greeks or Arabs, hoping to fare better that way. There are Greeks and Jews from the Byzantine Empire in the western part of the Khazar state. In one district the Jews (who were persecuted in the Greek Empire) outnumber everybody else, but only in this district. The same is true of Christians in another district, where the Khazars are called the "non-Christian population." Although the Khazars in the state outnumber the Greek and Jewish settlers five to one, this fact is lost, because the balance of forces and population figures are calculated not on the basis of the overall situation but by district.

These districts' representatives to the court are in proportion not to the number of people they stand for but to the number of districts, which means there are always more non-Khazars than Khazars at the court, although not in the state as a whole. Given this situation and this balance of forces, promotions hinge on blind obedience to the non-Khazar representatives. Just avoiding the Khazar name is already a recommendation in itself, enabling one to take the first step at court. The next step requires fiercely attacking the Khazars and subordinating their interests to those of the Greeks, Jews, Turkmen, Arabs, or Goths, as the Slavs are called in these parts. Why this is so is hard to say. A 9th-century Arab chronicler writes: "A Khazar contemporary of mine recently made an unusual statement to me: Only a part of the future reaches us Khazars, the toughest and most impenetrable part, which is hardest to master, and we brave it sideways, like a strong wind; or the moldering, worn debris and waste of the future that spreads imperceptibly, spilling over our feet like a puddle. Only the most inexorable part of the future ever reaches us, or only that part of the future that is already smoothed and trampled by use. We never know who gets the better, unchewed part in the general distribution and looting of the future...."

To understand these words, one must remember that

the kaghan does not allow the younger generation to come to power until it reaches the age of fifty-five, but this applies only to the Khazars. Others advance more quickly, because the kaghan, himself a Khazar, believes they cannot be dangerous since they are so few in number. According to the latest court decree, ranks in the Khazar administration are reduced, not reassigned, when they are vacated by a man of the kaghan's age or by a foreigner. In a few years, by the time the next generation of fifty-five-year-old Khazars is eligible, these state titles will already have been given to others, or will have lost their importance and not even be worth the taking.

There is a place in Itil, the Khazar capital, where, when two people (who may be quite unknown to each other) cross paths, they assume each other's name and fate, and each lives out the rest of his or her life in the role of the other, as though they had swapped caps. The most numerous among those waiting in this line to exchange their fate with someone, with anyone else, are always the Khazars.

In the war capital, an area with the largest Khazar population and the most densely populated region in the land, awards and decorations are distributed equally among all the inhabitants, with care always taken that an equal number of decorations is given to the Greeks and Goths and Arabs and Jews living in the Khazar Empire. The same applies to the Russians and others, and to the Khazars themselves, who share their own decorations and monetary prizes in equal parts with others, even though they themselves are the most numerous. But in the southern provinces, where there are Greeks, or in the western regions, inhabited by Jews, or in the East, where there are Persians, Saracens, and others, decorations are conferred only upon these peoples' representatives, not upon the Khazars, because these provinces or districts are considered non-Khazar, although there are just as many Khazars as anybody else there. And so in their own part of the state the Khazars share their bread with everybody, but in the rest of the land nobody gives them even a crumb.

As the most numerous, the Khazars shoulder most of the military duty, but the commanders come from the other nations, in equal proportion. Soldiers are told that only in combat do men live in balance and harmony, and that the rest is not worthy of attention. Thus, the Khazars are responsible for maintaining the state and its unity; they are duty-bound to protect and fight for the empire, while, of course, the others—the Jews, Arabs, Greeks, Goths, and Persians living in Khazaria—pull in their own individual direction, toward their parent nations.

Understandably, when war looms, these relations change. Then the Khazars are given greater freedom, and treated more leniently, and their past victories are glorified, for they are good soldiers. They can thrust a spear or a sword with their feet, slay with two hands at once, and are never just right- or left-handed, because both their hands have been trained for war since childhood. As soon as there is war, all the other peoples immediately join up with their parent countries: the Greeks rampage with Byzantine troops and seek enosis, union with the Christian matrix; the Arabs cross over to the side of the caliph and his fleet; the Persians seek the uncircumcised. After each war all this is quickly forgotten; the Khazars acknowledge the ranks earned by foreign peoples in enemy armies, but the Khazars themselves revert to dyed bread.

Dyed bread is the sign of the Khazars' position in the Khazar state. The Khazars produce it, because they inhabit the grain-growing regions of the state. The starving populace at the foot of the Caucasus massif eats dyed bread, which is sold for next to nothing. Undyed bread, which is also made by the Khazars, is paid for in gold. The Khazars are allowed to buy only the expensive, undyed bread. Should any Khazar violate this rule and buy the cheap, dyed bread, which is strictly forbidden them, it will show in their excrement. Special customs services periodically check Khazar latrines and punish violators of this law.

KHAZAR POLEMIC[v] —Dimasci writes that during the polemic, which was to decide what confession the Khazars were to adopt, there was great unrest in the land. During the debate at the sumptuous court of the Khazar kaghan,[v] the Khazar state started to walk. It was completely in motion. Nobody could meet anybody twice in the same place. A witness saw a crowd of people carrying huge rocks and asking: Where should we put them? They were the frontier stones of the Khazar Empire, the boundary markers. For Princess Ateh[v] had ordered that boundary markers be carried, that they not touch the ground until it was decided what would happen to the Khazar faith. Exactly when this happened has not been established, but Al-Bakri[c] notes that the Khazars adopted Islam before other religions, and that this was in the year 737 after Isa. Whether the conversion to Islam coincided with the polemic is a different question. It obviously did not. Thus, the year of the polemic remains unknown, but its essence is perfectly clear. Under strong pressure to adopt one of the three religions—Islam, Christianity, or Judaism—the kaghan summoned to his court three learned men—a Jew who had been expelled from the caliphate, a Greek theologist from the university in Constantinople, and one of the Arab interpreters of the Koran. The latter, named Farabi Ibn Kora,⊗ was the last to join the polemic, because he had had trouble getting to the kaghan's court. Therefore, the first to speak were the Christian and Hebrew representatives, and the Greek began winning the kaghan over to his side. A man with soupy eyes and freckled hair, he sat at the royal table and said:

"In a barrel the most important thing is the hole; in a jug, what is not the jug; in the soul, what is not man; in the head, what is not the head, which is to say the word. . . . Now, listen, you who do not feed on silence.

"Unlike the Saracens or Jews, in giving you the cross we Greeks will not take your word as security. You are not required to take our Greek language with the cross. On the contrary, you may keep your Khazar language. But know that this will not be the case if you adopt Judaism or the law of Mohammed. If you adopt either of those religions, you will also have to adopt their language."

Upon hearing these words, the kaghan was prepared to accept the tenets of the Greek, but then Princess Ateh spoke up and said:

A man who sells birds told me that living in a town on the Caspian shores are two renowned artists—a father and a son. The father is a painter, the man told me, and you will recognize his work by seeing the bluest of all blues you have ever seen. His son is a poet, and you will recognize his poems by feeling that you have heard them before, not from somebody else but from a plant or an animal. . . .

I put on my traveling rings and set out for the Caspian shores. When I reached the town, I made inquiries and found the two men. I recognized them immediately from the bird vendor's description: the father painted glorious pictures, and the son wrote marvelous poems in a lovely, entirely unknown (to me) language. I liked them both but they also liked me, and asked: "Which of the two of us will you choose?"

"I have chosen the son," I told them, "because he doesn't need a translator."

But the Greek would not let himself be pulled by the earring, and remarked that we humans are whole because we are made of two who are lame, and that women can see because they are composed of two who are one-eyed. As an illustration he told the following story:

When I was a young man, I fell in love with a girl. She didn't notice me, but I didn't give up, and one evening I spoke of my love so passionately to Sofia (that was her name) that she embraced me and I felt her tears on my cheek. I immediately knew from their taste that she was blind, but that didn't bother me. We were still embracing when suddenly horse hoofs could be heard thudding through the nearby woods.

"Is that a white horse whose hoofs can be heard through our kisses?" she asked me.

"We don't and won't know," I replied, "until it comes out of the forest."

"You haven't understood a thing," she said, and at that moment a white horse emerged from the woods.

"Yes, I have, I've understood everything," I responded, and asked her the color of my eyes.

"Green," she said.

"Look, my eyes are blue...."

The kaghan was impressed by the Greek representative's story, and he was on the verge of adopting the Christian God when, sensing what was happening, Princess Ateh decided to leave. Before going, she turned to the kaghan and said:

This morning my master asked me whether I felt in my

heart as he did in his. I had long nails with silver thimbles that whistled and I was smoking nargileh, blowing green smoke rings.

In answer to my master's question, I replied, "No!"—and my pipe dropped from my mouth.

My master departed, disheartened, because he didn't know that as I watched him go I was thinking: It would have been the same had I said yes!

The kaghan flinched at these words and realized that, although the Greek was wearing the voice of an angel instead of shoes, the truth was on the other side. Finally he turned to the caliph's man, Farabi Ibn Kora, and asked him for his interpretation of the dream he had dreamed on one of the previous nights. An angel had come to him in his dream with the message that God was pleased by his intentions, but not by his deeds. Then Farabi Ibn Kora asked the kaghan:

"In your dream, was it an angel of recognition or an angel of revelation? Did it appear in the form of an apple tree or something else?"

When the kaghan answered that it had been neither, Ibn Kora remarked:

"Of course it was neither, because it was a third angel. That third angel is Adam Ruhani, and you and your priests are trying to lift yourselves up to him. Those are your intentions, and they are good. But you are trying to achieve this by conceiving Adam as a book being written by your dreams and your dream hunters. Those are your deeds and they are wrong, for you perform them by creating your own book in the absence of the Holy Book. Since the Holy Book is given to us, accept it from us, share it with us, and discard your own. . . ."

Upon hearing these words, the kaghan embraced Farabi Ibn Kora, and that put an end to it all. He adopted Islam, doffed his shoes, prayed to Allah, and ordered the name bestowed upon him by Khazar tradition, before his birth, to be burned.

K ORA, FARABI IBN (8th and 9th centuries)—the Islamic representative in the Khazar polemic.▽ Reports about him are scarce and contradictory. He is not mentioned by Al-Bakri, the most important Islamic chronicler of the Khazar polemic. This is believed to be out of respect for Ibn Kora himself. That is, Ibn Kora did not like to have names mentioned in his presence, not even his own. He believed that a world without names was clearer and purer. The same name conceals both love and hate, both life and death. He was fond of saying that this revelation had come to him once when a fly was drowning in his eye as he watched a fish, and thus the fish fed on the fly. According to some records, Ibn Kora never even reached the Khazar capital and did not take part in the famous polemic, although he had been invited to join. Al-Bakri claims that the Jewish participant in the polemic had dispatched a man to poison or slay Ibn Kora, but according to other sources, Farabi was detained on the way and arrived only after the debate was already over. However, the outcome of the polemic shows that the Islamic representative was very much present at the court of the Khazar kaghan. When the participants were surprised to see Ibn Kora, for some of them thought that he was dead and that his rings should be prepared for his funeral feast, he calmly crossed his legs, looked at them with eyes like two shallow dishes of onion soup, and said:

Long ago, when I was a child, I saw two butterflies collide in a meadow; specks of colored powder shifted from one wing to the other, they flew off, and I forgot all about it. Last night on the road, a man mistook me for someone else, and struck me with his saber. Before I continued my journey, my cheek showed not blood but butterfly powder. . . .

One of the principal arguments believed to have been used by Farabi Ibn Kora in the name of Islam has been preserved. The Khazar ruler showed the representatives of the three religions—the Jew, the Arab, and the Greek —a coin. It was triangular; one side bore a denomination of five tears (which is how the Khazars marked their money), and the other the image of a man on a bier showing a bunch of rods to three young men. The kaghan asked the dervish, the rabbi, and the monk to interpret the scene on the coin for him. According to Islamic sources, the Christian representative in the polemic said that it had to do with an old Greek story: the father on his death bier shows his sons that they can be strong only if they stay together, like the unbreakable bunch of rods, but they are easy to break one by one if they are separated. The Jew said that the scene represented the limbs of the human body, which maintain the body only through common effort. Farabi Ibn Kora disagreed with both these interpretations. He claimed that the triangular numisma had been minted in hell, and that therefore the scene on it could not be interpreted as his predecessors had done. It depicted a murderer who, because of his crime, had been condemned to drink poison and was already lying on the bier prepared for him. Standing in front of him were three demons: Asmodeus, the demon of the Hebrew Gehenna, Ahriman-Shaitan, the devil of the Islamic Djehenem, and Satan, the devil of the Christian hell. The murderer held three rods in his hand, meaning that he would be killed if the three demons protected the murder victim, and saved if the demons decided against his victim. The message of the triangular coin was, therefore, clear. Hell had sent it to earth as a warning to men. A victim not represented by any of the three demons, the Islamic, the Hebrew, or the Christian, would remain unavenged, and his murderer would be spared. The most dangerous thing, therefore, is not to belong to any of these three worlds, as was the case with the Khazars and their kaghan. Then you are entirely without protection and can be killed by anyone, with no one having to pay for it. . . .

Farabi Ibn Kora was clearly trying to show the kaghan that it was essential and unquestionably useful for him and his people to abandon their faith and convert to one of the three powerful confessions, depending on which representative was best able to interpret the world for him and offer the truest answers to his questions. Farabi Ibn Kora's interpretation of the scene seemed the most persuasive, and the kaghan accepted his arguments, submitted to Islamic teaching, removed his belt, and prayed to Allah.

Those Islamic sources that believed Ibn Kora never took part in the polemic and never even reached the court of the Khazar kaghan, because he had been poisoned en route, cite a certain text that, they say, could be his biography. Ibn Kora was convinced that his entire life had already been inscribed in a book and was patterned according to a story told long, long ago. He read *A Thousand and One Nights* and a thousand and two other similar stories, but nowhere did he find the one that he lived his life by. He had a horse so swift that its ears flew like birds, even when it stood in place. Then one day the caliph of Samaria sent him to Itil to win over the Khazar kaghan to Islam. Ibn Kora started preparing for his mission. Among other things, he obtained the poems of the Khazar Princess Ateh$^\nabla$ and found one that seemed to be what he had so long been looking for, the story that had patterned his life. The only thing that did not fit and that surprised Ibn Kora was that the text spoke of a woman, not a man. Everything else fit; even the kaghan's court was called a "school." Ibn Kora translated the account into Arabic, thinking how the truth was merely a trick. The translation reads as follows:

NOTE ABOUT THE TRAVELER AND THE SCHOOL

The traveler has a passport that is considered western in the East and eastern in the West. Her passport therefore causes suspicion in both East and West; it casts two shadows; to the right it is masculine and to the left feminine. At the bottom of a forest furrowed with paths she looks for the famous school at the end of a long journey, a school where she is to pass her greatest test. Her navel is like the navel of unbaked bread, and her journey so long that it eats up the years. On finally reaching the forest, she meets two men and asks them the way. They gaze at her, leaning on their weapons, and remain silent, although they say they know where the school is. Then one of them points with his finger and says: "Go that way, and at the first crossing turn left, and then left again, and it will bring you right to the school." The traveler thanks them, thinking it was a good thing they had not checked her travel document, because then they would certainly be suspicious of her as a foreigner and would wonder what her real purpose was. She continues down the path, takes the first left turn, and then left again; it is not at all difficult to follow the directions, but the second path on the left leads not to the school but to a large swamp. And in front of the swamp stand two smiling, armed men whom she already knows. They apologize through their smile and say:

"We gave you the wrong directions: you should have

turned right at the first crossing, and then right again, and there is the school. But we had to find out whether you really did not know the way or were just pretending. However, it is late now, and you can't reach the school today. And that means not ever. Because the school will no longer exist as of tomorrow. You have missed your entire life's destination because of this small test, but you must realize that we had to take this precaution, for the security of others and to protect ourselves against any evil intent on the part of travelers looking for the school. But don't blame yourself either. Had you taken the opposite direction and gone right instead of left, it wouldn't have changed anything, because then we would have known that you were deceiving us and that you did know the way to the school even though you were inquiring about directions, and we would have had to check up on you: your purpose would have been clearly suspect, since you were concealing it from us. So you really can't get to the school either way. But you haven't sacrificed your life in vain: it has been used to verify something in the world, and that is no small matter. . . ."

The men talked, and the traveler had one consolation —she had not shown her passport, and the men by the huge swamp had no idea what color it really was. But, at the same time, she had thus deceived them and hindered their investigation, which meant that her life had actually been sacrificed in vain after all. Of course, it was in vain from their point of view in one way and from her point of view in another. What did she care about their checking?

It all comes out the same anyway. And so the purpose of her being, which no longer awaited her, must inevitably shift against the flow of time; now she starts thinking that the purpose was not in the school itself but somewhere along the way to the school, as vain as the actual search was. Suddenly her memory of this search becomes more and more beautiful; looking back, she begins to see the many beauties of the trip, and she concludes that the crucial thing happened not at the end of the road, in front of the school, but somewhere much earlier on, during the first half of the journey, which she would never have thought of had the trip not been in vain. In the rearrangement of her memories, dealing with her legacy like an agent on the market, she begins to pay attention to new details, barely registered in her mind. She looks for the most important details, constantly narrowing down their number, until, by ruthless reduction and increasingly strict selection, she arrives at a single scene from her memory:

A table, and on it a glass of wine colored with another wine. Freshly caught snipe roasted on camel droppings. Still nutritious from the bird's dream the night before. Hot bread which has the dark face of your father and the navel of your mother. And cheese from the milk of young and old island sheep. On the table by the food a candle with a drop of flame on the top; next to it the Holy Book and the month of Jemaz-ul-aker flowing through it.

K U —*Driopteria filix chazarica,* a type of fruit from the Caspian Sea. Daubmannus ✧ wrote the following about this fruit: The Khazars ▽ cultivate a kind of fruit that grows nowhere else in the world. It is covered with something resembling fish scales, or the scales of a cone; it grows on very tall trees, and the fruits on the branches look like the live fish innkeepers hang up by the fins above the doorway to indicate that they serve fish chowder. Sometimes the fruit releases voices that sound like a chaffinch. It has a very cold and somewhat salty taste. Since it is so light and carries a pit that pulsates like a heart, when it drops from the branch in autumn it floats for a while, fluttering its feathers as though swimming through the waves of the wind. Boys aim their slingshots at it, and even hawks are sometimes fooled and take it away in their beaks, thinking it is a fish. This explains the Khazar saying "The Arabs will eat us thinking, like the hawk, that we are fish, but we are *ku.*" The word *ku*—the name of this fruit —was the only word the devil left in the memory of the Khazar Princess Ateh▽ after she forgot her own language.

Sometimes, at night, you can hear the sound *ku-ku!* That is Princess Ateh uttering the only word she knows and weeping as she tries to remember her forgotten poems.

MASUDI, YUSUF (mid-17th century to September 25, 1689)—famous lute player and one of the writers of this book.

Sources: In his edition Daubmannus✿ included some information about Masudi gleaned from 17th-century music manuscripts. According to these sources, Masudi thrice forgot his name and thrice changed his trade, but his memory was preserved by those whom first he had disowned—the musicians in Anatolia. The lute schools in Izmir and Kula were the breeding grounds of legends about Masudi in the 18th century, and these legends were taught along with his famous fingering. Masudi had preserved the transcript of an Arabic version of *The Khazar Dictionary,* which he added to in his own hand, dipping his pen in Ethiopian coffee. He strained to speak, as if trying to urinate after having just peed.

Masudi came from an Anatolian family. It is said that he was taught to play by a woman who was left-handed and inverted the strings on her instrument. There is no doubt that the fingering[G] used by Anatolian minstrels in the 17th and 18th centuries was originally his. Legend has it that he possessed the gift of being able to judge an instrument before even hearing it. The presence of an untuned lute in the house upset him so much that it made him nauseated. He would string and tune his instrument by the stars. He knew that with time the player's left hand would forget its job, but the right hand never. However, he abandoned music at a very early age, and a tale about this has been preserved.

Three nights running he dreamed that a different member of his family was dying. First it was his father, then his wife, and then his brother. Finally, on the fourth night, he dreamed that his second wife had died, she with the dappled eyes that changed color in the cold like flowers. Before she shut them, her two eyes looked like two yellow grapes whose seeds showed through. She lay with a candle in her navel and her hair tied around her chin to stop her from smiling. He woke up and never dreamed another dream for the rest of his life. He was appalled. He did not have a second wife at all. He went to a dervish and asked him what to think of such a dream. The dervish opened the Book and read out the following words:

"Oh, my beloved son! Speak not of your dream to your brothers! They will hatch a plot against you."

Dissatisfied with this answer, Masudi asked his one and only wife what she thought the dream meant, and she replied:

"Do not mention your dream to anyone! Your dream will be carried out against the person you tell, not against you."

Masudi then decided to seek out one of the dream hunters,[†] somebody who might know about such matters firsthand. He was told that dream hunters had become scarce, even more so than before, and that he was more likely to find one if he headed east rather than west, because they all traced their origins and skills from the Khazar[∇] tribe that once used to live on the fringe of the Caucasus, where the grass grows black.

Masudi took his lute and followed the seashore, heading east. He thought, Better to trick a man before he wishes you good morning; afterward it is too late. And so he hurriedly embarked on his hunt of the dream hunters. One night he was awakened from his sleep. Standing before him was an old man whose beard was tipped with gray, like the back of a hedgehog. The stranger inquired whether in his dreams Masudi had by any chance seen a woman with dappled eyes, the color of white wine.

"They change color like flowers in the cold!" explained the unknown visitor. Yes, Masudi said, he had seen her.

"And what happened?"

"She died."

"How do you know?"

"She died in my dream, before my eyes, as my second wife. She lay with a candle in her navel and her face tied up with her hair."

Upon hearing these words, the old man sobbed and said in a broken voice: "Died! I've been following her from Basra. Her apparition keeps moving from dream to dream, and I've been trailing after her for three years, tracking those who dream of her."

And then Masudi realized that standing before him was the man he had been looking for.

"You've traveled that far for a woman—are you a dream hunter?"

"Me a dream hunter?" said the old man in surprise. "What kind of a question is that? Why, you are the dream hunter. I'm just an ordinary admirer of your art. Characters who roam from dream to dream can die only in the dreams of a born dream hunter. You, the dream hunters, are graves, not us. She traveled thousands of miles to die in your dream. But now you will dream no more. Now all you can do is go on your own hunt. But not for a woman with wine-colored eyes. She is dead for you and everybody else. You have to go in pursuit of a new prey...."

And so it was from the old man that Masudi received his first instruction in his new vocation and learned all there was to know about dream hunters. "With access to good written and oral sources," cautioned the old man, "one can become proficient in this skill. It is like that Sufi who performed *tauba*, repented, and found his *makkam*, following all the rules. Anybody can do that much. But only somebody born to it can really succeed in this job, somebody whom God Himself helps to achieve heavenly enlightenment—*khal*. The best dream hunters were the Khazars, but they have long since disappeared. Only their art has been preserved, and, in part, their dictionary telling of that art. They could track all those who appeared in people's dreams and hunt them like wild game from person to person, even in the dreams of animals or demons...."

"How is that done?" asked Masudi.

"Surely you have noticed that before falling asleep, in that double-edged realm between consciousness and dreams, man adjusts his relationship to the gravitation of the earth? His thoughts break free from the pull of the earth in proportion to the increased force with which the earth's gravitation acts on his body. It is then that the screen between thoughts and the world becomes porous, letting man's thoughts sift free, like sieves that have three different thicknesses. In that brief instant when the chill most easily slips into the human body, man's thoughts brim over and can be read with little difficulty. People who observe someone dropping off to sleep will be able, even without practice, to catch what he is thinking at that moment and to whom it refers. And if, through painstaking practice, you master this art of observing man's soul at the moment when it opens, you will be able to follow that moment of opening ever longer and ever deeper into the dream, and to hunt in it as in the water of open eyes. This is the making of a dream hunter.

"These confessors of dreamers, as the Khazars used to call them, carefully noted down their observations of dreams, the way observers of the skies do in some places, or like those who read fate in the sun and stars. Everything connected with this art, along with biographies of the most prominent hunters and the captured prey, was collected on the orders of the Khazar Princess Ateh,$^\nabla$ the protectress of the dream hunters, in the form of the Khazar encyclopedia or dictionary. The dream hunters passed on this Khazar dictionary from one generation to the next, and each had to add to it. It was toward this end that many centuries ago they founded a school in Basra, the 'fraternity of the pure' or 'friends of fidelity'; this sect, which did not disclose its names, issued the *Calendar of Philosophers* and *The Khazar Encyclopedia*. But Caliph Mostandji burned these books along with those of the school's Islamic branch and the writings of Avicenna. And so the original version of *The Khazar Dictionary,* founded by Princess Ateh, has not been preserved. The text of the dictionary that I obtained is only an Arabic translation, and it is all I can give you. You may take it, but you must learn all the entries, because, if you do not know the dictionary of your art well enough, you may lose the most important game of your hunt. But beware—in dream hunting the words of the Khazar dictionary are like a lion's tracks in the sand to the ordinary hunter."

So spoke the old man to Masudi, and along with the dictionary he gave him the following advice:

"Anybody can strum at the lute, but only the happy few endowed by the heavens can become dream hunters. Leave your instrument! The lute was invented by a Jew; Lamko was his name. Forget it and go for the hunt! If your prey doesn't die in somebody else's dream, as one did in mine, it will lead you to your goal!"

"But what is the purpose of hunting dreams?" asked Masudi.

"The goal of dream hunters is to understand that every awakening is just one step in the many releases from dreaming. He who understands that his day is merely another person's night, that his two eyes are another person's one, will search for the real day, which enables true awakening from one's own reality, just as one awakens from a dream, and this leads to a condition where man is even more wakeful than when conscious. Then he will finally see that he has one eye as opposed to those with two, and is blind compared with those who are awake...."

And then the old man confided to Masudi:

THE TALE OF ADAM RUHANI

If all human dreams could be assembled together, they would form a huge man, a human being the size of a continent. This would not be just any man, it would be Adam Ruhani, the heavenly Adam, man's angel ancestor, of whom the imams speak. In the beginning, this Adam-before-Adam was the third mind of the world, but he was so carried away with himself that he went astray; when he recovered from his vertigo, he cast Iblis and Ahriman, his fellow travelers in iniquity, into hell and returned to the heavens, where he was now no longer the third but the tenth mind, because in the meantime seven heavenly cherubim had overtaken him on the ladder of angels. And so Adam-the-precursor found himself seven rungs behind on the ladder, this being the measure of how behind himself he was, and that is how time was born: time is the part of eternity that runs late. This angelical Adam, or pre-Adam, who was both man and woman at once, this third angel who became the tenth angel, is forever trying to reach himself, and at moments he even succeeds, but then he falls again, and he is still drifting today between the tenth and second rung on the ladder of reason.

Man's dreams are the part of human nature that goes back to this Adam-the-precursor, this heavenly angel, because he thought the way we dream. He was as swift as we can be only in our dreams; our dreams are woven out of his angelic speed. And he spoke the way we speak in our dreams, without the present or the past tense, only the future. And, like us when we dream, he could neither kill nor sow seed. Hence, dream hunters plunge into other people's dreams and sleep and from them extract little pieces of Adam-the-precursor's being, composing them into a whole, into so-called Khazar dictionaries, with the aim of having all these assembled books incarnate on earth the enormous body of Adam Ruhani. If we follow our angel precursor when he is ascending the heavenly ladder, we approach God Himself, and if we have the misfortune to follow him when he falls, we move away from God, but we can know neither one nor the other. We depend on luck, always in the hope that our contact with him will be when he is on his way to the second rung on the ladder of reason, so that he might pull us up high, closer to Truth.

Thus, our calling as dream hunters can bring unimaginable benefit or terrible misfortune. But that depends not on us. Ours is to try. The rest is a matter of technique.

Finally, one more word of warning. The paths that hurry through other people's dreams occasionally conceal signs to show that Adam-the-precursor is rising or falling in his climb. These signs are the people who dream of each other. Hence, the ultimate goal of every dream hunter is to find such a pair and to get to know them as well as possible, because two such people always constitute small parts of Adam's body from different phases and are at different levels on the ladder of reason. Except, of course, the highest, second level, where God spat into Adam's mouth and clothed his tongue in four salivas. So, as soon as you come upon two people who dream of each other, you have reached your goal! And later do not forget to leave your reports and additions to the Khazar dictionary where all successful dream hunters leave theirs—in the mosque in Basra dedicated to the prophetess Rabbia. . . .

Thus spoke the old man to Masudi. And so Masudi abandoned his music to become a dream hunter.

The first thing he did was to sit down and read all the notes on the Khazars given to him in the form of a dictionary. The first page of this book said:

"In this, as in all houses, not everybody will be equally welcomed or honored. Some will be seated at the head of the table, the choicest offerings will be laid out before them, and they will be the first to see what is being brought to the table, the first to choose. Others will be seated in the draft where every mouthful they take has at least two smells and two tastes. Still others will be given ordinary seats, where all bites and all mouths are the same. And, forsooth, there will be those seated behind the door with plain soup, and they will be given to eat as much as the narrator gets from the story he tells, which is to say nothing."

Then, following the Arabic letters, *The Khazar Dictionary* formed a chain of biographies of Khazar and other figures, especially those who had taken part in the Khazar tribe's conversion to Islam. The central figure, the dervish and sage who had carried out this conversion, was called Farabi Ibn Kora,[℮] and the dictionary discussed him at length. However, in other places there were gaping holes. The Khazar kaghan who had summoned to his court the three priests—the Arab, the Jew, and the Christian—wanted a dream interpreted for him. But not all three of these participants in the Khazar polemic[∇] were equally familiar to Islamic sources on the Khazar question or to the Arabic translator of *The Khazar Dictionary*. One could not help noticing that Islamic sources did not mention by name the Christian and Hebrew dream hunters and participants in the debate, and information about them was in any case scarcer than was that about the Arab representative, Ibn Kora, who had argued in favor of Islam. While studying *The Khazar Dictionary* (and that did not take long), Masudi wondered who those other two were. Did any of the Christians perhaps know of their dream reader and representative of the Greek faith in the quadripartite talks at the Khazar court? Had his name been preserved? Did any of the Jewish rabbis know something about the other participant, about their own representative in the debate? Had no Greek or Jew informed himself about the Christian or Hebrew sage in the debate, as Masudi and those before him had done about the Islamic representative? These foreigners' arguments, Masudi observed and then wrote down, did not appear to be as forceful and exhaustive as Farabi Ibn Kora's. Was that because Ibn Kora's arguments really were more persuasive and comprehensive than theirs, or were theirs stronger than his in Hebrew and Christian books about the Khazars, assuming such exist? Perhaps they ignore us as we ignore them? Perhaps the only way to compile a Khazar encyclopedia or dictionary on the Khazar question would be to assemble all three stories about the three dream hunters and thus obtain one truth? Then *The Khazar Dictionary* could alphabetize certain entries with the names and biographies of the Christian and Jewish participants in the Khazar polemic, and this could include information about other chroniclers of the polemic, those from the Jewish and Greek sides. Because how is Adam Ruhani to be created if parts of his body are missing?

Contemplating these possibilities, Masudi shivered. He was afraid of open cupboards and chests with his clothes sticking out, and he would shut them every time he sat down with his dictionary. He began searching for Hebrew and Greek manuscripts relating to the Khazars: the words "Holy Book" could be read in the folds of his turban, but he ran after infidels and bribed Greeks and Jews on his way, learning their languages like looking glasses that give a different reflection of the world. And he learned to look at his reflection in these looking glasses. His Khazar file grew, and he intended one day to add to it the lives of the prey he hunted, a report on his part of the job, his small contribution to the huge body of Adam Ruhani. But, being a true hunter, he did not know what kind of game it would be.

The month of Rabbi-ul-aker came around, and in it the third jum'a, and for the first time Masudi saw into other people's dreams. He spent the night at an inn, next to a man whose face was invisible but who could be heard softly singing a song. At first Masudi was perplexed, but his hearing was swifter than his mind. He was a feminine key with a hole in its shaft, looking for a masculine lock with a bolt in its keyhole. And he had found it. The man lying there next to him in the dark was not singing at all; somebody inside him was singing, somebody the man in the shadows was dreaming about. . . . It was so quiet in the inn that the hair of the dreamer could be heard splitting somewhere in the dark next to Masudi. And then, imperceptibly, as if passing through a looking glass, Masudi stepped into a spacious dream, floored with sand, exposed to the rain and the wind, full of wild dogs and thirsty camels. He realized immediately that he was in danger of being mutilated and attacked from behind. All the same, he stepped onto the sand, which rose and fell in flows and ebbs, following the breathing of the dreamer. In one corner of the dream sat a man carving a lute out of a piece of wood that for years had been floating in a stream, its roots turned toward the mouth of the river. Now it was dry. Masudi deduced that the man was making the instrument the way they used to three hundred years ago, before this method had been abandoned. So the dream was older than the dreamer. Every so often the man in the dream would interrupt his work to take a bite of pilaf, and each bite moved him at least a hundred steps away from Masudi. As the man receded, a view opened up into the bottom of the dream, where there was a little light giving off an unbearable stench. Behind the light was a kind of graveyard where two men were burying a horse. One was the man who had been singing. But now Masudi did not just hear the song; he suddenly found himself looking at the singer. A young man, half of whose mustache was gray, appeared in the dream of the man lying next to him. Masudi knew that Serbian dogs bite first and bark later, that Walachian dogs bite without making a sound, and that Turkish dogs bark and then bite. The man in the dream belonged to none of these three species. He remembered the song; on the morrow the most important thing would be to catch the next dreamer visited by this young man with a half-gray mustache. Masudi immediately knew how. He assembled several lute players and singers, like a crew of herdsmen, and taught them to sing and play as he instructed them. He wore different-colored rings, each color corresponding to a note on the ten-note scale he used. He would show the singers one of his fingers, depending on the color of the ring, and it would call forth the voice it sought, just as every animal chooses its own kind of food; then they sang unerringly, although they had never heard the song before. They sang in public places—in front of wells, in city squares, and by fountains—and the song became a human bait for passers-by who carried Masudi's hunted prey inside them at night. They would stop as though the sun were sending them moonrays and listen as though bewitched.

As he tracked his prey from place to place along the shores of the Black Sea, Masudi began recognizing those who dreamed the dream he was looking for. Curious changes occurred when the number of people visited in their dreams by the young man with the half-gray mustache grew; in speech, verbs assumed more importance than nouns, and the latter were omitted wherever possible. Occasionally people dreamed of the young man in groups. Some Armenian merchants saw him in a dream, under gallows erected on an ox cart. He was passing through a lovely town built of stone, and the hangman picked at the young man's beard. Then some soldiers saw him burying horses in a beautiful horse graveyard overlooking the sea; they saw him with a woman, whose face was unidentifiable in the dream except for small patches, the size of silver coins, where the young man with the half-gray mustache had left the trace of a kiss on her cheeks. . . . And then suddenly the prey he was hunting would disappear from sight, its trail lost. Masudi did the only thing he could do—he put down in his *Khazar Dictionary* everything he had observed the last time, and now these writings, old and new, traveled with him, alphabetized in a green feedbag that got heavier and heavier. And still he had the feeling that many dreams being dreamed in his immediate proximity were simply slipping by, that he was not catching them all and dividing them up among the dreamers. The number of dreams was bigger than the number of dreamers. Finally Masudi turned his attention to his camel. Gazing into the animal's dream, he saw this young man with the callused forehead and strange two-toned mustache like an affliction upon his face. Up above was one of the constellations that never bathe in the sea. He stood by the window, reading a book tossed between his feet on the floor. The title of the book was *Liber Cosri,* ✿ but Masudi did not know what the words meant as he gazed through closed eyes into the dream of the camel. This was the moment when the hunt brought him to the one-time Khazar border. Black grass grew in the fields.

Now more and more people were again admitting the young man with the *Liber Cosri* into their dreams for the night. Masudi realized that sometimes the same dream, with the same people in it, was dreamed by entire generations or classes of society, but he also realized that some dreams slowly become twisted and disappear, that they were more frequent in the past than in his lifetime. These common dreams were obviously aging. Yet here at the border his hunt was turning into something new. Long ago he had noticed that the young man with the half-gray mustache would lend a fistful of silver to everyone whose dream he visited. And he gave it under very favorable terms, with an annual one-percent interest rate. In this remote spot of Asia Minor the loan was sometimes akin to a promissory note, because it was believed that dreamers must be honest with one another in the presence of the one about whom they were dreaming, for he holds all the account books in his hand. In other words, there was something akin to an accurately kept double accounting system, which covered and pooled capital from the conscious and the unconscious, based on the tacit agreement of the participants in the transaction. . . .

In a small town that for Masudi had no name, he entered the tent of a Persian who was performing at a Thursdaysite. The crowd, packed so tightly not even an egg could drop to the ground, was ringed around a pile of rugs, on which braziers were placed; a naked little girl was brought before the spectators. Moaning softly, she held a chaffinch in each hand, then opened her left hand and, the instant the bird made to fly off, caught it with lightning speed. She suffered from an unusual disease: her left hand was faster than her right. She claimed her left hand was so fast that it would die before she did: "I'll never be buried with my left hand! I can already see it lying without me in a small grave, without a marker or a name, like a ship without a rudder. . . ."

The Persian then asked everyone to dream about the little girl that evening so that she might recover, and he described in detail what he wanted them to dream. The crowd dispersed; Masudi was the first to leave, feeling as though he had a bone in his tongue, just as he had written in his *Khazar Notebook,* dipping his pen in

scalding-hot Abyssinian coffee. There was nothing for
him here. The Persian obviously had a notebook of his
own. He was a dream hunter too. Adam Ruhani could
obviously be served in various ways. Was Masudi's the
right one?

And then came the month of Jemaz-ul-ewel, and the
second jum'a in it. A new town, stark and hot, shrouded
in the mist of the river, stood in the sand. The mist
concealed it from sight, but in the water under the mist
each of its minarets could be seen impaled in the rapids.
A deep, three-day-old silence hung over the shore behind
the mist, and this silence, the town, and the thirsty water
aroused in Masudi a masculine urge. He was starving for
feminine bread that day. One of the rustlers he had sent
into town to sing reported he had found something. This
time the dreamer was a woman.

"Follow the main street until you smell ginger. That's
how you'll recognize her house: she uses ginger in her
cooking."

Masudi walked down to the houses and stopped at the
smell of ginger. A woman was sitting by the fire, her
kettle of broth babbling like bursting boils. Children
were standing in line with their plates and dogs, waiting.
She ladled out the broth to the children and animals,
and immediately Masudi knew that she was portioning
out dreams from the kettle. Her lips changed color, and
her bottom lip was the shape of an upside-down bench.
She was lying on the remains of a half-eaten fish, like a
desert dog on the bones of its prey, when Masudi went
up to her, and she offered him a ladleful, but he shook
his head with a smile. "I cannot dream any more," he
said, and she left the kettle.

She looked like a heron dreaming it was a woman.
Masudi lay down on the ground next to her, his nails
numb, his gaze crippled and broken. They were alone
now; they could hear the hornets sharpening their sting-

ers on the dry bark of the tree. He wanted to kiss the woman, but suddenly her face completely changed, as though a different cheek were receiving his kiss. When he asked her what was wrong, she simply said: "Oh, those are just days. Pay no mind, they flit across my face ten times faster than across yours, or your camel's. But your efforts to penetrate my cloak are in vain. It's not hiding what you're looking for. I do not have a black beaver. There are souls without bodies, called 'dybbuks' by the Jews and 'cabalas' by the Christians, but there are also bodies without a sex. Souls are sexless, whereas bodies are not. The only sexless bodies are those that have been divested of their sex by demons. That's what happened to me. A devil by the name of Ibn Haderash ⍟ took away my sex, but spared my life. In short, Cohen ✡ is my only lover now."

"Who is Cohen?" Masudi asked.

"The Jew I dream about and you pursue. The young man with a mustache that is one-half gray. He has a body imprisoned in three souls; I have a soul imprisoned in flesh, and I can share it with no one but him, when he enters my dream. He's a good lover—I can't complain. Anyway, he's the only one who still remembers me; nobody visits my dreams any more except him. . . ."

And so for the first time Masudi met somebody who knew the name of his prey. Cohen was the young man's name.

"How do you know?" Masudi asked, just to be sure.

"I heard it. Somebody called out to him, and he answered to that name."

"In your dream?"

"In my dream. That was the night he set out for Constantinople. But take heed: the Constantinople of our thoughts is always one hundred pepper fields west of the real Constantinople."

The woman then reached into her blouse, took out

something like a fruit but resembling a small fish, and offered it to Masudi, saying:

"This is a *ku;* [C] do you want to taste it, or would you prefer something else?"

"I'd like you to dream of Cohen in front of me," said Masudi, to which the woman replied in surprise:

"Well, you are very modest in your requests. Too modest, considering the circumstances, but you are obviously unaware of it. However, I will fulfill your wish: I will dream this dream especially for you, and I make you a present of it. But be very careful from now on: the woman who is pursuing the person you are dreaming of will catch you."

Then she lowered her head on the dog, her face and hands scratched from the countless looks that had grazed her through the centuries, and into her dream admitted Cohen, who said:

"Intentio tua grata et accepta est Creatori, sed opera tua non sunt accepta. . . ."

Masudi's peregrinations were at an end; he had received more from the woman than from anyone ever before, and, as though he had sprouted leaves, he rushed to saddle his camel and hurry back to Constantinople. His prey was waiting for him in the capital. And just as Masudi was calculating the edge he had gained in this last hunt, his own camel turned its head and spat in his eye. He whipped the camel in the face with dampened reins until it vomited the water from both its humps, but he never resolved the puzzle of its behavior that day.

The road stuck to his shoes and, remembering Cohen's words like a musical refrain, since the words themselves were incomprehensible to him, he thought how he would have to wash his shoes at the first inn he came upon: the roads lured the shoes that trod them by day until the shoes had returned all the mud they had taken away.

A Christian monk who knew no other language but Greek told Masudi that the words he remembered were Latin, and directed him to the local rabbi. The rabbi translated Cohen's sentence for Masudi:

"Your intention is good and acceptable to the Creator, but your deeds are not!"

And so Masudi realized that his wish was coming true and that his was the right way. He now recognized the sentence. He had known it in Arabic long ago, for it was the same sentence the angel had spoken to the Khazar kaghan all those hundreds of years ago. Masudi knew that Cohen was one of the two he was searching for, because Cohen was using Hebrew legend to trace the Khazars, just as Masudi was using Islamic. Cohen was the man Masudi had prophesied when he was poring over his Khazar dictionary. The dictionary and the dreams formed a natural whole.

But just now, when Masudi was on the brink of a great discovery, when his prey had proved to be almost his twin in the quest for Khazar stories, Masudi completely forsook his *Khazar Dictionary* and never returned to it again. This is how it happened.

They had stumbled upon an inn; darkness was falling in reddish flakes, and Masudi was breathing deeply on his bed. His own body looked to him like a ship riding the waves. Somebody in the next room was playing the lute. Later, Anatolian lute players would tell the legend of that night and that music. Masudi immediately recognized the lute as an exquisite specimen. It was made from the wood of a tree that had not been felled with an ax, so the sound in the wood had not been killed. Moreover, it had been found in some high country, where the sound of water does not reach the woods. And, finally, the belly of the instrument was made not of wood but of some kind of animal matter. Masudi could tell the difference, just as wine drinkers know the difference between inebriation on white wine and on red. Masudi recognized the melody the unknown musician was playing; it was an extremely rare tune, and he was surprised to hear this particular song in such an out-of-the-way place. There was an extremely difficult section in this song, and in the days when he had still played the lute, Masudi had devised a special fingering for it, one that was used widely by lute players. However, the anonymous player was using another, still better fingering; Masudi could not figure out what it was, could not find the key to it. He was stunned. He waited for the section to come around again, and when it did he finally understood. Instead of ten, the player was using eleven fingers for that section. Masudi knew now that it was the shaitan playing, because the devil uses his ten fingers and tail to play.

"Has he caught up with me or I with him?" Masudi muttered to himself, rushing into the room next door. There he found a man with slender fingers all the same length. Snakes of gray slithered through his beard. His name was Yabir Ibn Akshany, and lying there in front of him was an instrument made out of white tortoise-shell.

"Show me!" Masudi sputtered. "Show me! What I heard is impossible. . . ."

Yabir Ibn Akshany yawned, opening his mouth very slowly, as though giving birth to an invisible child that he formed with his mouth and tongue.

"Show you what?" he retorted, bursting into laughter. "The tail? But you're not interested in the song or the music—you abandoned that a long time ago. Now you are a reader of dreams. It is me you're interested in. You

want the devil to help you. Because, as the Book says, the
shaitan sees God, people don't. So what would you like
to know about me? I ride an ostrich, and when I go on
foot I take an escort of demons with me, little devils, one
of whom is a poet. He wrote poems centuries before
Allah created the first humans, Adem and Hava. His
verse tells about us shaitans and the devil's seed. But I
hope you won't take them too seriously, because the
words in the poems are not the real words. The real
word is always like an apple with a snake wrapped
around the tree, its roots in the earth and crest in the
sky. I will tell you something else about me and about
you.

"Let us look at some of the facts known to any reader
of the Koran. Like other devils, I am made of fire,
whereas you are made of mud. The only strength I have
comes from what I poured into you and what I take out
of you, because one can find in truth only as much as
one puts into it. But this is by no means a small amount
—there is room in truth for everything. You humans
will turn into whatever you want if you reach paradise,
but on earth you are imprisoned in one and the same
form, the form constructed by your birth. We, on the
other hand, assume whatever form we like on earth,
changing it at will, but as soon as we cross the river of
Khevser into heaven, we are forever condemned to be
what we really are, shaitans. But, because our origin is in
fire, our memory cannot entirely fade like yours, mixed
in clay. And that is the fundamental difference between
me as a devil and you as a man. Allah created you using
both hands, and me with only one, but my race of shaitans appeared before your human race. The important
difference between me and you, therefore, is one of time.
Although our sufferings go in pairs, my race came before
yours to Djehenem, to hell. And after you humans, a

new, third species will arrive. So your torment will forever be shorter than mine, because Allah has already
heeded the coming third species, who will cry out to
Him for us and for you: 'Punish the former doubly, to
lessen our torment!' In other words, torment is not inex-
haustible. This is the crux, this is the beginning of what
cannot be found in books, and this is where I can be of
help to you. Listen closely. Our death is older than your
death. My shaitan race has longer experience in dying
than your human race and remembers that experience
better. That is why I know and can tell you more about
death than anybody of your race, no matter how wise
and experienced he may be. We have lived with death
longer than you. So listen now, if you have a gold ring
in your ear, and take advantage of the opportunity. Because he who speaks today can do so again tomorrow,
but he who listens can do so only once, when he is
spoken to." Then Akshany related to Masudi:

THE STORY OF
CHILDREN'S DEATHS

The death of the child is always a model for the death
of the parent. A mother gives birth in order to give life
to her child; a child dies in order to shape the death of
its father. When the son dies before the father, the father's death is widowed; it will be crippled, without a
model. That is why we demons die so easily: we have no
offspring, no model has been set for our death. People
without children die easily, because their entire endeavor
in eternity is just a single extinguishment in a single
instant. In short, the future deaths of the children are
mirrored in the deaths of the parents, like a two-way
law. Only death is inherited backward, against the matrix of time, passed on from young to old, from son to

father—ancestors inherit death from descendants like a
rank of nobility. The hereditary cell of death—the coat
of arms of destruction—follows the course of time from
the future into the past, linking death with birth, time
with eternity, Adam Ruhani with himself. Death, therefore, falls within the nature of an inherited family phe-
nomenon. This is not a matter of inheriting black
eyelashes or catching chicken pox. It is a question of how
the individual experiences death, not what he dies from.
A man may die by the sword, from disease, or of old
age, but he always experiences something entirely different in the process. It is always somebody else's future
death he experiences, never his own: as we said, the
death of his children. He turns death into a common,
family affair, so to speak. A childless person will have
only his own death. Just that one. Conversely, a person
who has children will have not his own but his children's
deaths, many times over. The death of people with many
children is terrible, because it multiplies, since life and
death need not be in a ratio of one to one. I'll give you
an example. Many centuries ago, a monk by the name of
Mokaddasa Al-Safer ℰ ✿ lived in a Khazar monastery.
The way he prayed in the course of his long life in the
monastery, where there were ten thousand virgins, was
to impregnate all these nuns. And he had as many children. Do you know what he died of? He swallowed a
bee. And do you know how he died? He died in ten
thousand ways at once; he had a ten-thousand-fold
death. He died once for each of his children. They did
not have to bury him. His deaths tore him into such
shreds that nothing was left of him except this story.

It's like that well-known fable about the bundle of
sticks, a fable you humans misunderstand. The father on
his deathbed who summons his sons and shows them
how easy it is to break a single rod, is really showing

them how easy it is for a person with one son to die. And when the father shows his sons how hard it is to break a bundle of sticks, he is really showing them what a hard job it will be for him to die. He is showing how painful it is when you leave behind many children, when their deaths proliferate, because the father experiences all their agonies beforehand. The more sticks in the bundle, the more vulnerable you are, not stronger. Not to mention the death of women and their offspring—that is of an entirely different breed, not of the same variety as the death of men, and therefore it follows different laws. . . .

"That is more or less this secret of secrets, as seen from the vantage point of us shaitans, we who have somewhat more experience with death than you humans. Think about it, because you are a dream hunter and, if you are careful, you will get a chance to see all this for yourself."

"How do you mean?" asked Masudi.

"The objective of your hunt, as a dream hunter scavenging that rubbish heap, is to find two people who dream about each other. The one who sleeps always dreams the reality of the other, who is awake. Am I right?"

"Yes."

"Now, imagine that the one who is awake dies, because there is no reality more brutal than death. The person dreaming this one's reality is actually dreaming his death, because the latter's reality at that moment is that of dying. So our dreamer can see somebody dying as if on the palm of his hand, but he himself won't die. Yet he will never again wake up, because the person who is dying will no longer be around to dream about his life and to be the silk spinner who weaves the thread of his own reality. So the one dreaming about the death of the person who is awake can no longer wake himself and tell us what he saw in his dream, or what death looks like from the personal experience of one who is dying, even when he has direct insight into that experience. You, as a reader of dreams, have the power to read his dream and find there all you want to know about death, to cross-check and add to my experience and the experience of my species. Anybody can play music or write a dictionary. Leave that to others, because people like you, who can peer into that crack between one view and the other, that crack where death rules supreme, are few and far between. Use your gift as a dream hunter to land a big catch. It is you who command; be careful, therefore, what decision you take," Yabir Ibn Akshany said, winding up his story with the words of the Holy Book.

Outside, night had bled and day was breaking. The fountain was gurgling in front of the caravansarai. It had a phallic-shaped pipe made out of bronze with two metal eggs tufted with iron hairs, and the tip that went into the mouth was smooth. Masudi drank his fill and once again changed his vocation. He stopped writing his *Khazar Dictionary* and taking notes on the life of his Jewish wanderer. He would have thrown away his feedbag of papers written with his coffee-dipped pen had he not needed them as a handbook for hunting the truth about death. And so he continued to hunt his old prey with a new goal.

It was the first jum'a ertesi in the month of Safer, and Masudi's thoughts were like falling leaves: one by one they peeled off their stalk and fell; he followed them for a while as they floated before him, and then they sank to the bottom of their autumn forever. He paid and dismissed his minstrels and singers, sat with his eyes closed, leaning against the trunk of a palm tree, his boots burning the soles of his feet; between himself and the wind he felt only an icy, acrid sweat. He dipped a boiled egg in the sweat to salt it. The coming Saturday was for him as good as Friday, and he sensed clearly what had to be done. He knew that Cohen was going to Constantinople, so he did not have to pursue him any farther than that or hunt among the highways and byways of other people's dreams, where they peed on, raped, and trampled Masudi like cattle. A much more important and difficult question was how to find Cohen in Constantinople, the city of cities. But in the end he would not have to look for him there: somebody else would do it for him. No, he had to find the person Cohen was dreaming of. And that person—if he thought about it—could only be one man, the man Masudi already had intuited.

"Just as the fragrance of linden honey in rose-hip tea interferes with the fragrance of the tea itself, so," thought Masudi, "there is something obstructing my view of how people around me are dreaming of Cohen. There is somebody else there, an intruder...."

Masudi had long since decided that, besides himself and his study of Arab sources on the Khazar race, somewhere in the world there were at least two others. One of them, Cohen, studied Hebrew sources on the conversion of the Khazars, and the as-yet-unidentified third person was certainly involved with Christian sources on the same issue. Now he had to find that third person: a Greek, or some Christian, a learned man interested in Khazar affairs. He would be the person Cohen himself was looking for in Constantinople. It was the third man that had to be found. And Masudi immediately knew how he would do it. But just as he had worked it all out and was about to set off, Masudi again stumbled into somebody's dream, now hunting involuntarily. There were no people or animals around him this time. Just sand, a waterless expanse stretching out like the sky, and behind it the city of cities. But the powerful rush of water, running deep to the heart, sweet and deadly, roared through the dream, and Masudi was to remember it, because the roar spilled into all the folds of his turban, which had been wrapped to form a word from the fifth sura of the Holy Book. Masudi saw that the seasons were not the same in the world and in the dream. He decided, therefore, that the palm tree he was leaning against was doing the dreaming. It was dreaming of water. Nothing else happened in the dream, just the rush of the river deftly folded, like a glaringly white turban. . . . Masudi entered Constantinople in the scorching heat at the end of the month of Shaban and went to the city's main marketplace to sell a scroll of *The Khazar Dictionary*. The only offer came from a Greek monk by the name of Theoctist Nikolsky,[A] who took it to his master. The latter did not question the price, bought it, and asked if there was more. Masudi now knew he had found the third lexicographer he had been looking for, the one who dreamed of Cohen and who would serve as his bait to catch Cohen. Because he was certainly the reason for Cohen's coming to Constantinople. The wealthy buyer of the Khazar scroll from Masudi's feedbag was a diplomat working in Constantinople for the English envoy to the Porte, and his name was Avram Brankovich.[†] He was a Christian from Erdély, in Walachia, a highly respected and splendidly dressed man, as big as a well. Masudi offered to work for him and was taken on as a valet. Since Avram Effendi worked in his library by night and slept by day, that very first morning Masudi seized the opportunity of peering into Brankovich's dream. In Avram Brankovich's dream, Cohen rode a horse and a camel in turn, spoke Spanish, and was nearing Constantinople. This was the first time anyone had dreamed of Cohen by day. Brankovich and Cohen obviously took turns dreaming of each other. And so the circle closed and the moment of decision began.

"Good!" thought Masudi. "When you tie up your camel, milk it dry, because you never know whom it will serve tomorrow!" And he started inquiring about his master's children. He learned that Avram Effendi had two sons at home in Erdély, that the younger of the two suffered from some disease of the hair and would die when the last hair on his head fell off. Avram's other son already sported a saber. His name was Grgur Brankovich,[†] and he had already been in several battles. . . . That was all, but it was enough for Masudi. "The rest is just a matter of time and of waiting," he thought, and he began passing the time by forgetting his first love— music. He forgot not song by song, but piece by piece of these songs. First to fade from his memory were the lowest tones; the wave of oblivion rose like the tide to ever-higher sounds; then the flesh of the songs vanished and all that was left was the skeleton of their rhythm. Finally he began forgetting his Khazar notes, word by word, and was not too sad when one of Brankovich's servants tossed his dictionary into the fire. . . .

But then something unforeseen happened. Like the green woodpecker that can fly backward, from head to tail, in the last jum'a of the month of Shawwal. Avram Effendi departed from Constantinople. He left his diplomatic service and, with his entire suite and servants in tow, went to war on the Danube. In the year 1689 after Isa, in Kladovo, they found lodgings in the camp of Prince Badensky, and Brankovich joined his service. Masudi did not know what to think or do, because his Jew had gone not to Kladovo but to Constantinople, and this upset Masudi's plans. He sat on the banks of the Danube spinning his turban. And then he heard the rushing roar of the river. The water ran deep beneath him, but he recognized its scream; it fit perfectly into the folds of his turban, which formed one word from the fifth sura of the Koran. It was the same water that the palm tree in the sand near Constantinople had dreamed about a few months ago, and now Masudi knew everything was all right again and that he would indeed end his journey at the Danube. For days he sat shooting dice in a trench with one of Brankovich's scribes. The scribe was losing heavily, but he would not stop playing even when Turkish cannons shelled the trenches, for he lived in the hope that he would win back what he had lost. Masudi himself had no desire to leave, because behind his back Brankovich was again dreaming of Cohen. Cohen was riding through the roar of the river rushing through Brankovich's dream, and Masudi knew that the roar came from the same Danube that could be heard when he was awake. Then the wind spattered him with mud, and he sensed it would happen. A Turkish detachment reeking of urine stormed their trench as they were shooting the dice, and while the janissaries slaughtered right and left, Masudi desperately searched their faces for the young man whose mustache was one-half gray. Suddenly he saw him. He saw the same Cohen he had hunted in other people's dreams—with red hair and a tight smile beneath that half-gray mustache, advancing in small steps, a feedbag slung over his shoulder. That instant, the soldiers slashed the scribe to pieces, plunged their spears into the sleeping Avram Brankovich, and moved in on Masudi. Cohen rescued him. At the sight of Brankovich, Cohen collapsed on the ground, sheets of paper flying from his feedbag, strewn everywhere. Masudi knew immediately that Cohen had fallen into the deepest sleep, from which he would never awake.

"Is the interpreter dead?" the Turkish pasha asked the troops with an almost gleeful note in his voice. Masudi replied in Arabic:

"No, he is asleep," and this prolonged Masudi's life by an extra day. His response surprised the pasha, who asked how Masudi knew that. And Masudi spoke as Yabir Ibn Akshany had spoken to him. To wit, that it was he, Masudi, who tied and loosened the reins of other people's dreams, that he had followed to this place his medium, who served as a kind of bait for the hunt, and who was now dying from a spear wound, and that he begged his own life be spared until morning so that he could follow Cohen's dream, because Cohen was now dreaming about Brankovich's death.

"Let him live until that one there wakes up," said the pasha. The soldiers hoisted Cohen's sleeping body onto Masudi's back, and he went with them to the Turkish side, hauling his catch. Toted like that, Cohen did indeed dream of Brankovich, and Masudi felt as though he had two bodies to carry, not one. In his dream, the young man slung across Masudi's back saw Avram Effendi as he was when awake, because Cohen's dream was still Brankovich's wakeful reality. If ever Brankovich was awake, it was now, with a spear piercing his body: in death there is no sleep. And now came the chance Yabir Ibn Akshany had been talking about. Masudi hunted Cohen's dream while the young man dreamed of Brankovich's death, as until then he had been dreaming of Brankovich's life.

And so it was. Masudi spent that day and night tracking Cohen's dreams like stars in the roof of his mouth. And, they say, he saw Brankovich's death the way Brankovich saw it himself. By morning, his eyelashes had turned gray, his ears trembled, and his nails were long and smelled. He was thinking so rapidly he did not even notice the man slash his waist with a single flourish of the sword, and his belt slipped off without even unwinding. The saber left a sinuous cut, and a terrible winding gash gaped open like a mouth uttering an incomprehensible word, the scream of flesh. They say that those who saw it never forgot that ghastly winding slash of the saber, and those who remembered it say that they later recognized it in a book called *The Finest Signatures of the Saber,* written by somebody named Averkie Skila,[†] who collected and illustrated the most famous strokes in fencing. The book, printed in Venice in 1702, gives this particular stroke the name of one of the stars in the constellation of Aries. Whether such a terrible death was worth it to Masudi, and what he confided to the pasha before dying, nobody knows. Whether he crossed the Sirat bridge, which, finer than a strand of hair and sharper than a saber, crosses hell into heaven, is known only to those who no longer speak. According to one legend, Masudi's music went to heaven and he himself to hell, saying: "More than anything else I wish I had never sung a single song; then, like other lowlife and scum, I would have entered paradise! Music led me astray when I was within reach of the truth." The Danube ripples over Masudi's grave, and the carved inscription reads:

Everything I earned and learned has gone with the tap of a spoon against the teeth.

MOKADDASA AL-SAFER[✼] (9th, 10th, and 11th centuries)—Khazar priest in a nunnery. During his long life he and a monk from another monastery played chess without a board or pieces. They played one move a year on the vast stretch of space from the Caspian to the Black Sea, and they took turns releasing the hawk to attack the animals they used for pieces. They counted not only the square where the animals were caught, but also the above-sea-level altitude of the hunting ground. Mokaddasa Al-Safer was one of the Khazars' best dream hunters. He is believed to have shaped one of Adam Ruhani's strands of hair in his dictionary of dreams (see "Masudi, Yusuf" ©).

His manner of prayer and the religious order to which he belonged led him to impregnate ten thousand virgin nuns. The last of them, Princess Ateh,▽ according to the legend, sent him the key of her bedchamber, a small, feminine key with a gold coin in place of a handle. That key cost Mokaddasa Al-Safer his life, because it made the kaghan jealous. He died imprisoned in a cage suspended over water.

Muawia, Dr. Abu Kabir (1930–1982)—Arab Hebraist, professor at Cairo University. His field was the comparative study of Middle Eastern religions. He studied at the university in Jerusalem, did his doctorate in the United States on "Hebrew Thought in 11th-Century Spain and the Teachings of the Mutakallim." He was a handsome man, whose shoulders were so broad he could not make his elbows touch. He knew most of Judah Halevi's ✿ poems by heart and was sure that *The Khazar Dictionary* printed by Daubmannus ✿ in 1691 was still to be found on some old shelf. To give credence to this claim, he reconstructed its whereabouts in the 17th and later centuries, then drew up a concise list of all copies that had been destroyed and the few that

had been released into circulation, only to conclude that at least two copies of the last edition were still in existence. But he never managed to trace them, even though he could swallow an egg by just looking at it. When, in a burst of creative energy, he was publishing his three thousandth work, the Israeli-Egyptian war broke out in 1967. He went to war as an officer of the Egyptian army, was wounded and captured. His military papers attest to severe head and body wounds, one of which left him permanently impotent. When he returned home, his face was swathed in confused smiles, which he trailed behind him like a scarf. He took off his uniform in a hotel and for the first time saw his scars in a copper mirror. They smelled of bird droppings. He realized that he would never again be able to lie next to a woman. Dressing slowly, he thought: "I was a cook for more than thirty years, and bit by bit I prepared and put together this dish I have become: I was my own baker and dough, and kneaded myself into the bread I wanted; now another cook has suddenly appeared with a knife and, within a split second, has whipped me up into an entirely different, unknown dish. Now I am the Lord's sister—I don't exist!"

And he did not return to his family in Cairo or resume his job at the university. He moved into his father's empty house in Alexandria, where he lived in a hurry, and watched the white air bubbles under his nails escape into the world like those that come out of fish gills. He buried his hair, wore Bedouin sandals that left hoofprints in their wake, and one night, when the raindrops were as big as an ox eye, he dreamed his last dream and jotted it down:

Two women saw a tiny white-spotted animal, like a chalked face on two spindly legs, flit out across the lane from the underbrush by the stream, and they cried: "Look, that's (they said its name)! They must have killed someone in her family, or destroyed her home. She always looks prettier and more radiant when she's horror-stricken. She should be given a book and a pencil or some jam now. She'll take it to read or to write something, not on paper but on a flower. . . .

That was Dr. Abu Kabir Muawia's dream. He dreamed it again the following night and, as after the first time, he could not remember the animal's name. Then he redreamed all of his dreams one by one, but in reverse order. First the one from the day before last, then the one before that, and before that, and so on down the line, quickly, until he had done with all his dreams of bygone years in only one night. After thirty-seven nights he had finished the job, because he had reached his earliest childhood dreams, the ones he could no longer remember when awake, and he came to the conclusion that his servant, the mulatto Aslan, who wiped dirty dishes with his beard, shat only when he swam, and could slice bread with his bare feet, resembled him now more than he resembled himself of thirty-seven years ago. And this brought him to his last dream. Time, in his nights, like Khazar time, flowed from the end to the beginning of life and then expired. After that he never dreamed again. He was clean, and ready for a new life. Then he began going every evening to the Bar by the Bitch.

They charged only for the chair at the Bar by the Bitch, for they served no drinks or food, and riffraff came here to drink and eat what they brought themselves or to sit down at a table and get some sleep. Sometimes the place was packed, but nobody uttered a word. The place had no bar, no kitchen, no hearth, and no waiters, only a man at the door who charged for the chairs. Muawia took a seat amid the other customers, lit his pipe, and engaged in an exercise: he did not let a single thought last longer than the smoke coming out of his pipe. He inhaled the stink and watched the people around him stuff their faces with moldy buns known as "ripped pants," or with pumpkin jam with grapes; he watched them pass each mouthful through a bitter look and wipe their teeth with a handkerchief; he saw how their shirts burst open when they turned in their sleep.

Watching them, he thought how the material used for every second of his time and theirs was a tattered second from past centuries; the past was built into this present time, and the present was made up of the past, because that was the only material there was. These countless seconds of the past, carried like stones into various structures over the centuries, were, if we cared to look closely, clearly recognizable in our present-day hours, the way today we recognize and put on the market a gold coin from the times of Vespasian. . . .

Such thoughts did not serve to relieve any of his pains. Relief came from these people, who expected nothing more of the future than that it trick others as it had already tricked them. This rabble of worried masticators helped him find his way in his new life. It was soothing to know that very few of these people, who reeked from here to Asia Minor, could be unhappier than he was. The Bar by the Bitch was the right place for Muawia. With its sea-salt-polished tables and its fish-oil lamps, it looked at least seventy years older than it was, and it soothed Muawia to know this, because he could not stand anything to do with himself or his own time. And since his profession, which he loathed as much as his present, awaited him in his past, he slipped into a kind of semipast, where opal and jade are still half-sisters, and where the cuckoo bird still counts the days man has left to live, where knives are still forged with both edges blunt. . . .

After dining on beef and goat ears, he would go to the long-unopened rooms of his father's house, where deep into the night he would leaf through English and French newspapers printed in Alexandria at the end of the 19th century. Crouching on his heels and feeling the nutritious darkness of the meat flow through him, he would read the papers with thirsty interest, because they could have nothing to do with him. The advertisements were ideal for this purpose.

Night after night he pored over advertisements put in the papers by people who had long since died; offers that were now meaningless glistened in a dust that was older than he. These yellowed pages advertised French brandy for gout, and water for the mouths of men and women; August Ziegler of Hungary announced that his specialized shop for hospitals, doctors, and midwives had cures for upset stomachs, stockings for varicose veins, and inflatable rubber soles. The descendant of a 16th-century caliph was selling the family's fifteen-hundred-room palace, situated on the most beautiful part of the Tunisian coast, in the sea, only twenty meters below the water's surface. It could be viewed daily in fair weather with a southern wind called the *taram*. An unnamed elderly lady was selling an alarm clock that woke you up with rose scent or cow dung; there was an advertisement for glass hair or armbands that swallowed your hand as soon as you put them on. The Christian Pharmacy by the Holy Trinity Church was advertising Dr. Leman's lotion for freckles, celandine, and lupus scabs, powder to give camels, horses, and sheep an appetite and prevent foal disease, mange, and cattle exhaustion due to guzzling water. Somebody who did not give his name was looking to buy a Jewish soul on credit; he wanted one of the lowest order, called *nephesh*. A prominent architect offered to build, at very low cost, a luxurious custom-ordered summer home in heaven; the keys would be turned over to the owner during his lifetime, as soon as he had settled his accounts—not with the builder, but with the rabble of Cairo. A lotion was recommended to counteract going bald on a honeymoon; there was for sale a magic word that could be transformed into a lizard or a Chinese rose; there was a reasonably priced foot of land from which the rainbow could be seen at night every third jum'a in the month of Rabbi-ul-aker. Like getting rid of bugs, once she gets rid of her pimples, freckles, and beauty marks, every woman becomes more beautiful with the aid of Rony & Son English whitener. A porcelain set for green tea in the form of a Persian hen and chicks was for sale, along with a wooden bowl under which the soul of the seventh imam had spent some time. . . .

Countless names and addresses of no-longer-existing companies, sellers and shops that had long since shut down, covered the yellowing newspaper pages, and Dr. Muawia plunged into that bygone world as into a new grace-saving generation that was uninterested in his troubles and woes. One evening in 1971, when each tooth in his mouth felt like a separate letter, Dr. Muawia sat down and answered an advertisement from 1896. He carefully wrote out the name and address—an Alexandria street he was not sure still existed—and put his reply in the mail. From then on, every evening, he would answer another ad from the end of the 19th century. Piles of letters were sent out into the unknown. Then one morning the first reply arrived. The respondent wrote that, although he no longer sold the advertised French Touroul patent for home economics, which Dr. Muawia had mentioned in his letter, he did have something else to offer. And the very next morning a girl and a parrot called on Muawia in connection with the advertisement; they sang a duet about wooden clogs. Then the parrot sang a solo piece in a language unknown to Muawia. When Muawia asked which of the two was for sale, the girl said he could choose. Dr. Muawia looked at the girl—she had pretty eyes and breasts like two sunny-side-up eggs. He roused himself from his lethargy, instructed Aslan to clear out one of the large rooms in the attic, placed in it a glass hoop, and bought the parrot. Gradually, as replies to his letters began arriving from all sorts of heirs to the one-time advertisers, the room filled up. In it were now numerous oddly shaped, undefined pieces of furniture, a huge camel saddle, a woman's dress with bells in place of buttons, an iron cage in which to hang people from the ceiling, two mirrors, one of which was somewhat late in reflecting movements and the other cracked, an old manuscript of a song written in some unknown script and unknown language. The song was:

> Zaludu feiglicfemi farchalo od freeche
>   Kadeu gniemu ti obarzani uecche
> Umifto tuoyogha, ça ifkah ya freto
>   Obras moi ftobiegha od glietana glieto
> Uarechiamti darouoy, ereni fnami ni
>   Okade obarz tuoi za moife zamini.

A year later the attic room was full, and Dr. Muawia was astonished when one morning he entered and realized that the objects were beginning to make sense. Some of his acquisitions were obviously equipment for something that looked like a hospital. But an ancient, unusual hospital that did not use modern-day methods. Muawia's sanatorium had seats with strange slits in them, benches with iron rings for people to tie themselves to when they sat down, wooden visors with slits for just the left eye or right, or for a third eye on the forehead. Muawia moved these objects to another room. He called in a colleague from the medical school and showed them to him. This was the first time since the 1967 war that he had seen one of his university friends. The man stared at the objects and said: "One evening a dead man returned from the grave to dine with his family. He was just as stupid as when alive. Death had made him none the wiser. . . . This equipment is too antiquated for a dream clinic, for recovering the sight used in dreams. Because, according to some beliefs, we use a different eye in our sleep from the one we use when we are awake. . . ."

Dr. Muawia smiled at these words and focused his attention on the objects that had been left in the first large room with the parrot. But, as compared with the room that housed protective equipment against blindness in dreams, here it was harder to establish a connection between these articles. He spent a long time trying to find some common denominator for all the things, and eventually decided on a method he had used in his previous life as a scholar. He decided to use a computer. He telephoned one of his former associates in Cairo, an expert in calculating probability, and asked him to feed the computer with the names of all the objects he had listed in his letter. Three days later the computer produced its findings, and Dr. Muawia received the report from Cairo. With regard to the poem, the computer could only say that it had been written in a Slavic language on a sheet of paper from the year 1660 bearing the watermark of a lamb under a flag with a three-leaf clover. The other objects, such as the parrot, the belled camel saddle, the dried fruit in the shape of a fishlike pine cone, the cage for people, and so on, had one common denominator. Based on the scanty information fed into the computer, mostly from Dr. Muawia's own study, it transpired that all these objects had been mentioned in the now-lost *Khazar Dictionary.*

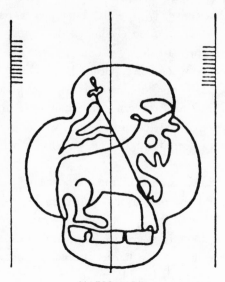

WATERMARK
FROM DR. ABU KABIR MUAWIA'S COLLECTION

And so Dr. Muawia was back where he had started from when he went to war. He went once more to the Bar by the Bitch, lit his pipe, looked around, put it out, and returned to his old job at the university in Cairo. Waiting for him on his desk was a pile of letters and invitations to various conferences. He chose one and started preparing a paper for a meeting due to be held in Constantinople in October 1982 on "The Cultures of the Black Sea Shores in the Middle Ages." He reread Judah Halevi on the Khazars, wrote his paper, and left for Constantinople, thinking that he might meet somebody there who knew a bit more about the Khazar story than he did. The murderer of Dr. Muawia in Constantinople told him as he aimed his gun:

"Open your mouth so your teeth won't be ruined!"

Dr. Muawia opened his mouth and was shot dead.

The murderer had taken such perfect aim that Dr. Mu-awia's teeth were left intact.

MUSIC MASON —The Khazars had masons who cut and mounted enormous pieces of rock salt on the paths of the winds. On the path of each of the forty Khazar winds (half of which were fresh, half sweet) an arrangement of saline marble was built, and when the annual seasonal winds reappeared, people would gather at these sites to hear which of the masons had composed the most beautiful song. For, as they caressed the rocks, slipped through their crevices, and skirted their tops, the winds always played a different tune, until the marble and the masons disappeared forever, washed away by the rains, whipped by the glances of passers-by, and licked by the tongues of rams and bulls.

One of these music masons, an Arab, set off with a Jew and a Khazar to hear how his stone would sing with the coming spring. At a temple where common dreams are dreamed in a group, the Jew and the Khazar came to blows and perished in the fight. The Arab, who had been sleeping inside the temple, was accused of killing the Jew, because it was known that he was the Jew's neighbor and that they could not stand each other. And so the Jews sought his death. The Arab thought: "Whoever causes offense on three sides will not escape on the fourth. Because in the Khazar state Greeks are protected by Christian law, Jews by Jewish, and Arabs by Islamic law, by laws that are much mightier than the Khazar state. . . ." Therefore, the Arab defended himself by claiming . . . (here the text is damaged). And so, instead of receiving the death sentence, he was put to work as a galley slave, and he lived long enough to hear the music of the marbles before they collapsed in a silence so solid it could smash your forehead.

MUSTAJ-BEG SABLJAK (7th century) —one of the Turkish commanders in Trebinje. Contemporaries say that Mustaj-Beg Sabljak could not keep food down and that, like a turtledove, he ate and excreted simultaneously. On his military campaigns he took along wet nurses to breast-feed him. But he did not mix with women, or with people in general; he could lie only with the dying, so they brought to his tent dying women, men, and children, who had been purchased, bathed, and dressed for this purpose. Only with them could he spend the night, as though he was afraid of impregnating anyone who might live. He was wont to say that he made children for the other world, not this.

"I never know," he wailed, "whose heaven and whose hell I'm making them for. They'll wander off to the Jewish angels or Christian devils, and I will never see them in the other world when I go to heaven. . . ."

He explained his proclivity, in very simple terms, to a dervish: "When death and love, this and the other world, are placed so close to each other, a good deal can be learned about both. It's like those monkeys that periodically go to the other world; when they return, their every bite is pure wisdom. Is it any wonder, then, that some people give these monkeys their hands to bite and then read the truth from the toothmarks? I don't need that kind of bite. . . ."

And so, in addition to horses, which he loved but did not ride, Mustaj-Beg Sabljak purchased the dying, whom he did not love but rode. He had a fine horse cemetery near the sea, cut out of marble and tended by a Dubrovnik Jew named Samuel Cohen.✣ This Jew left behind a note about what took place in Sabljak Pasha's camp during the campaign in Walachia.

One of the pasha's soldiers was suspected of an offense, but there was no solid evidence against him. He was the only one to survive his unit's battle against the enemy on the banks of the Danube. According to the commander, the soldier had saved his neck by deserting the field of battle. According to the soldier, they were attacked at night; all of the assailants were stark naked; he was the only one to stand up and fight, and he survived precisely because he did not let fear get the better of him. They brought him to Sabljak to judge whether he was guilty or innocent. The soldier's sleeve was ripped off; he was led up to the pasha, who, like everyone else in this mute investigation, uttered not one word throughout the trial. The pasha suddenly pounced on the young man like a beast, took a huge bite out of his forearm, and then, just as suddenly, turned indifferently away from the poor wretch, who was immediately led out of the tent. The pasha had not even seen the soldier properly or exchanged a single word with him, but he calmly chewed the piece of his flesh, with the strained expression of a man trying to remember the taste of some food he had not eaten for a long while, or trying to judge a wine. He spat out the meat—a sign for them to slay the man outside, because it was taken as proof of his guilt.

"Since I have not been in the pasha's service for long," wrote Cohen at the end of his note, "I have not seen many trials, but I know that when the pasha swallows the piece of bitten-off flesh the charges are immediately dropped and the man is acquitted."

Sabljak Pasha had a large, irregular build, as though he wore his skin over his clothes, and a turban between his hair and his skull.

THE
YELLOW
BOOK

HEBREW SOURCES
ON THE
KHAZAR QUESTION

ATEH[▽] (8th century)—name of the Khazar princess who lived at the time of the Judaization of the Khazars.[▽] Daubmannus✿ gives the Hebrew version of her name and the meaning of each letter in the name of At'h:

אטה

The letters can also be used to get some idea of what the Khazar princess was like.

"Aleph," the first letter of her name, denotes the Supreme Crown, wisdom—i.e., gazing up and gazing down, like a mother at her child. Consequently, Ateh did not need to taste her lover's seed to know whether his offspring would be male or female, because everything above and everything below is part of the secret of wisdom, which is incalculable. "Aleph" is the beginning; it embraces all other letters, and is the beginning manifestation of the seven days of the week.

"Teth" is the ninth letter of the Jewish alphabet and its numerical value is "an ordinary nine." In the book *Temunah* "teth" designates the Sabbath, which means it is under the sign of the planet Saturn and divine rest; thus, it also means "bride," inasmuch as Saturday is a bride, stemming from the sentence in Ezekiel 14:23; it is connected with broom sweeping, which stands for destruction and the loss of godlessness, and it denotes strength as well. Princess Ateh helped the Hebrew representative in the famous Khazar polemic;[▽] she wore, attached to her belt, the skull of her lover Mokaddasa Al-Safer, ℭ✿ she fed it with hot, spicy earth and salt water, and she planted cornflowers in its eye sockets so that in the other world he might see the blue colors.

"He" is the fourth letter of God's name. It symbolizes the hand, power, a strong swing, cruelty (the left hand), and mercy (the right), the vine that is lifted from the ground and hung to face the sky.

Princess Ateh spoke eloquently during the Khazar polemic. She said: "Thoughts whirled from the sky on me like snow. Afterward I was barely able to warm up and return to life...."

Princess Ateh helped Isaac Sangari, ✿ the Hebrew participant in the Khazar polemic, by out-arguing the Arab participant, and so the Khazar kaghan opted for the Jewish faith. Some believe that Ateh wrote poems and that they were preserved in the "Khazar books" used by Judah Halevi, ✿ the Jewish chronicler of the Khazar polemic. According to other sources, Ateh was the first to compile the dictionary or encyclopedia of the Khazars, providing extensive information about their history, religion, and dream hunters. [†] Composed as a cycle of poems arranged in alphabetical order, it even described the polemic at the court of the Khazar ruler in poetic form. Asked who would win in the polemic, Princess Ateh said, "When two warriors clash, the one that takes longer to nurse his wounds is the victor." *The Khazar Dictionary* rose like yeast around the princess's collection, which, according to one source, was called *On the Passions of Words.* If all this is true, then Princess Ateh was the first author of this book, its procreator, but this original Khazar dictionary did not yet include the present three languages; it was still one dictionary and one language. Very little of that original dictionary has reached the present one, no more than one dog's sadness can be conveyed to another by children imitating its whimpering.

When, thanks to Princess Ateh, the kaghan accepted the prayer mantle and the Torah, the other participants in the polemic were incensed. The Islamic demon pun-

ished Princess Ateh by condemning her to forget her
Khazar language and all her poems. She even forgot the
name of her lover; all that her memory retained was the
name of a fish-shaped fruit. But before this actually happened, Princess Ateh, sensing the coming danger, ordered a large number of parrots that could imitate
human speech. One parrot was brought to the court for
every word in *The Khazar Dictionary,* each was taught
an entry from the book and could, at any time of night
or day, recite by heart the lines referring to that word.
Of course, since the verses were in the Khazar language,
this was the language in which the parrots recited them.
When the Khazar faith was abandoned and the Khazar
language suddenly began to die out, Ateh released all the
parrots versed in the Khazar dictionary. She told them,
"Go and teach your poems to other birds, because soon
nobody here will know them. . . ." The birds flew away
to the Black Sea forest, where they taught their poems to
other parrots, and these taught them to yet others, until
there came a moment when the poems and the Khazar
language were known only to parrots. In the 17th century a parrot caught on the shores of the Black Sea could
recite several poems in an incomprehensible language
that its owner, a diplomat in Constantinople by the name
of Avram Brankovich,[†] claimed to be the Khazar language. He ordered one of the scribes to take down everything the parrot said, hoping to discover the "parrot
poems," the poetry of Princess Ateh. It seems that this is
how the parrot poems reached the Daubmannus edition
of *The Khazar Dictionary.*

   It must be said that Princess Ateh was the protectress
of the most powerful sect of Khazar priests, the so-called
hunters or readers of dreams. Her encyclopedia was
really nothing more than an attempt to compile the records kept over the centuries by dream hunters who

wrote down their experiences. Her lover, although young and his eyes still new, was one of the most celebrated members of this sect. One of Princess Ateh's poems was dedicated to this sect of archpriests:

When at night we fall asleep, we all turn into actors and step each time onto a different stage to play our part. And by day? By day, when we are awake, we learn our part. Sometimes, when we do not learn it well, we dare not appear on the stage and instead hide behind other actors, who for the moment know their lines and moves better than we do.

And you, you come to the theater to watch our performance, not to act in it. May your eye behold me when I am well rehearsed, for no one is either wise or beautiful all seven days of the week.

There is also a story that the Jewish representatives at the Khazar court saved Princess Ateh from the fury of the Arab and Greek missionaries by arranging to have her lover, the Khazar archpriest of the dream hunters' sect, punished in her stead. She accepted, and he was banished and imprisoned in a cage that hangs above water. However, even this did not spare the princess from punishment.

Betrothal contract of samuel COHEN AND LIDISIA SAROUK (17th century) —The betrothal contract is kept in the Dubrovnik Archive, in the file of the local Sephardi Samuel Cohen. ✿ It reads:

"Under good auspices and at the blessed hour, Mistress Lidisia, daughter of the honorable old Mr. Shelom Sarouk, may he rest in paradise, resident of the city of Thessalonica, is hereby betrothed to Samuel Cohen, under the following terms. First: the mother of the girl,

Madame Siti, blessed be she among women, gives as a dowry to the said daughter Lidisia one Spanish mattress, befitting her circumstances and dignity, and a maiden's trousseau. Second: the marriage is to take place within two and a half years of today. The parties have agreed that if, for whatever reason, the said Master Samuel should not appear to marry Mistress Lidisia within this period, be it for reasons of his own or because of powers beyond his control, all jewelry and objects he has bestowed upon his betrothed shall thereafter be considered hers in the eyes of the law and justice, and he shall have no right to appeal or complaint. These articles are specified as being the following: the bracelets on her wrists, necklaces, rings, cap, stockings, and toe warmers, totaling twenty-four in all. Worth the sum of two thousand two hundred akches, this is all a final gift to the said maiden if he fails to marry her within the appointed period of time. Furthermore, the said Mr. Samuel Cohen is bound by strict oath, like everyone who swears under the threat of excommunication, not to embrace or enter into matrimony with any woman in the world other than his betrothed Lidisia.

"Drawn up and confirmed under the rule of law, Mr. Samuel Cohen takes the oath on this Monday, in the first quarter moon of the month of Shevat in the year 5442, and everything is hereby forever and faithfully guaranteed.

"Judges Avram Hadida, Shelomo Adroke, and Josef Bahar Israel Alevi."

On the back of this document, a Dubrovnik informer had penned several comments about Cohen. One states that in a conversation held in the Stradun on March 2, 1680, Cohen said the following;

"The Khazars used fishing nets for sails on some of the ships in their flotilla, and these ships sailed like any other. When the Greek asked the Khazar priest how they accomplished this, a Jew standing nearby replied in their stead: 'It's simple. They catch in those nets something other than the wind.' "

The other comment written by the Dubrovnik informer refers to the noblewoman Ephrosinia Lukarevich. ✿ In May of that same year, Samuel Cohen met Lady Ephrosinia on Lucharitse Street and asked her the following question:

"Are you always beautiful, or just not on Friday evenings, when souls change, because that is when you won't let me see you?"

In reply, Lady Ephrosinia Lukarevich took a small candle from under her belt, held it in front of her eyes, squinted with one, and looked at the wick with the other. That look spelled Cohen's name in the air, lit the wick, and illuminated her way home.

Cohen, Samuel (1660–September 24, 1689) —a Dubrovnik Jew, one of the authors of this book. Banished from the city in 1689 en route to Constantinople, he died after falling into a coma from which he never awoke.

Sources: A picture of Cohen, who lived in the Dubrovnik ghetto, can be composed from the Dubrovnik police reports, written in the stark Italian style of a people with no mother tongue; from the court papers and depositions of the actors Nikola Rigi and Antun Krivonosovich; and from the list of items found in Cohen's apartment, drawn up in his absence for the Jewish community of Dubrovnik, the transcript of which was found in the Dubrovnik Archives' *Processi politici e criminali 1680–1689*. We know about the last days of Cohen's life from the bits of information sent to Dubrovnik from the files of the Belgrade Sephardim. With them goes a ring on which Cohen, in 1688, inscribed the year 1689, the year of his death. In order to complete the picture, these facts must be compared with the reports of the Dubrovnik emissaries who had been sent by Matia Marin Bunich, the envoy of the Republic of St.

Basil in Vienna, to follow the Austro-Turkish battle at Kladovo in 1689; they wrote only two or three sentences about Cohen, noting that they had found "more hay than horses."

Samuel Cohen's contemporaries describe him as a tall man, with red eyes and a half-gray mustache despite his youth. "He's felt cold ever since I've known him. But he's warmed up a bit in the past couple of years," his mother, Clara, once said of him. She claimed that he traveled vast distances in his dreams at night and would sometimes wake up tired and dusty, or would limp until he had rested from his dream. His mother said she felt a strange unease when Cohen slept, because he behaved in his dreams not like a Jew but like a nonbeliever who rides in his sleep even on the Sabbath, sometimes singing the Eighth Psalm, the one sung when you want to find something you have lost, but singing it in the Christian way. Besides Hebrew, he also spoke Italian, Latin, and Serbian, but when he dreamed at night he mumbled in some strange language he could not speak when awake, a language that turned out to be Walachian. At his interment, his left forearm revealed a terrible scar that looked as though it came from a bite. He longed to visit Jerusalem, and in his dreams did indeed see a city on the shores of time, walked through its straw-strewn streets that deadened sound, lived in a tower full of cupboards as big as a small church, and listened to the rain of the fountains. But he soon realized that the town he was dreaming about and had been convinced was Jerusalem was not the holy city at all, but Constantinople; this was evident from an engraving of Constantinople that he had in his collection of old maps of heaven and earth, towns and stars, in which he recognized the streets, squares, and towers of his dream. Cohen had indubitable virtues, but, in the opinion of Madame Clara, they did not lean toward the practical. He would calculate the speed of the wind from the shadows of the clouds, he had a good head for relations, actions, and numbers, but easily forgot faces, names, and objects. The people of Dubrovnik remembered him as always standing in the same spot, at the window of his little room in the ghetto, his eyes lowered. In fact, he kept books on the floor of his room and would read them standing up, turning the pages with his bare toes. Sabljak Pasha [℮] of Trebinje had heard that there was a Jew in Dubrovnik who made fine wigs for horses, and that is how Cohen joined the pasha's service, in which he lived up to his reputation. He kept the pasha's horse graveyard in good order above the sea and braided the wigs worn by the pasha's black horses for holidays and on military campaigns. Cohen was content with his work. He seldom saw the pasha, but he did encounter the pasha's men, who were quick with their swords and smooth in the saddle. Comparing himself with them, he noticed that somehow he was faster in his sleep than when awake. He tested this impression in his own singularly meticulous way. In his dream he saw himself standing alone under an apple tree, his sword unsheathed. It was autumn in his dream and he was waiting, with blade in hand, for the wind to blow. When it did, the apples began thudding down, like horse's hoofs. As the first one fell, he sliced it in mid-air with his sword. He awoke to the same autumn of his dream, borrowed a sword, and went under the bridge by the Pile Gate. An apple tree stood there, and he waited for the wind to blow. When it did, and the apples began falling, he knew he would not be able to spike any of them with his sword. He turned out to be right, confirming that he was swifter and quicker with his sword in his sleep than when awake. Maybe that was because he practiced in his dreams. He often dreamed he was in the dark, that in his right hand he held a sword and wrapped around his left hand a camel rein, which was being pulled at the other end by someone in the darkness. His ears were full of the dense darkness, and through it he could hear somebody unsheathing a sword in the blackness and inching the steel toward his face; unerringly he sensed it coming and met it head on with his own weapon, blocking the invisible, whistling blade that swooped out of the blackness and fell clanging against his saber.

Suspicions concerning Samuel Cohen and the punishments that followed came from various quarters and for various reasons. He was accused of impermissible engagement in a religious dispute with the Dubrovnik Jesuits, of having a relationship with a Christian noblewoman, and of propagating the heretical teachings of the Essenes, not to mention the testimony of a monk that, within full view of the entire Stradun, Cohen had swallowed a soaring bird with his left eye.

It started with Samuel Cohen's highly unusual visit to the Jesuit monastery in Dubrovnik on April 23, 1689, and it ended with prison. That morning Cohen had been seen rushing up the steps to the Jesuits, placing his pipe between his teeth through a smile, because he had seen the pipe being smoked in his sleep and begun smoking it on awakening. He rang the bell at the monastery and, when the door was opened, immediately began asking the monks about a Christian missionary and saint who was approximately eight hundred years older than he, whose name he did not know, but whose biography he knew by heart; he knew that the man had been schooled in Thessalonica and Constantinople and hated icons, that he had learned Hebrew somewhere in the Crimea, and that he converted the misguided to Christianity in the Khazar Empire, taking along his brother to help him. He had died in Rome, Cohen said, in the year 869.

Cohen asked the monks if they knew the name of this saint and if they could direct him to his biography. But the Jesuits did not even let Cohen through the door. They listened to what he had to say, constantly making the sign of the cross over his mouth, and sent for the guards to put him in the dungeon. For, ever since 1606, when the synod at the Church of Our Lady had passed a decision against the Jews, it was forbidden in Dubrovnik for inhabitants of the ghetto to engage in any kind of discussion about the Christian faith, this offense being punishable by thirty days in prison. While Cohen served his thirty days, smoothing the rough bench with his ear, two noteworthy things occurred. The Jewish municipality decided to make an inventory of Cohen's papers, and a woman appeared who took an interest in Cohen's fate.

Every afternoon at five o'clock when the shadow of the Mincheta turret fell on the other side of the rampart, Lady Ephrosinia Lukarevich, ✿ a respected noblewoman from Lucharitse Street, would pick up her porcelain pipe, fill it with the yellowest tobacco, which had been kept in raisins over the winter, light it with a lump of myrrh or a pine splinter from the island of Lastovo, give a silver coin to a boy from the Stradun, and send the lighted pipe to Samuel Cohen in prison. The boy would give it to Cohen, who, when he had finished smoking, would send it back to Lady Ephrosinia.

This Lady Ephrosinia, born into the aristocratic Getaldich-Kruhoradich family, had married into the upperclass Luccari family of Dubrovnik, and was as famous for her striking beauty as for the fact that nobody had ever seen her hands. It was rumored that she had two thumbs on each hand, that is to say a second thumb in the place of a little finger, so that there was no way to tell which was her left hand and which her right. They say this could be seen clearly on a portrait completed without her knowledge depicting her clasping a book to her breast with her two-thumbed hands. This story notwithstanding, Lady Ephrosinia lived like everybody else of her class; she did not, as they say, have one ear heavier than the other. But every so often, as though possessed, she would allow herself to visit and attend the maskeratas performed by the Jews in the ghetto. At the time, the Dubrovnik authorities had not yet banned these Jewish plays, and once Lady Ephrosinia even lent the ghetto comedians and clowns one of her dresses, "blue with yellow and red ribbons," for the leading female role, which was played by a man. In February 1687 the female role in the "shepherd's play" went to Samuel Cohen, who played the shepherdess wearing Lady Luccari's blue dress. In their reports to the Dubrovnik authorities, informants observed that the "Judeo Cohen" had behaved oddly, "in a way not befitting a comedy." Dressed up as a shepherdess, "decked out in ribbons and lace, blue and red, made up so that not even his face could be recognized," Cohen was supposed to recite a declaration of love, "told in verse," to a shepherd. But in the middle of the play he turned to Lady Ephrosinia (whose dress he was wearing) and to everyone's astonishment presented her with a mirror and the following "words of love":

> In vain do you this good mirror send me
>> When the image I see there is not of thee;
> When I find not the image I seek, thine own,
>> But one that flees from year to year, mine alone.
> Your gift I return, for sleep now escapes me,
>> Since 'tis not your image but mine that I see.

Lady Ephrosinia received this gesture surprisingly calmly and richly rewarded the players with oranges. When with the spring came confirmation time, and Lady Luccari brought her daughter to church, all the world could see that she was also carrying a doll attired in a blue dress made of the yellow-and-red-ribboned one that the "Judeo Cohen had recited in at the maskerata in the ghetto." Cohen pointed at the doll and cried out that this was his daughter receiving Communion, and that the child of his love was being led into a temple, Christian though it be. That same evening, Lady Ephrosinia met Samuel Cohen in front of the Church of Our Lady just as the ghetto was closing; she gave him the tip of her belt to kiss, led him away on the belt as though it were a rein, and when they reached the first shadow gave him a key, pointing to the house in Prieko where she would wait for him the next evening.

At the appointed hour Cohen arrived, to find a door whose keyhole was above the door handle; the only way to unlock it was to insert the key with its notched side up and then push the door handle up. He found himself standing in a narrow hallway in which the right wall was like any other, but the left was composed of small square stone pillars and, fanning out, it veered off in cascades to the left. Looking over these small pillars, Cohen could see into the distance and the open space; down below, the sea rumbled somewhere far away in the moonlight. But the sea was not lying on its back; it hung straight, like a curtain, its bottom end tucked in, wavy and hemmed with foam. Attached at a right angle to the pillars was something that looked like an iron fence, which prevented anyone from getting too close. Cohen deduced that the entire left wall of the hallway was actually a staircase placed with its flat side against the floor, making it unusable, because the steps stood upright, to the left of the foot, not under it. He followed the staired wall, which took him farther and farther away from the right side of the hallway, and somewhere in the middle he suddenly lost the ground from under his feet. He fell against one of the step-pillars and when he tried to get up realized that he could not get a footing on the floor because, although unchanged, it had turned into a wall. Meanwhile, the staired wall, which was the same as before, had turned into a usable staircase, and the light that had glowed at the back of the hallway now shone high above Cohen. He had no problem in climbing the stairs toward the light and the room on the upper floor. Before going in, he peered over the railing and down below saw the sea as he knew it, spilling with a roar into the abyss beneath his feet. When he entered the room, Lady Ephrosinia was sitting barefooted and weeping into her hair. On top of a three-legged stool in front of her was a peasant shoe, an *opanak,* containing a small loaf of bread and, in its nose, a burning wax candle. Lady Ephrosinia's bare breasts showed through her long hair; they had lashes and brows like eyes, and they dripped a dark milk like a threatening glance. She broke off crusts of bread with her double-thumbed hands and dropped them into her lap. As they became wet with her tears and her milk, she tossed them onto the floor in front of her feet, which had teeth instead of toenails. Curling the soles of her feet, she voraciously chewed at the food with those teeth, but since there was no way for her to swallow it, the masticated morsels of food rolled in the dust on the floor. . . .

She saw Cohen, pressed him against her, and led him into the bedchamber. That night she took him as her lover, nursed him on her black milk, and said:

"You'll age if you suck too hard, because what flows out of me is time. It gives you strength up to a point, and then it weakens you. . . ."

After spending the night with her, Cohen decided to convert to her Christian faith. He spoke about it in open rapture, and the story spread, but nothing happened. When he confided his intentions to Lady Ephrosinia, she told him:

"Please don't do it, because, if you must know, I my-

self am not of the Christian faith; that is to say, I am
only temporarily a Christian, by marriage. Actually, in a
very complicated way, I am of your own, Jewish world.
You may have sometimes noticed in the Stradun a familiar cloak on an entirely unfamiliar person. We all
wear such cloaks, including me. I am the devil; my name
is 'sleep.' I come from the Hebrew hell, from Gehenna;
I reside on the left side of the temple, among the spirits
of evil; I am the seed of Gebhurah, of whom it is written:
atque hic in illo creata est Gehenna.' I am the first Eve; I
am called Lilith; I knew the name Jehovah and quarreled with Him. Ever since, I have been drifting in His
shadow, among the seven meanings of the Torah. I was
created in my present form, the one you see and like on
me, by mixing together the truth and earth; I have three
fathers and no mother. And I must not walk backward.
If you kiss my brow, I will die. If you convert to Christianity, you will die for me. The satans of the Christian
Hades will take you over; they will take care of you, not
I. You would be lost to me forever and beyond my reach.
Not just in this life, but in other, future lives as well. . . ."

And so the Dubrovnik Sephardi Samuel Cohen remained what he was. But when he stopped, the rumors
did not. His name traveled faster than his person, and
things were already happening to it that had yet to happen to Cohen. The cup spilled over at the carnival in
1689 on the Sunday of the Holy Apostles. Right after the
carnival, the Dubrovnik actor Nikola Rigi was put on
trial for offenses committed by his troupe during the
carnival. He was accused of ridiculing the prominent
Dubrovnik Jew Papo-Samuel and other Jews in the pageant, of using them in the maskerata, and of abusing
Samuel Cohen in front of the entire town. The actor
defended himself by saying that he had had no idea
Cohen was behind the carnival mask. As the young do

every year when the wind changes hue, Rigi and the actor Krivonosovich prepared the "Judiata," a carnival play featuring a Jew. But that year Bozho Popov-Saraka and the other landed gentry pulled out, so the common people decided to prepare the masks themselves. They hired an ox cart and put a scaffold on it; Krivonosovich, who had played the Jew before, got himself a shirt made of sailcloth and a hat of fishnet, used hemp to make a red beard, and wrote the testament read in the "Judiata" by the Jew before he dies. They met at the appointed hour in their (masked) disguises, and Rigi swore to the court that he thought that riding in the cart, as in earlier carnival years, was Krivonosovich disguised as a Jew, standing under the scaffold and submitting to the blows, the spitting, and other humiliations envisaged by the play. All the actors, including the hangman and the Jew, piled into the cart and rode through town, from the black monks to the white, performing the play. They went through the Stradun, then headed for Our Lady and Lucharitse Street. At the big fountain, Rigi, playing the hangman, broke the nose off the supposed Jew's mask (behind which he thought was Krivonosovich); at Tabor he singed his beard; at the small fountain he exhorted the crowd to spit at him; at the court in front of the palace (ante Palatium) he ripped off his hand (made out of a sock filled with straw) and noticed nothing unusual except that the rattling of the cart brought bursts of whistling from the Jew's mouth. In front of the Lukarevich home on Lucharitse Street the scenario called for the "Judeo" to be hanged; Rigi put the noose around his neck, still convinced that behind the mask was Krivonosovich. But instead of the testament the man behind the mask read out a poem or something—God knows what it was—and, with the noose around his neck, addressed it to Lady Ephrosinia Lukarevich, who was standing on the balcony of her palazzo, her hair freshly washed with woodpecker egg. What he read was nothing like the testament of the Jew in the "Judiata"; on the contrary, it went as follows:

Autumn is your ornament, a necklace for your breast;
  Winter is the belt that against your skin is pressed;
Spring is no different from the garments you wear;
  Your shoes are the summer after spring's care.
Time amasses and you have more and more clothes;
  Every new year bringing its own burden of woes;
Discard all garments, all seasons of the year;
  Before my joyous flame does all but disappear.

Only then—because these words were more appropriate for a maskerata (with its declarations of love) than for a "Judiata," and certainly did not sound like the Jew's testament—did the actors and spectators realize that something was wrong; only then did Rigi think to remove the mask from the reader. To the astonishment of one and all, when the mask was lifted it revealed not the actor Krivonosovich but a real Jew from the ghetto, Samuel Cohen. This Judeo had willingly suffered all the blows, spitting, and humiliations in place of Krivonosovich, and Nikola Rigi could in no way be held responsible, because he had not known that the mask was worn by Cohen, who had bribed Krivonosovich to let him take his place. And so, to everybody's surprise, it was established that Rigi was not to blame for the abuse of Samuel Cohen or for the insults hurled at him, but, on the contrary, that Samuel Cohen had infringed upon the law that forbids Jews to mix with Christians in the carnival pageant. Since Cohen had only recently completed a stint in prison for having visited the Jesuits, the latest verdict came as a finger tilting the scales, for it banished from town this Judeo, whose "hair hung heavy" and who tended a horse graveyard for the Turks somewhere in Herzegovina. The only thing that was uncertain was whether the Jewish community would stand behind Cohen and protect him, which would postpone if not alter the entire matter. And so Cohen was sent back to prison while everybody waited for the ghetto to have its say.

In the ghetto it was decided not to wait, as if for a fire in winter. In the second moon of the month of Iyar that year, Rabbi Abraham Papo and Isaac Nehama went to examine and list the papers and books in Cohen's room; his visit to the monks had disturbed not only the Jesuits but the ghetto as well.

When they arrived, nobody was there. They rang the bell and could tell from its sound that the key was inside. It was attached to the tongue of the bell. Inside, a candle was burning in the room, although Cohen's mother was out. They found a mortar for cinammon, a sleeping net strung up so close to the ceiling that a book could be propped against it to read, an hourglass filled with lavender-scented sand, a three-pronged oil lamp with an inscription on each prong bearing the names of man's three souls: *nephesh, ruah,* and *neshamah.* On the windowsill were potted plants, whose species led the visitors to believe that they were a kind protected by the stars under the constellation of Cancer. On the shelves lining the walls were a lute, a saber, and 132 covers made of red, blue, black, and white sackcloth, containing Cohen's manuscripts or transcripts of other writings. A plate bore instructions, written with a pen dipped in sealing wax, for waking up easily and quickly: "To become fully awake it suffices to write out any word whatsoever, for writing is in itself a supranatural and godly, not a human, act." Written on the ceiling above the sleeping net were various letters and words spelled out in the course of waking up. Among the books, the visitors' attention was drawn to three found on the floor by the window where Cohen used to read. He had obviously leafed through them

in turn, reading polygamously. Lying on the floor
was a Cracow edition of the book *De illustribus familiis*
(1585) by the Dubrovnik poet Dr. Didak Isaiah
Cohen (died in 1599), known as Didak Pir; next to it was
Aron Cohen's book *Zeḳan Aron (The Beard of Aron)*,
printed in Venice in 1637, with a transcript of Aron's hymn
to Isaac Yushurun (died in the dungeons of Dubrovnik); and beside that was *The Good Oil (Semen Atov)*
by Shalamun Oeph, Aron Cohen's grandfather. The
books had obviously been selected for family reasons, but
this fact revealed nothing more. Rabbi Abraham Papo
opened the window, and the soft southern breeze swept
into the room. The rabbi opened one of the books, listened for a moment to the pages rustling in the breeze,
and then said to Isaac Nehama, "Listen! Doesn't it sound
as if the pages are murmuring the word *nephesh, nephesh,
nephesh?*"

The rabbi let the next book speak, and its rustling
pages could be heard loud and clear, saying the word
ruah, ruah, ruah.

"If the third book utters the word *neshamah*," said
Papo, "then we'll know that the books are calling Cohen's souls."

And as soon as Abraham Papo opened the third book,
both men heard it whisper the word *neshamah, neshamah,
neshamah.*

"The books are arguing over something in this room,"
Rabbi Papo declared. "There are some things here that
want to destroy some others."

They sat down and stared at the room. Suddenly
flames shot up from the oil lamp, as though summoned
by the rustling pages of the books. One of the flames
separated from the lamp, weeping in two voices, and
Rabbi Papo said:

"That is Cohen's first and youngest soul crying for his
body, and his body crying for his soul."

This soul then moved to the lute on the shelf and began plucking its strings, playing soft music to accompany its weeping. "Sometimes in the early evening," wept Cohen's soul, "if the last glimmers of sunlight catch your eyes, a passing butterfly may look like a distant bird, or fleeting joy like soaring sorrow...."

Then the second flame elongated into human form, stood in front of the mirror, and began dressing and rubbing on whitener. It took the balsams, brazilwood, and scented ointments to the mirror, as though only in the looking glass could it tell their color, but when putting on the whitener it turned its face away from the mirror, as though afraid of injury. When it had finished, it was completely transformed into the image of Cohen, with his red eyes and half-gray mustache. Then it took the saber from the shelf and joined the first soul. But Cohen's third soul, the oldest of the three, flickered like a firefly or small flame high up by the ceiling. While the first two souls leaned against the shelf with the manuscripts, the third stayed hostilely in its ceiling corner, scratching at the letters inscribed above the sleeping net, where it was written:

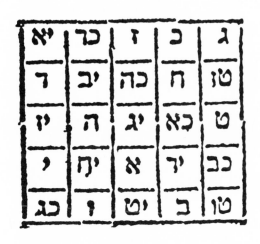

Rabbi Papo and Isaac Nehama decided that Cohen's souls had quarreled over the bags containing the manuscripts, but there were so many that they could not examine them all. Said Rabbi Abraham:

"Are you thinking what I'm thinking about the colors of those bags?"

"Aren't they the colors of a flame?" said Nehama thoughtfully. "Let's compare them with a candle. It has several flames—blue, red, black. This tricolored flame burns and is always in contact with the burning wick and oil. It is tipped by another, white flame, which does not burn yet shines, supported by the tricolored flame below; in other words, fire nourishing fire. Moses stood on the mountain in the white flame that shines but does not burn, while we stand at the foot of the mountain in the tricolored flame, which devours and burns everything except the white flame that stands as the symbol of the greatest and most secret wisdom. Therefore, let us look inside the white covers!"

There were not many, just enough for one feedbag. They found an edition by Judah Halevi,✧ printed in Basel in 1660, with a translation from the Arabic into Hebrew by Rabbi Judah ben Tibbon✧ and the printer's Latin version. The other covers contained Cohen's manuscripts. The first to catch the visitor's eye was:

A NOTE ON ADAM CADMON

The Khazars saw letters in people's dreams, and in them they looked for primordial man, for Adam Cadmon, who was both man and woman and born before eternity. They believed that to every person belongs one letter of the alphabet, that each of these letters constitutes part of Adam Cadmon's body on earth, and that these letters converge in people's dreams and come to life in Adam's body. But these letters and the language they designate are not what we know and use. The Khazars believed they knew the boundary line between the two languages and scripts, between God's word *davar* and our own human word. The borderline, they claimed, runs between verbs and nouns! The tetragram—God's secret name, concealed in the Alexandrian septinarius behind the innocent word *kyrios,* is not a noun at all, but a verb. One should also remember that Abraham took into account the verbs used by the Lord when He created the world, not the nouns. The language we use is made up of two unequal forces, with radically different origins, because the verb, the logos, the law, the concept of good conduct and proper, correct behavior preceded the actual creation of the world and everything that was to act and communicate in it. Nouns appeared only after the creatures of this world were created, to designate them. Hence, names are like the bell on the cap; they come after Adam, who says in his 139th Psalm, "There is not a word in my tongue, but, lo, O Lord, thou knowest it altogether." The fact that nouns are destined to lie in the nature of human names is only further proof that they do not belong to the same order of words that create God's name. For God's name (Torah) is a verb, not a noun, and that verb starts with "aleph." God looked at the Torah when He created the world, and so the word with which the world begins is a verb. Our language, therefore, has two levels—a divine level and another one that is of dubious origin, probably connected to Gehenna, to the expanse north of the Lord. Thus language and the letters of language already contain hell and heaven, the past and the future.

The letters of language! Here we come to the bottom of the shadow. The earth's alphabet mirrors heaven's and shares the fate of language. If we use both nouns and

verbs together, although verbs are infinitely above nouns
—the two are not equal in either age or origin, since
verbs appeared before and nouns after the creation—
then all this also applies to the alphabet. Thus, the letters
used to write nouns and the letters used to designate
verbs cannot be of the same ilk and since time imme-
morial have been divided into two orders of signs, but
our eyes today confuse them, because oblivion lies in the
eye. Just as each letter of the earth's alphabet corresponds
with a part of the human body, so each letter of the
heavenly alphabet corresponds with a part of the body of
Adam Cadmon, and the white space between the letters
denotes the rhythm of the body's movements. However,
since parallelism between the divine and the human alphabet is impermissible, the one always retreats to make
room for the other, just as the other pulls back to let the
former expand. This also applies to the letters of the
Bible—the Bible is always breathing. At moments, it is
the verbs that shine and then, as soon as they retreat, the
black letters of the nouns appear, only we cannot see it,
just as we cannot read what the black flames write on
the white. So it is too with the body of Adam Cadmon,
which alternates between filling our being and deserting
it, like the ebbing tide, depending on whether the heavenly alphabet is on the rise or on the wane. The letters
of our alphabet appear in our waking consciousness and
those of the heavenly alphabet in our dreams, strewn like
light and sand on the waters of the earth at the moment
when the divine letters rise to push back the human
letters from our sleeping eye. For in dreams one thinks
with the eyes and the ears; speech has no nouns, just
verbs; only in dreams is every person a zaddik, never a
murderer. . . . I, Samuel Cohen, the author of these lines,
plunge like the Khazar dream hunters into spheres situated on the dark side of the world, trying to extract the

trapped divine sparks. But it may happen that my own soul gets trapped there as well. Out of the letters I collect there, and those collected by others before me, I am putting together a book that, as the Khazar dream hunters said, will constitute the body of Adam Cadmon on earth. . . .

Staring at each other in the half-dark, the two men emptied the remaining white sacks but found nothing in them except several dozen alphabetized words, something Cohen called *The Khazar Dictionary* (*Lexicon Cosri*), which they took to be alphabetized information about the Khazars, their religion, their customs, and everybody associated with them, their history, and their conversion to Judaism. The material was similar to that compiled many centuries before by Judah Halevi in his book about the Khazars, but Cohen had gone a step further by trying to find out more about Halevi's unnamed Christian and Islamic participants in the Khazar polemic.[▽] He tried to discover their names and their arguments, and to compile their biographies for his dictionary, which, he believed, ought to include entries neglected by Jewish sources on the Khazar question. And so there was a rough outline for the life of a Christian preacher and missionary, clearly the same person Cohen had inquired about with the Jesuits, but since Cohen had been unable to discover his name it could not be included in the dictionary. "Judah Halevi," wrote Cohen in an annotation to this unfinished biography, "his publisher, and other Hebrew commentators and sources mention by name only one of the three participants in the religious polemic at the court of the Khazar kaghan—the Jewish representative, Isaac Sangari,[✿] who interpreted the dream about the angel's visit to the Khazar ruler. He-brew sources do not name the Christian or Islamic participants in the polemic; they merely say that one is a philosopher; as for the other, the Arab, they do not even mention whether he was killed before or after the polemic. Perhaps," wrote Cohen, "there is somebody else out there in the world collecting papers and information about the Khazars, like Judah Halevi, and compiling sources or a dictionary, like me. Perhaps he is not of our faith, but a Christian or a person of Islamic law. Perhaps there are two other people somewhere out there in the world searching for me the way I'm searching for them. Perhaps they are dreaming of me, as I of them, and craving for what I know, because my truth is a secret to them, just as theirs is the hidden answer to my questions. It is not in vain that people say that every dream is a sixtieth part of the truth. Perhaps it is not in vain that I dream of Constantinople and of myself there in an entirely different version of my real self—smooth in the saddle and quick with the sword, a bit lame, and pious in a different way from the way I actually am. The Talmud says: 'Let him go forth to have his dream interpreted before three men!' Who are my three? Apart from myself, is the second not perhaps the Christian searching for the Khazars, and the third, the Moslem? Are there three religions in my souls rather than one? Will two of my souls go to hell, and only one to heaven? Or, as always when learning the book about the creation of the world, three are necessary and one is not enough, and I rightly yearn for the other two as perhaps they yearn for the third. I don't know, but I do know and have reliably experienced that my three souls are warring inside me and one of them carries a sword and is already in Constantinople; the second hesitates, weeps, and sings while playing the lute; the third is against me. The third does not appear, or is not yet reaching me. And so I dream only of the first, the one bearing the sword; I do not dream of the second one, with the lute. Because, as Raav Hisda says, 'A dream that is not interpreted is like a letter that has not been read,' but I turn that around and say, 'An unread letter is like an undreamed dream.' How many dreams have been sent to me that I never received and dreamed? I do not know, but I do know that one of my souls can trace the origin of another by looking at a sleeping man's brow. I feel that pieces of my soul can meet among other humans beings, among camels, among rocks and plants; somebody's dream has taken material from the body of my soul and is using it to build its own house somewhere far, far away. Because the self-improvement of my souls requires the cooperation of other souls, souls helping souls. I know, my Khazar dictionary includes all ten numbers and twenty-two letters of the Hebrew alphabet; the world can be created out of them but, lo, I cannot do it. I am missing certain names, and as a result some of the letters will not be filled. How I would love to use only verbs instead of nouns for the entries in my dictionary! But a man cannot do that, because the letters that designate verbs come from Elohim, are unknown to us, and are divine, not human; only letters designating nouns and names, those that come from the devil in Gehenna, build my dictionary and are accessible to me. I must, therefore, keep to names and the devil. . . ."

"Baal halomot!" cried Rabbi Papo, looking up from Cohen's papers. "Is he delirious?"

"I think something else," replied Nehama, putting out the candle.

"What do you think?" asked Rabbi Papo, putting out the three-branched lamp, as each soul whispered its name before it vanished.

"I am wondering," replied Nehama in the inky blackness that made him confuse the darkness of the room with a dark mouth, "I am wondering whether Zemlin, Kavalla, or Thessalonica is for him."

"Thessalonica, the Jewish mother?" asked Rabbi Papo in surprise.

"Certainly not. He should be sent as a sapper to Siderokapsi!"

"We'll send him to his betrothed in Thessalonica," decided the other old man thoughtfully, and they left without turning on the light.

Outside a southerly wind greeted them, salting their eyes.

And so Samuel Cohen's fate was sealed. He was banished from Dubrovnik and, as the police reports show, he bade farewell to his acquaintances "on the Day of St. Thomas the Apostle in 1689, in a heat that makes cattle tails molt, and fills the Stradun with bird feathers." That evening, Lady Ephrosinia dressed up like a man the way whores do and stepped out. Cohen was walking for the last time from the pharmacy toward the Sponza Palace when, from the shadows of the Garishte arch, she tossed him a silver coin. He picked it up and moved toward her in the dark. At first he mistook her for a man and was startled, but as soon as her fingers touched him he recognized her.

"Don't go," she said. "Everything can be arranged with the judges. You need only say so. There is no exile that cannot be replaced with a few days in maritime prison. I will wrap a few golden pieces in the beard of the right person, and we will not have to part."

"I don't have to go because I've been banished," replied Cohen. "That paper of theirs means about as much as the song spewed by a flying swallow. I have to go because it's high time. Ever since childhood I've been dreaming that I'm fighting with my sword in the dark, limping. I dream in a language I do not understand when I'm awake. It has been twenty-two years now, and it's time for my dream to come true and be explained. It's now or never. And it will come true at the place where I dream it—in Constantinople. For it is not by chance that I see in my dream those crooked streets made to kill the wind, those towers and the water beneath them. . . ."

"If we never meet again in this life," replied Lady Ephrosinia, "then we shall see each other in some future life. Perhaps we are only the roots of souls that will sprout from us one day. Perhaps your soul is pregnant and will give birth to my soul. But first they must both travel their assigned paths. . . ."

"Even if that were so, we would not recognize each other in that future world. Yours is not Adam's soul, a soul banished to those of all subsequent generations and doomed to die again and again with each one of us."

"Then we shall meet in some other way. And I will tell you how to recognize me. I will be a male then, but I will have the same hands I have now—each with two thumbs, so that it can be both my right hand and my left. . . ."

And with these words Lady Ephrosinia kissed Cohen's ring, and they parted forever. Her death, which followed shortly afterward, was so terrible that poems were written about it. However, Cohen could not be suspected because at the time of her death he had himself already fallen into a coma, into a dream of no return and no awakening.

At first it was thought that Cohen would go to his betrothed, Lidisia, in Thessalonica and marry her there, as advised by the Jewish community in Dubrovnik. But this is not what he did. He filled his pipe that evening and smoked it in the morning in the Trebinje camp of Sabljak Pasha, who was getting ready to march on Walachia. Thus, in spite of everything, Cohen headed for Constantinople. But he never got there. Eyewitnesses from the pasha's entourage, bribed by the Dubrovnik Jews with plant dye for their wool to tell them about Cohen's end, say the following.

That year the pasha traveled north with his entourage, while the clouds above drifted south, as though to take away their memory. That in itself was not a good omen. They watched their hounds race through the scents of the Bosnian woods as through the seasons of the year and came upon a Šabac inn the night of the eclipse. One of the pasha's steeds had broken its leg, and he summoned his keeper of the horse graveyard. Cohen was fast asleep and did not hear the summons, so the pasha lashed him between the eyes with his whip, drawing the blow as if out of a well, with such force that his arm bracelets snapped. Cohen instantly woke up and rushed off to do his job. Here all trace of Cohen is temporarily lost, because from the pasha's camp he went to Belgrade, which was being held by Austrian troops. There he is known to have visited the huge two-story house of the Turkish Sephardim, with the drafts howling through its corridors—the Jewish home, the *abheham,* with its more than one hundred rooms, fifty kitchens, and thirty cellars. In the streets of the city built between two rivers he watched children in paid fights draw blood from one another like cocks, as the circle of spectators placed their bets. He stayed at an old inn, in one of the forty-seven rooms belonging to the local German Jews, the Ashkenazi, and there he found a book about interpreting dreams, written in Ladino. At dusk he watched the bell towers plow the clouds above Belgrade.

"When they reach the end of the sky," he jotted down, "they turn around and head back through fresh clouds. . . ."

When Sabljak Pasha's troops reached the Danube, one of the four heavenly rivers—symbolizing the allegorical level in the Bible—Cohen rejoined them. And then something happened that was to win Cohen great favor with the pasha. The pasha had brought along on his campaign a well-paid Greek, a cannon forger. With his molds and equipment the Greek had stayed one day's walk behind the troops, and at the sound of the first skirmishes with the Serbs and Austrians, the pasha ordered that a cannon be forged in Djerdap; it was to have a range of three thousand elbows, and each cannonball was to be the size of two Egyptian scales. "Because," said the pasha, "from the roar of the cannon chicks will die in their eggs, foxes will miscarry, and honey will turn sour in the beehives." He ordered Cohen to bring the Greek. But it was the Sabbath, and Cohen, instead of riding off, went to bed. . . .

The next morning Cohen chose a camel, the offspring of a double-humped male and a single-humped female, which had spent the summer covered with tar and was now ready to travel. He also took along a "joy" horse, the kind they let loose on mares for foreplay before the mares are turned over to the stallions. By riding the camel and the horse in turn, Cohen completed a two-day ride in one and arrived as ordered. When the astonished pasha asked him where he had learned to ride and who had taught him, Cohen replied that he practiced in his sleep. The pasha was greatly pleased by this answer, and he gave Cohen a gift—a nose ring. When the cannon was forged, it began pounding Austrian positions. Sabljak ordered his men to charge, and they swooped down on the Serbian positions, and with them Cohen, who instead of a saber carried a feedbag, although it was known to contain no valuables, just some old, neatly penned sheets of paper in white covers.

"Under a sky as thick as porridge," an eyewitness related, "we stormed a trench where we found only three men, the others having fled. Two soldiers were throwing dice, oblivious to our attack. In front of the tent next to them was a splendidly attired horseman who seemed to be in a delirium of sleep, and the only ones to attack us were his dogs. In a flash our boys slew one of the dice players and rammed a spear into the sleeping horseman. He raised himself up on his elbow, the spear protruding from his body, and looked at Cohen. That gaze felled Cohen like a bullet; his papers spilled out of his feedbag. The pasha asked whether Cohen had been killed, to which the other dice player replied in Arabic:

" 'If his name is Cohen, then it was not a bullet that hit him; it was sleep that knocked him off his feet. . . . ' "

This proved to be true, and these unusual words spared the dice player's life for that day. Because the human word is like hunger—it is not always of the same power. . . .

The statement about Samuel Cohen the Jew from the Dubrovnik ghetto ends with a report on his last dream, concerning the heavy, deep coma into which he plunged as into a dense sea of no return. That last report on

Samuel Cohen was made to Sabljak Pasha by the dice player whose life had been spared in the battlefield. What he told the pasha remains forever sewn into a silk tent on the Danube, and only fragments of that talk have reached us through the green rainproof material. The dice player's name was Yusuf Masudi,[℮] and he was a dream reader. He could catch a hare in people's dreams, let alone a man, and he was in the employ of the horseman who had been woken up by the spear. Now, this horseman was a prominent and affluent man named Avram Brankovich;[†] his greyhounds alone were worth a shipload of gunpowder. Masudi made an incredible claim about this man. He assured Sabljak Pasha that in his heavy sleep Cohen was dreaming of this very same Avram Brankovich.

"You say you're a dream reader?" asked the pasha. "Well, then, can you read Cohen's dream?"

"Of course I can. I already see what he is dreaming: since Brankovich is dying, he's dreaming of Brankovich's death."

These words seemed to excite the pasha.

"That means," he quickly concluded, "that Cohen can now experience what no mortal can: by dreaming of Brankovich dying, he can experience death and yet stay alive?"

"That's right," said Masudi, "but he cannot wake up to tell us what he saw in the dream."

"But you can see his dreaming of that death. . . ."

"Yes, I can, and tomorrow I will report to you on how it is to die and what a man feels. . . ."

Sabljak Pasha never discovered, nor will we, whether the dice player said this in order to prolong his life by an extra day, or because he really could see into Cohen's dream and find Brankovich's death there. But the pasha felt it was worth a try. He would say that every tomorrow is worth an unused horseshoe and every yesterday the used shoe off a camel, so he let Masudi live one more day.

Cohen spent the night sleeping for the last time; his huge nose peered like a bird's body through the smile of his sleep, and that smile looked like a leftover from a dinner eaten long, long ago. Masudi did not leave his pillow until the morning, and when day broke the Anatolian was changed by his vigil, as though he had been whipped in the dreams he had read. And what he had read in them was this.

It was as though Brankovich was not dying from his spear wound at all. In fact, he did not even feel it. He felt many more wounds than just one, and their number rapidly multiplied. He felt he was standing high up on a stone pillar, counting. It was spring, bringing the wind that plaits the branches of the willow trees, and all the willows from the river Mureşul to the rivers Tisa and Danube wore braids. Arrows seemed to be piercing his body, but it all happened backward: with each arrow he felt first the wound, then the penetrating stab; then the pain would stop, something would whistle through the air, and finally there was the zing of the bow string as it released the arrow. Dying, he counted the arrows from one to seventeen and then fell from the pillar and stopped counting. He fell against something hard, immovable, and vast. But it was not the ground: it was death. The collision sent his wounds flying in all directions, so that one could no longer feel another, and only then did he hit the ground, already dead.

And then, in that same death, he died a second time, although it did not look as if there were any more room for even the slightest pain. In between the stabs of the arrow he was dying once again, but completely differently; now he was dying the premature death of a boy, and his only fear was that he would not be fast enough to complete the huge job (because death is hard work) and to finish with this second death before the time came to fall off the pillar. And so he hurried. He lay in that motionless rush behind the colored heating stove built like a small toy church with red and golden cupolas. Searing and icy pains surged from him into the room, as though the years were fighting to break free of his body in quick succession. The dark spread like dampness, every room in the house darkening differently; only the windows were still invested with the last light of day, hardly distinguishable from the darkness in the room. Someone with a candle was coming from the invisible vestibule and, as if the frame had as many black doors as a book has pages, he leafed through them briefly, shifting the light as he came in. Then something started pouring out of him, and he peed out his entire past, until he was empty. Like rising water, night crept up from the ground to the sky, and suddenly all his hair fell out, as though a fur hat had been knocked off his head, which was already dead.

And now Brankovich's third death appeared in Cohen's dream. It was barely noticeable, shrouded by something that could have been mounds of time. Hundreds of years seemed to stand between Brankovich's first two deaths and this third, which was barely visible from where Masudi was standing. At first Masudi thought that Brankovich was now dying the death of his foster son, Petkutin, but since he knew how Petkutin had ended he quickly realized that this was not Petkutin's death. The third death was swift and short. Brankovich was lying in a strange bed, and a man took a pillow and began smothering him with it. But Brankovich could think of only one thing: he had to reach the egg on the little table by the bed and crack it. Brankovich did not know why this had to be done, but as the man smothered him with the pillow, he knew that this alone was important. He also realized that humanity had discovered its yesterday and tomorrow very belatedly, a million years after its appearance

—first tomorrow, and then yesterday. It discovered them one night long ago, when the present started dying out in the darkness, caught and almost stifled between the past and the future, which that evening had swelled until they almost merged. That is what it was like now. The present was fading, smothered by two converging eternities—the past and the future—and Brankovich died for the third time, exactly when the past and the future collided inside him, crushing him just as he was about to crush that egg. . . .

Suddenly Cohen's dream was as barren as a dry riverbed. It was time to wake up, but there was nobody left to dream Cohen's own reality, as he had done during Brankovich's lifetime. And so what happened to Cohen had to happen. Masudi saw how, in Cohen's dream, which was turning into a death rattle, all the names of all the things around him began dropping off like hats, and the world was left as virgin pure as on its first day in the beginning. Only the first ten numbers and the letters of the alphabet designating verbs glittered like golden tears above the things surrounding Cohen. And it was then he learned that the numbers of the Ten Commandments are also verbs, that they are the last to be forgotten when one is forgetting a language and remain as an echo when even the Commandments themselves vanish from memory.

That moment Cohen awoke in his death, and the path before Masudi disappeared, because a veil descended over the horizon on which, written with water from the river Yabok, were the following words:

"For your dreams are the days in the nights."

Selected Bibliography: Anonymous, *Lexicon Cosri, continens colloquium seu disputationem de religione,* Regiemonti Borussiae excudebat typographus Ioannes Daubmannus, Anno 1691, passim; for Cohen's ancestors see: M. Pantic, *"Sin vjerenik jedne matere . . . ,"* Anali Historijskog instituta Jugoslavenske akademije znanosti i umetnosti in Dubrovnik, 1953, vol. II, pp. 209–216.

Daubmannus, Joannes (17th cen-
tury)—"*typographus* Ioannes Daubmannus," a Polish
printer. In the first half of the 17th century he published
a Polish-Latin dictionary in Prussia, but the same name
also appears on the title page of another dictionary, published in 1691 under the title *Lexicon Cosri—continens
colloquium seu disputationem de religione.* . . . Thus,
Daubmannus also appears as the first publisher of the
book whose second edition the reader now has in his
hands. The very next year, in 1692, the Inquisition had
ordered the Daubmannus edition of *The Khazar Dictionary* destroyed, but two copies escaped this fate
and remained in circulation. Daubmannus probably obtained the material for his dictionary of three dictionaries on the Khazar question from a monk of the
Eastern Christian order, but he himself added to this
material and therefore appears not only as the publisher of *The Khazar Dictionary* but also as its editor.
This can be seen from the languages used in the edition. The accompanying Latin text was probably written by Daubmannus, because it is unlikely that the
monk knew Latin. The dictionary itself, however,
was printed in Arabic, Hebrew, and Greek, as well as
Serbian, this being how the text was submitted to the
publisher.

But a German source claims that the Daubmannus
who published the 1691 *Khazar Dictionary* was not the
same Daubmannus who published the Polish dictionary
in the first half of the 17th century. According to this

Prussian source, the younger Daubmannus had been crippled in early childhood by a disease. At the time he was called not Joannes Daubmannus but Jacob Tam David ben Yahya, which was his real name. "May he be cursed day and night" were the words a woman who sold paints and dyes reportedly hurled at him. Why the curse was uttered is unknown, but it was effective. It was the beginning of the first month of Adar when the boy returned home in the snow, curved like a saber. From then on he dragged one arm along the ground, and in the other carried his head by the hair, because it would not sit straight on its own. That is why he went into printing: it was a job in which he could lean his head on his shoulder without its bothering him; indeed, that position was even useful. He smiled, said, "The dark is like the light," and was hired by the real Daubmannus, the elder Joannes. He never regretted it. Just as Adam christened the days in the week, so he gave names to each of the seven arts of bookbinding, sang as he picked the letters out of the wooden box, and for each letter had a different song. To look at him, one would not have thought that he was at war with his affliction. But it happened that a well-known healer was passing through Prussia just then, one of those rare people who knew how Elohim had wedded Adam to his soul. So Daubmannus the elder sent his Jacob Tam David to the healer to be cured. Jacob was already a young man; he had a broad, what they called "well-salted" smile on his face, different-colored stockings on each leg, and in the month of Elul, faster than the hens could lay them, he ate scrambled eggs from a furnace where in summer the eggs were kept in the draft of the chimney. When he heard about going to the healer, his eyes glinted in the blade of the knife with which he was cutting the bread; he tied his mustache into a knot and rushed off, carrying his head in his hand. It is not known how long he stayed abroad, but during one sunny day, Jacob Tam David ben Yahya returned from Germany hale and hearty, straight and tall, but under a new name. He had taken the name of his benefactor Daubmannus the elder, who had sent him away as a hunchback and now welcomed him back with joy and these words: "One cannot speak about half the soul. Otherwise we could keep one half in heaven and the other in hell. You are the living proof."

Indeed, with his new name the young Daubmannus began a new life. But his life was as two-faced as the double bottom of an Erdély plate. Daubmannus the younger continued to dress foppishly and carry two caps to the fairs, one under his belt and the other on his head, changing them periodically to look handsomer. He was, in truth, a handsome man; he had flaxen hair that had grown in the month of Iyar, and had as many attractive faces as the month of Sivan has thirty different days. People felt it was time for him to marry. But ever since he had regained his health, that familiar smile of his had left his face. That smile, which he would blow away in the morning when he entered the printer's shop, would, as it used to, be waiting for him in the evening at the shop door like a dog, but he would catch it in flight with his upper lip, as if keeping a fake mustache in place. That, in fact, is how he wore his smile. It was rumored that when he had discarded his hunched back and stood up straight, the printer had fallen prey to fear. He was afraid—it was whispered—of the height from which he now observed the world, of the new vistas he could not recognize, and especially of his equality with other people, over whom he now towered, he who had once been the lowest of the low in the streets.

Beneath these street rumors coursed others, graver still, told in hushed whispers, and they were as heavy as the silt at the bottom of the river. According to one of these terrible stories, the source of Daubmannus' erstwhile youthful cheerfulness and spirit, despite his affliction, was the fact that, hunched and bent as he was, he could reach down and suck at himself, and so he learned that the male seed tastes like a woman's milk. This was how he kept renewing himself. But once he stood up straight and tall, this became impossible. . . . These were just the sorts of stories that make a person's past as opaque as his future, but everyone could see that since his recovery young Daubmannus often played an unusual joke on the boys in the workshop. He would interrupt his work for a minute, touch the ground with one hand, and with the other take hold of his head by the hair and then stand it up straight. It was then that the old, well-salted smile would spread across his face and the former ben Yahya would sing out as he had not been heard to sing in a long, long time. It was not hard to guess what had happened: in order to be healed, the printer had had to give up more than it was worth, and it was not in vain that he said, "Germany returns to me in my sleep like an undigested lunch." Worst of all, he no longer enjoyed the work in the printing shop. He would fill his rifle with the type letters and go hunting. But the decisive moment, like the stone that separates the water of one stream into two seas, was again his encounter with a woman. She came from far away, wore violet dresses like the Jewish women in Greece under the Turks, and was the widow of a Romaniot who had once made kachkaval cheese near Kavalla. Daubmannus caught sight of her in the street. Their hearts met in their eyes, but when he extended two fingers toward her she said, "Nonkosher birds are recognized by the way they separate their claws on a branch into pairs rather than into three and one. . . ." And she refused him. This was the last straw. Daubmannus the younger completely lost his head. He had already decided to abandon everything and leave town when the elder Daubmannus suddenly died. One evening a Christian monk walked into the shop Daubmannus the younger had now inherited, carrying three heads of cabbage on a spit and bacon in a bag. He sat himself down by the hearth, where a kettle of water was boiling, threw some salt and the bacon into it, sliced the cabbage, and said, "My ears are filled with the words of God, and my mouth with cabbage."

His name was Nikolsky[A] and he had once been a scribe at the St. Nicholas Monastery by the same Morava River in which long ago the maenads had torn Orpheus apart. He asked Daubmannus whether he would like to publish a book whose content was rather strange, so much so that nobody would probably dare print it. Daubmannus the elder or ben Yahya would have turned down such an offer without thinking twice, but Daubmannus the younger, confused as he was, realized that this might be his chance. He agreed, and Nikolsky began dictating the dictionary from memory until, at the end of seven days, he had dictated the entire book, all the while eating cabbage with his incisors, which were so long they seemed to grow out of his nose. When Daubmannus received the manuscript, he gave it unread to the typesetter and said, "Knowledge is a perishable commodity; it can turn sour in a second. Like the future." As soon as the dictionary was typeset, Daubmannus printed one copy with the poisonous printer's dye and immediately sat down to read it. The more he read, the stronger the effect of the poison, and Daubmannus' body became more and more crooked. Every consonant in the book seemed to strike at some part of his body. The hunched back returned; his bones reverted to the original position in which they had grown and locked long ago around his bowels; as he read, his bowels reassumed the position they had been accustomed to since childhood; the pains that had paid for his health now subsided; his head once again dropped into the palm of his left hand, while the right dropped to the ground, and as he touched it Daubmannus' face lit up again as in his childhood, beaming with a forgotten smile of beatitude that gathered together all his years. And then he died. Through this blissful smile the last letters he had read in the book dropped out of his mouth: *Verbum caro factum est,* "The Word became flesh."

H ALEVI, JUDAH (Arabic, Abulhassan al Lavi, "little Halevi") (1075–1141)—the principal Hebrew chronicler of the Khazar polemic,$^\nabla$ one of the three leading Hebrew poets of Spain. Born in southern Castile in Tudela, and following the wishes of his father, Samuel Halevi, Judah received a comprehensive education in Moorish Spain. "There is only one wisdom," Halevi was later to write; "the wisdom spread through the sphere of the universe is no greater than the wisdom contained in the tiniest of animals. Except the former—composed of pure matter, which is constant and hence diverse in kind —can be destroyed only by the Creator who made it, whereas animals are made of matter that is subject to various kinds of influence, and so the wisdom in them is subject to heat, cold, and everything else that affects their nature." Halevi studied medicine at Isaac Alphasy's Talmudic school in Lucena, and spoke both Castilian and Arabic. In Arabic he studied philosophy, which was under the influence of the ancient Greeks, and about which he wrote, "It has colors but no fruits, and while feeding the mind it gives nothing to the emotions." Hence, Halevi believed that no philosopher can ever become a prophet. Although medicine was his profession, Halevi devoted a great deal of attention to literature and the Hebrew tradition in magic, and he spent his life in various parts of Spain, keeping company with the poets, rabbis, and scholars of his time. He contended that female organs were inverted male organs, and that the Book says as much, only in a different way: "Man is aleph, mem, shin; woman is aleph, shin, mem. The wheel turns forward and backward; on the up nothing better than joy; on the down nothing worse than injustice. . . ." An expert on the Talmud, Halevi traced the origin of the alliteration in God's name and offered to modern biblical exegesis outlines for sourcing the letters "J" and "E." His was the saying: "Vowels are the soul in the body of consonants." He warned that there are knots in time, the "hearts of the years," which beat to the rhythm of time, space, and human beings, and corresponding with these knots are acts, works that are in tune with time. He believed that the differences in things stem from their essence. Somebody might ask: "Why did He not create me as an angel?" And, with just as much right, a worm might ask: "Why did Thou not create me as a man?" Ever since he was thirteen, Halevi had known that the past is on the stern, the future on the bow, that the ship is swifter than the river, the heart faster than the ship, but that they do not move in the same direction. Some one thousand poems believed to be his have been preserved, along with some of his letters to friends, who told him, "He who takes a bite in his mouth will not be able to say his name; he who says his name will make the bite in his mouth bitter." From Castile Halevi moved to Córdoba, which was held by the Arabs at the time, and where for centuries there had been an interest in the Khazars. He worked as a doctor, and it was there that he wrote many of his early poems. He wrote in Arabic versification and inscribed his name in acrostics. "I am the sea with its stormy waves," he wrote of himself. The "collection" of his poems was discovered in Tunis, in a manuscript later completed from other sources. In the 18th century he was translated into German by Herder and Mendelssohn. In 1141 Halevi wrote his famous book on the Khazars (*Kitab al Khazari*). The first pages of the book describe the polemic at the court of the Khazar kaghan[▽] between the Islamic doctor, the Christian philosopher, and the Jewish rabbi on the meaning of a dream. Later chapters leave only two of the participants in the discussion—the rabbi and the Khazar kaghan—and the book becomes what its subtitle says: *The Book of Arguments and Proofs in Defense of the Jewish Faith*. While writing this book, Halevi did the same as its protagonist—he decided to leave Spain and go to the East, for he wanted to see Jerusalem. "My heart yearns for the East," he wrote at the time, "but I am riveted to the distant West. . . . Adornments of the earth, joys of the world, oh, how I am drawn to you . . . though your empire be no more, though in place of your healing balsams only scorpions and snakes now swarm." He traveled via Granada, Alexandria, Tyre, and Damascus, and, legend has it, snakes left their signature in the sands of his journey. It was on this trip that he wrote his most mature poems, among them the famous *Song of Zion,* which is read in synagogues on the Day of the Holy Abba. He landed on the holy shores of his original homeland and died within reach of his destination. According to one account, just as he laid eyes on Jerusalem he was trampled to death by Saracen horses. Writing about the clash between Christianity and Islam, he said: "There is no port in either East or West where we might find peace. . . . Whether Ismael wins or the Edomites"—Christians —"prevail, my fate remains the same—to suffer." There is a legend that Halevi's gravestone bore this inscription: "Where have you flown, O faith, O nobility, modesty,

and wisdom? We lie beneath this stone; we are insepa-
rable from Judah even in the grave." Thus Halevi
proved the saying "All roads to Palestine, none from it."

Halevi wrote his famous book about the Khazars in
Arabic, and it was not printed in Hebrew translation
until 1506. It had several reprints in both the Arabic
original and the Hebrew translations by ben Tibbon✿
(1167) and Judah ben Isaac the Cardinal. The Hebrew
translation published in Venice in 1547 and 1594 was
impaired by censorship (especially the second of these
two editions), but it included a commentary by Judah
Muscato and is therefore considered an important edition. In the 17th century, John Buxtorf translated Halevi's book on the Khazars into Latin. It was the censored
version of Halevi's work that reached the broader European public through this Latin translation. This edition
posits the arguments of Isaac Sangari,✿ the Hebrew participant in the Khazar polemic, against the anonymous
Islamic and Christian participants. However, the foreword to this censored version claims that Halevi wrote:
"I am often asked what arguments and answers I might
give to philosophers whose views differ from ours, to
people of other faiths (except the Christians) and to the
heretics in our midst who deviate from the Jewish faith
as it is generally accepted, and I remembered what I had
heard about the views and proofs given by a certain
scholar in the polemic with the Khazar king, the one
who adopted Judaism four hundred years ago." Obviously, the parenthetical "except the Christians" was inserted at a later date, because of the censors, for, contrary
to this comment, Halevi did speak in his book about the
Christian faith. That is, he spoke about three religions—
Christianity, Islam, and Judaism—using the image of
a tree to symbolize them. On that tree, he said, the
branches with their leaves and flowers represent Christianity and Islam, while the root is Judaism. Moreover,

despite the fact that the name of the Christian participant in the polemic is omitted, his title has been kept—Philosopher. The term Philosopher, as both Hebrew and Christian (Greek) sources call the Christian participant, is actually a Byzantine university title and should not be taken in the usual sense of the word.

However, the Basel edition of Halevi's book, in John Buxtorf's Latin translation, won great popularity, and the publisher received letters in connection with its publication. In his 1691 *Khazar Dictionary,* Daubmannus notes that among those to comment on Halevi's book at the time was a Dubrovnik Jew by the name of Samuel Cohen. ✿ The Latin version of Halevi's book was followed by translations into Spanish, German, and English. A critical edition of the Arabic original with a comparative Hebrew translation came out in Leipzig in 1887. Hirschfeld remarked that, in discussing the nature of the soul, one of the sources Halevi used was a text by Ibn Sina (Avicenna).

Halevi soon became so popular that legends were told about him. Halevi is believed to have had no sons, just one daughter, whose own son carried his grandfather's name. This, according to the Russian Jewish encyclopedia, disproves the story that Halevi's daughter married the prominent scientist Abraham ben Ezra, because Ezra's son was not called Judah. This story can be found in Yiddish in Simon Akiba ben Joseph's book *Maseh ha Shem,* which says that the famous grammarian and poet of Toledo, Abraham ben Ezra (died in 1167), wedded Halevi's daughter in Khazaria. Daubmannus cites the following legend about that wedding:

Abraham ben Ezra lived in a little house by the sea. Aromatic plants always grew around it, and since the winds could not disperse the scents they carried them like carpets from place to place. One day, Abraham ben Ezra noticed that the scents had changed. That was because he felt fear. At first the fear inside him was as deep as his youngest soul; then it descended to Ezra's middle-aged, and then to his third, oldest soul. Finally, the fear ran deeper than the souls in ben Ezra, and he could no longer stand it in the house. He wanted to leave, but when he opened the door he found that a cobweb had been spun across the entryway during the night. It was like any other cobweb, except it was red. When he tried to remove it, he noticed that the beautifully spun web was made of hair. He began to search for the owner. Although he found no clue, in town he noticed a foreign woman walking with her father. She had long red hair, but she paid no attention to ben Ezra. The next morning, ben Ezra again felt fear, and again he found a red cobweb spun across his door. When he met the girl that day, he offered her two bouquets of myrtle.

She smiled and asked:

"How did you discover me?"

"I immediately noticed," he said, "that inside me were three fears, not one."

Bibliography: John Buxtorf, "Praefacio" to the Basel edition of Halevi's book in Latin (*Liber Cosri,* Basilae, 1660); *Lexicon Cosri, continens colloquium seu disputationem de religione,* Regiemonti Borussiae excudebat typographus Ioannes Daubmannus, Anno 1691 (destroyed edition); *Evreiskaya enciklopedia,* St. Petersburg, 1906–1913, vol. I, pp. 1–16, includes an extensive article and bibliography on Halevi; a selected bibliography comes with the edition J. Halevi, *The Kuzari (Kitab al Khazari),* New York, 1968, pp. 311–313; the latest bilingual edition of the poems has been put out by Arno Press, New York, 1973; *Encyclopedia Judaica,* Jerusalem, 1971.

KAGHAN—title of the Khazar ruler; comes from the Jewish word *cohen,* which means "priest." The first kaghan after the Khazar Empire adopted Judaism was Sabriel, and his wife was Serah. The name of the kaghan who staged the Khazar polemic[v] and summoned to his court Jews, Greeks, and Arabs to interpret his dream is not known. According to the Hebrew sources cited by Daubmannus, prior to the Khazars' conversion to Judaism the kaghan had a dream that he recounted to his daughter, or sister, Princess Ateh,[v] in these words:

"I dreamed I was wading through waist-high water, reading a book. The water was the Kura River, muddy, full of weeds, the kind you drink through your hair or beard. Whenever a big wave comes along I lift up my book to keep it from getting wet, and then continue reading. The deep is nearby, and I have to finish reading before I reach it. Just then an angel appears, a bird perched on its hand, and it says to me, 'The Lord is pleased by your intentions, but not by your deeds.' Then I wake up and open my eyes. Even awake I am waist-high in water, in that same muddy Kura River with its weeds, I'm holding the same book, and before me stands the angel from my dream. That same angel, with the bird. I quickly shut my eyes, but the river, the angel, the bird, and everything else are still there. I open my eyes —the same thing again. Horrible. I read from the book in my hand—'Let him who puts on shoes not boast'— and there I shut my eyes, but still see the end of the sentence: '. . . like him who has taken them off.' That very same moment the angel's bird flew off and I opened my eyes. I could see the bird soaring away. And then I realized there was no more shutting of your eyes to the truth, no salvation in being blindfolded, no dream and reality, no being awake or asleep. Everything is one and the same continuing eternal day and world, coiling around you like a snake. That is when I saw vast, remote happiness as being small but close; when I perceived the great cause as empty, and the small as my love. . . . And did what I did."

KHAZARS$^\triangledown$ —a warrior people who settled
in the Caucasus between the 7th and 10th centuries, had
a powerful state, ships sailing two seas, the Caspian and
the Black, as many winds as there are fish, three capitals
(summer, winter, and wartime), and years as towering
as the pine trees. They preached a faith unknown
today, worshipped salt, carved their temples into underground salt rocks or saline hills. According to Halevi,✿ they adopted Judaism in the year 740, and the last
Khazar kaghan, Joseph, even made contact with the
Spanish Jews, because he sailed on the seventh day, when
the earth curses man and its malediction drives ships
away from shore. These ties were broken in the year 970,
when the Russians captured the Khazar capital and destroyed the Khazar state. Some Khazars subsequently
merged with the East European Jews, others with the
Arabs, Turks, and Greeks, so that today we know only
about that small oasis of Khazar people who, without
either a religion or a language of their own, continued to
live in autonomous districts in Eastern and Central Eu-
rope until the outbreak of World War II (1939), and
then entirely disappeared. The Jewish version of their
name is Kuzari (plural Kuzarim). It is generally held
that only the Khazar nobility adopted Judaism; however,
between the 7th and 10th centuries, in the Pannonian
plains, there was a center for Judaization that is sometimes attributed to the Khazars (Chelarevo†). Around
the year 800, in Westphalia, Druthmar of Aquitaine
mentions *"gentes Hunorum que ab et gazari vocantur,"*
stressing that they were circumcised, were of the faith of
Moses, and were strong. In the 12th century, Cinnamus
said that the Khazars lived by the law of Moses, albeit
not always orthodoxly. The Jewish kaghans were men-

tioned as early as the 10th century by Arab sources (Ibn Rustah, Al-Istakhri, Ibn Hawqal).

A text known as the "Khazar Correspondence" provides interesting information about the Khazars. This text is preserved in at least two versions, one of which is more detailed than the other; it has yet to be fully elucidated by scholars. Kept at Oxford and written in the Hebrew language, it is the correspondence of Joseph the king of the Khazars and Hasdai Ibn Shaprut of Moorish Spain, who wrote to the Khazar king in the middle of the 10th century, asking him to reply to the following questions:

1. Is there a Jewish state anywhere in the world?
2. How did the Jews come to Khazaria?
3. How did the Khazars' conversion to the Jewish faith take place?
4. Where does the king of the Khazars live?
5. What tribe does he belong to?
6. What is his role in wars?
7. Does he suspend war on the Sabbath?
8. Does the Khazar king possess any information whatsoever about the possible end of the world?

The reply explains the Khazar polemic,▽ which preceded the Khazars' conversion to Judaism.

There is another source in connection with this polemic, but it has not been preserved. In his entry on the Khazars, Daubmannus✿ cites the manuscript *On Khazar Affairs* (probably a Latin version). The closing words of this text show that its oldest sections relate to a report that probably served to brief the Hebrew representative, Rabbi Isaac Sangari, prior to his departure on his Khazar mission, where he participated in the celebrated polemic. The preserved parts of the text read:

ON THE NAME KHAZARS: The Khazar state is

called the "kaghan's empire" or the "kaghanate," and
gone from its name is that of the original Khazar Empire, which preceded the kaghanate and built it with the
sword. Khazars are grudgingly called by this name in
their own state. They always avoid the Khazar name
and use some other. In regions near the Crimea, where
there is also a Greek population, the Khazars are known
as the "non-Greek population" or as "Greeks who have
not joined Christianity"; in the South, where there are
also Jews, Khazars are called the "non-Jewish group"; in
the East, which has a partly Arab population, the Khazars are called the "non-Islamized people." Khazars who
have adopted one of the foreign faiths (Jewish, Greek, or
Arab) are no longer called Khazars, but are counted as
Jews, Greeks, or Arabs. The accidental few who happen
to convert to the Khazar faith are addressed in Khazar
circles by their preconversion names; in other words,
they are still considered Greeks, Jews, or Arabs, even
though they are now of the Khazar faith. For instance,
instead of saying that some man was a Khazar, a Greek
recently put it like this: "In the kaghanate, Khazar-
speaking people who have not converted to the Greek
faith are called future Jews." One can find in the Khazar
state learned Jews, Greeks, or Arabs who know a great
deal about the Khazars' past, books, and monuments,
who speak of them at length and with praise; some of
them even write Khazar history; but the Khazars themselves are not permitted to speak about their own past or
write books about it.

THE KHAZAR LANGUAGE is musical, and the
poems I heard recited in it sounded lovely, but I do not
remember them; it is said they were composed by a
Khazar princess. The language has seven genders; along
with the masculine, feminine, and neuter, there are also
genders for eunuchs, for sexless women (those whom the

Arab shaitan blighted and robbed), for those who change sex, be they males who switch to female or the other way around, and for lepers, who along with their disease must adopt a new form of speech to reveal their malady as soon as they engage in conversation. Girls have a different accent from boys, and men from women: boys learn Arabic, Hebrew, or Greek depending on whether they live in a Greek-populated region, in an area where there are Jews mixed with Khazars, or the territory of the Saracens and Persians. Consequently, the Jewish "kamesh," "holem," and "shurek," the big, medium, and small "u" and middle "a," come through when boys speak the Khazar language. Girls, on the other hand, do not learn Hebrew, Greek, or Arabic, and their accent is different and purer. As is known, when a people vanishes, the first to disappear are the upper classes, and with them literature; all that remains are books of law, which the people know by heart. The same can be said of the Khazars. In their capital, sermons in the Khazar language are expensive, whereas in Hebrew, Arabic, or Greek they are cheap or free of charge. Curiously, once they are outside their state the Khazars are reluctant to reveal their Khazar origin, preferring to avoid one another and conceal the fact that they speak and understand the Khazar language, hiding it from their own compatriots even more than from foreigners. In the country itself, people not proficient in the Khazar language, which is the official language, are more highly regarded in the civil and administrative services. Consequently, even people who are fluent in the Khazar language will often deliberately speak it incorrectly, with a foreign accent, from which they derive a manifest advantage. Even with translators—for instance, from Khazar into Hebrew, or Greek into Khazar—the people selected are those who make mistakes in the Khazar language or pretend to do so.

JUDICIARY: Under Khazar law, the sentence for the same crime is in the Jewish-populated part of the state one to two years labor as a galley slave, in the Arab-inhabited part of the empire half a year, in the Greek-inhabited region no punishment, and in the central part of the state, which alone is called the "Khazar district" (although the Khazars are everywhere the largest group), beheading.

SALT AND SLEEP: The letters of the Khazar alphabet take their names from salted foods, and the numbers from types of salt; the Khazars recognize seven types of salt. Only the salty regard of God does not cause aging; otherwise the Khazars believe that aging comes from looking at one's own body or another's, because looks plow and tear through bodies with the most varied and lethal tools, creating their passions, hates, plans, and cravings. The Khazars pray by weeping, for tears are a part of God, by virtue of always having a bit of salt at the bottom, just as shells hold pearls. Sometimes women take a handkerchief and fold it until it can be folded no more; that is a prayer. The Khazars also follow the cult of sleep. They believe that anyone who has lost salt cannot fall asleep, which is why such attention is paid to sleep. But that is not all; there is something I could not fully grasp, like a road you cannot hear from the noise of the cart. They believe that the people who inhabit every man's past lie as though enslaved and cursed in his memory; they can take no other step than the one they once took, can meet no one but the people they once met, cannot even grow old. The only freedom allowed ancestors, allowed entire bygone nations of fathers and mothers retained in memories, is occasional respite in our dreams. There, in our dreams, these figures from our memories acquire some measure of freedom; they move around a little, meet a new face, change partners in their hates and loves, and assume a small illusion of life.

Hence, sleep occupies a prominent place in the Khazar faith, because in dreams the past, forever captured within itself, gains freedom and new promise.

MIGRATIONS: The old Khazar tribes are believed to have resettled once every ten generations and with every migration to have become more a nation of traders and less a nation of warriors. Suddenly, instead of being quick with their sword and lance, they could work out the price of a ship, a house, or a meadow in jingling ducats or spilling silver. Many explanations have been given for this, but the one I find most convincing says that they became infertile during this cycle and had to move in order to maintain the species and renew fertility. As soon as their fertility was revived, they would return to their homeland and again pick up their spears.

RELIGIOUS CUSTOMS: The Khazar kaghan does not allow religion to interfere with state or military affairs. He says, "If a saber had two tips, it would be called a pickax." This attitude is the same whether the faith in question is the Khazar, the Jewish, the Greek, or the Arab. But where the shoe fits some it pinches others. Whereas our own, the Greek, and the Arab faiths dropped roots in other states as well and enjoy strong foreign protection from our fellow tribesmen and other nations, the Khazar faith is without such foreign protection, so, when pressure is brought to bear, it suffers the most; in other words, the first three flourish at its expense. A case in point is the kaghan's recent attempt to reduce monastic landholdings in the country and cut down the number of temples by ten for each religion. Since there were fewer Khazar temples than Jewish, Arab, or Greek temples to start with, the Khazar church was the most severely affected. This can be seen at every step. Khazar cemeteries, for instance, are dying out. In areas of the state inhabited by Greeks (like the Crimea), by Jews (as in Tamatarkha), or by Arabs and Persians (along the Persian border), Khazar cemeteries are increasingly being placed under lock and key, Khazar burial rites are denied, and the roads teem with dying Khazars heading for the area around Itil, the capital, where Khazar cemeteries still function. Their souls tremble in their throats as they take to the road. "The past is not deep enough behind us," lament the Khazar priests, who, of course, see what is happening. "Our people have to await maturity, so that the past can sufficiently increase its stocks and create a broad enough basis to build the future successfully."

It is interesting that in the Khazar Empire there are Greeks and Armenians who are of the same Christian faith but are constantly at one another's throats. However, the result of their arguments is always the same and bespeaks their wisdom: after every conflict, the Greeks and Armenians demand separate temples. Since the Khazar state approves these expansions, the two sides come out of every conflict reinforced and with double the number of their temples, which, of course, works to the detriment of the Khazars and their faith.

THE KHAZAR DICTIONARY embraces the books of the dream hunters, a very powerful Khazar religious sect. The dictionary is a kind of Holy Scripture, a Bible to them. Complete with biographies of various personages of the male and female sex, *The Khazar Dictionary* is a mosaic portrait of a single character whom we call Adam Cadmon. Here are two fragments from the dictionary:

"The truth is transparent and goes unnoticed, whereas lies are opaque and let in neither light nor gaze. There is a third version, where the two mix, and this is the most customary. With one eye we see through the truth, and that gaze is lost forever in infinity; with the other eye we do not see even an inch through the lies, and that gaze can penetrate no further, but remains on earth and ours; and so we push through life sideways. Hence, the truth cannot be understood on its own, like a lie, but only by comparing it with lies, by comparing the white space with the letters of our Book, because the white spaces in *The Khazar Dictionary* mark the translucent places of the divine truth and name (Adam Cadmon), and the black letters between the white spaces are where our eyes cannot penetrate beyond the surface."

"Letters can also be compared with items of clothing. In winter you put on wools or furs, a scarf, a hat with its winter lining turned out, and you button yourself up; in summer you are in cotton, you discard your heavy wear; in between summer and winter you add to or take away from your clothing. So it is with reading. In the various seasons of your years, the content of your books will differ, because you will combine the clothing in various ways. For the time being, *The Khazar Dictionary* is still just a heap of random letters, names, and pseudonyms (Adam Cadmon's). But with time you will dress and acquire more.... Dreams are the Friday to what in reality is called Saturday. They lead to It and are one with that day, and so it should be with each day (Thursday to Sunday, Monday to Wednesday, and so on). He who can read them together will have them and will have a part of the body (of Adam Cadmon) inside him...."

In the hope that my words will be of assistance to Rabbi Isaac, this is as much as I can say, I who am called Yabel on Friday, Tubalkain on Sunday, and Yubal only on the Sabbath. Having made this effort, I shall now rest, for remembering is permanent circumcision....

KHAZAR JAR —A Khazar dream reader who was still a novice in a monastery was given a jar as a present, and he placed it in his cell. That evening he dropped his ring into it, but when he looked for the ring in the morning it was not to be found. He stuck his hand inside the jar but could not reach the bottom. And since his arm was longer than the jar was deep, this surprised him. He picked up the jar; the floor beneath it was flat and revealed no opening, and the bottom of the jar was sealed like any other. He took a stick and tried to touch bottom with it, but to no avail; the bottom seemed to be escaping him. He thought, "I am, that is where my limit is," and asked his teacher Mokaddasa al-Safer ⚭ ⚭ to explain the meaning of the jar. The teacher picked up a pebble, dropped it into the jar, and counted. When he had reached seventy, a splash was heard from deep down in the jar, as though something had hit water, and the teacher said:

"I could tell you what your jar means, but ponder first whether it is worth it. As soon as I tell you, the jar will inevitably be worth less to you and less to others. No matter how much it is worth, it cannot be worth more than everything; yet, once I tell you what it is, it will no longer be all the things it is not, and what it is now."

When the novice agreed, the teacher picked up the stick and smashed the jar. The startled boy asked him why he had damaged it, and the teacher replied:

"The damage would be if I had first told you what the jar was for and had then smashed it. This way, you don't know its purpose and there is no damage done; it will continue to serve you as though it had never been smashed. . . ."

Indeed, the Khazar jar serves to this day, although it has long since ceased to exist.

K HAZAR POLEMIC[∇] —Hebrew sources cite this as the key event in the Khazars' conversion to Judaism. Since accounts of the event are scarce and contradictory, the exact date of the polemic is unknown, and the time of Judaization is confused with the moment when the three dream interpreters visited the Khazar capital. The earliest preserved account, dating from the 10th century, is the correspondence between the Khazar Kaghan Joseph (who already practiced Judaism) and Hasdai Ibn Shaprut, the minister of the caliph in Córdoba. Hasdai was a Jew and had asked the kaghan to describe the circumstances under which the Khazars had adopted the Jewish faith. According to this correspondence, it all took place under the reign of Kaghan Bulan, at the invitation of an angel, right after the capture of Ardabil (around 731). It was then, if this source is to be believed, that a debate on religions was conducted at the court of the Khazar kaghan. Since the Jewish envoy bested the Greek and the Arab representatives, the Khazars adopted Judaism under Kaghan Bulan's successor, Obadiah. The second source is a fragment of a Jewish letter found in 1912 in Cambridge, England. It comes from a manuscript belonging to the Cairo Synagogue (ed. Schechter). The letter was written in approximately 950 by a Jew of Khazar origin to Minister Shaprut, as a supplement to Kaghan Bulan's letter to the same personage at the court in Córdoba. This source contends that the Judaization of the Khazars took place before the polemic and that it happened as follows. A nonpracticing Jew returned from war a hero and became the Khazar kaghan. His wife and her father expected that he would now accept the faith of his forefathers, but he himself said nothing. The turning point (according to Daubmannus✿) came one evening when the kaghan's wife said to him:

Beneath the heavenly equator in the valleys where the sweet and saline dew meet, there grows a huge poisonous fungus, and the tasty little edible mushrooms on its cap transform its contaminated blood into sweetness. The deer like to invigorate their masculine strength by nibbling these little mushrooms. But if they are careless and bite down too deep, they ingest some of the big poisonous fungus along with the little mushrooms, and then they die.

Every evening, when I kiss my beloved, I think: It is only natural that one day I will bite down too deep. . . .

Upon hearing these words, the kaghan began practicing Judaism. All this transpired before the polemic, which, according to this source, took place during the reign of the Byzantine Emperor Leo III (717–740). After the polemic, Judaism became fully established among the Khazars and neighboring peoples during the reign of Kaghan Sabriel, who is one and the same person with Kaghan Obadiah, because (according to Daubmannus) he was called Sabriel during the even years and Obadiah during the odd years of his rule.

The most exhaustive Hebrew source on the Khazar polemic is also the most important, although it is of a later date. This is the book *Al Khazari* by Judah Halevi,✿ the famous poet and chronicler of the Khazar polemic. He says that the polemic and the Khazars' conversion to the Jewish faith took place four centuries before the writing of his book, which would place it in the year 740. Finally, there is Bacher, who found that the impact of the Khazars' Judaization is reflected in midrash literature. The legends that told about the event especially flourished in the Crimea, the Taman peninsula, and Tamatarkha, known as a Jewish city in the Khazar Empire.

Briefly, the event that was these sources' object of interest took place in the following way. In the summer capital of the kaghan, on the Black Sea, where they whitewashed the pears on their branches in the autumn and picked them fresh in winter, three theologians were brought together: a Jewish rabbi, a Christian Greek, and an Arab mullah. The kaghan informed them of his decision to convert, along with all his people, to the religion of the one theologian who gave the most satisfactory interpretation of a dream. An angel had appeared in the Khazar kaghan's dream and had said to him: "God is pleased by your intentions, but not by your deeds." The debate centered on these words, and the Hebrew sources cited by Daubmannus describe the further course of events.

The Hebrew representative, Rabbi Isaac Sangari,✿ said nothing at first, letting the other two, the Greek and the Arab, speak. When it seemed that the kaghan was about to be swayed by the arguments of the Islamic representative, a Khazar princess by the name of Ateh▽ joined in the discussion, admonishing the Arab in these words:

You are too wise when you speak to me. I watch the clouds drift and disappear behind the mountains and recognize in them my fleeting thoughts. Tears sometimes trickle from them, but in the brief hours when the clouds part I see a patch of clear sky with your face at the bottom, because it is only then that there is nothing to prevent me from seeing you as you are.

In reply, the mullah told the kaghan that he was not suggesting any kind of trickery to the Khazars, but, rather, he was suggesting a holy book, the Koran, because the Khazars did not have the Holy Book: we have all learned to walk because we are made out of two lame legs, but you are still limping.

Princess Ateh then asked the Arab:

"Every book has a father and a mother. There is the father, who dies impregnating the mother and who gives the child a name. And there is the (book's) mother, who gives birth to the child, nurses it, and releases it into the world. Who is the mother of your Divine Book?"

When the Arab was unable to answer this question, merely repeating that he was not suggesting trickery, he was suggesting the Holy Book, which is the messenger of love between God and man, Princess Ateh wound up the discussion with these words:

The Persian shah and the Greek emperor decided to exchange lavish gifts as a sign of peace. One gift-bearing legation set out from Constantinople and the other from Isfahan. They met in Baghdad, where they learned that Nadir, the Persian shah, had been deposed, and that the Greek emperor had died. The two legations were thus compelled to stay in Baghdad for a while, not knowing what to do with the treasures they were bearing, and fearing for their lives at every step. Seeing that bit by bit they were beginning to spend the treasure, they consulted on what to do. One of them said:

"Whatever we do will be wrong. So let us each take one ducat and throw away the rest. . . ."

Which is what they did.

And what are we to do with our love, the love we send one another through our messengers? Will that too not remain in the hands of the messengers who take a ducat each and throw the rest away?

Having heard her words, the kaghan decided that the princess was right, and he rejected the Arab, saying, as quoted by Halevi:

"Why do Christians and Moslems, who have divided the inhabited part of the world between them, war against one another, each serving his own god of pure intent, by fasting and praying, like monks or recluses? And they accomplish everything by killing, believing that this is the most devout way to bring them closer to God. They wage war, believing that heaven and eternal bliss will be their reward. Yet not both convictions can be accepted."

The kaghan reached the following conclusion:

"Your caliph has fleets of green-sailed ships and soldiers who chew on both sides. If we cross over to his religion, how many Khazars will be left? It is better for us, since convert we must, to join the Jews expelled by the Greeks, to join the poor and the wandering who came here from Khorezm during the time of Kitabia. Their only army is what they can fit into a temple or onto a scroll."

The kaghan then turned to the Hebrew representative and asked him what he had to say about his religion. Rabbi Isaac Sangari replied that the Khazars did not have to convert to a new religion at all: they could keep their old one. His words caused general surprise, so the rabbi explained:

"You are not Khazars. You are Jews and should return to your rightful place: to the living God of your ancestors."

Only then did the rabbi begin to expound on his teachings to the kaghan. The days dripped like rain, and he talked and talked. First he told the kaghan about the seven things created before the creation of the world: heaven, the Torah, justice, Israel, the Throne of Glory, Jerusalem, and the Messiah, the son of David. Then he enumerated the most exalted things: the spirit of living God, air from the spirit, water from the wind, and fire from the water. And then he listed the three mothers: in the universe—air, water, and fire; in the soul—the chest, stomach, and head; in the year—moisture, frost, and heat. And the seven double consonants: "beth," "gimel," "daleth," "kaf," "peh," "resh," and "tav," which are: in the universe—Saturn, Jupiter, Mars, the sun, Venus, Mercury, and the moon; in the soul—wisdom, wealth, power, life, mercy, progeny, and peace; and in the year —the Sabbath, Thursday, Tuesday, Sunday, Friday, Wednesday, and Monday. . . .

And the kaghan began to understand the language spoken to Adam by God in heaven, and he said: "The wine I am pressing now will be drunk by others after me."

The kaghan's lengthy talks with Rabbi Isaac can be found in Judah Halevi's book on the Khazars, where the kaghan's conversion is described in the following way:

"Afterward, says the history of the Khazars, the Khazar kaghan departed with his vizier for the barren mountains by the sea. One night they came upon a cave where some Jews were celebrating Passover. They told them who they were, adopted their faith, were circumcised in the cave, and then returned home, eager to learn Jewish law. But they kept their conversion secret until the occasion presented itself for them to disclose the entire affair slowly to a handful of intimate friends. When the number of these friends increased, they made it public and persuaded the rest of the Khazars to adopt the Jewish faith. They sent for teachers and books from other countries and began studying the Torah. . . ."

In fact, the Khazars' conversion to Judaism evolved in two phases. The first came immediately after the Khazar victory over the Arabs at Ardabil, south of the Caucasus, in the year 730, when they used the plundered booty to build a temple modeled after the biblical one. In approximately 740, Judaism was adopted in certain external forms. Kaghan Bulan invited rabbis from other countries to cultivate the Jewish faith among the Khazars. This early Judaism of the Khazars appears to have included the Khorezm people, who, when the Hursat Uprising was crushed, had fled in the sixties or eighties of the 8th century to the Khazar court, led by the rabbi.

The reform of this original Judaism was undertaken around the year 800, by Kaghan Obadiah, who began building synagogues and schools, where the Khazars learned about the Torah, Mishnah, Talmud, and Jewish liturgy; in other words, rabbinical Judaism was introduced.

In a way, the Arabs played a decisive role in the entire process. Leading figures in the Khazar state adopted Judaism at a time when Islamic influence had declined because of the power struggle between two dynasties in the Arab caliphate—the Omayyad and the Abbasid. Consequently, Masudi's claim that the king of the Khazars became a Jew during the reign of Caliph Harun Al-Rashid (786–809) checks out with the time of the reform of Judaism undertaken by the Khazar Kaghan Obadiah.

L I B E R C O S R I —title of the Latin translation of Judah Halevi's ✿ book about the Khazars, which appeared in 1660. The translator, John Buxtorf (1599–1664), gave a comparative Hebrew version along with his own Latin translation. Buxtorf was the son of a father who carried the same name and surname and was introduced to the biblical, rabbinical, and medieval Hebrew language at an early age. He also translated Maimonides into Latin (Basel, 1629) and took part in a lengthy public debate with Louis Capella on biblical diacritical marks and letters denoting vowels. He published his translation of Halevi's book in Basel in 1660, and the foreword shows that he worked from the Venetian editions of ben Tibbon's * Hebrew translation. Like Halevi, he believed that vowels are the souls of letters and that there are three vowels to each of the twenty-two consonants. Reading is really like trying to hit one tossed stone with another; the consonants are the stones, the vowels their velocity. In his opinion, seven numbers were brought onto Noah's ark during the flood, and they were shaped like a dove because it can count to seven. But these numbers bore the mark of vowels, not consonants.

Although known of since 1577, the "Khazar Correspondence" did not reach the broader public until Buxtorf's 1660 translation of Halevi, to which he appended Hasdai Ibn Shaprut's letter and Khazar King Joseph's reply.

TITLE PAGE OF HALEVI'S BOOK ON THE KHAZARS
(8TH-CENTURY BASEL EDITION)

LUKAREVICH (LUCCARI), EPHROSINIA
(17th century)—Born into the Getaldich-Kruhoradich
family of Dubrovnik landed gentry, she married a noble-
man from the Luccari family. In her palazzo she kept a
caged jaybird, whose presence in the house was medici-
nal, and on the wall a Greek clock that played hymns
and psalms on holidays. She was wont to say that opening every new door in life is as uncertain as dealing cards,
and about her rich husband she said that he dined on
silence and water. She was known for her uninhibited
behavior and was beautiful; she defended herself by saying with a smile that flesh and honor do not go together.
She had two thumbs on each hand, and always wore
gloves, even at meals. She liked red, blue, and yellow
foods, and wore dresses in these same colors. She had
two children, a boy and a girl. One night, watching
through the window that separated her room from her
mother's, the seven-year-old daughter saw her mother
give birth. Attended by her caged bird, Lady Ephrosinia
gave birth to a bearded little old man with spurs on his
bare feet, who entered the world crying, "A hungry
Greek will even to heaven go," bit off his own umbilical
cord, and rushed off, grabbing not clothes but a cap and
calling for his sister by name. The little girl was struck
dumb, could be neither led nor pushed, and was removed from sight to Konavlje. These things were said
to happen to Lady Ephrosinia because she had sat on
bread and was secretly having an affair with a Jew
named Samuel Cohen ✿ from the Dubrovnik ghetto. To
accusations about her free ways, Lady Ephrosinia coldly
replied that she accepted lectures from no one.

"The truth be told, if I could choose from one

hundred charming, strong, and noble dark-maned lords, whose days were not fleeing, then tempted might I be. But in Ragusa not even one hundred such fifers can in a hundred years be found! And who has one hundred years to wait?"

The other accusations she did not even answer. Namely, it was said that she had been Mora as a girl, became a witch when she married, and after her death would be a vampire for three years. Not everybody believed this third part, because it was held that vampires were most often Turks, less often Greeks, and never Jews. And it was whispered that Lady Ephrosinia was secretly of Moses' faith.

Be that as it may, when Samuel Cohen was banished from Dubrovnik, Lady Ephrosinia did not take it lightly: it was said that she would die of sorrow, and that every night she held her fist, the thumbs clenched on either side, like a rock against her heart. But, instead of dying, one morning she disappeared from Dubrovnik; she was subsequently seen in Konavlje, then at Dance sitting on a grave at high noon combing her hair, and later traveling north to Belgrade and down to the Danube in search of her lover. When she heard that Cohen had died at Kladovo, she did not return home. She cut off and buried her hair, and no one knows what happened to her after that. Her death is believed to be described in a long, sad folk poem, recorded in Kotor in 1721 and preserved only in Italian translation under the title *The Latin Maiden and the Walachian Count Dracula.* Although the translation is damaged, the heroine of the poem is believed to represent Lady Ephrosinia, and Count Dracula a person by the name of Vlad Malescu, who actually lived in Transylvania in the 17th and 18th centuries. Briefly, the poem imparts the following information:

The white reeds were already sprouting when a beautiful,

sorrowful woman went down to the Danube to search for her beloved, who had been sent to war. When she heard he had been killed, she went to Count Dracula, who looks through tomorrow's eye and is the most costly healer of sorrow. He had an almost black skull under his hair, a wrinkle of silence on his face, and an enormous penis, which on holidays he tied to a chaffinch and let the bird carry for him on the long silk thread as it flew ahead. Tucked under his belt was a small scrap of shell with which he could skin a living man to perfection; he could then dress him again in the same skin, holding him by the pigtail. He concocted potions for a sweet death, and his court was constantly besieged by vampires dousing candles and asking Dracula to let them die once more. Death was their only remaining contact with life. The knobs on the doors leading into his living quarters turned of their own accord, and in front of his court a small whirlwind drew everything within reach into its kneading swirl. It had been whirling here for seven thousand years now, and moistening its center or eye was the moonlight which had shone as brightly as noon for all these seven thousand years. When the young woman arrived, Count Dracula's servants were sitting in the shade of the whirlwind drinking; one of them would take a swig from a jug while the other emitted long sounds resembling a song, and the first one drank until the other took a breath. Then they reversed roles. In honor of the visitor, they sang first an evensong, then a harvest song, and lastly a song sung "heads together," which went as follows:

"Every spring, when the birds start counting the fish in the Danube, a white reed grows at the mouth of the river into the sea. (It grows only for the three days that the fresh and the salt water intermingle, its seeds are swifter than any other, it blossoms faster than a turtle moves, reaching heights that overtake the ants crawling up it. On dry land, the seed of the white reed can lie dormant for up to two hundred *years, but when it encounters the damp, it germinates in less than an hour, within three to four hours it reaches the height of one meter, then it thickens, and by the end of the day you can no longer put your hands around it. By the morning it is as thick as a man's waist and as tall as a house, and fishermen often tie their nets to the white reed, which, as it grows, pulls the nets out of the water by itself. Birds know that the white reed also grows in the entrails, and they are careful not to swallow its seed or its shoot. Still, boatmen and shepherds will sometimes see a bird being torn apart in the sky, and they know that this is because the bird, in some fit of madness or avian grief, reminiscent of a human lie, has pecked at the seed of the white reed, which then sprouted inside it and tore it asunder in the sky. Something like tooth-marks are always found near the root of the white reed; the shepherds say that the white reed grows not from the soil but from the mouth of some underwater demon that whistles and talks through it, luring birds and other greedy creatures to its seed. That is why the white reed is not used to make flutes: one does not blow another's flute. Other fishermen say that, instead of using their own seed, birds sometimes impregnate their mates with the seed of the white reed; thus is the egg of death renewed on earth. . . ."*

When the song was over, the girl let her greyhounds loose on the foxes, entered Count Dracula's tower alone, and gave him a bag of gold so he would heal her sorrow. He embraced her, led her into the bedchamber, and did not let her go until the greyhounds had returned from their fox hunt. It was morning when they parted; in the evening the shepherds found the greyhounds whimpering by the Danube in front of a lovely young woman torn to pieces like a bird that had been impregnated with the seed of the white reed. Only her silken dress still clung to the huge stalk that had already spread its roots and rustled through her hair. The girl had given birth to a mercurial daughter—her own death. In that

death her beauty was divided into whey and curdled milk,
and at the bottom was a mouth holding the root of the reed.

Mokaddasa al-Safer℮ (8th and 9th
centuries)—the best of the dream readers and dream
hunters.† Legend has it that he put together the masculine part of the Khazar encyclopedia, while the feminine
part was compiled by Princess Ateh.▽ Al-Safer did not
want to write his part of the encyclopedia (or Khazar
dictionary) for his contemporaries or descendants, and so
he compiled it in the ancient 5th-century Khazar language, which none of his contemporaries understood; he
wrote it exclusively for his ancestors, for those who had
once dreamed about their part of Adam Cadmon's body,
the part that will never be dreamed again. The Khazar
Princess Ateh was Al-Safer's mistress, and there is a
legend about how he laved her breasts with his beard
dipped in wine. Al-Safer ended up in captivity, and
the reason for it, according to one source, was a misun-
derstanding between Princess Ateh and the Khazar
kaghan. The argument was caused by a letter the
princess had written and never sent, but which had
fallen into the kaghan's hands all the same. Since it referred to Al-Safer, it aroused jealousy and anger in the
kaghan. It said:

I planted roses in your boots; I have a wallflower growing
out of your hat. As I await you in my lone and eternal night,
the days snow upon me like shreds of torn missives. I put
them together and read out your loving words letter by letter.
But I read only the little I can, because an unknown hand-
writing sometimes appears, and a piece of some other letter
gets mixed up with yours: somebody else's day and letter
interferes with my night. I await your return, when letters

and days will no longer be necessary. And I wonder: will the other one still write to me then, or will it still be night?

According to other sources (which Daubmannus ✿ connects with the manuscript of the Cairo Synagogue), this letter or poem was never intended for the kaghan, but for Al-Safer himself, and it referred to him and Adam Cadmon. In any event, the letter aroused the jealousy or political suspicions of the Khazar kaghan (because the dream hunters were Princess Ateh's strong opposition party, which put up resistance to the kaghan). Al-Safer was punished by being locked in an iron cage and suspended from a tree. Every year, through her dreams, Princess Ateh sent him the key to her bedchamber, but all she could do to ease his plight was to bribe the demons to have someone briefly replace Al-Safer in the cage. And so Al-Safer's life consisted partly of the lives of other people, who alternated in lending him a few of their own weeks. Meanwhile, the lovers exchanged messages in a special way of their own: he would scratch a few words with his teeth on the back of a tortoise or a crab caught from the river underneath his cage and would then return them to the water, and she would answer in the same way, sending her messages of love inscribed on living tortoises into the river that merges with the sea underneath the cage. When the devil divested Princess Ateh of her memory and obliged her to forget the Khazar language, she stopped writing, but Al-Safer continued sending messages, trying to remind her of his name and the words of her poems.

Several hundred years after this event, two tortoises with messages inscribed on them were caught on the shores of the Caspian Sea, messages from a woman and a man who had loved each other. The tortoises were still together, and the messages of the loving couple could be read on their backs. The man's message read:

You are like the girl who always rose late; when she married in the next village and for the first time had to rise early, she saw the hoarfrost on the fields and said to her mother-in-law, "We don't have that in our village!" Like her, you think there is no love in the world, because you have never been awake early enough to encounter it, although every morning it is there on time. . . .

The woman's message was shorter, amounting to just a few words:

My native land is silence, my food—muteness. I sit in my name like an oarsman in a boat. I hate you so much I can't sleep.

Mokaddasa was buried in a grave shaped like a goat.

SANGARI, ISAAC (8th century)—rabbi, Hebrew representative in the Khazar polemic.▽ It is not until the 13th century that he is mentioned as an expert on the Cabala and as having led the Khazars▽ to Judaism. He made a point of stressing the values of the Hebrew language, but he knew many other languages as well. He believed that the differences between languages lay in the following: all languages except God's are the languages of suffering, the dictionaries of pain. "I have noticed," he said, "that my sufferings are drained through a rupture in time or in myself, for otherwise they would be more numerous by now. The same holds true for languages." R. Gedaliah (c. 1587) established that the answers given by Isaac Sangari at the Khazar court were delivered in the Khazar language. According to Halevi,✿ Sangari used the teachings of Rabbi Nahum the Scribe, who recorded how the sages learned from the prophets. "I heard it from Rabbi Mayash," wrote Rabbi Nahum, said Sangari to the kaghan as recorded by Halevi, "I heard it from Rabbi Mayash, who learned it from the 'pairs,' who had received it from the prophets as a command given to Moses on Mount Sinai. They were careful not to pass on the teachings of individuals, as can be seen from the last words uttered to his son by an old man on his deathbed:

" 'My son, in future, defer the opinions I taught you to four designated men.' 'Why,' asked the son, 'did you not defer your own opinions?' 'Because,' replied the old man, 'my opinions were taken from many who had in turn learned from many. And so I upheld my own tradition, and they upheld theirs. But you have learned from only one person, from me. And it is better to ignore the teaching of one person and accept that of several. . . .' "

It is said that Sangari thwarted the arrival of the Arab participant in the polemic at the Khazar court by arranging to have the polemic held at a time when comets could not help the Arab and when his entire faith could fit into a jug of water. Sangari himself almost did not make it to the polemic. Daubmannus ✿ recounts the following story:

Isaac Sangari set sail for the Khazar capital. But his ship was attacked by the Saracens, who began killing everything in sight. Jews jumped overboard to save themselves, but the pirates killed them with their oars. Only Isaac Sangari stayed calmly on board. Surprised, the Saracens asked him why he did not jump into the waves like the others.

"I can't swim," Sangari lied, and that saved his neck. Instead of slaying him, the pirates shoved him into the sea and sailed away.

"The heart in the soul is like a king in war," Isaac Sangari observed, "but sometimes even in war man must act like the heart in the soul."

Thus, Sangari finally arrived at the Khazar court, and

during the polemic with the Christian and Islamic representatives he explained a dream to the Khazar kaghan, thereby persuading him to convert along with the other Khazars to the Jewish faith, a faith that expects more of the future than of the past. He explained the words spoken by the angel to the kaghan in his dream, the words "God is pleased by your intentions, but not by your deeds," comparing them to the story of Adam's son Seth.

"There is a tremendous difference," said Isaac Sangari to the kaghan, "between Adam, who was created by Jehovah, and his son Seth, who was created by Adam. Seth and all people after him are God's intention, but man's deed. Hence, a distinction should be made between intent and deed. The intention in man remains pure, godly, the verb or logos, which precedes the act as the concept of the act, but the deed is earthly; it bears the name Seth. In it, virtues and vices are inside one another like a set of hollow dolls. This is the only way to uncover man, by lifting one hollow doll from the next, the bigger bell from the smaller. So you should not feel that the angel who spoke those words in your dream was admonishing you; on the contrary, nothing could be further from the truth. He simply wanted to draw your attention to your true nature. . . ."

SCHULTZ, DR. DOROTHEA (Cracow, 1944–   )—Slavist, university professor in Jerusalem, maiden name Kwaszniewska. Her records at Jagellonian University in Poland, where she graduated, and at Yale University in the United States, where she earned her doctorate, give no details about her origin. The daughter of a Jewish mother and a Polish father, Kwaszniewska was born in Cracow under unusual circumstances. Her mother had left her a written note which had belonged to Dorothea's father: "My heart is my daughter; I orient myself by the stars, and my heart by the moon and by the pain that lies at the end of all speed...." Kwaszniewska never discovered who had written these words. Her mother's brother, Ashkenaz Scholem, disappeared in the Jewish pogrom in 1943 during the German occupation of Poland, but he managed to save his sister before disappearing. Taking matters into his own hands, he got her forged papers in the name of a Polish woman, and then he married her. The wedding took place in Warsaw, in the Church of St. Thomas, and it was considered a marriage between a converted Jew and a Polish woman. He was smoking his mint tea instead of tobacco when he was taken away, and his sister and wife, Ana Scholem, who was still taken for a Polish woman and indeed carried the maiden name of one Ana Zakiewicz, promptly divorced her husband (and brother, a fact known only to her), thereby saving her skin. She immediately remarried. Her second husband was a widower named Kwaszniewski who had eyes like freckled eggshells, a feeble tongue, but horned thoughts. They had only one child—Dorothea Kwaszniewska. After getting her degree in Slavic studies, Dorothea went to the United States, where she later obtained her doctorate in Old Slavonic literature. But when Isaac Schultz, whom she knew from her student days, moved to Israel, she went there to join him. In 1967 he was wounded in the Israeli-Egyptian war, and the very next year she married him, lived in Tel Aviv and Jerusalem, conducted courses in the history of early Christianity among the Slavs, but kept mailing letters to herself in Poland. She addressed them to the street where she used to live in Cracow, and these letters, which Kwaszniewska, now Mrs. Schultz,

wrote to herself were kept by her former Cracow land-
lady unopened in Poland, in the hope that one day she
would be able to hand them over to Dorothea. Except
for one or two, the letters are short and represent a kind
of diary kept by Dr. Dorothea Schultz from 1968 to 1982.
They have to do with the Khazars, inasmuch as the last
letter, written from detentive custody in Istanbul, touches
upon the Khazar polemic.[▽] The letters are given here in
chronological order.

1

Tel Aviv, August 21, 1967

Dear Dotty,

I have the feeling here that I'm gorging myself at the
expense of others and fasting at my own. I write these
lines knowing that you have already grown younger than
me there in your Cracow, in that room of ours where it
was always Friday, where they stuffed us with cinnamon
as though we were apples. If you ever get this letter,
you'll be older than me when you read it.

Isaac is better; he's lying in some hospital on the
battlefield, but he's improving rapidly, and his handwriting shows it. He writes that he dreams of the
"Cracow silence, three days long, twice heated over,
and a little burned at the bottom." We'll be seeing
each other soon, and I am afraid of that meeting, not
only because of his injuries, of which I still know nothing, but also because we are all trees planted in our own
shadows.

I'm glad that you, who do not love Isaac, have remained there, far away from us. Now it's easier for you
and me to love each other.

2

Jerusalem, September 1968

Dotty,

Just a few lines. Always remember—you work because you don't know how to live. If you knew how to live, you would not work, and science wouldn't exist for you. But everybody taught us only how to work, not how to live. I don't know how to live either. I walked my dogs down an unfamiliar path in the woods. The branches touched overhead. Reaching for their food—for light, the trees built beauty. From my food all I can build is memories. I will not be made beautiful by my hunger. What binds me to the trees is something they know how to do and I don't. All that binds the trees to me is my dogs, who love me more tonight than other nights. For their hunger is more beautiful when they are hungry from the trees than hungry from me. Where does your science fit into all this? All you need to know to get ahead in science is the last word in your field. With beauty it's not like that.

Isaac is back. His scars don't show when he's dressed; he's as handsome as he used to be and resembles a dog who has learned to sing the Cracow song. He prefers my right breast to my left, and we sleep indecently. He has those long legs with which he bounded up the steps in Wawel, and which he clasps around one knee and then the other when he sits. He pronounces my name the way it was used in the beginning, before all other uses, before it was worn thin by being passed from mouth to mouth. . . . Let's make an agreement: we'll split up our roles. You go on over there in Cracow being a scholar and I will stay here and learn how to live.

$$\overline{3}$$

Haifa, March 1971

My dear, unforgettable Dorothea,

It's been so long since I've seen you, who knows whether I would know you now. Maybe you don't know me any more either and don't think of me in those rooms where the door handles catch at your sleeve. I remember the Polish woods and imagine you running through yesterday's rain, whose drops ring louder from the branches above than the branches below. I remember you as a little girl and see how quickly you grow, faster than your nails and your hair; growing with you, but faster than you and inside you, is hate for our mother. Did we have to hate her so much? The sand here arouses my desire, but I have been feeling strange with Isaac for some time now. This feeling has nothing to do with him or with our love. It has to do with something else. With his injury. He reads in bed; I lie next to him in the tent and turn out the light when I desire him. He lies still for a few moments, peering at the book in the dark, and I can hear his thoughts gallop cross the invisible lines. And then he turns to me. But as soon as we touch I feel the terrible scar of his wound. After we've made love, we lie there, each staring into our own separate darkness. The other evening I asked him:

"Did it happen at night?"

"What?" he replied, although he knew what I meant.

"When you were wounded."

"It happened at night."

"And you don't know what it was?"

"No, but I think it was a bayonet."

Perhaps you won't understand all this, Dotty, young

and inexperienced as you are. A bird foraging for food in the swamps and marshes sinks rapidly if it doesn't move. It has to keep pulling its feet out of the mire to move on, regardless of whether it has caught something or not. And the same applies to us and to our love. We have to move on, we can't stay where we are, because we'll sink.

$$\overline{4}$$

Jerusalem, October 1974

Dear Dotty,

I've been reading about how the Slavs descended to the sea with their spears in their boots. And I've been thinking how Cracow is changing, in a rash of new orthographic and linguistic mistakes, sisters to the progress of words. I've been thinking how you stay the same and how Isaac and I are losing each other more and more. I don't dare tell him. Whenever we make love, no matter how good it is or what we do, I can feel on my breast and my belly the mark of that bayonet. I feel it in advance; it's come between Isaac and me in our bed. Is it possible that in a matter of seconds a person can sign himself with a bayonet on another's body and leave his portrait forever imprinted on another's flesh? I have to keep hunting for my own thoughts. They're mine not when they're born but when I catch them, if I manage to do so before they escape me. That wound resembles a mouth, and whenever Isaac and I make love—in fact, as soon as we touch—the tip of my breast falls into that scar as if into a toothless mouth. I lie beside Isaac and look at the spot in the dark where he is sleeping. The smell of clover screens the smell of the barn. I wait for him to stir; that is when dreams thin out, and then

I can wake him up, because he won't regret it. Some dreams are costly and others are rubbish. I wake him up and ask:

"Was he left-handed?"

"I think so," he tells me drowsily but readily, and I see he knows what I mean. "They captured him, and in the morning they brought him to my tent to show him to me. He had a beard, green eyes, and a head wound. It was the wound they really wanted to show me. I had done it. With my rifle butt."

—
5

Haifa again, September 1975

Dotty,

You don't know how glad I am that you're over there in your Wawel and that you've been spared the horror that's been happening to me. Just imagine being in your husband's bed, making love to the person you love, and being nibbled and kissed by somebody else. Just imagine making love to your man, and all the time on your stomach you feel the welt of a wound, which has come between you and your love like a foreign limb. There lies and will always lie between Isaac and me a green-eyed, bearded Saracen! And he will respond to my every move before Isaac, because he's closer to my body than Isaac. And mind you, this Saracen is no invention! The beast is left-handed and prefers my left breast to my right! It's horrible, Dotty! You don't love Isaac the way I do, so maybe you can tell me how to explain it all to him. I left you and Poland and came here because of Isaac, only to discover in his arms a green-eyed monster who awakens at night, bites with his toothless mouth, and is hard even when Isaac isn't. Isaac sometimes makes me have an orgasm with this Arab! If you ever need him, just call! He'll come, he always can. . . .

Our wall clock, Dotty, is fast this autumn, and in the spring it will be slow. . . .

6

October '78

Dorothea,

In the morning, when the weather is good, Isaac carefully appraises the quality of the air. He checks its moisture content, sniffs at the wind, and watches to see whether it is cool at noon. When he senses that the moment is right, he fills his lungs with a special kind of select air, and in the evening lets it out through a song. He says one can't always sing well; songs are like the seasons. They come when it's their turn. . . . Isaac, my dear Dotty, can't fall. He's like a spider. A web is holding him to a place known to him alone. But I fall more and more often. The Arab rapes me in my husband's arms, and I no longer know where my pleasure comes from. The husband behind this Saracen looks different to me now; I've begun to see and understand him in a new, unbearable way. The past has suddenly changed; the more inroads the future makes, the more the past changes—it becomes more fraught with dangers and more unpredictable than the future, full of long-closed rooms from which live beasts increasingly emerge. And each of these beasts has its own name. The beast that will tear Isaac and me apart has its own name. Imagine, Dotty, I asked Isaac and he told me. He knew the name all along. The Arab's name is Abu Kabir Muawia. And he already started the job, somewhere at night, in the sand near a waterhole. Like all beasts.

7

Tel Aviv, November 1, 1978

My dear, forgotten Dotty,

You are coming back into my life in the most ghastly way. Over there in your Poland, where the fogs lie so heavy they sink into the water, you can't even dream of what I'm about to do to you. I am writing to you for the most selfish reasons. I often think I am lying wide-eyed in the dark, when in fact there is a light on in the room and Isaac is reading while my own eyes are shut. Still lying between the two of us in our bed is that third creature, but I tried my hand at a bit of cunning. It's difficult, because the space for battle is limited—there's Isaac's body. Avoiding the Arab's mouth, for months I inched across my husband's body from right to left. And just when I thought I had escaped the trap, I was ambushed on the other side of Isaac's body. Waiting for me there was the Arab's second mouth. Under the hair behind Isaac's ear I found another scar, and it was as though Abu Kabir Muawia had stuck his tongue between my teeth. Horrible! Now I'm trapped good and proper! Even if I do manage to escape one mouth, there is always the other one waiting for me on the other side of Isaac's body. How can I possibly think of Isaac? I can't caress him any more, out of fear that my mouth will touch the Saracen's. He has marked our lives. Could you think of having a child under such circumstances? The worst was the night before last. One of those Saracen kisses reminded me of our mother's kiss. I haven't thought of her for years, and now suddenly here she is to remind me of her. And with that vengeance! Let he who puts his shoes on not boast like he who takes them off, but how is one to stand it?

I asked Isaac openly whether the Egyptian was still alive. And what do you think he said? He's very much alive, and working in Cairo. He leaves behind his steps wherever he goes, like spit. I implore you, do something! You could save me from this intruder if only you would draw his lust away from me and to yourself, so Isaac and I could be saved. Don't forget that cursed name—Abu Kabir Muawia—and let's the two of us divide it up: you take your left-handed Arab to bed in your room over there in Cracow, and I will try to hold on to Isaac. . . .

8

Department of Slavic Studies
Yale University, USA
October 1980

Dear Miss Kwaszniewska,

This is your Dr. Schultz writing in between classes at the university. Isaac and I are fine. My ears are still full of his withered kisses. We have quieted down somewhat, and our beds are now on separate continents. I'm working hard. I've begun accepting invitations to conferences, something I hadn't done for almost a decade. I'm now getting ready for another trip, one that will bring me closer to you. In two years a conference is being held in Istanbul on the cultures of the Black Sea shores. I'm preparing a paper for it. Do you remember Professor Wyka and your senior thesis on "The Life of Cyril and Methodius, the Slav Enlighteners"? And do you remember Dvornik's study, which we used at the time? Well, he's put out a new, amended edition (1969), and I'm reading it with immense interest. My paper will be about Cyril's[†] and Methodius'[†] Khazar mission, the one where the most important documents—the writings of Cyril himself—have been lost. The anonymous compiler of

Cyril's biography says that Cyril recorded the arguments
he used in the Khazar polemic at the kaghan's court in
separate books, in the "Khazar Orations." "If someone is
interested in the complete orations," writes Cyril's biog-
rapher, "he will find them in Cyril's books, which were
translated by our teacher and archbishop, Methodius, the
brother of Constantine the Philosopher, who divided
them into eight orations." Incredibly, the books with the
eight orations by Cyril (Constantine of Thessalonica), the
Christian saint and father of Slav literacy, written in
Greek and translated into the Slavonic language, disappeared without a trace! Could that be because they contained too many heretical elements? Did they perhaps
have iconoclastic overtones, which may have been effective in the polemic but were unlawful, and therefore
after the Khazar mission, they were removed from use?
I checked Ilyinski again, his well-known *Survey of the
Systematic Cyril-Methodius Bibliography* up to 1934, and
then his successors (Popruzhenko, Romanski, Ivanka Pet-
kovich, etc). I reread Moshin. And then I read all the
works they list about the Khazar question. And nowhere
is there any mention that Cyril's "Khazar Orations" at-
tracted anybody's particular attention. How could it have
all disappeared without a trace? Everyone has precon-
ceived ideas about this question. But along with the
Greek original there was also the Slavonic translation, from which one can only deduce that at one time
the work was in wide use. Not just during the Khazar
mission, but later as well; its arguments must have been
used in the Slav mission of the Thessalonica brothers,
and even in the polemic with the "Trilinguists." Otherwise, why would the "Khazar Orations" be translated
into Slavonic? I think it might be possible to track down
Cyril's "Khazar Orations" by taking a comparative approach to the entire matter. A systematic check of the
Islamic and Hebrew sources on the Khazar polemic

would be bound to reveal some mention of Cyril's "Khazar Orations." But that's not something I or a Slavist can do alone; a Hebraist and an Orientalist are needed for that as well. I looked through Dunlop (*History of Jewish Khazars,* 1954) but found nothing there that might help me trace the lost "Khazar Orations" of Constantine the Philosopher.

So, you see, you over there at your Jagellonian University are not the only one engaged in scholarship. I'm doing the same thing over here. I've finally gone back to my vocation and my youth, which tastes like fruit shipped by sea. I wear a straw, basket-shaped hat, and I can carry cherries from the market in it without taking it off my head. I age every time the Romanesque bell tower strikes midnight in Cracow, and I wake up every time daybreak strikes in Wawel. I envy you your eternal youth. How is your Abu Kabir Muawia? Does he have a pair of smoked-dry ears and a well-emptied nose, as in my dreams? Thank you for taking him in. You probably already know everything about him. Imagine, he's doing something very similar to your work and mine! He's like a colleague. He teaches comparative Middle Eastern religions at the University in Cairo and is interested in Hebrew history. Do you have the same problems I had with him?

> Love from your
> Dr. Schultz

9

Jerusalem, January 1981

Dotty,

Something unbelievable has happened. Upon my return from America, I discovered among my unopened mail a list of participants at that conference on the cultures of the Black Sea coast I told you about. And guess who's on the list! Or perhaps you already know, you with your prophetic little soul, which doesn't need a hairdresser to have its hair curled? The Arab, in flesh and blood, the one with the green eyes who drove me from my husband's bed. He's coming to the meeting in Istanbul. But I won't lie. He's not coming in order to see me. I'm going to finally see him. I've reckoned for a long time that our work intersects, and that if only I were to go to these conferences, our paths would be bound to cross as well. In my bag I'm carrying my paper on the Khazar mission of Cyril and Methodius, and underneath it is a .38-caliber model 36 S & W. Thank you for your fruitless efforts to take Dr. Abu Kabir Muawia upon yourself. Now I'm taking him over as my own responsibility. Love me as you don't love Isaac. I need this now more than ever before. Our common father will help me. . . .

<hr>

10

Istanbul, Kingston Hotel,
October 1, 1982

Dear Dorothea,
Our common father will help me, I wrote to you the last time. My poor little fool. What do you know about our common father? When I was your age I didn't know anything either. But my new years have given me time to think. Do you know who your real father was, my darling? That Pole who had a beard like grass, gave you the name Kwaszniewska, and bravely married your mother, Ana Scholem? I don't think so. Do you recall that man we could not remember? Do you recall an Ashkenaz Scholem, the young man from the picture,

with riding glasses on his nose and another pair of glasses in his vest? The one who smoked tea instead of tobacco and whose beautiful hair bit at his photographed ears. Who, they told us, used to say,"We shall be saved by our false victim." Do you recall the brother and first husband of our mother, Ana Scholem, allegedly née Zakiewicz, Scholem by marriage, and Kwaszniewska by remarriage? And do you know who was the real father of her daughters, of you and me? You've finally remembered, after all these years! Your uncle and your mother's brother could easily be our father to boot, no? Why couldn't he be the husband of our mother? Now, what do you think of that little equation, my lovely? Maybe Mrs. Scholem never had a man before getting married, and she could hardly remarry as a virgin, could she? Maybe that's why she appears in such strange ways, bringing horror with memories. Anyway her old age has not been wasted, and I think that, if that's what my mother did, then she was right a thousand times over, and if I can choose a father, then I prefer it to be my mother's brother rather than anybody else. Misfortune, my darling Dorothea, misfortune teaches us to read our lives backward. . . .

Here in Istanbul I've already met quite a few people. Since I don't want to appear strange in any way, I chat with everyone, as though I were opening my mouth to the rain. There's a colleague here at the conference by the name of Dr. Isailo Suk.[†] He's a medieval archeologist, knows Arabic well; we converse in English and joke in Polish, because he speaks Serbian and says he is the moth of his own clothes. His family has been moving the same tile stove from one house to another for a hundred years now, and he believes that the 21st century will differ from ours in that people will finally rise together against the boredom that today inundates them like putrid water. We carry the stone of boredom on our backs up a huge hill, like Sisyphus, says Dr. Suk. Hopefully the people of the future will stand up and rise against this plague, against boring schools, boring books, against boring music, boring science, boring meetings, and get this boredom out of their lives and work, as demanded by our original father, Adam. He talks like that, partly joking, he drinks wine but won't let his glass be refilled until it's empty, saying that a glass is not an icon lamp to be kept filled before it runs out. His textbooks are used all over the world, but he is not in a position to use them himself. He has to teach something else at the university. His extraordinary professional erudition is totally out of proportion with his minor reputation as a scholar. When I said as much to him, he laughed and explained:

"The point is, you can be either a great scientist or a great violinist (did you know that all great violinists, with the exception of Paganini, have always been Jews?) only if you and your accomplishments are supported and backed by one of the powerful internationals of today's world. The Hebrew, Islamic, or Catholic international. You belong to one of them. I do not, and that means I belong nowhere. All fish have long since slipped through my fingers."

"What are you talking about?" I asked him in bewilderment.

"That's a paraphrase of a Khazar text that is more than a thousand years old. Judging by the paper you'll be reading us, you have most certainly heard of the Khazars. So why are you so surprised? Have you never come across the Daubmannus edition?"

I must admit that he baffled me. Especially with his story about the Daubmannus edition of *The Khazar Dictionary*. If such a dictionary ever did exist, not a single copy, as far as I know, has been preserved.

Dear Dotty, I see the snow in Poland, I see the snow-flakes turn into tears in your eyes. I see the bread on the spoke with the wreath of onions, and the birds seeking warmth from the smoke above the houses. Dr. Suk says that time comes from the south and crosses the Danube at Trajan's Bridge. There's no snow here, and the clouds are like arrested waves spewing out their fish. Dr. Suk drew my attention to yet another thing. Staying in our hotel is a fine-looking Belgian family, the Van der Spaaks. It's a family such as we never had and I never will have. Father, mother, and son. Dr. Suk calls them "the holy family." Every morning at breakfast I watch them eat: they're well fed, and I heard Mr. Spaak joke that fleas don't go for fat cats. He plays sublimely on an instrument made out of white tortoiseshell, and his wife's preoccupation is painting. She paints with her left hand, and very well too, on everything in sight—on towels, glasses, knives, and her son's gloves. The boy is only just four. He wears his hair cut short, is called Manuil, and is forming his first sentences. As soon as he finishes his bun, he comes over to my table and stares at me as though he were in love. His eyes are pebbled with colors, like my own path, and he keeps asking me, "Did you recognize me?" I stroke his hair as though I were strok-ing a bird, and he kisses my fingers. He brings me the pipe of his father, who looks like a zaddik, and gives it to me to smoke. He likes all things that are red, blue, and yellow. And he likes foods that are these colors. I was horrified to see that he has a deformity: he has two thumbs on each hand. I never know which hand is his right and which is his left. But he's still oblivious to his appearance and doesn't hide his hands from me, al-though his parents make him wear gloves. Believe it or not, at moments they look perfectly natural to me and don't bother me at all.

And, indeed, why should anything bother me, when

at breakfast this morning we heard that Dr. Abu Kabir Muawia had arrived for the conference. "For the lips of a strange woman drop as a honeycomb, and her mouth is smoother than oil. But her end is bitter as wormwood, sharp as a two-edged sword. Her feet go down to death; her steps take hold on hell. . . ." So says the Bible.

11

Istanbul, October 8, 1982

Miss Dorothea Kwaszniewska—Cracow

I'm appalled by your selfishness and cruel verdict. You've destroyed Isaac's life and mine. I was always afraid of your science and sensed it would do me harm. I hope you know what happened and what you did. That morning I went down to breakfast resolved to shoot Muawia as soon as he appeared in the hotel garden, where we eat. I sat down and waited in anticipation. I watched the shadows of the birds overhead tumble down the garden walls. And then everything that there was no way of predicting happened. The man appeared, and I immediately knew who he was. He wore a face as dark as bread, had a head of graying hair, and looked as though he had fishbones in his mustache. But growing through the scar on his temple was a tuft of black hair that cannot turn gray. Dr. Muawia walked straight over to my table and asked if he could sit down. He had a noticeable limp, and one of his eyes was closed, like a small pursed mouth. I was petrified. I released the safety catch on the revolver in my handbag and was on my guard. Only four-year-old Manuil was with us in the garden; he was playing under a nearby table.

"Certainly," I said, and the man put something on the table that was to change my life forever. It was an ordinary pile of paper.

He knows the subject of my report—he said, sitting down—and wants to ask me something in connection with my field of work. We spoke in English. He was shivering; he was colder than I was, his teeth were chattering, but he did nothing to hide or stop it. He warmed his fingers on his pipe and blew smoke into his sleeves. He quickly explained what it was all about. It was about Cyril's "Khazar Orations."

"I have read through everything dealing with the 'Khazar Orations,' " he said, "and I have found no mention of these texts being still in existence. Is it possible that nobody knows that fragments of Cyril's 'Khazar Orations' were preserved and even printed a few hundred years ago?"

I was flabbergasted. What this man was saying would be the greatest discovery to have been made in my field, in Slavistics, since its inception as a science. If it was true.

"Where did you ever get such an idea?" I asked in astonishment, giving my own explanation with a strange feeling of uncertainty.

"Cyril's 'Khazar Orations,' " I said, "are known to science only through the mention made of them in Cyril's biography, which is how we know that they existed at all. There can be no question of some preserved manuscript or even published text of these speeches."

"That's what I wanted to check," said Dr. Muawia. "Now it will be known that precisely the opposite is true...."

And he gave me a few of the Xeroxed sheets of paper lying on the table in front of him. *As he passed them to me, his thumb brushed mine and I trembled from the touch. I had the sensation that our past and our future were in our fingers and that they had touched. And so, when I began to read the proffered pages, I at one moment lost the train of thought in the text and drowned it in my own feelings. In these seconds of absence and self-oblivion, centuries passed*

*with every read but uncomprehended and unabsorbed line,
and when, after a few moments, I came to and re-established
contact with the text, I knew that the reader who returns
from the open seas of his feelings is no longer the same reader
who embarked on that sea only a short while ago. I gained
and learned more by not reading than by reading those pages,
and when I asked Dr. Muawia where he had got them he
said something that astonished me even more.*

"You needn't ask where I got them. They were found
in the 12th century by a fellow tribesman of yours, Judah
Halevi the poet, who included them in his book about
the Khazars. Describing the famous polemic, he cited the
words of the Christian participant in the debate, calling
him Philosopher, which is how the same personage is
called by the writer of Cyril's life in connection with the
same polemic. Cyril's name, like that of the Arab participant, was omitted by this Jewish source, which gives
only the university title of the Christian participant, and
that's why nobody ever looked for Cyril's text in Judah
Halevi's Khazar chronicle."

I looked at Dr. Muawia as though he were somebody
who had nothing to do with that wounded man of the
green eyes who had seated himself at my table only a
few minutes ago. It was all so convincing, so simple, it
all fit in so well with everything science knows about this
question, that it's a wonder nobody had ever thought of
looking for the text in this way before.

"There's a slight problem here," I finally said to Dr.
Muawia. "Halevi's book refers to the 8th century, but
Cyril's Khazar missions didn't take place until the 9th
century, until the year 861."

"He who knows the right way can also take a short-
cut!" observed Dr. Muawia. "We are not interested in
dates but in whether Halevi, who lived after Cyril's time,
had access to Cyril's 'Khazar Orations' when he wrote
his book about the Khazars. And whether he used them

in his book, there where he cites the words of the Christian participant in the Khazar polemic. Let me say right off that in Halevi's book the Christian sage's speech has unquestionable similarities to the preserved fragments of Cyril's own arguments. I know you've translated Cyril's life into English, so you'll easily recognize these sections. For instance, whose text is this? It speaks about man being midway between angel and animal. . . ."

Naturally, I recognized it immediately and recited it by heart:

" 'As the All-Creator, God created man midway between angel and animal—separating him by speech and reason from animals, and by anger and lust from angels, and whichever of these parts he nears, he comes closer to those above or those below. . . .' That," I said, "is from the life of Cyril, in the section on his Agaren mission."

"Correct, but it also appears in the fifth part of Halevi's book, in the polemic with the Philosopher. There are other such similarities. Most important of all is that the speech itself, which in the Khazar polemic Halevi attributes to the Christian participant, dwells on matters which Cyril, according to his biography, raised in that polemic. Both texts talk about the Holy Trinity and the laws that preceded Moses, about eating forbidden kinds of meat, and, lastly, about doctors who heal contrary to the way they should. They give the same argument, that the soul is at its strongest when the body is at its weakest (around the age of fifty), etc. Finally, the Khazar kaghan reproaches the Arab and Hebrew participants in the polemic, again according to Halevi, because their books of revelation (Koran and Torah) are written in languages that mean nothing to the Khazars, Hindus, or other peoples who do not understand them. This is one of the basic arguments given in the life of Cyril against the Trilinguists (who accept only Greek, Hebrew, and Latin as liturgical languages), and clearly here the kaghan was influenced by the Christian participant in the polemic, expressing convictions which we know to have been really Cyril's. Halevi merely conveyed them.

"Finally, there are two last points to be made. First, we do not know everything that was actually said in the lost 'Khazar Orations' of Constantine of Thessalonica (Cyril), and we do not know what Halevi's book has taken from them. In other words, it's reasonable to assume that there is more than I have mentioned here. Second, the section of Halevi's book that deals with the Christian participant in the polemic is damaged. It has not been preserved in the Arabic original, only in its later Hebrew translation, while, as is known, the printed editions of Halevi's book, especially those from the 16th century, were subjected to Christian censorship.

"In short, Halevi's book on the Khazars preserved in part, although we do not know to what extent, Cyril's 'Khazar Orations.' Our conference here in Istanbul," concluded Dr. Muawia, "will be attended by a Dr. Isailo Suk, who is fluent in Arabic and studies Islamic sources on the Khazar polemic. He told me he has a 17th-century Khazar dictionary published by somebody named Daubmannus, and that it shows that Halevi used Cyril's 'Khazar Orations.' I came to ask you whether you would talk to Dr. Suk. He won't talk to me. He says he's only interested in Arabs from a thousand and more years ago. He has no time for others. Would you help me to contact Dr. Suk and clear up this matter? . . ."

Dr. Abu Kabir Muawia finished his speech, and suddenly the various lines of thought in my mind came together like lightning. If you forget the direction time follows, there's always love as a compass. Time always abandons it. After so many years, I was again seized by your cursed thirst for science, and I betrayed Isaac. Instead of firing the gun, I rushed out to call Dr. Suk, leaving behind my papers and underneath them the gun. There was nobody in the lobby; in the kitchen somebody was toasting a slice of bread over the fire and eating. I saw Van der Spaak coming out of one of the rooms and realized that the room was Dr. Suk's. I knocked, but nobody answered. Rapid footsteps were pattering somewhere behind me, and between them could be felt the heat of female flesh. I knocked again, and the door swung ajar. At first all I saw was a small night table with some kind of egg and a key on a saucer. I pushed the door open a bit farther and screamed. Dr. Suk was lying in bed, smothered by a pillow. He was lying there, biting his mustache as though he were racing against the wind. I ran out screaming, and suddenly there was a shot from the garden. It was just one shot, but I heard it with each ear separately. I immediately recognized the sound of my own gun. I flew down into the garden, only to find Dr. Muawia lying on the gravel, his head blown off. . . . At the next table, the gloved boy was sipping his chocolate milk as though nothing had happened. . . . There was nobody else in the garden.

I was immediately taken into custody, the Smith & Wesson on which they found my fingerprints was taken as evidence, and I was accused of the premeditated murder of Dr. Abu Kabir Muawia. I am writing this letter from prison, where I'm being kept in detention, and I still don't understand what happened. In my mouth I have a fresh-water spring and a double-edged sword. . . . Who killed Dr. Muawia? Imagine, the indictment reads: "A Jewess murders an Arab in revenge!" The entire Islamic international, the entire Egyptian and Turkish public, will rise against me. "Your Lord will deliver you to your enemies to be beaten; you will encounter them on one road and flee them on seven. . . ." How do you prove that you didn't do what you had actually intended to do? You have to find a thundering lie, one as fearful and strong as the father of rain, to prove the truth. Horns in place of eyes are needed by anybody who wants to invent such a lie. If I find it, I'll live, and then I'll bring you from Cracow to me in Israel and return to the science of our youth. "We shall be saved by our false

---

מאמר ראשון 9

ה'הודיעם די'לי במד־ שהוא
גראה משפלותם ומיעוטם
ושהכל מואסים אותם וקרא
לחכם מחכמי אדום ושאל
אותו על חכמתו וכישתו ו
ואמר לו אני מאמין בחדוש
הנבראות ובקדמו' הבורא' ית'
ושהוא' ברא העולם כלו
בש' ימים ושבכל המדברים
צאצא' אדם אליו הם מ
מתיחסים כלם ושיש־לבורא
השגחה על הבראים והדבקות
במדברים יקצף ורחמ'ם
ודבור והראות והגלות לנביאיו
חסדיו והוא שוכן בתוך
רצוי מהמוני בני אדם' וכללי
של דבר אני מאמין בכל מד־
שבא בתורת ובספרי בני
ישראל אשר אין ספק ב
באמתתם בעבור פרסומם
והתמדתם והגלותם בהמונינ־
גדולים [ ] ובאחריתם ו
ובעקבותם נגשמה האלהות
והי'ה עובר ברחם בתולד־
מנשיאות בני ישראל וילדד־
אותו אנוש־ הנראה אלקי
הנסתר נביא שלוח בנראד־
אלוד־ שלוח בנסתר והוא
המשיח הנקרא בן אלקים
והוא האב והבן והוא רוח
הקדש ואנחנו מיחדים א
אמתתו ואם נראה על לשוננו
השלוש נאמין בו האחד' נ
ומשמנו

COSRI PARS I.

Ad Judæos quod attinet, satis mihi est cognita illorum humilitas, vilitas, paucitas; & quòd illos ab omnibus reprobari & contemni videmus (*ut non opus sit, illos audire*).

Accersivit itaq; Sapientem ex Edomæis, (*h.e. è* [1.] *Chriſtianis*) & quæsivit ex eo de Sapientiâ & Operibus seu Actionibus ipsius. Qui ei dixit; Ego credo Innovationem Creaturarum (*i. e. omnia eſſe creata, non ab æterno*), & Æternitatem Creatoris Benedicti; quòd sc. ille Mundum totum creaverit spatio sex dierum; quòd omnes homines rationales sint progenies Adami, ab illo familiam suam ducentes; quòd sit Providentia Dei super res creatas, quòd item adhæreat rationalibus (*.h.e. se communicet .cum hominibus*): credo etiam Dei iram; amorem, misericordiam, sermonem, visionem, revelationem Prophetis & viris sanctis factam; denique, quòd Deus habitet inter.eos qui accepti ipsi sunt ex humano genere. Summa: Credo omnia quæ scripta sunt in Lege & libris Israëlitarum, de quorum veritate nullus est dubitandi locus, eò quòd illa publicata, vel, publicè gesta, continuè conservata & propagata, revelataque sint in maxima hominum turba & frequentia. [Et [2.]] in extremo ac fine illorum (*Reipublicæ & Ecclesiæ Judæorum*) incorporata (*incarnata*) est Deitas, transiens in uterum virginis cujusdam è primariis inter Israëlitas, quæ genuit eum Hominem visibiliter, Deum latenter, Prophetam missum visibiliter, Deum missum occultè. Hicque fuit Messias, dictus Filius Dei, qui est Pater, Filius, & Spiritus Sanctus, cujus Essentiam unicam esse credimus & fatemur. Licet enim ex verbis nostris videatur, nos Trinitatem vel Tres Deos credere, credimus tamen unitatem. Habitatio au-

victim," said one of our two fathers. . . . It's hard enough
to endure His mercy, let alone His anger.

P.S. I'm enclosing the Philosopher's rejoinders
from Halevi's book on the Kazars (*Liber Cosri* ✿),
which Dr. Muawia claimed were fragments of the lost
"Khazar Orations" of Constantine the Philosopher,
St. Cyril:

Cosri Pars I.

tem ejus fuit inter filios Israël, summo ipsorum cum honore, quandiu Res Divina ipsis
adhæsit (*durante Templo*), donec illi rebel-
larunt contra Messiam istum, eumque cruci-
fixerunt. Tum conversa fuit Ira Divina
continua super eos, gratia verò & Benevo-
lentia super paucos (*è Judæis*) qui sequuti
sunt Messiam, & postea etiam super alios
populos, qui hos paucos sunt sequuti &
imitati, è quibus nos sumus. Et quamvis
non simus Israëlitæ, longè potiori tamen
jure. nobis nomen Israëlitarum debetur,
quia nos ambulamus secundum verba Messiæ, & Duodecim Sociorum (*h. e. Discipulo-
rum vel Apostolorum*) ejus è filiis Israël, loco
Duodecim tribuum, prout etiam populus
magnus è filiis Israëlis sunt sequuti illos
Duodecim, qui fuerunt quasi Pasta populi Christiani. Unde nos digni facti
sumus Dignitate Israëlitarum, & penes
nos nunc est potentia & robur in terris,
omnesque populi vocantur ad fidem hanc,
& jubentur adhærére ei, atque magnificare
& exaltare Messiam, ejusque Lignum (*h. e.
Crucem*) venerari, in quo crucifixus fuit, &
similia: Judiciaque & Statuta nostra sunt
partim Præcepta Simeonis socii (*h. e. Petri
Apostoli*), & partim Statuta Legis, quam
nos discimus, & de cujus veritate nullo mo-
do dubitari potest, quin à Deo sit profecta.
Nam in ipso Evangelio in verbis Messiæ
habetur; *Non veni ut destruam præceptum ali-
quod ex præceptis filiorum Israël, & Mosis, Pro-
pheta ipsorum, sed veni, ut illa impleam & confir-
mem, Matth. 5.*]

NOTÆ.

[٭.] *Ubi prima editio habet* אֱדוֹם, h. e. Christianum; *pro eo in secundâ
substitu.*

מאמר ראשון ١٥
וּמִשָּׁכְנוּ בְּתוֹךְ בְּנֵי יִשְׂרָאֵל ٭
לכבוד להם כאשר הירה
הענין האלקי נדבק בהם עד
רח יו המוניהם במשיח הזה
ותלוהו ושב הקצף מתמיד
עליר׳ ועל המונם זהרצון
ליחידים ההולכים אחרי
המשיח ואחרי כן לאומות
ההולכים אחרי היחידים
האלה ואנחנו מהם ואם
לא נהיה מבני ישראל אבחנו
יותר ראוי׳׳ שנקרא בני ישראל
מפני שאנחנו הולכים אחרי
דברי המשיח וחביריו מבני
ישראל שנים עשר במקום
השבטים ואחר כן הלכו עם
רב מבני ישראל אחרי השנים
עשר זהם זהי כמחמצרץ
לאומת הנוצרים הינינו אנו
ראויים למעלת בני ישראל
היתה לנו הגבורה והעצמה
בארצות וכל האומות נקראים
אל האמונה הזאת ומצווים
להדבק בה׳ ולגדל ולרומם
למשיח ולגדל אר׳ עצו אשר
נתלה עליו והדומר׳ לזה
דיניגו וחקינו ממצורץ שמעון
והבר וחוקים מן התורה
אשר אנו לומדים אותה ואין
ספק באמתתה שהיא מאת
האלקים : וכבר בא באון
גליון בדבר׳ המשיח לא באתי
לסתור כצור׳ ממצור׳ בני
ישראל ומשה נביאם אבל
באתי לחזק ולאמצם [:

TIBBON, JUDAH BEN (12th century)—
translator of Judah Halevi's *Book on the Khazars* from
Arabic into Hebrew. The translation appeared in 1167,
and there are two explanations for its unevenness: that
later, printed versions were castrated in the hands of the
Christian Inquisition, and that the whole thing depended
not just on Tibbon, but on circumstances.

The translation was faithful when ben Tibbon was in
love with his betrothed, good when he was angry, wordy
if the winds blew, profound in winter, expository and
paraphrased if it rained, and wrong if he was happy.

When he finished a chapter, Tibbon would do as the
ancient Alexandrian translators of the Bible had done—
he would have someone read him the translation while
walking away from him, and Tibbon would stand still
and listen. With distance, parts of the text were lost in
the wind and around corners, the rest echoing back
through the bushes and trees; screened by doors and
railings, it shed nouns and vowels, tripped on stairs, and
finally, having begun as a male voice, would end its
journey as a female voice, with only verbs and numbers
still audible in the distance. Then, when the reader returned, the entire process would be reversed, and Tibbon
would correct the translation on the basis of the impres-
sions he had derived from this reading walk.

APPENDIX I

Father Theoctist Nikolsky penned his dying confession to Patriarch Arsen III Charnoyevich of Peć in the pitch dark, somewhere in Poland, using a mixture of gunpowder and saliva, and a quick Cyrillic hand, while the innkeeper's wife scolded and cursed him through the bolted door.

"You know, Your Holiness," Theoctist wrote to the Patriarch, "that I am condemned to having a good memory, which my future constantly fills and my past never empties. I was born in 1641 in the village of the St. John Monastery on the day of St. Spiridon, the patron saint of potters, into a family which on its table always had two-handed bowls and in them food for the soul and food for the heart. Just as my brother sleeps holding the wooden spoon in his hand, so in my memory I hold all the eyes that have ever seen me since I came into being. The moment I noticed that the clouds over Mt. Ovchar resumed the same position every five years and recognized clouds seen five autumns past now returning to the sky, I was gripped by fear and began to hide my affliction, for a memory such as mine is a punishment. In the meantime, I learned Turkish from the coins of Constantinople, Hebrew from the merchants of Dubrovnik, and how to read from icons. I was driven to keep remembrances by something like thirst—not thirst for water, because water cannot quench it, but a different, passing kind of thirst that is allayed only by hunger. Yet, not hunger for food, but a different kind of hunger, and in vain I searched, like a sheep for a salty wall, to discover what hunger it was that could save me from thirst. For I was afraid of memory; I knew that our memories and reminiscences are like icebergs. We see only the tips in passing, but the mass of land under water slips by unseen and inaccessible. We do not feel their immeasurable weight simply because they lie submerged in time, as in water. But, if we carelessly find ourselves in their way, we shall run aground against our own past and be ship-wrecked. That is why I never even touched any of this profusion that fell into me like snow into the Morava River. And then, to my astonishment, it happened that my memory betrayed me, albeit only for a second. At first I was ecstatic, but later I bitterly regretted it, for I saw where it was leading. It happened this way.

"In my eighteenth year, my father sent me to St. John Monastery and said to me in parting: 'When fasting, do not take a single word into your mouth, so that at least your mouth, if not your ears, may be cleansed of words. For words come not from the head or the soul but from the world, from sticky tongues and malodorous jaws; they have all long since been picked dry, spewed out, and become pulp from constant chewing. They have not been whole in a long while and have been carried by countless mouths from tooth to tooth. . . .' The monks at St. John's took me in, said I had too many bones in too tight a soul, and set me to work transcribing books. I sat in a cell full of books with black ribbons marking the last pages the monks had read before dying, and I worked. Then word reached us that a new calligrapher had arrived at the nearby Nicholas Monastery.

"The path to Nicholas runs along the Morava, be-tween the steep banks and the water. Since it is the only road to the monastery, at least one boot or pair of hoofs

is bound to get muddy. And it is from this muddy boot
that the monks can tell where visitors to the monastery
have come from: from the sea or from Mt. Rudnik,
splashing the water from the west downstream along the
Morava with their right foot, or from the east, upstream
with their left. On the Sunday of St. Thomas in 1661,
we heard that to the Nicholas Monastery had come a
man whose left boot was wet and muddy; he was robust
and handsome, had eyes the shape of eggs, a beard so
long it would take an evening to burn, and hair pulled
down over his eyes like a tattered fur hat. The man was
called Nikon Sevast,[†] and he soon became the head calligrapher at Nicholas, for he had already developed a
masterful skill somewhere. He was of the armory guild,
but his job was harmless: he drew flags, archery tar-
gets, and shields, making pictures that were doomed
to be destroyed by bullets, arrows, or swords. He said
he was in Nicholas only temporarily, on his way to
Constantinople.

"Three St. Michael's winds blew on the Day of St.
Cyricaus the Recluse, each replete with its own birds—
one with starlings, another with the last swallows, and
the third with sparrow hawks. Cold smells intermingled
with the warm, and word reached St. John's that the
new calligrapher at the Nicholas Monastery had painted
an icon that everyone in the gorge was rushing to see. I
got up myself to see how the Lord of the Universe
holding the Baby Jesus on His knee had been painted on
the monastery wall. I went in with the others and took a
good look at what had been painted. Afterward, at supper, I saw Nikon Sevast for the first time, and his beautiful face reminded me of somebody I know well but
couldn't find among the faces around me. There was no
such face in my memories, although they all suddenly
lay spread out before me like open cards, or in my

dreams, where they lay like a closed deck whose every card I could flip over at will. Nowhere was such a face to be found.

"The sound of an ax ricocheting off a beech tree rang out somewhere in the mountains; an ax ricochets one way off a beech tree and another off an elm, and this was the season for felling both beech and elm. I remembered perfectly those sounds from the first evening I had heard them, in a blizzard a decade ago; I remembered the birds, now long dead, that had flown through that blizzard and dropped heavily into the wet snow; but for the life of me I could not remember what I had seen on that face just a few minutes ago. I could not remember a single feature of Nikon's face, not a single color, not even whether he had a beard. That was the first and last time in my life that my memory had let me down. It was all so extraordinary and incredible that soon enough I easily found a reason for it. There could be only one: what is not of this world cannot be remembered; it is retained in the memory no more than the loach that is swallowed by the duck. Before leaving, I again scanned the faces and looked Nikon straight in the mouth, and I was gripped by fear, as if my every look could be bitten off. Indeed, that is precisely what he did, his mouth snapping slightly as he took a bite. And so with a nipped gaze I returned to St. John's.

"I went back to transcribing books, but at one moment I felt as if I had more words in my saliva than the man who had written the book. And so I began adding to the transcribed manuscript a word here, two there, sentence by sentence. It was Tuesday, and my words that first evening were sour and brittle under my teeth, but the following evenings I noticed that as autumn progressed my words ripened day by day, like a fruit, each time becoming juicier, fuller, and sweeter, filled with a core that was both pleasant and invigorating. On the seventh evening, it was as if I were hurrying so that my fruit would not be overripe, would not drop or droop; to the Life of St. Petka Paraskeva I added an entire page, one not to be found in any of the excerpts I was transcribing. Instead of discovering and investigating my misdeed, the monks began asking me to do more and more transcribing, preferring my books, with the insertions, to books by other scribes, of whom there were many in the Ovchar Gorge. I took courage and decided to see the thing through to the end. Not only did I add stories to the Lives, I began inventing new recluses, adding new miracles, and my transcriptions began selling at a higher price than the books from which they had been transcribed. Little by little I felt the tremendous power I held in my inkwell, and I let it flow at will. And then I reached a conclusion: Every writer can with no trouble kill his hero in just two lines. To kill a reader, someone of flesh and blood, it suffices to turn him for a moment into the hero of the book, into the protagonist of the biography. The rest is simple. . . .

"At the time there lived in the Monastery of the Visitation a young monk by the name of Longin. He lived an ascetic life and felt like a swan with its wings spread open waiting for the wind to blow and take it sailing across the water. Not even Adam, who gave names to the days, could have had as perfect an ear as he. He had eyes like the wasps that transmit the holy fire: one eye masculine, the other feminine, and each with a sting. He aimed at goodness like a hawk at a chicken. And he was fond of saying: 'We can all easily choose for a model somebody better than ourselves; from the spirits could be made Jacob's ladder, climbing from earth to heaven; everything would be connected and arranged with ease and joy, because it is not difficult for man to follow and obey someone better than he. All evil comes from the fact that in this world we are constantly tempted to obey and take for our model those who are worse than we. . . .' When he commissioned me to transcribe the Life of St. Peter of Corishia, who after five days of fasting saw unaging light, it was dusk and the birds streaked down into their nests in the bushes like black lightning. My thoughts soared up at the same speed, and I felt the strength was not in me to combat my burgeoning sense of power. I sat down to transcribe the Life of St. Peter of Corishia, and when I reached the part about the days of the fast, instead of 5 I wrote 50 and gave the transcription to the young monk. He took it, singing, and read it that same evening; the next day, word spread through the gorge that the monk Longin had embarked upon a major fast. . . .

"On the fifty-first day, when they buried Longin at the Annunciation in the foothills, I decided never to take pen in hand again. I looked with horror at the inkwell and thought: Too many bones in too tight a soul. And I decided to repent of my sin. In the morning I went to the prior and asked him to have me assigned to the Nicholas Monastery scriptorium as an assistant to the head calligrapher, Nikon Sevast. He did so, and Nikon led me into the writing room, with its smell of pumpkin seeds and sage blossoms, which the monks believe know how to pray. From other monasteries or from traveling merchants from the Ukraine, the monks would borrow, for four or five days, the kinds of books Nicholas did not have, and would give them to me to learn by heart quickly. Then they would return the books to their owners, and for months, day after day, I would dictate the memorized books to the head calligrapher, Nikon. And he would sharpen his pens and say that green is the only color that is not of plant origin—it alone is obtained from iron—all other colors he extracted from plants and decorated the books we wrote with various floral letters. Thus began my companionship with Nikon, like the masculine days in the week. He did everything with his left hand, hiding what it was doing from his right. We wrote by day. When there was no work, he would paint on the walls of the monastery, but he quickly abandoned icon painting and devoted himself entirely to writing books. Thus, we descended into our life slowly, night after night, for years.

"On the Day of St. Eustace of Serbia in 1683, the frost came out to sow its millet, the dogs were allowed in bed, and boots and smiling teeth cracked from the cold. In the green sky the jackdaws froze in mid-flight and dropped like stones, leaving only their cries in the air. The tongue felt the icy lips, which no longer felt the tongue. The winds howled from the other side of the Morava River, which was stilled by ice, while along the banks the ice lay unmowed, full of icicled reeds, traveler's joy, and sedge, as though the ice were growing a silver beard. The drooping willow branches were caught in the frozen river, encaging the trees. Out of the mist came the lonely crows that fly in place, painfully extracting their wings from the white skein of the salty damp. And flying high over the frost-divided hills and into the sky beyond, bidding farewell to the landscape, were Nikon's thoughts and mine, as fleeting as quick summer clouds, and in them our memories passed as slowly as a winter illness. And then in March, on the first Sunday of Lent, we heated a kettle of brandy in the boiling beans; we drank, ate, and left Nicholas forever. We came upon Belgrade with the first and last snow of that year, and we stood through the Mass for the proto-martyrs of Belgrade—Stratonik, Donat, and Hermil—and started a new life.

"We became traveling scribes and began moving our pens and inkwells across the waters and boundaries of the empires. We worked less and less for the church as we had books to transcribe in more and more languages. We started transcribing books not only for men but for women as well, because masculine and feminine stories cannot have the same ending. We left behind rivers and plains (taking only their names with us), decaying gazes, iron rings with keys in the ear, paths strewn with straw knotted by the beaks of birds, wooden spoons that smoke, and forks made of spoons, and on Tuesday, All Saints Day, in 1684 we arrived in the imperial city of Vienna. The big bell on St. Stephen's Cathedral began striking the hours—the small ones hurriedly, as though dropping knives from the bell tower, and the big ones solemnly, as though laying eggs in the night around the temple. And when in the semidarkness we went in under that tower, over the echoing flagstones dropped chandeliers from long threads like illuminated spiders, and around them rose the smell of wax, filling the church to the stone walls, the way a body fills clothes. One could see nothing, but as one's gaze climbed up through the tower, the dark became thicker and thicker, and in the dense blackness up there one expected the thread holding the light down in the bottom of the church to snap at any minute. . . . Here we found new work and met our noble lord Avram of Brankovich,[†] a man who led with his pen and built churches with his sword. I shall say just a word or two about him, because he was feared as much as he was loved.

"People used to say: 'Brankovich is not alone.' They believed that when he was young he did not wash for forty days, that he had put his foot into the devil's plate and become a warlock. A whip of hair grew on each of his shoulders; he became clairvoyant, sleepy in March, lucky; he could jump far with his body and farther still with his soul, which, while the body slept, flew like a flock of doves, led winds, chased clouds, brought and carried off hail, and protected the crops and cattle, milk and wheat against warlocks from across the sea, not letting them wrest the harvest away from his region. Hence, people believed that Brankovich met with the angels, and about him they said, 'Where warlocks spread there is bread.' He belonged, they claimed, to the warlocks of the second camp, along with the Skadar viziers and the beys of Plav and Gusinje, and in a clash with the warlocks of Trebinje he repulsed Mustaj-Beg Sabljak Pasha, ᵉ who belonged to the third camp. In that battle, in which he carried sand, feathers, and a bucket as his weapons, Brankovich was wounded in the leg; after that he took a black horse, the sultan of all horses, which neighed in its sleep and was also a warlock. The lame Brankovich would go off into heavenly battle riding the soul of his horse transformed into straw. They also say that in Constantinople he confessed and admitted to being a warlock, after which he ceased being one, and the cattle in Transylvania no longer walked backward when he passed by the pens. . . .

"This man, who slept so soundly that they watched over him to ensure nobody would turn him around and put his head where his feet were (for then he would never wake up again), this man who is buried on his stomach and loved even after death, took us on as scribes and led us into his and his uncle Count George Brankovich's library. And we got lost amid the books as we would in a street of blind alleys and twisted stairs. We scoured Vienna's markets and cellars to buy for Kyr

Avram manuscripts in Arabic, Hebrew, and Greek, and, looking at Vienna's houses, I noticed that they stood one next to the other like the books on Brankovich's library shelves. I thought how houses are like books: so many of them around you, yet you only look at a few and visit or reside in fewer still. Usually you get sent to an inn, a lodging place, a tent rented for the night, or a cellar. Seldom, if at all, does it happen that a storm accidentally drives you back to the same house you used long ago, so that as you spend the night there you remember where you once slept and how everything, although still the same, was different then, how spring dawned through that window and autumn walked out of that door. . . .

"On the eve of St. Peter's and Paul's Day in 1685, the fourth Sunday after All Souls, our Master Avram of Brankovich hired his services as a diplomat to the English legation in Turkey, and we moved to Constantinople. We were received in a tower over the Bosporus, where our master had already settled in with his sabers, camel saddles, rugs, and cupboards as tall as a church, with his fasting eyes the color of damp sand. On Paternoster he had a temple built in that tower to St. Angelina the Despot, great-grandmother to himself and to his uncle Count George, and for a valet he brought in an Anatolian who used his long pigtail as a whip and kept buckshot in the tip of his plait. The new servant, named Yusuf Masudi, © taught our Master Avram Arabic and watched over his dreams. He brought with him some kind of feedbag full of penned pieces of paper, and he was rumored to be a reader of dreams or hunter of shadows, which is what some call those who flagellate one another with human dreams. Nikon and I spent the entire first year stocking the master's shelves and cases with books and manuscripts, which still smelled of the camels and horses that had brought them from Vienna.

Once, when the valet Masudi was keeping his vigil in Kyr Avram's bedroom, I snatched Masudi's feedbag and read and memorized the entire manuscript letter by letter without understanding a word, because it was in Arabic. I know only that it was in the form of a dictionary or glossary arranged according to the Arabic alphabet, that it zigzagged like a crab and read like the jaybird that flies backward. . . .

"The actual city and its bridges over the water did not surprise me. As soon as we arrived in Constantinople, I began recognizing in the street faces, hate, women and clouds, animals, love that I had fled long ago, eyes I had met once and remembered forever. I decided that nothing happens in the flow of time, that the world does not change through the years but inside itself and through space simultaneously—it changes in countless forms, shuffling them like cards and assigning the past of some as lessons to the future or present of others. Here all of a person's recollections, remembrances, and overall present are lived in various places and in various people at one and the same time. One should not consider all those nights around us, I thought, as being one and the same night, for they are not: they are thousands upon hundreds of thousands of nights, which, instead of traveling through time, one after another, like birds, calendars, or clocks, evolve simultaneously. My night next to your night is not the same night even by the calendar. For the papists in Rome and here, today is Assumption Day, but for Christians of the Eastern rite, for Greeks and those of the autonomous faith, it is the Day of the Translation of the Relics of the Archdeacon St. Steven the Beardless; for some this year of 1688 will end fifteen days earlier; for the Jews in the ghettos it is already the year 5447, while for the Arabs it is only the year 905. We the seven servants of Kyr Avram will use up a whole week of nights by dawn. We shall collect a whole September of nights from here to Topcisaray, but from Aya-Sofia to Vlaherna, October is already being spent. Somewhere our Kyr Avram's dreams are coming to life, while elsewhere somebody is dreaming Kyr Avram's reality, and who knows whether our Kyr Brankovich came here to Constantinople not to work as an interpreter for the English consul to the Porte, but to see the person whose real life he dreams of, the person who in his own dreams is spending Kyr Avram's life. For there is no man's reality around us that someone else is not dreaming about somewhere in this human ocean tonight, nor is there somebody's dream that is not becoming the reality of another. If one were to go from here to the Bosporus, from street to street, one would count all the seasons of a year from date to date, because autumn and spring and all the seasons of a human life are not the same for everyone, because nobody is old or young every day, and an entire life could be gathered like the fire of a candle's flames, and if you blow it out not even a breath remains between birth and death. If you knew exactly where to go, you would this very night find someone who was experiencing your waking days and nights, one who eats your next day's lunch, another who mourns your losses of eight years ago or kisses your future wife, and a fourth who is dying exactly the same death you will die. And if you were to move faster and delve deeper and wider, you would see that a whole infinity of nights is evolving over an immense expanse this evening. Time that has elapsed in one town is only just beginning in another, and one can travel between these two towns forward and backward through time. In a male town you can meet in life a woman who in a female town is already dead, or vice versa. Not individual lives, but all future and past times, all the branches of eternity, are already here, broken up into tiny morsels and divided among people and their dreams. The immense body of Adam, the original man, stirs in its sleep and breathes. Humanity chews up time all at once, not waiting for tomorrow. Time, then, does not exist here. It comes and washes over this world somewhere from the other side. . . .

" 'From where?' Nikon asked me right then, as if he had heard my thoughts, but I kept silent. I kept silent because I knew from where. Time comes not from the ground but from the underground. Time belongs to Satan; he carries it like a skein in the pocket of the devil, unravels it when his mysterious economies so dictate, and it should be wrested away from him. For, if one can ask and receive eternity from God, then we can take the opposite of eternity—time—only from Satan. . . .

"On the Day of Jude the Apostle, the brother of the Lord, Kyr Avram assembled us and told us we would be leaving Constantinople. Everything had been said, the travel orders issued, when suddenly a brief but violent argument broke out between Nikon and that Anatolian Masudi, and Nikon began fluttering his lower lids upward like a bird. Angry as he was, he grabbed Masudi's feedbag, already packed for the journey (the one with the Arabic glossary, which I already knew by heart), and hurled it into the fire. Masudi was not very upset; he simply turned to Kyr Avram and said:

" 'Look at him, Sire; that one fucks with his tail, and he does it from the rear, with his back turned, so he doesn't see the person he is impregnating. And he has no partition dividing his nostrils.'

"At that moment all eyes turned to Nikon. Kyr

Avram took the mirror from the wall and shoved it under his nose as if he were a corpse. We all bent closer and, true enough, the mirror revealed that Nikon had no dividing wall between his nostrils. The others had now learned what I had long known—that my colleague and head calligrapher Nikon Sevast was one and the same with Satan. Indeed, he himself did not deny it now. But, unlike the others, I did not look at his nose. I looked at the mirror and discovered what must have been long known to everyone around me. Nikon Sevast's face, which had so reminded me of one I had seen before, was practically identical to mine. We roamed the world like twins, making God's bread with the devil's tear.

"That evening I thought, Now is the moment! When a man spends his life napping, nobody next to him ever figures that one day he will wake up. And so it was with Nikon. I am not like those who wake up in fright when their hand falls out of their sleep and onto the floor, but I was afraid of Sevast. His teeth held a perfect picture of my bones. All the same, I went. I knew that the devil always walks one step behind man, so I trod in his every step and he did not notice me. I had remarked long ago that, of all the papers in Kyr Avram Brankovich's enormous library, he devoted particular attention to the Khazar glossary, a kind of alphabetical book of material on the origin and collapse, customs and wars of an extinct nation, which we scribes had been instructed to put in order. Avram Brankovich took a special interest in this nation; he would buy up old documents with no thought of the cost and would bribe people to catch the 'tongues' of those who knew something about the Khazars,[▽] or would send people out to hunt the dream hunters, who derived their skills from the ancient Khazar sorcerers. This glossary caught my attention because, of all the thousands of volumes in Brankovich's library, it was this book that interested Nikon. I learned Brankovich's *Kha-*

zar *Dictionary* by heart and began observing what Nikon did with it. Until that evening, Nikon had not done anything unusual. But now, after the incident with the mirror, he went alone to the upper floor of the tower, took the parrot, placed it on a lamp, and sat down to listen to what the parrot had to say. Kyr Avram's parrot often recited poems believed by our master to be those of the Khazar Princess Ateh,$^\triangledown$ and we scribes were under orders to write down for Kyr Avram's Khazar glossary everything the bird said. That evening, however, Sevast did not write. He merely listened, and the bird said:

Sometimes bygone springs, full of warmth and scents, blossom yet again inside us. And we carry them through the winter, protecting them with our chests. Then, one day, those bygone springs begin protecting our chests from the frost when we find ourselves on the other side of the window, where winter is not just a picture. It is now the ninth winter that I have had such a spring inside me, and it is still keeping me warm. Imagine, in this winter, two such springs touching like the scents of two meadows. That is what we need instead of overcoats. . . .

"When the bird stopped its recital, I felt terribly alone, hidden as I was, without spring in my soul, and only the remembrance of a shared youth with Nikon Sevast remained as a kind of light in my memory. A lovely light, I thought, when Nikon took the bird and sliced off its tongue with a knife. Then he went to Avram Brankovich's *Khazar Dictionary* and started burning it in the fire, page by page. Including the last page, on which was written in Kyr Avram's hand:

Note on Adam, the Brother of Christ

The Khazars believed that the first and last man, Adam, elder brother to Christ and younger brother to Satan, was created out of seven parts. Satan created him: he made his flesh from the earth, his bones from stones, his eyes quick to evil from water, his blood from the dew, his breath from the winds, his thoughts from the clouds, and his mind from the speed of angels. But he could not come to life until his real and second father, God, breathed a soul into him. When the soul entered him, Adam's left thumb touched his right, the masculine touching the feminine, and he came to life. Of two worlds—the invisible, spiritual one created by God and the visible, material one built by the unjust economies of the devil—only Adam was the child of both creators and the work of both worlds. Satan then enclosed two fallen angels in his body, and such was the lust that grew inside them that not until the world's end will they be able to gratify and allay it. The first angel was named Adam and the second Eve. Eve had nets instead of eyes and a rope in place of a tongue. The latter was in the shape of the Great Loop or chains. Adam immediately began to age, because his soul was a migratory bird, dividing itself between and migrating to different times. At first Adam was made of only two times—the masculine and the feminine in him. Then of four (belonging to Eve and his sons, Cain, Abel, and Seth). But later the particles of time enclosed in the human form steadily multiplied, and Adam's body multiplied, until it became an enormous state, like the state of nature. Only different in composition. All his life, the last mortal will search inside Adam's head for an exit, but he will not find it, because the way in and out of Adam's body was found only by Christ. Adam's immense body lies not in space but in time. Now, it is not easy to slip into miracles as into shoes or to make a shovel out of words. Therefore, not only does Adam's soul migrate to all later generations (for the migration of the soul is always the migration of only one single soul, Adam's), but all the deaths of Adam's descendants migrate and return to Adam's death, like particles forming a huge death commensurate in size to Adam's body and life. Imagine white birds migrating and black birds returning from migration. When his last descendant dies, Adam himself will die, for in him are repeated the deaths of all his children. And then, as in the fable of the crow and the feather, earth, stone, water, dew, wind, cloud, and angel will come, and all will take from Adam what is theirs and empty him out. And then woe upon those who have deserted Adam's body, the body of man's first father, for they will not be able to die with him or like him. They will become not people but something else.

Hence the Khazar dream hunters search for the original man, for Adam, and assemble their dictionaries, glossaries, or alphabeticons. However, one must know that what the Khazars call a dream is not what we mean by a dream. Our dreams are remembered until one looks at the window; as soon as one looks, they disperse and are forever gone. With the Khazars it is not like that.

They believe that in the life of every man there are knot points, small parts of time like keys. Hence, every Khazar had his own stick and in the course of his life would put notches on it, carving states of clear consciousness or moments of the sublime fulfillment of life. Each of these markings was named after an animal or a precious stone. And called a "dream." To the Khazars, therefore, a dream was not just the day of our nights; it could also be the mysterious starry night of our days. Dream hunters, or dream readers, were priests who interpreted these markings and used them to create dictionaries or biographies, but not in the ancient sense of the words, not like Plutarch or Cornelius Nepos. These were collections of nameless biographies compiled from those moments of enlightenment where man becomes part of

Adam's body. If only for a moment in his life, every man becomes a part of Adam, and when all these moments are assembled, one gets the body of Adam on earth, not in form but in time, because only one part of time is illuminated, accessible, and usable. Adam's piece of time. The rest lies for us in darkness and serves somebody else. Our future is like the tentacles of a snail: as soon as it touches something hard it withdraws, and it sees only when it comes all the way out. Adam always sees like that, because he who knows all deaths of all people, in advance until the end of the world, also knows the world's future. Thus, it is only by joining Adam's body that we ourselves become all-seeing and joint owners of our future. Therein lies the basic difference between Satan and Adam: the devil does not see the future. That is why the Khazars searched for Adam's body, why the feminine and masculine books of the Khazar dream hunters were a bit like Adam's icons, in which the feminine marked his body, the masculine his blood. The Khazars knew, of course, that their sorcerers could not encompass the entire body or depict it in their dictionary-icons. In fact, they often painted two icons without any face, but with two thumbs—the left and the right, Adam's feminine and masculine thumb. For each part captured in the dictionaries could be put into motion and come to life only after the touching of two fingers, the masculine and the feminine. Therefore, in their dictionaries the Khazars paid particular attention to mastering these two parts of Adam's body, and it is believed that they even succeeded, but did not have enough time for the other parts. Adam has, however, and he waits. Just as his souls migrate to his children and return to his body as the deaths of those children, so part of his immense body-state can at any moment and in every one of us be killed again or revived. It only takes the prophetic touch of the fingers, the masculine and the feminine, provided we have built at least a part of Adam's body behind these fingers. That we have become a part of it. . . .

"Avram Brankovich's words rang in my ears all through the journey, which we undertook during a drought, when the Danube at the mouth of the Black Sea was like the Danube in Regensburg, and in Regensburg it was like the Danube in Schwartzwald, at its source. His words still rang when we reached the battlefield and when I saw how the wind drove the cannon smoke swiftly and the mist slowly across the Danube. Then, on the thirteenth Sunday after All Souls in 1689, the drought stopped, and we saw the greatest rain in our lives. The Danube again flowed as deep as the sky above it, and the rain stood vertically in the river, like the railings of a high fence, separating our camp from the Turkish. And here, in camp, on the battlefield, it dawned on me that each of us had come to the Danube for a different reason, and that I could tell what each of us was lying in wait for. Nikon had become a different man ever since he had burned Masudi's and Brankovich's dictionary. Nothing interested him any more; he had the 'fifth Our Father' read out to him, the one read for suicides, and one by one he threw his writing tools into the water. He and Masudi were shooting dice on a checkered scarf, with Nikon losing enormous amounts of money, like somebody who had given up all thought of life. And I felt he was bidding farewell to life and hoping that death would befall him here more easily than somewhere else. Kyr Avram Brankovich had not come to the Danube to fight, although he was a past master at fighting and fought well again now. He ob-

viously had an appointment with somebody here on the
Danube. Masudi sat shooting dice, but he was waiting to
see whom Kyr Avram was going to meet here, at Djerdap, enduring the blood and the rain, and that fatal day
on the Erection of the Holy Cross, when the Turkish
cannons increased their thunder. As for Kyr Avram's
saber instructor, the Copt by the name of Averkie Skila,[†]
he stayed by the Danube under Turkish fire because it
gave him a chance, without risk of punishment, to try
out on enemy soldiers or on our own (it was all the same
to him) a new saber stroke, a stroke he had been practicing for a long time but had not yet been able to test on
live flesh and bones. And I, I sat there with them, because I was waiting for the third part of *The Khazar
Dictionary*. I already knew the first two parts by heart—
Masudi's, the Islamic, and Kyr Avram's, the Greek part
—and I was now waiting to see whether someone would
appear with the third, Hebrew part of the glossary, since
it was evident from the first two parts that a third followed. Nikon had burned the first two and was no
longer afraid that the third would be added to them, so
his job was done. But, knowing the first two parts by
heart, I wanted to see the third, and I did not know how
it would be. I put my faith in Kyr Avram, who, it
seemed to me, was waiting for the same thing as I. But
he did not live to see it. The Turks soon killed Brankovich and Nikon in battle, and captured Masudi. Appear-
ing with the Turks at the scene of the battle was a
red-eyed young man with folded eyebrows like wings.
One half of his mustache was gray and the other red. He
ran, his brows dusty, his beard smeared with streaming
snot. Who would ever think, I mused, watching him,
that his time too deserves a watch! But I knew he was
my man. Suddenly he collapsed as though felled, and
out of the bag he had been holding spilled pages filled

with minute handwriting. After the battle, when every-body had moved off, I left my shelter and picked up the strewn papers. I crossed the Danube and in Walachia, at the Delski Monastery, I read the Hebrew pages from the bag, trying not to comprehend or interpret anything written on them. Then I went to Poland to do what Nikon Sevast had so wanted to prevent. I sought out a printer and sold him all three Khazar dictionaries: the Hebrew, found in the battlefield; the Greek, assembled on the orders of Avram Brankovich; and the Arabic, brought by Masudi, the reader of dreams. The printer's name was Daubmannus;✿ he suffered from a disease that did not develop and bring death until the fifth gen-eration, like a protracted game of cards. He paid me two months' rent, food, and buttons for my shirt, and I wrote down everything I had learned by heart. I was now again doing my job of narrator, and for the first time after so many years, also the other, long-abandoned job of Nikon Sevast, that of scribe. On Holy Innocents' Day in 1690, I finished the job, amid the kind of snow and frost that make your nails peel. Using Brankovich's alphabeticon, Masudi's glossary, and the Jewish encyclopedia from the red-eyed lad's bag, I composed something like *The Kha-zar Dictionary* and gave it to the printer. Daubmannus took all three books—the red, the green, and the yellow —and said he would print them.

"Whether he did or not I do not know, nor do I rightly know, Your Holiness, whether I did right to do what I did. But I now know that I am still hungry for writing and that from this hunger my thirst for remem-bering has passed. It is as though I were turning into the calligrapher Nikon Sevast. . . ."

APPENDIX II

Istanbul

October 18, 1982

Virginia Ateh, waitress at the Kingston Hotel, witness
in the case of Dr. Dorothea Schultz, approached the
bench and made the following statement:

"On the said day (October 2, 1982) the weather was
sunny and I was very upset. Veins of salt air were coming in from the Bosporus, and with them rapid thoughts
snaked their way into slow thoughts. The Kingston
Hotel garden, where breakfast is served in fine weather,
is quadrangular. One corner is sunny, the other has a
cultivated bed with flowers, the third is windy, and in
the fourth corner there is a stone well and beside it a
pillar. I usually stand behind the pillar, because I know
that guests don't like being watched when they eat. It's
no wonder. I, for instance, know immediately, when
watching a guest having breakfast, that a soft-boiled egg
will sustain him to bathe before noon, fish to go to
Topcisaray before nightfall, and a glass of wine to smile
before bed, a smile that will never reach the nearsighted
mirrors of the hotel room. From this spot by the well,
you can see the steps leading into the garden, and you
can always keep your eye on who's coming and going. It
has one more advantage. Just as all water from the surrounding drainpipes pours into the well, so all voices
from the garden also reach it, and if you tilt your ear a

bit toward the well opening, you can quite clearly hear
every word spoken in the garden. You can hear when a
bird pecks a fly, or a shell cracks on a boiled egg; you
can recognize the forks calling out to one another always
in the same and the glasses each in a different voice.
Since before calling the waitress guests usually mention
in conversation the reason why they want me, I am able
to satisfy their wishes before they inform me of them,
because I have already heard them from the well. And
to know something a few seconds before others is a great
advantage and always of benefit. That morning, the first
to come to the garden were the guests from Room 18,
the Van der Spaak family, with Belgian passports, father,
mother, and son. The father is elderly; he plays nicely on
an instrument made of white tortoiseshell, and in the
evening its music could be heard. He's a bit eccentric
and always eats with his own two-pronged fork, which
he carries in his pocket. The mother is a young and
pretty woman, which was why I took a closer look at
her. And that is how I noticed that she was marked by a
defect—there was no partition in her nose. Every day
she would go to St. Sofia's, where she would make lovely
copies of the wall paintings. I asked her whether these
pictures served as notes for her husband's songs, but she
didn't understand. Her nearly four-year-old boy probably had a defect of his own. He always wore gloves, even
at meals. But it was something else that upset me. That
sunny morning I watched the Belgians come down the
said steps to breakfast. And I saw the following: the old
gentleman's face was unlike other faces."

Judge: How do you mean?
Witness: Join two left sides of the same face on a
photograph and of a handsome man you will make a
monster. Double up the sides of the soul and you will

get not a complete but rather two monstrous halves of the soul. Like the face, the soul has a left and a right side. You cannot make a two-legged person out of two left legs. The old gentleman's face had two left sides.

Judge: And that is why you were upset that morning?

Witness: Yes.

Judge: The court warns the witness to confine her testimony to the truth. What happened next?

Witness: I served the Van der Spaaks, telling them not to pick up the pepper and salt with the same hand, and after their meal they left, except for the boy, who stayed behind to play and drink his chocolate milk. Then Dr. Dorothea Schultz, present here, entered the garden and sat at her table. Before I managed to wait on her, the now dead Dr. Muawia went up to her table and sat down. You could see that her time was trickling like rain and his was falling heavily like snow. He was already covered up to his neck. I noticed that he wasn't wearing a tie, and that she sneaked a revolver out of her handbag, but after exchanging a few words with Dr. Muawia she put out her hand and he gave her a bundle of papers. Then she ran up the stairs to the rooms, leaving the weapon on the table, under the papers. All this upset me even more. Dr. Muawia had a childlike smile trapped in his beard that resembled an insect in amber and was singed by the green of his melancholy eyes. As though drawn by that smile, the boy from the Belgian family went up to Dr. Muawia's table. I remind the court that the child was not yet four. There was nobody else in the garden. The boy was wearing gloves, as usual, and Dr. Muawia asked him why he didn't take them off.

"Because this place makes me sick," the boy replied.

"Sick?" asked Dr. Muawia. "Sick of what?"

"Of your democracy!" said the boy—word for word. Then I moved still closer to the well and listened to their conversation, which seemed to me increasingly strange as it went on.

"What kind of democracy?"

"The kind you and your ilk protect. Look at the results of this democracy of yours. Before, big nations used to oppress small nations. Now it's the reverse. Now, in the name of democracy, small nations terrorize the big. Just look at the world around us. White America is afraid of blacks, the blacks are afraid of the Puerto Ricans, Jews of the Palestinians, the Arabs of the Jews, the Serbs of the Albanians, the Chinese of the Vietnamese, the English of the Irish. Small fish are nibbling the ears of big fish. Instead of minorities being terrorized, democracy has introduced a new fashion: now it's the majority of this planet's population that's being burdened.... Your democracy sucks...."

Judge: The court warns the witness not to make implausible statements. The witness is fined. You claim under oath that all this was said by a child who is not yet four years old?

Witness: Yes, I do, because I heard it with my own ears. Then I wanted to see what I was hearing, so I moved to a spot where I could watch from behind the pillar in the garden. The child grabbed Dr. Schultz's revolver from the table, spread-eagled his legs, crouched, and, holding the gun with both hands like a professional, aimed at Dr. Muawia, shouting:

"Open your mouth so your teeth won't be ruined!"

Stunned, Dr. Muawia really did open his mouth, and the child fired. I thought it was a toy gun, but Dr. Muawia toppled over on his chair. Blood gushed, and then I saw that one of Dr. Muawia's trouser legs was already dirty—he had one foot in the grave. The child threw down the weapon, went back to his table, and proceeded to finish his chocolate milk. Dr. Muawia didn't move, and the stream of blood tied itself into a knot under his chin. I thought then, "There, now he has a tie. . . ." Just before that, Mrs. Schultz let out a scream. Everyone knows what followed. Dr. Muawia was pronounced dead, his body was removed, and Dr. Schultz reported the death to another guest at our hotel, Dr. Isailo Suk. . . .

Prosecutor: "I thought then, 'There, now he has a tie. . . .' " I would like to express to the court my profound indignation at the way the witness expresses herself. What are you by nationality, Miss—or is it Mrs.?—Ateh?

Witness: That's hard to explain.

Prosecutor: Try, please.

Witness: I am Khazar.

Prosecutor: What did you say? I've never heard of a nation like that. What passport do you carry? Khazar?

Witness: No, Israeli.

Prosecutor: So, that's it. That's what I wanted to hear. How can you be Khazar and have an Israeli passport? Did you betray your people?

Witness (laughing): No, one might say just the opposite. The Khazars assimilated with the Jews and, along with everybody else, I accepted Judaism and an Israeli passport. What's the point of being alone in the world? If all Arabs became Jews, would you remain an Arab?

Prosecutor: No comment is necessary, and here I ask the questions. Your testimony is calculated to help the accused, who carries the same passport as you. I have no more questions. Nor, I hope, has the jury. . . .

Next to take the stand was the Van der Spaak family from Belgium. They agreed on three things. First, that it is ridiculous to believe the story that a three-year-old child ostensibly committed the murder. Second, that the investigation had established that Dr. Muawia was killed by a weapon bearing the fingerprints of only one person, Dr. Dorothea Schultz, and had also established that the said weapon (a .38-caliber model 36 Smith & Wesson) with which Dr. Muawia was killed belonged to Dr. Schultz. Third, Mrs. Spaak, as the main witness for the prosecution, claimed that Dr. Schultz had a motive for the murder of Dr. Muawia, and had come to Istanbul to kill him, which she did. Namely, the investigation established that during the Egyptian-Israeli war Dr. Muawia had seriously wounded Dr. Dorothea Schultz's husband. The motive is clear: murder in revenge. The testimony of the Kingston Hotel waitress could not be accepted as reliable. That was all.

On the basis of the evidence, the prosecutor asked that Dr. Dorothea Schultz be declared guilty of premeditated murder, entailing political motivations as well. Then the accused was brought before the court. Dr. Schultz made a very brief statement. She was not guilty of Dr. Muawia's death, and she could prove it. She had an alibi. Asked by the judge what kind of alibi, she replied: "At the time of Dr. Muawia's murder, I was murdering somebody else—Dr. Isailo Suk. I smothered him with a pillow in his bedroom."

During the investigation it had been established that Mr. Van der Spaak had also been seen in Dr. Suk's room that morning, at the time of death, but Dr. Schultz's confession absolved the Belgian of any responsibility.

The trial ended and the verdict was pronounced. Dr. Dorothea Schultz was acquitted of the charge that she had killed Dr. Abu Kabir Muawia in an act of premeditated murder and revenge, and was condemned for the

murder of Dr. Isailo Suk. Dr. Muawia's murder remained unresolved, while the Van der Spaak family was
set free. Virginia Ateh, the waitress at the Kingston
Hotel, was fined for trying to deceive the court and
mislead the investigation.

Dr. Dorothea Schultz was sentenced to six years' im-
prisonment in the casemates of Istanbul. She writes letters addressed to her own name in Cracow. All the
letters are examined, and they always end with the same
incomprehensible sentence: "Our false victim saved us
from death."

The search of Dr. Suk's room turned up no books or
papers. All that was found was an egg cracked at one
end. The dead man's fingers were caked with yolk,
indicating that the last thing he had done in life was to
crack the egg. Also discovered was an unusual gold-
handled key that, strangely enough, fitted the lock of a
room belonging to a Kingston Hotel employee. The
room of the waitress Virginia Ateh.

Found on the Van der Spaak family's table, and enclosed as evidence, was a bill written on the back of a
sheet of hotel stationery. It said:

$$
\begin{array}{r}
1689 \\
+ \quad 293 \\
\hline
= \quad 1982
\end{array}
$$

CLOSING NOTE ON THE
USEFULNESS OF THIS DICTIONARY

A book can be a vineyard watered with rain or a vineyard watered with wine. This one, like all dictionaries, is of the latter variety. A dictionary is a book that, while requiring little time every day, takes a lot of time through the years. This loss should not be underestimated. Especially if one takes into account that reading is, generally speaking, a dubious proposition. When used, a book can be cured or killed in the reading. It can be changed, fattened, or raped. Its course can be rechanneled; it is constantly losing something; you drop letters through the lines, pages through your fingers, as new ones keep growing before your eyes, like cabbage. If you put it down tomorrow, you may find it like a stove gone cold, with no hot supper waiting for you any more. Moreover, today people do not have enough solitude to be able to read books, even dictionaries, without harm. But to this too there is an end. A book is like a scale—it tilts first to the right until it tilts to the left, forever. Its weight thus shifts from the right hand to the left, and something similar has happened in the head—from the realm of hope, thoughts have moved to the realm of memory, and everything is over. The reader's ear may perhaps retain some of the saliva from the writer's mouth, words borne by the wind with a grain of sand at the bottom. Over the years, voices will settle around that grain, as in a shell, and one day it will turn into a pearl, into black goat-cheese, or into a void when the ears shut like a shell. And least of all does this depend on the sand.

In any event, to read such a thick book means to be alone for a long time, to be for a long time without the person whose presence you need, because four-handed reading is still not customary. This gives the writer a guilty conscience, and he will try to atone for it. Let that lovely woman with the quick eyes and languid hair who, in reading this dictionary and running through her fear as through a room, feels lonely, do the following. On the first Wednesday of the month, with the dictionary under her arm, let her go to the tea shop in the main square of town. Waiting for her there will be a young man who, like her, has just been overcome with a feeling of loneliness, wasting time by reading the same book. Let them sit down for a coffee together and compare the masculine and feminine exemplars of their books. They are different. When they compare the short passage in Dr. Dorothea Schultz's last letter, printed in italics in the one and the other exemplar, the book will fit together as a whole, like a game of dominoes, and they will need it no longer. Then let them give the lexicographer a good scolding, but let them be quick about it in the name of what comes next, for what comes next is their affair alone, and it is worth more than any reading.

I see how they lay their dinner out on top of the mailbox in the street and how they eat, embraced, sitting on their bicycles.

Belgrade, Regensburg, Belgrade
1978–1983

LIST OF ENTRIES

337

A NOTE ON THE TYPE

This book was set in a digitized version of Granjon, a type named in compliment to Robert Granjon, a type cutter and printer active, in Antwerp, Lyons, Rome, and Paris, from 1523 to 1590. Granjon, the boldest and the most original designer of his time, was one of the first to practice the trade of type founder apart from that of printer.

Linotype Granjon was designed by George W. Jones, who based his drawings on a face used by Claude Garamond (c. 1480–1561) in his beautiful French books. Granjon more closely resembles Garamond's own type than does any of the various modern faces that bear his name.

Composed by Dix Type Inc., Syracuse, New York
Printed and bound by R. R. Donnelley & Sons, Crawfordsville, Indiana
Typography and binding design by Iris Weinstein